MW01123988

One Small Step
an anthology
of discoveries

Edited by Tehani Wessely

READ ORDER

61	109	25	41
159	121	211	1
247 (10)	169 (12)	229	85
	71 (14)		133
			181
			257

GOODNOW LIBRARY
21 Concord Road
Sudbury, MA 01776

5113

First published in Australia in 2013
by FableCroft Publishing

http://fablecroft.com.au

This anthology © 2013 FableCroft Publishing

Cover design by Amanda Rainey
Design and layout by Tehani Wessely
Typeset in Sabon MT Pro and Footlight MT Light

Introduction ©2013 Marianne de Pierres
Always Greener ©2013 Michelle Marquardt
By Blood and Incantation ©2013 Lisa L. Hannett & Angela Slatter
Indigo Gold ©2013 Deborah Biancotti
Firefly Epilogue ©2013 Jodi Cleghorn
Daughters of Battendown ©2013 Cat Sparks
Baby Steps ©2013 Barbara Robson
Number 73 Glad Avenue ©2013 Suzanne J. Willis
Shadows ©2013 Kate Gordon
Original ©2013 Penelope Love
The Ships of Culwinna ©2013 Thoraiya Dyer
Cold White Daughter ©2013 Tansy Rayner Roberts
The Ways of the Wyrding Women ©2013 Rowena Cory Daniells
Winter's Heart ©2013 Faith Mudge
Sand and Seawater ©2013 Joanne Anderton & Rabia Gale
Ella and the Flame ©2013 Kathleen Jennings
Morning Star ©2013 D.K. Mok

All rights reserved. Without limiting the rights under copyright above, no part of this publication may be reproduced, stored in or introduced into a retrieval system, or transmitted in any form, or by any means (electronic, mechanical, photocopying, recording or otherwise), without the prior written permission of both the copyright owner and the above publisher of this book.

National Library of Australia Cataloguing-in-Publication entry (pbk)

Title:	One small step : an anthology of discoveries / Tehani Wessely (ed.) ; Thoraiya Dyer ... [et al]
ISBN:	9780987400000 (pbk.)
	9780987400017 (ebook)
Subjects:	Short stories, Australian.
	Science fiction, Australian.
	Fantasy fiction, Australian.
	Horror stories.
Dewey Number:	A823.01

The editor gratefully acknowledges the generous assistance given by Marianne de Pierres, Elizabeth Disney, Dirk Flinthart, Amanda Rainey, and the amazing authors — I never cease to be impressed by the depth of talent and professionalism among our Australian authors.

As always, Tehani would like to thank her ever-enduring husband and children for their patience and support, and for keeping her away from the computer when she should be.

ALSO EDITED BY TEHANI WESSELY...

The Bone Chime Song and other stories by Joanne Anderton
(FableCroft Publishing)

Epilogue (FableCroft Publishing)

To Spin a Darker Stair (FableCroft Publishing)

After the Rain (FableCroft Publishing)

Australis Imaginarium (FableCroft Publishing)

Worlds Next Door (FableCroft Publishing)

New Ceres Nights (with Alisa Krasnostein, Twelfth Planet Press)

Andromeda Spaceways Inflight Magazine
#4, #16, #27, #31, #36 (with Lucy Zinkiewicz) & **#37**
(Andromeda Spaceways Publishing Co-operative Ltd)

Shiny #4 and **#5**
(with Alisa Krasnostein and Ben Payne, webzine,
Twelfth Planet Press)

Contents

Foreword

Not so long ago, I attended a seminar on the topic of "Australian Victorian Female Crime Writers". I was struck by how many there had been, but more importantly, how I had never heard of them. History can be very selective in what it chooses to publicise.

When invited by Tehani Wessely from Fablecroft Publishing to write this foreword, I was thrilled to have the opportunity to help ensure that the current generation of Australian female genre writers don't suffer the same anonymity as their Victorian crime-writing sisters.

Within these covers is a collection of thought-provoking, entertaining and engrossing stories by a crop of talented writers who have earned the right, not only to be read, but to be remembered.

They have treated the concept of *One Small Step* imaginatively; between these pages you will find a gamut of speculative genres, from traditional fantasy, horror and science fiction to contemporary slipstream, and the telling of one small step towards either self-determination or self-realisation.

Reading this collection is like partaking in a strange intense dream that at the same time wonders if it might be real.

Mostly though, you cannot absorb *One Small Step* and be left unmoved. These are stories that provoke emotion; tales of prejudice, affliction, resurrection, survival and new beginnings. Each one so different from the last and yet all connected by characters with conviction.

Enjoy the feast between the covers, and then I urge you to talk to others about it. For it is only in our conversations and stories that we live on. It is in them that our legacy is transferred. It is in them that we make sense of the past, present and future. It is in them that the insights of our notable women storytellers will be recalled.

Marianne de Pierres
February 2013

ALWAYS GREENER
MICHELLE MARQUARDT

"They're ugly," I said, squinting at the aliens over the interweaving mesh of Grass. "Why did they have to put them here?"

Mark looked at me sideways. It was cramped on our side-by-side squashing boards and we were standing hip against hip, the dense wall of Grass around us. I could feel the calculation in his gaze. He wanted to argue with me, but was unwilling to risk another bout of shouting that would end in tears. I didn't think that would happen today, but my grief was an unpredictable thing and he was right to be wary of it.

In the end he just shrugged, reached out with a gloved hand and pushed aside more blades to get a better view. "I don't think the Council had anywhere else they could put them. The Grass makes a better prison than anything we've got in town, and who'd want them there anyway? The truce finishes in four days. One of their ships will come and get them before then. Better that happens out here with nobody about."

Nobody except us. I stared at the two figures as they moved slowly over the expanse of open rocky ground. Their three short fat legs inched their massive bodies along, while their varied arms balanced the building material above their tiny swiveling heads. They were pulling apart the last skeletal remains of the hut that had once stood at the highest point of the field, though there was no sign of what they'd done with any of the pieces.

"They're stupid too," I said. "That hut was the only shelter they had. What if we get early snow?"

Mark didn't point out that the few remaining uprights of the old hut would have provided little protection anyway. "Maybe they don't care about snow. Maybe engineers are designed to be weather-proof. It'd make sense."

"Maybe they'll just freeze." I waited for a twinge of satisfaction at the thought, but it didn't come. "I don't know why I came here," I said. "I hate them."

But I didn't really hate these sad slow creatures, despite all my intentions. They were builders and fixers, or so we had been told. A harmless variation of a species we still knew almost nothing about. They were trapped and alone and had probably been born to be slaves. These weren't the ones that had killed my dad. They hadn't flown the ships that had dropped in their thousands from the sky.

"I think they're starving," said Mark. "They've been stuck in that field for weeks."

My gaze followed the busy figures as they moved over the rocky terrain. "They don't look it."

"How would we know? I've brought them something to eat."

So that was what was in the lumpy rucksack on his back. "How do you know what aliens eat?"

He looked vaguely embarrassed. "I don't. I just brought stuff. I guess they can take what they want."

Stuff? What could his family possibly spare?

He opened the bag and we both stared inside. Some vegetable peelings, probably stolen out of the compost, an old shirt that was so cut up and tattered it couldn't even be used as rags, some bits of an old tyre. The plastic leg of a chair.

"You're going to give them that?"

He shrugged. "Better than nothing."

I didn't have an answer for that. "Alright," I said. "I want to see them." I wasn't sure where the words had come from, but as I said them I suddenly knew that I had to do it. "I want to see them up close."

I knew he wouldn't argue, because of what had happened to my dad, and I knew it was unfair of me to take advantage of it.

But lately I had stopped caring about fair, as though the weight of everything else had forced me to shed things, with consideration for other people the first to go.

Wordlessly he handed me the sack.

Part of me wanted to go up to where the Grass stopped and the bare rock began, to let them see that it was me who was bringing them these things. Another part wanted to stay back, within the razor sharp safety of the Grass.

In the end it was the vegetable peelings that made my decision for me; I had no way of throwing them any distance. So I walked to the edge, laying my squashing boards carefully before me to press the Grass down and provide safe passage. I felt exposed and a little foolish and I realised, when I was almost there, when the big lumbering shapes had stopped their progress and swiveled their tiny heads towards me, that in the Grass it was impossible to turn and run.

The two giants remained still as I reached the open ground and, still standing on my board, emptied the contents of my sack onto the stone. My offering seemed pitifully small as it scattered. When I looked up the aliens were heading straight for me.

The need to run was so sudden that I almost stepped off my board into the waiting blades, but a lifetime of careful movement stopped my raised foot at the last moment, made me step slowly back along the board I was on and onto the one that was lined up directly behind it. My gaze remained fixed on the hulking figures moving towards me. My throat tightened and my heartbeat pushed against my eardrums.

I lifted the board I'd just vacated and the Grass began to slowly rise, a curtain of safety before me.

The aliens had covered two thirds of the ground between us, moving faster than I'd ever seen them, their stumpy legs motoring along in coordinated swinging movements, rolling their bodies along, their tentacles and appendages clamped down to their sides, as though it would somehow make their ungainly bodies more aerodynamic.

I stopped my retreat three boardlengths out from the edge, twice again what I thought their longest tentacle could reach, and feeling a sudden light headed courage, turned to watch what they would do.

It wasn't me they were after, it was the things on the ground. They slowed as they approached, little heads craning forward, arms waving excitedly over my offering, as though they were frightened to touch. I saw for the first time that they had four eyes, two in the center and one on either side of their heads. I'd expected them to be like the pictures I'd seen of insect eyes, many faceted and cold, but these were big and soft and brown, like horses' eyes. They blinked every now and then, one at a time.

The one on the left seized a piece of tyre in one tentacle and inspected it carefully, first bringing it up to its eyes, then wiping it against its chest, where there was a moist looking patch between the armoured plates of its hide. Then, quite suddenly, a hole opened below the patch — it looked like a round, pink, fleshy mouth. In went the rubber and then the hole was gone.

"Cool." It was Mark's voice rising from his hiding place amid the Grass.

I found that I was grinning.

The other alien had wasted no time in imitating its fellow. Within a few seconds all the rubber was gone.

The shirt went into the same hole as the rubber, after being carefully divided between them. The vegetable scraps went into a different hole, further up, just below the head. When everything was gone and the questing tips of their tentacles had inspected every bit of ground, their heads turned towards me. There was a brief humming sound in the air, something that echoed inside my skull rather than through my ears, then they turned away and headed back to their collection of dismantled hut parts up the hill.

"Cool," said Mark again from behind me.

I watched their retreating forms. "I hate you," I said. "You had no right to come here." But the words felt hollow as they came out of my mouth and I didn't even know why I had said them. Was there something wrong with me? Some defect that prevented the self-righteous anger I knew that I was entitled to, that my father was entitled to? I suddenly felt I had betrayed him by helping these things, by failing to hate them the way I should.

In the distance, the tinny rattle of our yard bell sounded, calling me home. I reached back and grabbed the squashing board behind me. The track we'd made getting here over the Grass had already disappeared, blades springing back up neatly into place as though they'd never had our weight crushing them down.

I wanted to hate the Grass too, but I couldn't manage that either. Maybe if I'd been born on another world, like my parents, and hadn't always looked out over a dazzling velveted landscape of green. Our town looked like a scar to me, the bare earth around the houses stark and naked, the various Earth species that struggled to grow in the depleted soil all sickly and wrong. All around the Grass stretched out, perfect and unstoppable. I was proud of it in an odd way. I didn't tell my mother that. Every day since my father had died, the defeat had pushed itself a little further into the lines of her face. It sat in the distant unfocused look in her eyes and every aspect of the way she moved. I wanted to lift it away from her as though it were a clinging veil, to reveal the mother I remembered. But I didn't know how to begin and my concern for her had started shifting into anger.

The thought dragged at my movements as I made my way over the Grass towards the road, leather gloves protecting my hands from the blades as I replaced one board with another before me. There had been times, before The War, when I'd actually wished my father would leave, when the strained silences over the dinner table or the sudden vicious arguments had made me wish for peace, an end to the tension that sat like a live thing in the air between my parents. But the two of them had always worked it out in the end. There would be a huge fight and then the next morning it would all be gone. For a while at least.

It was gone forever now, and the guilt I felt at ever having wished it away sat like a small furtive animal in my mind, darting out when I least expected it.

At the road, Mark headed off in the opposite direction, waving a hand in farewell, boards tucked under his arm. I wasn't the only one who had clearing to do before dinner.

∞¥∞Ω∞¥∞

The small rectangle of our yard was empty when I got home, my mother probably inside preparing dinner. I grabbed the heavy secateurs from their hook by the back door without going in. There would be enough indoor time this evening for me to sit through.

I started with the track to the creek, like I did every day. The narrow path ran downhill from the end of our yard for about a hundred meters to the slow, twisting, rocky banks of the stream that cut across our claim. On every side was Grass, blades reaching inwards about waist high to swipe at the skin of anyone who wandered by without their leather coveralls on.

I started by cutting back the overhanging blades, needing both hands to close the secateurs on the fibrous stalks, tossing them back into the ocean of green as I did so, methodically working each side down to the slick mossy banks of the creek. Then I turned around and did the runners, green tendrils inching across the clean soil of the track. They grew about ten centimeters a day here, this close to water. I pulled them up, cut them off and threw them back to join their fellows.

My father told me once how amazing it had been to see this new world as they descended from space. How beautifully, dazzlingly green it had been. How the colonists had laughed and hugged one another with joy that their world seemed so rich and abundant.

You never could tell, he said, what you were getting, no matter how many bribes you'd paid. There were always stories of colonists being sent to desert planets, or frozen wastelands, or worse. After all why should the Earth authorities care? It wasn't as though you could go back and ask for a refund.

As it turned out, our world was a sort of wasteland after all. And he'd been right, we couldn't go back.

Once the track was cleared, I hauled water in buckets up to our straggly vegetable garden, which covered most of the cleared area of our yard. Something was still eating the cabbages. I examined the neat semicircular defects along the edges of the leaves and searched for the hundredth time for caterpillars or other insects. There was nothing. I suspected it was a fuzzer, one of the matted puff-ball rodents that lived in the underlayer of The Grass. The thing had obviously braved the exotic terrain of the open yard and developed a taste for something besides Grass stems, but there was nothing to make a trap with and no money for netting.

I hated cabbage anyway; it made the whole house stink like garbage for days.

Clearing the edges of the yard took longer. I was half way around when something caught my eye out in the grass. It was red; a red that I'd never seen before. Pure and vibrant, it glowed in the afternoon sun like a beacon a little more than a metre out in the sea of blades. I stared at it for long minutes trying to work out what it was. It had to be man-made to be a colour like that, though I couldn't remember seeing anything in the town that had ever been that red. How would it get out here, on our claim?

I reached out a gloved hand, shuffling up to the wall of the Grass. Blades pushed against my treated leather coveralls but none came as high as my face. I stretched as far as I dared, leaning out, careful not to overbalance, acutely aware that the further I stretched the closer my face came to the knife edges below me.

My fingers brushed the red thing and it swayed. It seemed to be attached to the Grass around it. A second attempt and I'd grabbed whatever it was attached to and pulled, but the Grass refused to break.

Carefully, I stretched out with my other hand, which held the secateurs. I'd need to cut the thing free of the Grass. It was much harder reaching out with both hands. I found myself standing on tiptoes in an effort to get more reach, my balance hanging by a thread. Then the secateurs bit into the Grass and the red thing came free. It did so with a sudden jerk and suddenly I was unbalanced and falling.

It happened in slow motion. I windmilled my arms, desperately trying to stay away from the wall of Grass before me. A picture came into my mind of Amy Rice, who had tripped and fallen face first into the Grass. It had cut off her nose and sliced open her lips and one of her eyes. I wanted to scream, to let out the fear and horror that had blossomed in my chest, but in this sluggish, treacle world I had no control over my body.

Then I fell, hard and backward, landing bottom first with a thump on the cleared soil of the yard.

For a few moments the world swayed and shifted around me as I sucked air down into my lungs. Then it all settled and I was able to look at the thing I held in my hand.

It was a flower; five luminescent, gently curving petals with a round yellow bulb at the centre. It was half way up a long stalk that must have come up from the Grass. There were more flower buds at intervals along its length, but none of them had opened.

Taking off my left glove, I carefully stroked a fingertip along one of the delicate petals. It was soft and warm and left a faint tingling sensation on my skin. Leaning close, I put my nose to it. There was no smell. I gazed at the wall of green before me. Now I was looking, I could see other stalks with buds. They looked almost exactly like normal blades; only slight symmetrical swellings gave them away.

I had never really thought that the grass might flower. It certainly hadn't in the sixteen years since colonists had been here. I'd seen flowers before. There were beds of them, carefully tended, around the Council chambers, seeds brought the vast distance from Earth. There were seeds in the Archives too, waiting for a time when ornamental vegetation was no longer a luxury only civic authorities could afford. Some people didn't think that time would come. Some thought that we would never win, that the Grass would consume us. Swallow us whole, the way it had swallowed almost every other thing on this world.

Unnatural, my father had called it. On land, he said, we had discovered only fifteen species of vegetation, four species of animal, thirty-two species of insect and twelve invertebrates. The seas, as though in compensation, teemed with life. Certainly most of the meat we ate was fish, brought overland along narrow, laboriously paved roads. It cost a lot; we hadn't eaten any since Dad died.

"Should have chosen the coast," my father had muttered whenever we'd painstakingly extended our yard, slashing the Grass at ground level, digging out the metre deep root systems, shredding and composting it all. It wouldn't even burn.

But the coast had problems of its own. Near Landfall something had come out of the sea one night. At least that's what they thought; the next day the whole town was empty with not a clue to where everyone had gone. There wasn't any blood, or signs of panic. There weren't any people either, but a few days later some bits washed up on the beach.

That town was deserted now, everything usable taken away to safer ground, leaving a pillaged skeleton, as though the things in the ocean had done more than just make a meal of the populace.

I looked down at the flower in my hand, feeling oddly as though this hostile world that was my home had given me a gift, a peace offering of some sort. Behind me the light in the house had come on.

I hurried to finish the rest of the yard, then tucked the flower inside my coveralls before going inside.

My mother was in the kitchen, doing something with vegetables. The food tasted different since Dad had died, as though the oppressive air of the house seeped into everything that was created there.

"Wash your hands, Jennifer." My mother's voice followed me as I ducked into my room. "Nina Sung just lost three fingers to that fungal infection that's going around."

I pulled the flower from inside my coveralls and put it into the glass of water that stood beside my bed. Even in the dimness of my room it seemed to glow. I stroked the petals and again felt the oddly pleasant tingling in my fingertips.

My mother's voice came again from the kitchen. "Dinner's on the table."

I left the flower in the darkness of my room.

I hated dinner; of all the times of day it was the worst. My mother and I sat across from one another at the table, under the single globe that we could only run at half intensity since two thirds of our solar array had gone offline. Neither of us spoke. The vegetable soup tasted bland and almost metallic, as though my mother had forgotten to put salt in it. Perhaps we'd run out of salt. I didn't dare ask.

It took me until the bottom of my soup bowl to muscle up the nerve to say what I'd been wanting to say for days.

"Mark says we should apply for a Council subsidy." The words came out in a rush, as though my normally unresponsive mother might jump in and cut me off. "He says we're entitled to one on account of Dad being killed in the fighting. He says we should be getting it already, but maybe there's been a mistake in the records or something."

My mother just sat there, her grey eyes focused a little to the left of my face, as though I wasn't really there at all.

"It'd help." I said. "Maybe we wouldn't have to sell any land."

The silence stretched further for a few moments. Then my mother said, "Have you been discussing our finances with your friends?" There was an edge to her voice that told me I should have kept my mouth shut.

"No, not really, it's just that…" How could I tell her that everyone knew we were in trouble, that I hadn't even needed to mention it.

"I don't want you seeing Mark Trenton anymore," said my mother, her gaze still on the space beside my head. "He's not a good influence on you. Besides, there's more than enough work to be done around here."

And with that, she got up and began to do the dishes, leaving her dinner half eaten on the table. In a fit of anger I grabbed it and ran with it to my room, where I drank it down straight from the bowl, before she could come and look for it.

I was sick of being hungry all the time. Sick of the pitying looks people gave me in town. Sick of my mother's misery. And I certainly wasn't going to do what she said. Pure rage washed through me, the emotion so strong it left me shaking. How dare she just give in? How dare she opt out and leave me with all of it? She had even stopped going out and looking for work. Was that my job now? What were we going to do when our coveralls and gloves wore out and there was no money to buy more? Or if one of us got sick?

I buried my face in the pillow on my bed and waited for my breathing to slow. My thoughts hung there, suddenly clear in my mind. This was my world and it wasn't going to defeat me, and neither my mother, nor anyone else was going to get in the way of that.

∞¥∞Ω∞¥∞

When I looked out my window the next morning the world had turned red. It was the red of the flower at my bedside, which now had every bud open. As far as I could see, the velvet green of the grass appeared as flashes in a sea of flowers. Every bud on every flower must have opened overnight, as though set on some internal timer.

"You were early," I said to the flower at my bedside and ran out into our yard.

My mother was already out there, standing completely still with her back to me, looking out over the blanket of colour. I went to join her, my bare feet silent in the dirt. When I was standing beside her I saw the shiny tracks of tears on her cheeks.

Without thinking I reached out and took her hand.

For a long time she didn't even look at me. Then she said. "Roses are red like that."

I didn't reply. I'd never seen a rose. No one had been able to make one grow here.

"He used to give me roses," my mother said. "Even though they were so expensive. He said I was worth it. We worked so hard to come here. We planned it together. It was what we wanted. We were going to do it together. How can things change so much?"

Her hand suddenly squeezed my own so tightly it hurt. I felt her start to shake.

"It's going to be okay." My voice sounded weak and uncertain in my ears. "We'll be okay."

"No." The word was a moan. "It's not okay. I can't. I just can't do this." My mother sank slowly to her knees, still holding my hand. Her breathing was coming in jerking sobs now, with horrible inhalations between, as though she couldn't draw the air down into her lungs. I stood fixed, my hand in hers, my toes digging down into the dirt beneath me, immobile but desperate to run, to cram myself under my bed and put my hands over my ears.

"I hate this place." She gasped the words out between breaths. "I've always hated it. From the moment my feet touched it I knew it was wrong. What are we going to do?"

I stood there, trapped, holding her hand as she cried, the red of our world around us.

∞¥∞Ω∞¥∞

"They really liked that wire," said Mark. "I wonder if there's a cook pot at home that Mum wouldn't miss."

"The chair was just as good."

Mark had managed to turn up with a coil of rusting wire and the other bits of the chair which had donated its leg earlier. I'd got the impression that he'd been the one who'd broken it and this was a handy way of destroying the evidence. The aliens had certainly made short work of it. They'd watched us expectantly as we'd approached this time, shuffling their massive frames forward but not coming too close until we'd deposited our offerings, as though they didn't want to scare us away. Their eager advance once we'd begun to retreat was evidence enough of their enthusiasm.

"What do you think they're building?"

We'd been speculating for the last half an hour as to the nature of the structure which was appearing on the hill. It consisted of a fragile looking four-legged framework standing more than two metres high. It didn't look very functional, particularly as shelter, and it had something hanging down from the centre of it by four poles. This part swayed every now and again in the gusts of the breeze.

"Maybe they're just bored," said Mark, "waiting for their people to come and get them. My dad says they're going to have to do it soon. The Aramaci have set a date for them to be out of the system."

The Aramaci were the race we'd negotiated with to protect our new planet, all those years ago when my parents had boarded their ship headed for the stars. Safe passage and military backup, in exchange for a one tenth share in our export tradings, no matter what they may be, for a thousand years. So when an alien race, bristling with attack craft, had arrived and advised us that the Grass belonged to them, we had triggered our distress beacon and, to everyone's surprise, the warships had arrived. I guess the Aramaci thought the planet had to contain something worthwhile for someone to attack it in the first place. Certainly this world was rightfully ours, allotted to Earth, but out in the fringes people didn't always pay a lot of attention to things like that.

We didn't even know the true name of the race that had attacked us, or why they had done so.

"You going to the War's End celebrations tomorrow?" said Mark. "I bet we could get hold of a whole lot of rubbish before the Recyclers come and pick it up. No one'd know."

I'd completely forgotten about the planned festivities that would be occurring the next day. There was going to be a fair. With so many people eating, drinking and enjoying themselves, we should be able to get our hands on all manner of disposables before the Recyclers snapped them up.

I thought about that as I made my way slowly home, hundreds of thousands of perfect red flowers swaying gently around me. The light had the heavy golden quality of late afternoon and the air smelled ever so faintly sweet. My feet seemed extraordinarily light on the road, and I was suddenly filled with optimism and hope. I was doing something important back on that stony hill, something that would go on to resonate through my life. Good would come of it, I was sure.

My feeling of optimism lasted until I reached home and remembered that my mother was waiting for me.

∞¥∞Ω∞¥∞

The day of the Wars End celebrations dawned bright but not clear and I woke to a faint dusting of gold on my pillow. I gazed at it in consternation for a moment before looking up at the flower on my bedside table. The table itself was also dusted with powder and all the small yellow bulbs at the center of my red flowers were gone.

It had to be pollen. It made sense; we hadn't discovered any pollinating insects on this planet, so the plants must have found a way to spread the pollen themselves. I giggled, suddenly finding the idea of exploding flower centers disproportionately funny. I imagined millions of them, all going off together. What was the sound of a million flowers exploding? Sitting up, I looked out the window. The air was hazed in gold, so thick it might have been fog. I laughed out loud.

When I came into the kitchen, my mother was cooking eggs. I stared at the two sizzling blobs of white and orange in amazement. "Where did those come from?"

"Suri Burton." My mother's voice was quietly surprised, as though she couldn't quite believe what she was saying. "She came to the door and gave them to us. Said she had extra and she thought we'd like them. Do you want to toast some bread?"

I had two slices of bread under the griller in a matter of seconds and started setting the table. The smell of the eggs was making me dizzy in anticipation. Everything seemed amazing this morning; bright and glowing and clear. Even the hazed gold of the sunlight streaming through the kitchen window was spectacular, pollen motes swirling lazily in the kitchen draughts. I gazed at them, entranced and suddenly I knew that today was going to be a perfect day.

∞¥∞Ω∞¥∞

The War's End celebrations were in Plenty, our hub town, more than twenty kilometres away. A special Council road train came and picked everyone up from the satellite settlements, its eight open-sided carriages wending slowly over dirt roads, enormous armoured tyres standing almost as tall as me. It would do the circuit continuously until the sun set on the day.

The mood in the carriages was effusive. People talked and laughed over the top of one another. Not even the babies cried. I sat in the midst of the press of people and drank it in, my gaze on the gold-tinged red fields around us. It was as though I'd been living in a dark damp hole and had suddenly been thrown out into warmth and light. In my hands I held my rucksack tightly, my collecting sack inside.

∞¥∞Ω∞¥∞

Plenty was packed with people. The town square had been turned into a market, stalls decorated with anything brightly coloured that people could find. Many had made wreaths and chains out of the Grass flowers, and loose red petals whirled in the breeze.

Mark appeared at my side as we got off the train. "Got any cash?" he asked, keeping his voice low so that my mother wouldn't hear.

I shook my head; we'd even brought a packed lunch, though in the euphoria of the morning I hadn't cared.

"Here," he pressed something into my palm. "My mum gave me heaps. Must've gone mad this morning. See you over by the games in half an hour."

Then he was gone, following his parents into the throng and I was left looking down at the five credit piece in my hand.

It was easy to convince my mother to let me explore on my own. There was free coffee, put on by the Council, and she didn't particularly want me hanging around while she sat and gossiped, so off I went. It was just as easy to grab the odd bit of rubbish when no one was looking and jam it in my sack, which soon bulged satisfyingly against my thigh. Half an hour later Mark was waiting by a stall where you had to throw rubber balls into barrels. Nobody was managing it very well. The balls kept bouncing out, but no one seemed to care as they laughed and shelled out credit for more attempts.

We both had a go at the rifle shooting; the solid butt of the gun was heavy against my shoulder as I lined up garishly painted paper fuzzers in the notched sight on the end of the muzzle. I laughed at the light kick of the recoil, even as I missed every time. Mark was giggling too, though he hit all his and we walked away with a big stick of fairy floss, pulling off chunks and shoving them into our mouths.

"Mum says this stuff used to be bright pink back on Earth," said Mark, holding up a pale golden tuft. "And just a little bit bitter, like it wasn't really food at all. She says they didn't care though, that they probably wouldn't have liked it any other way."

"Urghh." The idea of eating fake food as a treat seemed ridiculous.

Then, through the press of people, I saw something that made the world slow around me. My father stood in a gap in the crowd.

I stopped, unable to think, only able to stare as he turned in the sunlight and began to walk away. Then the crowds closed back in and he was gone.

For a moment I stood there, stunned and blinking, then I began to push my way towards where he'd been. It seemed I should call out, as though the words would stop him leaving, but part of me knew that this must be an illusion, another small miracle thrown up by this supernatural day.

I burst free of the crowds into a clearer space, my gaze frantically scanning faces. And there he was, standing less than twenty metres away. He looked the same as he always had, he even wore the same clothes — his best blue sweater and the khaki pants he'd brought from Earth and saved for special occasions.

I advanced slowly, afraid that if I ran it would break the spell and the illusion would dissolve before me. He was talking to a tall, brown-haired woman who I thought I might have seen before sometime, in some crowded adult place.

Step by step I drew nearer until I was standing less than two metres away, still mesmerised, watching all the little movements he made.

The woman noticed me first. She stopped talking and the smile faltered on her face. My father saw her looking and turned towards me.

It took a moment for him to pick me out of the background crowd. I waited for him to smile, speak my name, do any of the hundred familiar things that would prove to me that he was real.

His eyes widened as he saw me. But there was a confused, frightened look in them, as though he wasn't looking at the daughter he knew but something wrong that had taken her place. My own smile faded in response and I took a few steps closer, as though proximity could somehow change the expression in his eyes.

"Dad?" I said, the question coming into the word at the last moment.

He took a step backwards as though I was contagious. "Jessica." The horror was in his voice too. "What are you doing here?"

There was anger and accusation in the words. I shook my head against them, feeling the sudden sting of tears in my eyes. "Dad?" My voice sounded small and uncertain in my ears.

The woman beside my father reached out and took his arm. There was concern in her eyes and as she gave me a tentative smile I realised that her worry was for me. "Gary?" she said. "It's alright. We'll work through this. She's your daughter."

My father shrugged off the hand, his face drawing together in anger. "She said they wouldn't be here. I bet she planned it all along." He rounded from the woman onto me. "Did your mother tell you to come looking for me? Was that the plan? To come and beg me for money? I gave you the claim, didn't I? Wasn't that enough?"

I was crying in earnest now. My chest shaking, the tears running down my nose and into my mouth.

The woman grabbed my father's arm again. "For God's sake, she's just a child." She released her hold and came over to me, stooping down to my level and taking my shoulders in her big brown hands. "It's okay, honey. Your dad's just had a bit of a shock. He needs a couple of minutes to get over it. He feels bad about everything that's happened. He doesn't mean the things he said."

"But they said he was dead." My voice was a thick whisper through the crying. "Mum got a letter. He never came home. We lit candles every night." My mind was turning over and over, trying to understand, trying to see a way in which it had all been a mistake, a way where no one had lied to me, where my father hadn't walked out and not wanted to come back.

The woman had turned back towards my father. "Is that what she was told? That you were dead?"

He was shaking his head. "I didn't tell her anything. I have no idea what Mary told her. It just seemed best that I stayed away for a while."

"You mean you just left? Without even talking to her?" The woman was angry now too. "How could you be so gutless? God, if I'd known that was the way you'd dealt with it, I would have thought twice about letting you move in."

I couldn't stand it any longer. I pulled free of the woman's grasp and ran blindly into the crowd. My thoughts churned, tumbling over themselves out of sequence; relief that my father was alive falling beneath the knowledge that he had abandoned me; anger at my mother mixing with the understanding that I was not the only one that he had walked out on.

My vision was still blurred by tears and before I realised it I had escaped the crowds and was standing beyond the market square. The transport stop was before me, at the end of the street, the road train waiting to begin another loop. I looked down to where my fingers clutched tightly on the bag of odds and ends I'd so happily scavenged earlier.

I couldn't turn around and go back into the crowd. What would I say to Mark, or my mother, or worse still my father? I couldn't even bear the thought of it. I had to be far away from here. I jumped on the transport train as it began its trundling trip towards home.

∞¥∞Ω∞¥∞

By the time I reached the stone field it was mid-afternoon. It was awkward managing the squashing boards and my bulging sack at the same time, so my progress was slower than usual. That was good. It helped calm the horrible swirl in my mind. Worst of all, the magical euphoria that had infected everyone that day kept trying to push in. I resisted it because it felt perverse and wrong, but it only increased the muddle. I began to feel nauseous.

The two aliens waited patiently just out of touching distance while I emptied my loot onto the ground, though they were already waving their tentacles in anticipation. I think they knew I wasn't frightened of them anymore, because they were already inching forward as I began my retreat.

Perhaps because of everything else going on in my brain, I didn't pay enough attention to the boards beneath my feet. You have to place them just right, so there aren't any uneven clumps or hollows beneath them or they can tip when you stand on them and suddenly you're in serious trouble. The flowers made it harder than usual to judge how the Grass was arranged and whether there were any dips in the ground. I didn't test the stability of the board properly before transferring my weight onto it. My foot came down and the board tilted sharply to the side. My foot slid with it and suddenly I was falling.

I had a split second of realisation; I was dead. In my hurry to get here I hadn't gone home and put on my leather coveralls. No one knew where I was. I would bleed to death, quickly or slowly. I had time to hope that the Grass would hit a major artery and everything would be over in a minute or so. Then the tangle of green was rushing towards my face. In futile reflex, I closed my eyes.

Then everything stopped. Something clamped around my chest so tightly I could barely breath and I had the sensation of being lifted.

I opened my eyes just as I was set, feet first, on the stony ground.

The alien released the tentacle it had wrapped around my chest and the appendage retracted back into its body with a leathery shlupping noise. We gazed at one another. The two of them were only a metre away. I could have reached out and touched their knobbly, armoured hides. Their great dark eyes gazed at me. They looked expectant.

"Thanks," I said, unable to think of anything else to say.

The look of anticipation didn't change. Then the one on the right waved a tentacle at me, as though beckoning. They both turned, heads swiveling to look up the hill. The structure they had built sat there, outlined against the sky, the golden haze of the afternoon air around it.

The tentacle beckoned again and then both aliens turned and lumbered up the hill.

I stood there for a moment, gaze going to my boards, still lying in the Grass. I could get back on them and go home. I could wait in the silent house for my mother, questions and accusations going around and around in my head. Or I could stay. Part of me knew I should be cautious. If there was one rule about alien species it was that you could never predict what they would do. Part of me also knew that my mind wasn't working normally. The euphoric golden haze in the air had turned off my caution and my fear and these two beings in the field with me probably knew that.

I stared at my boards for a moment longer then turned and headed up the hill.

The aliens ahead of me were obviously excited and for a moment I wondered if they were as affected by the pollen as I was. They kept swiveling their little heads around, making sure I was following them. As I drew nearer to the structure they had made, my footsteps slowed. I'd expected a glued together mass of old hut beams and God knew what else, but this was more than that. Much more. It was all made out of the same material, for starters, something smooth-lined and luminous. Its poles and struts held the glow of the light, beautiful in their clean simplicity. My gaze went over the angles and lines and came to rest on what hung in the centre. It looked like a seat, but it wasn't the right size for either of my companions. I stared at it, my already overwhelmed brain trying to grasp the bizarre truth.

It was a swing. These two creatures from another world had built a swing. And they wanted me to use it.

They were looking at me, the expectation back in their eyes.

I took a step forward and they waved their tentacles in excitement.

I had to straddle the seat like a horse to sit on it. It yielded ever so slightly beneath my weight, as though the whole structure was flexible. Poles ran down to the sides and at the front and back, sloping inwards to a central axle above. I tilted my head upward and even that slight shift in weight sent the thing moving in a fluid arc, as though on perfectly oiled hinges. I gasped in surprise and without thinking shifted my weight forward and then back, feeling the seat and attached poles shift with me, magnifying my movements. Around me the landscape swayed. In reflex I pushed myself higher.

I'd been on swings before, but not like this. In the pollen-laden air, with the sea of red and green stretched out, it felt as though I could fly. Every movement of air took my breath away. Every pull of gravity as the swing reached its highest point, hung weightless for a moment, then dropped, was overwhelming. It felt as though my body couldn't hold the entire, startling experience of it. Everything else fell away, all the turmoil of the day, all the problems in my life, inconsequential. How could they matter when it felt this amazing to be alive?

I don't know how long I stayed on that swing. But when I finally allowed the everyday world to intrude, my face was wet with tears and my fingers ached from gripping. My legs shook as I stepped back onto the stony earth.

Two pairs of large dark eyes were still watching me and suddenly I was glad that we couldn't talk, because my fumbling words would have spoiled it all.

"I'm sorry," I said at last. "I'm sorry this happened to you."

One of them shuffled forward, eyes blinking in turn, and it reached a tentacle out to me, something wrapped in its tip. I held out my hand in automatic response.

A weight dropped into my palm. I stared down into flashing green. It was a stone, intricately faceted and coloured the blazing green of the Grass. Deep within, motes of red swirled and shifted. Somehow, I knew that they had made it, and now they had given it to me for some unfathomable reason that I would probably never know. I had never seen anything so beautiful, and I had never felt as undeserving as I did at that moment, as I said my clumsy goodbyes and walked away.

∞¥∞Ω∞¥∞

My mother came home late that night. I heard her footfalls come to my door and stop. I hunched beneath the bedclothes, pretending to be asleep while she stood there for an endless time. Eventually she went away.

Perhaps she didn't know what to say either.

∞¥∞Ω∞¥∞

The next morning I woke to an unnaturally bright room. I stared at the ceiling for a moment, sudden dread churning in my stomach, then raced to the window. Snow lay in a heavy suffocating blanket over the ground.

I pulled my coveralls over my nightdress in a matter of moments and ran from the house. Snow slid into my shoes and the icy air stung my skin. I didn't care. I slogged down the road towards the stone field, exertion burning the back of my throat, my breath clouding in the air before me. The world was silent and still, the sound of my breathing the only evidence of life. Around me the Grass was deep in snow, not a single flash of red in sight.

It was worse when I needed to leave the road. The snow was deep over the Grass and the boards skittered and slid. I stayed on my hands and knees, hoping that if I slipped the snow would shield me. Only a light drop in the landscaped defined the edge of the stone field, as Grass gave way to bare earth.

The field was empty.

I stood, gasping for breath, gazing over the unblemished blanket of white. There were no footprints, no signs of a ship landing. The swing still stood, its cross pieces and seat mantled in snow.

I stared at it for a long time before I noticed the two large bumps in the snow at its base.

I walked forward slowly, my feet punching down through the crust of the snow. Sun glittered over the perfect expanse of white and part of me felt that I was desecrating something sacred, that it should all be left as it was, silent and untouched in the morning sun. But I had to know.

Up close the mounds were more obvious. They were neatly side by side at the foot of the swing, as though the two of them had settled down together and waited patiently as the snow formed their shroud. I wanted to believe that they were just hibernating, that they had shut themselves down as protection and would wake when their ship came for them. But the truce was over. No one would come for them now. They would stay here, in this field on this foreign world, beneath the funeral monument they had built to bring a human child joy.

I cried for a time then left them there.

∞¥∞Ω∞¥∞

The stone field didn't hold the only death that day. The Grass, vulnerable as it reproduced, collapsed beneath the weight of the snow and turned to brown mush when the thaw came. It never got a chance to form seed, at least where we were. After the snows melted, I found I disliked the new brown, naked landscape around me, every hollow and rock exposed, but for the first time our claim was truly ours.

In other places the Grass remained. The Council analysed the pollen we had all been affected by and it started to become clear why a race might plant a world with such a thing and then travel light years to retrieve it.

I sold the stone they had given to me. I cried as I did it, even as I knew it was the right thing and that they would have approved. We bought chickens and rabbits for meat and eggs, seaweed to enrich our soil and seed for green manure. Our claim bloomed green for a few short weeks until it was all ploughed back in again and planted anew. The chickens roamed through the tilled soil, energetic blobs of life. We chose fruit trees and planted an orchard. We sowed three paddocks with fodder-weed and clover, in anticipation of the cows we were going to buy. The vegetable garden thrived and expanded and suddenly we had produce to sell. Somewhere during all of this, my mother began to smile again.

It was after that I went and saw my father. What he did still sits between us, despite the spoken apologies and forgiveness. I have no idea how to take the past and use it to strengthen our shared future, so the guilt and the resentment remain. But nothing is forever. I went back to the stone field once after the snow had melted. I felt I owed it to them, that I should make some attempt to bury anything that remained.

All that was left were a few small scattered pieces of metal, as though everything else had melted away with the snow. Even the swing was gone.

I stood there for a time looking out over the brown, muddy landscape around me. It was so ugly and so full of promise.

I turned and headed for home.

∞¥∞Ω∞¥∞

BY BLOOD AND INCANTATION
LISA L. HANNETT & ANGELA SLATTER

The cunning woman heats salted water, carefully stirring in clumps of bee propolis. Spoonfuls of honey. Rosemary sap. Aloe dew. Sweet-scented steam rises from the surface, softening the ever-dark wrinkles in her cheeks. She skirts the round hearth to gather ingredients, heels scuffling and scraping with each step. Old injuries, these, but persistent. When the woman was much younger, much less cunning, she could sprint. She could give frantic chase. Fast as a hare across her yard, *fast fast* down to the bog. She could splash in night-mud up to the thighs. She could dig in the mire, getting right down into the grime. Splashing, scooping, sobbing, searching. She could hobble herself on half-sunken blades, corroded silver, jagged bones. Ancestral offerings, once flashing in late afternoon sun, now glinting through the murk, so shiny and tempting. So dangerous underfoot.

She doesn't go far now. Doesn't flee the yard curving around her cottage, doesn't breach the hedge encircling the lot. She doesn't hare, or dash, or delve anywhere near the life-sucking wet. Instead, she spends her days tending circles. Bog, briar, yard. Cottage, hearth, wooden washtub. Circles within circles within circles. She keeps them intact, protected. Keeps herself, slump-shouldered Brona, at their centre. Forever staying put.

People come to see her, never vice-versa. She won't leave — and why should she? Her life, past and future, is here. She has all she needs. More: she has what *they* need. Herbs and remedies, blood and incantations. She never asks for payments. She will, however, accept gifts. Things left beside the hedge, close enough to the gate to accommodate her limp. Cupboards filled with food and other, useful, supplies. A log-pile always stacked. Ice chipped from the well in winter. Some gifts, though, should be greater than others. Warm-bodied thanks from grateful husbands, for instance — but this not so often now as before.

The men are younger than they once were. They are bashful. Reluctant. Their noses wrinkle at the threshold of her cottage, smelling something off.

The stink of years, Brona supposes. Loneliness. Desperation.

She doesn't force matters. She will exchange favours with whoever comes knocking, and will take no more than her due — knowing that service and offering must be commensurate in value.

"Leeches," she'd said, earlier this evening, to the maids who'd appeared on her doorstep. Two freckle-faced women, neither cunning. Steeped in the same stench that shoos potential lovers away. "Plucked from the deepest heart of the Grumnamagh — nowhere else. Bring as many as your legs can carry."

The pair had wanted to grumble, to negotiate — to debate! Brona had seen complaints in the slit of their gazes. But they'd taken the jars she'd forced on them, did as they were bid. A favour for a favour.

None would survive in the village, the cunning woman knows, if it wasn't for her.

If it wasn't for her, the bogs would be full.

Her gait assumes its usual cadence as she circumnavigates the fire. A few logs cupped in the packed-dirt floor, nestled deep. The cottage's pulsing heart, a blackened pot bubbling above its embers. She pads her hands with old linens, unhooks the cauldron. As always, it thuds to the ground between her mangled feet, much too heavy to carry when full. Grunting, she drags it behind her, over to the washtub discreetly kept behind a hazelrood screen.

Dried muck covers everything back here. Timber, tub and skin alike are stained a rich, rusty brown. Brona crouches, groaning, knees popping, and ladles scalding water into the bath, basting the contents.

Souls too, she thinks, fingernails tracing concentric lines onto the soaking leather. Round and round, she gouges targets for the leeches to grasp and suckle. *Souls are definitely circular. Here and gone and back again, never-ending.*

She sings under her breath while kneading the skin, keeping it supple and loose. The ladle dips in and out of the pot, splashes, washes, but does not clean. Brona wipes a grimy forearm across her brow, looks up at the dusty handprints smacked all over the walls. Tiny markings, so tiny. Evidence of a toddler's gumption and stubbornness. *If I can't go outside to play in the mud*, those handprints said, *then I'll make a sty in here.*

How many times had she slapped his greedy palms? Rapped his knuckles? "No, *a chuisle*. It's raining. No, my heart. It's too cold. No, my Cavan. You must remain with me."

Cavan, she thinks, splashing, scooping. *Cavan, my little hollow one.* Maybe tomorrow he'll help her to scrub it all away.

∞¥∞Ω∞¥∞

Nightjars squawk above the Grumnamagh. Pestering, scolding the maids for disturbing their slumber. And for singing so off-key.

"We're going to have scars. Hundreds of them," M'Amie moans, yet again, between verses. The old hag's song sloshes in her mouth, the words nonsensical slurping. Brona had said it wouldn't hurt a bit, but M'Amie knew she lied. Some swore the leeches of the Grum had tiny, tiny teeth. She winces at the sting of them on her legs, at her unwilling companion's splashing and scowling. The leeches must be paining her, too.

"I'm sure *she* could get rid of them — who knows at what price, though. You keen on asking?" Cora sounds both sly and aggrieved, as if what they want should be given free of charge. That's Cora all over.

M'Amie curses as she slices a toe. For a minute, she concentrates on placing her feet carefully. Hard *somethings* bump against her shins, scratch her calves. Twigs, maybe. Weeds. She plunges a hand into the blackness. Withdraws it, clutching tiny, naked bones. Evidence of drowned rabbits, she hopes. Stupid, innocent rabbits.

Released, the sepia-stained fragments land with a *plop*.

Moonlight makes M'Amie and Cora's white, white legs glow, beacons for the leeches. With her petticoats drawn up between her thighs, plump knees bobbing in and out of the bog, M'Amie clinks with each step. The empty jars in her satchel must be filled before dawn. Before she has to get back to stoke the kitchen's fires, and Cora has to make sure she does it. One night's gathering, Brona had said, and they'd be square. The witch happy with her worms, and their own troubles gone. One night's gathering, but a lifetime of tiny scars...

"Matthew will see them. He'll *know*," M'Amie says absently, eliciting a sound from Cora that's half spit, half angry air. "He'll know why."

"Keep your skirts down for once," Cora snaps. "Don't *present* yourself so openly. In broad daylight, even. Every time he finds you bent over the luncheon plates... Do it in the dark, for God's sake, and milord will be none the wiser."

M'Amie rolls her eyes, wanting to laugh at Cora for calling scruffy-cheeked Matthew *milord*. She snorts, pretending a midge has got up her nose when Cora's scowl deepens. It's only right, she supposes, that the housekeeper use his title... After all, Cora's not close to him the way M'Amie is, and she's a shrew besides. Nearly thirty, her stomach still flat and her chest not much better — and no chance of either changing. Cora's too old. Too stiff and formal. Married twelve years, womb ever as clean as the manor she sweeps, but still she claims she'll give that peat-farmer husband of hers a second pair of hands to wield spades. But if he hasn't managed to sow that quagmire by now, well, it's just not going to happen, is it? Most likely she wants an excuse to get out of work. To lie in with a bub, nestling and feeding, and leave all the hard slog to the younger, fitter, prettier maids. But servants, M'Amie thinks, even housekeepers, don't *convalesce*. They drop their little parcels, clean up their own messes before getting back to milord and milady's needs.

Cora's just snippy because she knows M'Amie has plenty of time. With her wide hips, heavy tits, and regular moons, M'Amie will always be fertile as a field after flood. As if that's such a good thing. As if that's such a boon.

But Cora doesn't know, does she? She has no idea. The bounty of Matthew's seed. How quickly it germinates, given the right conditions. She hasn't got a clue how anxious M'Amie is for what's growing to be gone… Cora, stiff, formal Cora, can't possibly imagine what that yearning feels like. Wanting so badly to undo something that's well and truly done.

So it was a surprise to find her at Brona's cottage, blushing, begging a favour. M'Amie hadn't heard what it was, but she could certainly guess. She'd giggled, seeing Cora so mortified, so debased. And the sound had caught the hedgewitch's attention. It had attracted her glare.

With one look, Brona had gleaned what M'Amie wanted. One look, and the old woman was laughing.

"Look at you two," she'd said, grasping their wrists, more firm than friendly. M'Amie and Cora didn't look anywhere but straight ahead. "You know, if you'd had a quiet word with each other back at the house, you might've timed this better." Brona had lifted an eyebrow at their silence. "I see," she'd said, after the moment dragged long. "You must know that secrets shared are secrets no longer." No response. "Good. That's good."

And as Brona told them what they were to do, what favours they could bestow, Cora and M'Amie had risked a sideways glance at one another. Knowing they would share naught.

Now, slopping through the Grum, her legs squirming black, M'Amie wonders if Cora thinks she visited the witch to advance herself. Or to buy a love potion? A ravishment spell? She grins, swallowing another snort. As if she's not got *natural* charms enough to keep Matthew where she wants him. As if she's the kind of girl who needs to resort to such *tactics*. She resumes her low chant, garbling, warbling. If she *was* that kind of girl she'd not be enlisting Brona to get rid of this babe. Maybe she'd be buying sweet-tasting poisons, treats for Matthew's goodwife and his bright-haired son. If she was that type of girl. Maybe she'd be slipping bespelled drops into his eyes after he comes, when he's soft and susceptible. To help him see her more clearly, to want her to be something more than a tumble taken whenever he fancies. If M'Amie was that kind of girl, she'd be doing much, much more than gathering poxy leeches beneath a witch's moon.

∞¥∞Ω∞¥∞

Little bitch, little bitch, thinks Cora. In her head it's a tune to rival the incantation she's mouthing at the witch's behest. *Little bitch, little bitch*, echo the nightjars.

Smarmy and smug, M'Amie is. Cora feels a bite, rips the bloodsucker from her hamstring before it gets too set in its suckling. *Firm and healthy and brimming with — what?* She tears another wyrm away, flicks it into a lidless jar. *With time*, answers a whisper, nagging from the back of her mind. *Young, elastic, fresh-bellied time.*

Cora stops singing. Drops a curse and a thumb-sized writher into silver-edged ripples.

"Start over," M'Amie says, wading over to squint into Cora's jar.

The housekeeper glares. "What?"

"The tune," the maid explains, so smug, so smarmy. The moon casts weird shadows across M'Amie's face, complicates it, but Cora can hear the girl's expression. "If you mess it up—" M'Amie widens her mulish eyes, shakes her head derisively "—you have to start over. The whole thing, three times through — *unbroken* — for each friggin' leech. If I have to do it proper, so do you."

Little bitch. Won't be so clever when that smooth chin turns to suet. When those cheeks sprout gin blossoms. When those tits start to droop no matter what she's about, and she can't stop it, and she finds she pisses her britches with every sneeze. When she's no longer the ripe apple everyone wants to pluck. When her man starts looking elsewhere, just as Cora's did and does.

Cole's taken to calling her 'The Burren' when she comes abed late, late at night. That is, when he bothers calling her much at all. Woman. Wife. Burren. Never Cora, never *a chuisle*. Thinks a bit of wordplay makes him smart. As if his own name wasn't perfectly apt.

Barren as the burren... Oh, the housekeeper knows what he's getting at — but he's wrong, of course. Cora's not *barren*. She has it in her to bear life — she's fallen pregnant more than a dozen times — she just can't keep the babe inside long enough for it to thrive.

M'Amie, though, the self-centred thing, doesn't have the faintest idea. She can't fathom what it was like — surviving all those sad, wet, painful fiascos. Erasing their presence. Moving on. Ever-hoping. Silly bint, hasn't been at the manor anywhere near long enough to know the years Cora swelled and failed. M'Amie hasn't yet seen a winter in this county, four months she's spent here more or less, and a lazier scullery maid Cora's never seen, though she moved herself fast enough into his lordship's good graces.

Little bitch, little bitch, let me come in. Oh, yes, while she's pert and willing, milord will ever be at her door, finding her in the corridor, the cupboard, the kitchen. Tossing the skirts over her head as and when he pleases. And she, stupid slut that she is, somehow has the sense to keep letting him in.

∞¥∞Ω∞¥∞

Brona has watched for their return, feigning patience. A blurred path skirts through the dust, the floor foot-polished. She has waited, shuffling between the window, its glass obscured by cobwebs and marsh-spatter, and the hazelrood screen. When the maids appear, trying and failing to step carefully from sturdy tussock to tussock, trying and failing to stay out of the oily water, dawn is still some hours away. The cunning woman has had no sleep. She stands vigil, ever awake.

The women tap twice at the entrance, quiet as a heartbeat. Brona forces herself to wait until they knock again, then twists the knob too hard. "Quickly," she says, ushering her supplicants in. "Close the door." With shaking hands, she nudges them towards the rickety table. Her ears drink in the sound of full bottles clacking in the satchel M'Amie still carries.

"Put them here," Brona says, pulling two jars from the girl's grasp. Brona places them carefully down, as far from the table's edge as possible. One jar, two, three — she reaches out, but there are no more.

Rather, she is given no more.

Cora and M'Amie stand, united for however brief a time, but united nonetheless. They hug the vessels to their chests, mouths set in identical determined lines.

"Give us what we came for, hedgewitch," says M'Amie.

"Give us what we're owed," says Cora through gritted teeth.

"Gifts," Brona reminds them. "Favours. Let there be no talk of *owing*."

Her brain is fuddled and fuzzy with exhaustion. Through the glass, in the jars' swirling myriad contents, she thinks she can see … can see … slinking, slithering forms, yes. But more, something more. A shape. A boy? So small, so small. Wispy, spinning. She catches strange glimpses, shadows spiralling around ghostly, slow-forming limbs. She blinks and the vision is gone.

Hallucinations, Brona thinks. *Exhaustion.*

She shakes her head.

"I've never broken a bargain," she says. She points to a tidy shelf across the room where she laid the gifts out carefully, hours earlier. Piles of feverfue, baaras, cures for water elf disease. Two miniature clay tokens shaped like curled babes. A puddle of colourful silk ribbons.

At last, M'Amie hands over the satchel. Cora relinquishes the remaining bottles, and the two of them retreat to collect their due.

For a moment, Brona loses herself in arranging, lining up, assessing the trove. *This will have to do*, she thinks. *It must be enough. It must.* Behind her, the room has gone quiet.

"What now?" she asks, feeling the weight of two gazes. "You think I have nothing better to do than fuss about the roundness or flatness of your bellies? Wear the charms and the ribbons, steep the herbs in boiled water then drink it all down, every drop." She recites an enchantment they must speak before and after the drinking, then gets them to repeat it. Brona thinks she gets it right — doesn't care much if she hasn't. No sooner does the spell leave her lips than it is gone from her mind. She does not watch them leave.

∞¥∞Ω∞¥∞

Come dawn, poisonous eels churn inside M'Amie's gut. Stoats gnaw at her innards. Wasps sting her tender parts, burning and shredding. *That's some flushing Brona's worked*, she thinks, breath seething through clenched teeth. She balls up on her cot, hipbone scything into the thin mattress. A huge round softness prevents her from properly folding. Sweat-soaked, she unfurls, gritting through pain. She fumbles for candle and match. Eyes gummy and heavy-lidded, M'Amie squints against spark and flame. Squints and squints but cannot seem to focus, to clear away the big white blob that's blocking all view of her thighs.

Bloody witch! M'Amie's belly hasn't gone down; it has bloated even further! She coughs and coughs, and coughs become sobs. Quiet, stifled whimpers. Inhuman snuffling. There are talons inside her. There are knives. Rocking back and forth, she wipes drips from her nose. Gapes, mouth pried but not moaning. Heaving silently at the sight. *I look five months gone now, not two.*

She feels the taut flesh, the stretched bulb of her middle, feels it chafing against her shift. *Things* move within her. Eels? Stoats? Wasps? No, no. Nightmares. An angry babe. Pangs lance through her, and now she moans. Loud and long. Like a poisoned cat, she's filled with noxious gas, bile, putrescence. No matter how she farts, how she writhes, the sensation does not ease. And the stench! Mud and decay. Loam and wild garlic. Fungus. Things buried, unearthed.

M'Amie moves slowly, gingerly down the servants' staircase and comes into the empty kitchen. Tonight, for the first time, she has avoided Matthew. Heavens forbid he see her — smell her! — like this. The hearth is cold, but the girl can't make it to the fireplace, much less dig kindling from the bottom of the chip-box, or cast about for flint and steel. She stumbles, falls to her knees on Cora's perfectly-swept tiles.

Cursed witch. Sped the child along instead of slowing... Instead of stopping it altogether! Between her thighs, there is wetness. Stickiness. *It's coming*, she guesses, too afraid to check. *No, please no.* The liquid is warm and carries a tang of iron. Rats nibble on her intestines. A clot of maggots presses, pushes, roils to get out.

M'Amie can't bear to look, can't bear to see the baby's crowning.

She crawls away from the hearth, towards the comfort of the large pantry. *A good place for a scullery maid to hide,* she thinks. Dry and dark and safe. She makes a nest of apple sacks and bags of flour. Curls like a bitch on the hard floor to whelp her pup in secret.

She imagines the look on Matthew's face when he realises what's happened. What she's done. Not the pregnancy. The trying to get rid of it.

With her face buried, cheeks grating against rough hemp, M'Amie howls.

∞¥∞Ω∞¥∞

Cora had gone from Brona's hovel straight to her quarters. Straight to her own small corner of milord's great manor, and into her husband's bed. Convinced, at last, they'd conceive a child who would stay. Who would cling to her, and hold fast.

At first Cole is surprised by her enthusiasm. Then fervent. Eager. Delighted as Cora slides up and down on him. She isn't dry tonight; her nethers don't rasp against his. For once, this isn't a brief, grunted rutting. Cora is liquid on top of him. She slurps and sloshes. Cole groans and moans with each glide of her. And he thrusts and thrusts and thrusts and hollers. Growls. Slaps.

"What is this, woman?" he shouts, punching her off of him. She splays on the bed while he scrambles away, scrubbing at his red-soaked cock, yanking up his red-soaked trousers. The feather bed, a wedding gift from Cora's mother, is awash with crimson.

There should be no blood until a baby is born, she thinks, smearing the scarlet on her bloomers, staring at it blankly. Her husband retreats, head moving from side to side like a confused hound. Seeing the bewilderment on Cora's face, Cole hesitates, and hope rises in her that he might, just this once, offer some sympathy. Some care. What he gives is his broad back. The door closing behind him as expressive as Cole is ever likely to be.

Cora inhales deeply, gathers herself. She has felt this before. Has no doubt she'll experience it again. Down the hall, she grabs thick rags and a worn calico belt from the linen cupboard, into which she struggles, refusing to cry.

In the pantry, there is dried nettle and yarrow to staunch the flow. Her feet are leaden on the stairs.

She doesn't give M'Amie a second thought until she reaches the kitchen. Sees the carmine trail dragging from the fireplace to the closed pantry door. It takes all her strength to push it open. To step aside and let a sliver of morning light splash across the girl's shivering, huddled form. Her twisted, desperate face. The bloat in her nightdress. The blood.

Little bitch, she thinks again, but half-heartedly. *Little bitch, little bitch, that baby should've been mine.*

Might be it still can…

Cora grabs the herbs she needs, enough for herself and for the ailing maid. "Come. Now," she says. She'll make a quick poultice for each of them, jam it between M'Amie's legs herself if she has to — the girl can't lose the baby. A tisane, too, to slow things down, to keep the child within. The baby *must* be saved. Her grip on M'Amie's arm — her young, plump arm — is harder than it needs to be. The maid squirms, but Cora's hold tightens.

"Get up," she says, adding a boot to her command. "We're going back."

∞¥∞Ω∞¥∞

When tipped, the jars' contents glide into the tub, graceful and playful as otters. The cunning woman stirs once or twice with a long wooden spoon, then abandons it in favour of flesh upon flesh. Water froths with the flickering slickering of overfed leeches. Brona's lips twitch with a twickering smile. Once they've all latched, round mouths to round tracings, she hooks them in place with careful, precise whispers. Fixes them to Cavan's skin.

Her fingers, though soak-shrivelled and thick at the knuckles, are nimble. Submerged in the tub, they squeeze and stroke. Careful of the wyrms' tender flesh, so delicate when engorged. They frisk gently, rubbing and tugging. Quick, confident motions. Ones she's practised many times before, when accepting and returning favours. Giving and taking comforts. She milks the leeches, resisting the urge to clench, to rush. Rushing doesn't return any favours. Rushing takes more than it gives. Time. Effort. Joys. Boys.

Her fingers work and work, massaging. Coaxing spurts of her son's soul from wriggling fat bodies, grey-white gouts of the spirit the leeches have feasted on in the Grumnamagh all these years. She lifts a flaccid thigh from the preserving fluids, pinning a leech with her thumb. Has the boyish hide stretched? Has her son grown while she wasn't looking? Cavan, dear hollow one, always in such a hurry. Always rushing.

She strokes and strokes and strokes.

He's filling out, she thinks, the slurry in her veins slurping and sloshing through a heart that hasn't beat so quickly since the child rushed his life short. Barely three, and he hadn't quite learned to run, hadn't toughened his muscles. But he could plod, stomp, *hurry* from place to place. He could sneak though the smallest gaps: in the cottage's siding, the sapling briars, blades of grass on the soggy shores. Cavan hadn't been a runner, not quite, but he'd sure had a stride on him. An inexorable, unforgettable stride.

One small step into the Grum and Cavan's foot caught on a dented brass arm-ring. Or a sword bowed by time. A thief's crooked ribcage. Brona had imagined it thousands of times. She could picture it perfectly. The twist of her son's ankle, shackled to muck. Nightjars taking up his screech, sending it back, beak-shrill. Surprise turned panic, just for a second, before his precious face was swallowed. Gone beneath the surface with the other treasures and bones, gone gone until Brona had woken from her untimely doze. Until she'd splashed and scooped and sobbed and searched, having slept just a minute — just a few minutes — drowsing in the afternoon heat... Until she'd liberated his limp shell from the drowning-shallows.

Until now, at last, when she'd harvested every last skerrick of his soul from the wet.

It's working.

Soon there is meat to him, not just wrinkled skin, not just leather. *Finally.* Certain of it now, her hands are a blur. *Finally, it's working.*

Another moment and Cavan's torso begins to lift on its own. His limbs flail, contorting into grotesque positions. Brona slips her hands under his legs, feels sinew and cord. Not toddler's legs, pudgy even as they stretched into boyhood. The knees, once pink and dimpled, are wizened and black, bending backwards like a nag's. They press into her palms, sharp and knobbly. Covered in a pelt of slimy hair.

Not to worry, she tells herself, a bit too quickly. *It's just a bit of sludge, a bit of soul-scum. We'll scrub you up nicely, my boy, once the spirit's settled. Not to worry.*

Webbing gums the spaces between Cavan's fingers and toes. Now his cheeks and chin lengthen, equine. Once-bright irises are muddied; orbs of gold and rust bulge from the sockets, wide-set and rolling with a wild horse's glare.

The thing whinnies, shakes its weedy mane, claps its scaled hands against the walls. *Splat splat splat*, erasing the five-fingered prints with its own. The leeches, spent, fall off the swollen skin. *Splat splat splat* into the filthy water, too exhausted to flee as the púca flips onto its belly and plunges face-first into the tub.

Púca.

Brona doesn't gasp — she doesn't believe it. *Will not.*

She grabs a cake of lye and lard, and starts to grind it across her son's spine, shoulder blades, ribs. *We'll scrub you up nicely... Not to worry...* But Cavan's ears point and droop. Bristles sprout from his neck and spike all the way down to his long-tailed rump. And the smell — oh, the smell! — sweat and rot and meat. Mouthfuls at a time, he crunches and slurps and snorts all the leeches until the bath is depleted. There are none left to restore him, none to rescue. Left too long in the Grum, the boy's spirit has diluted, decayed, mingled with unsavoury wights. Mischief-makers with a mind to drown their riders, not carry them safely across bog and fens. Letting loose a loud burp, the beast rolls over and smiles. His teeth are wood-tinged and covered in moss.

Not púca, Brona thinks, unable to deny what's in front of her. *Kelpie. Look how he runs—*

And it is this speed — as he leaps out of the tub, past hazelrood wickers and cunning woman alike, and skitters across the cottage — this unnatural pace, that convinces Brona the creature is not her boy. *Her* Cavan scuttled, meandered, waddled. He did not rear or gallop.

∞¥∞Ω∞¥∞

The cottage door opens.

"Close it! Close it!" Brona cries, hobbling, a small-stepper, just like her son. "Stupid girls," she says, startling Cora and M'Amie. The fury in her voice overwhelms their own ire, cuts it down and makes it stillborn. "He's getting out! He's taken my son!"

The women stare at the creature hurtling towards them. Black fairytale incarnate, legend made flesh, nightmare given form. Their concerns, their aches and agonies give way to self-preservation; despite Brona's exhortations they scamper out of the thing's way. The cunning woman's scream is something to hear. Fast and shrill, it doesn't waste its time in the shanty's cramped space, but shoots through the narrow door, almost as quick as the kelpie with his jumping, kicking gait.

Brona can guess why the women have returned so soon. In her haste, she was careless. Inattentive in distraction. She'd given them the wrong herbs. Too few or too many ribbons. Perhaps she'd spoken the words for another bewitching. Her fingers on the clay were sluggish, too slow to quicken the manikins. She had not repaid the girls' favour with her own.

Even so, Brona *is* cunning. These dull maids are helpless without her, she knows — just as she is without them. Even so, even so. She hasn't yet got what she wants, what she needs. But neither have they.

"Catch it! Catch him! Or you'll have no remedy from me, though you beg until the last sunset!"

The women scurry as quickly as they can, both with bellies aching and hearts dimmed. Their feet, driven by misery, fear, despair, thud the packed earth, chasing after the kelpie. The fae colt lets loose shattering cries, mocking laughter as it teases, now trotting, now cantering, now slowing almost to a walk. Giving the women a chance to catch up. Making them believe they've a hope of grabbing his long tail, pulling him to a halt.

Brona shuffles along behind, still some distance away, her feet aching, aching, aching. She can only see what happens from afar; her shouts make no difference. Even so, even so. She screeches her son's name. Sees his fall recreated, just as she's imagined so many times.

One small misstep.

His hoof catches on a dented brass arm-ring. Or a sword bowed by time. A thief's crooked ribcage. It doesn't matter, she realises. There was nothing she could do. Nothing she can do. He is caught, well and truly. He flails and topples, with M'Amie and Cora close behind.

M'Amie leaps clumsily after the creature, tries to balance her new-found weight, fails. She lands on top of him, begins to tip, to tumble. Cora, anxious as a mother hen, follows in M'Amie's wake, close enough to touch. To wrangle. Her attack is more confident, her aim more precise. She reaches past the snorting, struggling kelpie. Scoops her arms around the pregnant girl, and keeps her from falling.

Dragging Cora with her, M'Amie wraps her hands — her strong, red-skinned, scullery maid's hands — around the kelpie's throat and begins to squeeze. The creature thrashes, its hooves catching at her shins and ankles. Still, M'Amie squeezes. Frail bones give way beneath her fingers. Tighter, and its cries diminish, muffle, mewl. Its scrunched face, purple and white, covered in mucus. Shrivelled as an old man's.

M'Amie squeezes and squeezes and squeezes until the last gasp soughs from the kelpie's mouth, until the rough hairy body goes limp at last, until its substance melts away, and M'Amie is left with nothing more than a brown, desiccated skin sack that once held a boy.

Even then, her grip does not loosen — nor does Cora's, who has encircled the girl's broad waist, holding her up, arms cradling the distended belly. Protective and protecting.

Brona puffs up to them, cheeks wan and wet. She takes in the depleted skin. The women's depleted expressions. Splashing, scooping, sniffling, she slouches beneath the weight of all she has done. All she still needs to do.

Her feet throb, soles shredding again and again, but she refuses the crutch of the women's arms. Instead, she takes the leather draped across them. Strokes it, folds it, cradles it in the crook of her elbow.

"That's good blood you're wasting there," she says, gesturing at the spill on Cora's skirts, the seep on M'Amie's arse. "We'll need that to fix this mess. We'll need as much as we can get."

∞¥∞Ω∞¥∞

INDIGO GOLD
DEBORAH BIANCOTTI

"Don't you hate that, Kaneko?"

He said it like they were in the middle of a conversation.

Ai Kaneko looked up from her desk. Looked up, squinted, took off her glasses, and leaned back so she could see him better. Merv was wide, but also tall. He had the bulk of a man who really shouldn't loom over desks blocking out the dawn.

"I'm suppose to say, 'hate what, exactly, Merv', aren't I?" Kaneko asked. She tried and failed to keep the frustration out of her voice.

"It's good you're playing along," Merv replied. "Keep it up. Let's pretend I'm the boss around here for a while."

He dropped a scrap of paper on her desk. Literally a scrap, since it was torn from the bottom of a broadsheet. It was the story of a car-jacking in the southern suburbs. He'd made a note in thick blue marker over the top of it.

Merv really was the boss, so she had to pick it up and try to decode what he'd written.

"Something, something," she muttered, "and then another something, and a phone number."

"Oh, yeah, coming back to our earlier conversation. This is what you're meant to hate," Merv said. "When crackpots call taking credit for crimes that've already been solved."

"That's what this is?"

Merv shrugged. "It's *something*."

"You want me to ring up and ask what kind of crackpot they are?" Kaneko offered.

"I want you to call up, get an address, and go meet her."

"Why?"

"Because she's got one hell of a story. And you know what stories do?" Merv asked.

Kaneko didn't bother to suppress her sigh. "They sell papers, Merv."

"Right. Go make a story, Kaneko."

She got to her feet. "And if there's nothing there to report?"

"I said *make* the story, Kaneko, not find the story. Be a journalist."

She waited too long to come up with a witty response. By the time she opened her mouth, Merv was checking his pockets.

"Wait, here's another one," he said.

"Another what?" Something sour-tasting lodged in the back of her mouth.

"Another guy claiming to have some kind of special, super-duper power." He found the scrap of paper and was holding it at arm's length. "Says he can find numbers. Whatever that means."

"*Find* them? What, even the imaginary ones?"

Merv didn't take the bait. "You tell me, it's your story."

He dropped the scrap of paper on the desk in front of her. It had been folded and refolded, the burr of the edges eating away at the numbers marked in heavy pen.

"Kaneko, story-maker, Kaneko, lone journo-warrior," he said.

"Is that racist, Merv?" she asked. "I think that's racist."

Merv took a step backwards. Kaneko liked when he did that. She resumed her seat and leaned back, staring up at him.

"Why are you filling up my time with these fakers?" she asked.

"Fakers?" Merv looked hurt, and the hurt looked almost genuine. "You see this second number here?"

He pointed to the folded scrap of paper on the desk.

"Yeah?" she said.

He leaned in and whispered loud enough to be heard two desks away, "You should ask them about fakers."

Kaneko returned his dramatic whisper with one of her own. "Who is this 'they', Merv?"

"The cops. Turns out, there's a taskforce."

"Wait, they've set up a *taskforce?* You sure about that?"

"And abracadabra!" Merv straightened. "I knew we'd make our story in the end."

Kaneko hesitated. "Great."

She surprised herself by meaning it.

Merv said, "Be careful with the numbers guy. Sounds like a real nut."

∞¥∞Ω∞¥∞

She dialled the second number first. It was answered on the first ring. That could be a good sign or a bad one. It meant someone who was keen to talk, or someone who was keen to get the talking done so they could hang up the phone.

A deep woman's voice answered. "Detective Palmer here."

"Detective Palmer? Of the … special powers taskforce?"

Kaneko held her breath. Palmer might've been doing that also.

"Depends," Palmer said a moment later. "Who's calling?"

"My name is Ai Kaneko—"

"What's your interest, Ai?"

Nothing for it. "I'm calling from *City Tribune*—"

The line went dead. Just like that, like Palmer had been holding her thumb over the phone cradle the whole time.

Kaneko pulled the phone from her ear. Great. One of those stories where she got to chase her own tail. She loved those.

She called the 'numbers' guy and listened to his voicemail message. His voice was smooth and old. He could have been a radio announcer, back when having a good voice meant something to the trade. She left her number and a message that she was calling about a report he'd made to the City Tribune. Then she headed for the door.

∞¥∞Ω∞¥∞

"Got a drink, love?"

The alley smelled of piss and muck. In the middle of it — sprawled indifferently, like he was lounging on a sofa — was a man, dirty from his matted hair to his bare feet. His toenails were long and yellow and his beard was so full of grit it stood out straight across his chest like a bib.

"No. Sorry," Kaneko replied.

It was dark in the alley; even the pavement was dark, a giant oil spill of a spot, filled with the mess of a life lived in the open. In contrast, the quiet, suburban street two metres away looked to be lit by Klieg lights.

Kaneko wrote *Klieg lights* in her Moleskin.

"What's your name?" she asked.

"Who's asking?"

"I'm Ai Kaneko," she said. "I'm a journalist for the *City Tribune*."

"You're what?"

"You can call me Annie," Kaneko said. "And you are?"

"I'm the King around here."

Kaneko breathed shallowly, not wanting to take in the smell of the place. Already it was in her clothes and coating her skin like an oil bath.

"Well, that's great," Kaneko said.

"Isn't it, though?" The man grinned.

Impossible to judge his age. His face was unlined but his hair was grey. Kaneko put him somewhere between forty and sixty. Maybe seventy; his eyes were rimed with some kind of gummy glaze. He wasn't who she had come to see, he just happened to be in this miserable alley when she moved through it for a better view of the apartment block.

She wrote *the stink of human detritus, the age-old smell of waste and loss in a city too long grown used to it.* Her writing was uneven, more a scrawl than actual words. It didn't matter. One prompt by a pen mark on a page and the smell would come flooding back.

The apartment block was old and plain, four storeys high and about a dozen metres wide. Not wide enough, Kaneko would've thought, for the sixteen letterboxes lined up on the front wall. It looked like it had been dropped there, a forgotten building that was all red brick and corners, windows added as an afterthought. *Like a coffin standing on its end,* she thought. *Like a place people came when they didn't care about living anymore.*

She wrote *coffin* on the page.

She'd already been all the way to the top to knock on the door of Number 14. No answer. So she'd come down to do a perimeter sweep. This kind of otherwise useless rummaging in alleys could help with the setting, and setting helped mood and mood made stories. And stories, Merv assured her, sold newspapers.

She made a note in her notebook about the oily residue under her feet. *Will I ever get the smell outta my shoes?* is what she wrote.

"Hey, Your Majesty," she said.

"Yup?"

"Do you know anything about the residents of this building?"

"Junkies," the King said, with venom.

"Okay. Know anything about the woman in Number 14? Tipsy Burrows?"

He snorted. "What kind of name is Tipsy?"

"Well," Kaneko began, but realised she didn't have an answer.

"What's she look like?" the man asked.

"I haven't met her."

He frowned hard and a spiderweb of lines opened up along his face. "Don't be bringing me this rubbish. How'm I s'posed to know who she is if you can't describe her?"

"Sorry, yeah," Kaneko said. *You sound like my boss.* "Thought I'd ask."

She decided to try the apartment again. It had to be better than standing in filth.

This time when she entered the building, she could hear a washing machine on one of the floors and a television blaring through the thin walls. People were awake. That was a good sign.

She knocked loudly at Number 14.

"Yeah?" A tired voice, barely muffled by the thin door.

Kaneko leaned forward. "Tipsy Burrows?"

"Yeah?"

"I'm Ai Kaneko, from the *City Tribune*. You called about a story?"

The door opened. Kaneko thought she heard three or four other doors open at the same time. She didn't turn around, only kept her smile fixed on the girl. She was young, very young, smeared in mascara and lipstick, sallow underneath that with a fine face that would look like vulnerability to a camera. Kaneko would have described her as slim but for the round knobs of her wrists and the clavicle jutting out above her flat chest. Gaunt was a better word. She wrote *gaunt*.

"Tipsy?"

Tipsy wore very little, some kind of singlet top over shorts where the pockets hung lower than the denim. The shorts looked like they should be tight, but they ballooned stiffly, held up by Tipsy's pronounced hipbones and some kind of inbuilt gravity defiance.

"Yeah?"

Kaneko said, "I understand you know something about a murder that took place last week?"

Tipsy perked up. "Hey. Yeah, I rang that newspaper."

"And here I am," Kaneko replied. "I'm from that newspaper."

"Hey!"

Tipsy invited Kaneko in and then curled on her bed, the only piece of furniture in the tiny bedsit. To one side was a kitchen bench. To the other was what appeared to be a bathroom. In the middle was a window that looked grimy inside and out. The place smelled of stale air and takeaway *something* but it still smelled better than the alley.

"What's your name, again?" Tipsy asked.

"Ai Kaneko."

Tipsy frowned. "What kind of name is that?"

There was nothing in her voice but curiosity, so Kaneko told her it was Japanese. Then she pulled out her phone.

"Can I take a photo?" Kaneko asked.

"Of what?"

"Of you, in your home. It's just a memory prompt for later, when I write your story. I won't publish it."

"But you'll write the story, right?"

Kaneko had met this kind before. Almost exclusively this kind whenever Merv dropped one of his notes on her desk. They wanted to be famous, but they wanted the fame to be flattering, and they wanted to make sure of that first. Tipsy Burrows probably would consent to a photo, but only after she fixed her make-up and put on some even more revealing clothes.

"Don't worry about it," Kaneko said. "Just an idea." She looked down at her phone like she might be checking a number and hit the camera button with the side of her thumb. Tipsy didn't seem to notice.

"Let's start with your age," Kaneko smiled. She looked around for a clean place to lean and chose the edge of the windowsill. When Tipsy looked at her blankly she added, "How old are you?"

"Eighteen," Tipsy replied, too quickly.

Kaneko scratched *18* onto her notepad with a question mark beside it.

"And you have a power?" Kaneko prompted. "You can find dead bodies?"

"Not really," Tipsy said.

Kaneko gave her a look she hoped was politely curious.

"I mean, I guess? I can find *things*, right?" Tipsy said. "But not people. Not unless they're dead."

The girl had an upward inflection that made her hard to follow. Everything sounded like the beginning of something else.

"That must be useful," Kaneko commented.

"Yeah? Think I could make some money from it?"

"You need money?"

Tipsy scratched at one long, limp arm. "Yeah. I could do with some."

"I could maybe pay you for this interview, how's that sound?"

"Yeah?"

"It depends, though."

"On what?"

"How interesting your story is. To my readers."

Tipsy's face fell. "What do your readers want to know?"

"That you're legitimate."

"What's that mean, like do I pay taxes?"

"No," Kaneko smiled, trying to soothe the expression of panic on the girl's face. "It means, can you really find lost things?"

"I found the body, right?"

Kaneko made another note. "How?"

"I seen it, in my mind. And I told the cops where to find it."

"And they found it, right where you said?" Kaneko asked.

"Exactly," said Tipsy. "Just like I said."

"And you didn't put the body there? Obviously." Kaneko tried to look casual. "I have to ask."

Tipsy looked at her like she was crazy. "The guy was strangled or something. You think I look like I could strangle someone?"

Kaneko wanted to say, *You look ragged, like your arms and legs are nothing but meat. But your wrists are all bone. Your head might snap your neck any minute, just the sheer weight of that giant lump of gristle teetering on top of your shoulders could send the whole structure cascading down. But you could be strong for all that, and there's no telling what someone on speed can do.*

But she didn't. She threw Tipsy a tight smile. "How long have you been able to find people?"

"Not people, things." Tipsy reminded her.

"Right."

"You know that saint who helps you find lost things?"

Kaneko reflected. "Saint Anthony?"

"Okay?" Tipsy shrugged. "I think about things and I see them and then I find them."

"Can you find something if I ask you to?" Kaneko said.

Tipsy looked dubious.

"If I can test your ability," Kaneko said, "then I'll know it's worth paying for your story."

Tipsy smiled. Her smile was full of hunger. "How much?"

Kaneko gestured. "I don't know. How far would a hundred bucks go?"

A light came on behind the girl's eyes. "Sometimes it takes a while to find stuff, though. I can't always do it right away."

"I'd like you to try."

"You could come back tomorrow, maybe?"

"Let's try now," Kaneko said.

Tipsy looked like she wanted to argue, but Kaneko put steel into her voice and it seemed to hold the girl.

"I guess I can try?" Tipsy said at last.

Kaneko took a breath. She pretended to be thinking.

"A hatpin," she said. "Can you find a hatpin?"

"What's a hatpin?" Tipsy asked.

There was something feline about her face, Kaneko thought. She wrote *feline* on her notepad.

"I'll describe it. It's a long pin, like this," she indicated the length on the inside of her arm. "It's white, Satsuma—"

"What?"

"A kind of Japanese pottery."

"From your country?"

I was born here, this is my country. "It was my aunt's. Anyhow, it's a long pin with a large bauble on the end. Ivory-coloured with a gold dragon. The glaze ... well, that's probably enough, right? How much do you need?"

Tipsy stared at her, unblinking. "What's a hatpin, again?"

Kaneko felt her chest tighten. "Never mind. How about we try something you know? Can you tell me where my phone is right now?"

"In your bag?"

"Well, it's in my hand. But close enough," Kaneko said.

The girl's face fell. She shrugged and began pulling on a scraggly wisp of hair beside her ear.

Kaneko said, "How'd you really find the body, Tipsy?"

"I guess it just happened?"

Tipsy wasn't looking at her anymore; she was looking at her bare toes, curled over the side of the bed.

Tipsy's answers were too vague. Like the girl's thoughts were sliding around in her oversized skull.

"Anything else for my story, Tipsy?" Kaneko prompted.

"My sister," she offered up, "she says I'm like the next step of human evolution. Like in the future we'll all be psychic."

Her words ran together in her excitement.

"Maybe," Kaneko said. "I think you mean stage, though."

"What?"

"The next *stage of* human evolution. That's more colloquially widespread, I believe. Or ... anyway. I'm being pedantic," Kaneko caught the girl's agonised expression behind the smeared make-up mess of her face. The expression looked permanent. "She could be right. Your sister."

Tipsy, beamed. "They call us indigo kids."

"Who does?"

"Like, doctors and stuff."

"Indigo children, that stuff from the seventies?" Kaneko almost laughed.

"Maybe, I dunno."

"Tipsy, have you ever been diagnosed with an illness? Like, learning disability, ADHD, schizophrenia? Psychopathy?"

"No?" Tipsy gave her a wounded look.

"Because a lot of those kids they called indigo children were. They were meant to be the first wave of supernatural evolution, come to save the world. But they were mostly just spoilt brats."

"I'm not a brat," Tipsy pouted.

"No," Kaneko agreed. "And I don't think you found that body, either. Am I right?"

Tipsy's lip trembled and her eyes narrowed. She kept her gaze on Kaneko though tears began to line her eyes.

"I didn't think so," Kaneko said gently.

She shut her notebook and made to leave.

"That mean I won't get any money?" Tipsy asked.

"Not for this."

Make the story, don't find the story. Some bedsit-living, broken kid with no future and no idea what to do beyond the next dollar. She left Tipsy curled on the corner of the bed.

∞¥∞Ω∞¥∞

Downstairs, she turned into the alley.

"Hey. You still the King?" she called.

"Always," he called back. "You still looking for the girl with the drunken name?"

"Not anymore."

"You bring *me* a drink this time?"

"Not this time." Kaneko squatted beside him. "Is there another name by which I can call you? For my story."

"Yeah," the King looked dubious. "I guess you can call me Rick. If you have to."

"I wonder if you can help me, Rick," Kaneko said. "I'm looking for something."

"It's not like, your conscience or your sense of humour or something?"

Kaneko let out a huff of surprise. "No. None of those."

"Good. I don't do those."

"It's a hatpin."

Rick grunted. "Didn't think Japanese women wore hatpins. You mean a hairpin?"

"No," Kaneko smiled. "My family made them. But you're right, Rick, we mostly didn't wear them. They were for export."

She described the pin in detail and with more hope than when she'd tried with Tipsy. She explained the raised gold dragon, hand-painted, the bearded nostrils, the flare of its claws. The hatpin was the only thing she'd ever lost that she wanted back, barring her youthful optimism, and Rick had already said he didn't do that kind of thing.

Rick's face relaxed. He gazed into some kind of middle-distance that had Kaneko checking over her shoulder. But by the end of the hatpin's description, something sly and dark entered his eyes.

"What's in it for me?" he asked.

"I could give you some money, pay for your story."

He looked interested. "How much?"

"Depends how good you are."

He grinned. "*Whoop de doo*, darling."

"The hatpin first, though," Kaneko reminded him.

"That? It's under the floorboards."

"Which floorboards?"

Rick frowned. "There's a hole under a rug. A red and white rug. Under a bed."

Kaneko felt her stomach lurch. "I know where that is. I know exactly."

"There's your fancy Japanese hatpin, then."

He was beaming. Kaneko fished in her wallet and pulled out a twenty dollar note. Her hands were shaking. She pulled out another note, a fifty.

"Thanks, Rick." She held both notes out. "Tell me. Do you know a young woman who lives in this building? Skinny, wears a lot of make-up."

"Can you believe the shit kids put on their faces?" Rick spat, roundly, at the dumpster. "Rots your head, that stuff."

"Yeah, well. She's Tipsy. You ever tell her about your ability?"

"Maybe." Rick's face grew hard. "Why?"

"I think she's trying to sell your story."

"For money? Rotten bloody junkie."

"Rick. Why'd you even tell her?" Kaneko asked.

He shrugged and looked away, his eyes rolling. "Had to tell someone. Couldn't let the body just rot there."

"You didn't want to tell the police?"

"Bloody cops. Never find one when you need one. That's irony, right? Guess I could find a dead one, though." Rick gave her a thoughtful look. "Never knew I could find bodies. Just things."

"How long have you been able to find things?"

He shrugged. "I was always finding stuff, even when I was a kid. Me Mum lost stuff, I found it. Earrings. Bank statements. Remember bank statements?" He said it like bank statements had been wiped from the face of the Earth.

"Have you ever known other people with powers like yours?" Kaneko asked.

Rick's gaze had become unfixed. "Some. Hey, you believe all that stuff they're saying in the papers? About human beings evolving?"

"I'm a journalist," she smiled. "I'm not paid to believe."

"Well, none of us are paid for that, Annie."

"Is paid, none *is* paid," she muttered, then cursed herself. It was a bad habit, correcting people.

Rick winked, like he got it. "Whatever."

Kaneko thanked him and stood. "How long have you been on the streets, Rick?"

"Since I was young. Ran away from home. Got lost. Been lost ever since," he chuckled and stroked his beard with grubby fingers. "Lucky to get this little pocket of heaven, hey?" He gestured around the alley, its stink and grime.

"Undoubtedly," Kaneko agreed. "One more question. For the story."

"Yeah?"

"What's your last name?"

She wondered if he even remembered. This was a guy who'd been living on the streets since he was a kid, who thought bank statements had ceased to exist.

"Gold," he said, his head jerking up. "Rick Gold. I sound like a rock star, hey? Always thought I'd be a rock star. The junk got me, though."

Kaneko wrote *GOLD*.

"But it's a good power I got. Most of the time." Rick smiled. "If only I could bottle it, hey, sweetheart? Make a fortune."

∞¥∞Ω∞¥∞

On the way to her car, Kaneko's phone rang. It was Merv.

"And how are you this morning?" he asked. "It's still morning, isn't it? And *where* are you, my lovely?"

"Heading back to the office. You sold me a bum steer, Merv. That girl you sent me to is a faker."

"A good journalist can always make a story."

"Yeah," Kaneko muttered, more to herself, "I made a story, all right."

Merv apparently didn't hear her. Merv didn't hear a lot of things.

"Was she a looker, at least?" he asked. "We can send a photographer."

Kaneko ignored him. "I did come across something interesting. But I'm not sure how much the subject is going to like the attention."

She got in the car and switched her phone to the other hand.

Merv grunted. "Go with the more photogenic one."

"She was faking!"

"So make the story about that," Merv said expansively. "Tell the story of the people who *aren't* superheroes. Show us the ones who've been left behind, the ones faking it, not making it. The ones lying to make themselves look like they're still top of the food chain. Give us the human *soul*, Kaneko."

She drove the car forward and pulled up at lights, listening to Merv drone on about the human soul. Kaneko closed her eyes and leaned back, trying to imagine she was someplace else.

"And that numbers nut called here looking for you," Merv said. "I gave him your mobile number. What's the deal, giving out a desk number? No self-respecting journalist is ever at her desk."

The drivers in the traffic behind Kaneko began to hit their horns. She jumped and moved her car into the intersection. She wanted to tell Merv to go screw himself, but she was afraid he wouldn't hear her over the noise of the horns. She sped forward, trying to outpace the traffic.

"Thanks, Merv. Give out my number to every crazy in the book, why don't you?"

She dropped the phone into her bag and drove until she reached her apartment block.

∞¥∞Ω∞¥∞

Inside the apartment, she dumped her bag by the door and headed upstairs to the bedroom.

Underneath the bed was the red and white striped rug, just like Rick had said. She shifted it aside, but couldn't find the gap Rick had mentioned. So she lifted one of the bed legs and kicked the rug out from under. Then she got down on her side and reached a hand underneath, feeling for a space. The floorboards were old and split and the join between each board and its neighbour was wide from age and warping. But not wide enough for a Satsuma bauble. She squeezed herself further in, sliding her hand under the loose rug.

There was an uneven space where a knot in the wood must have worked loose. She pressed it with her fingertips, trying to figure out its size. Then she slid further in until her head was under the bed and she was flat on her stomach with one arm extended. Downstairs, her phone began to ring. Kaneko swore.

Curling her fingers into the small gap in the floor, she felt something hard and cold and round. She inched closer. With two fingers, she traced the shape of the bauble down to the long metal pin at the end. The hatpin. She tried to lift it, but the bauble stayed stuck beneath the floor.

Gently she pulled the hatpin until she found a spot where the gap widened and she could draw it free. She clutched the pin close. The golden dragon watched her, his lips pulled back in a grimace, his long moustache lifted by some invisible breeze. Even in the dark under the bed, he shone. The five tiny claws on each foot sparked with light. The cracklature of the Satsuma glaze around him made him, in contrast, seem long and lithe and smooth.

Her phone was ringing again. Kaneko pulled herself free of the bed and the ringing got louder. Then she realised the noise was coming up the stairs towards her.

She scrambled to her feet, clasping the pin in her hand, the dragon pressed to the web of her thumb.

A shadow stepped into the room, and then the man who owned it.

"Who are you?" she asked.

"Your next appointment," the man smiled.

He raised the phone and shook it, like he was expecting it to rattle. He was pale and bald. *A shop dummy before they applied the wig, as featureless and bland as a canvas, as uncanny as a walking corpse.*

He said, "I got your number."

"But how'd you know my address?" Not even Merv was dumb enough to share that information.

"I followed the numbers," the man said. "The ringing of your phone. See? It's my gift."

Freak.

Kaneko found herself taking two steps back for every step he took forward. Her back was against the wall before he'd even taken four steps. She slid sideways, the hatpin clenched stupidly between both hands.

"Let's get this straight," Kaneko said. "You look like you're planning something violent. Is that right?"

The man grinned. "You're very direct."

"That's right. And I want you to know, if you try something on me, they'll find you."

"How?"

"I've got your number, too, remember? My boss spoke to you."

"Who'd believe it?" he asked. "We haven't met, we've never spoken, you've never come to my house. Don't you see? I could be anyone. But it's very unlikely I'm the person who owns the phone number in your phone."

"The police might believe it," she said. "They have a taskforce for people with creepy powers like yours."

He hesitated, but just for an instant. Then he laughed.

"Oh? That should make all the difference."

He lunged and she whirled. She leapt over the bed and towards the stairs behind him. He came for her. She ran, one hand to the wall. She'd made it down five steps before he had her. He wrenched a fistful of her hair and she spun. She screamed. She reached up her hands to save herself.

∞¥∞Ω∞¥∞

"And you stabbed him with a hatpin?" the detective asked.

"Yes, Detective Palmer. A hatpin," Kaneko replied.

Detective Palmer had a habit of wincing whenever Kaneko spoke. She had brown skin and dark eyes and a long brown plait like a cable that hung straight at her back.

Kaneko memorised the word *cable*, determined to use it later.

"How many times?" Palmer winced.

"What?"

"How many times did you stab him with the hatpin?"

Kaneko shrugged. "Enough that he stopped coming for me."

She held her hands still in her lap. There was blood to her elbows, blood on her skirt, her shirt, blood — sprayed and dried — across her face. She could feel it catching at the sides of her eyes when she blinked. She tried not to blink.

Palmer was looking at Kaneko's hands.

Kaneko said, "Is that going to be a problem?"

"Could be. Depends."

"On whether I have previous convictions, that sort of thing? Whether I'm a good person?"

Palmer made a note in a small, black notebook. "Depends who's doing the deciding."

"Right."

"You'd never met him before?" Palmer asked.

"He said he had my number." Kaneko replied.

Detective Palmer nodded. Just like that, she nodded. As if she'd heard it all before.

One of the paramedics handed Kaneko an ice pack. Not knowing quite what to do with it, she pressed it to her temple. She tried not to look at the browning smears on her arm.

She asked, "Who else can do that? Just, hear a number and follow it to a phone? Across miles?"

Palmer winced. "No one I know."

"Right," Kaneko said. "Right. That's good, I guess."

There was a pause, during which time Kaneko's mind was blessedly, remarkably blank for the first time in a long time. She felt swept clean.

Palmer stood beside her. Not even waiting. Just standing.

"You believe me, though, right?" Kaneko asked her.

"Yeah. I believe you."

Kaneko let out her breath. She pressed the ice bag to an ache along the top of her shoulder. Her notebook was open across her knee. She'd grabbed it before she'd even reached for the phone. But the open page of the notebook held nothing but blood-red smears.

Around her, the forensics team dusted the balustrade for prints and took photos of the spatter on the steps. *Spatter*. Not a big enough word for the mess the stranger had left behind.

She watched someone bag the fallen hatpin.

"Will I get that back?" she asked.

Palmer glanced up at the forensics team. "Eventually. It's a nice example. Satsuma, right?"

"Yeah. Family heirloom."

"Nobody wears hatpins anymore," Palmer lamented.

"Nobody wears hats," Kaneko reasoned. "It's all baseball caps nowdays. Is he dead?"

"Oh, he's dead all right. You doubted it?"

"The hatpin's so small."

"Sometimes location is all that matters," Palmer told her.

"Good." Kaneko reversed the ice bag, letting the cold numb her. "I mean…"

"I know." Palmer made another note in her notebook and looked up, like she was seeing the room for the first time.

"Will I be charged?" Kaneko asked.

"I can't say for sure."

But the detective fixed Kaneko with her gaze and gave a slow shake of her head. *No.*

"I don't understand why he came after me," Kaneko said. "I mean, why *me?*"

"He probably figured he'd found the perfect randomiser," Palmer replied. "Random victim, random crime. Worst damn things to try and solve."

"It's a good thing you guys came, then," Kaneko said. "You taking this back to the taskforce?"

Palmer looked at her. "This is the taskforce."

She nodded at her partner, an overweight man in a sagging trench coat. He was crouched on the staircase with the forensics team.

"That's it?" Kaneko asked.

Palmer nodded.

Kaneko said, "Off the record, though. There's more of you, right?"

Palmer shook her head.

There was quiet.

"So, this taskforce—" Kaneko began.

"Forget it," Palmer flipped her notebook closed and put it into a pocket of her jacket. "I'm not here to be interviewed."

"Might make a difference to people if they knew the police are already on the trail of ... whatever it is that's giving people these powers."

"Might make a difference to the bad guys, too," Palmer replied. "But it's not my call."

"I've got a superpower, too," Kaneko said.

Palmer raised her eyebrows in a kind of *this will be interesting* expression. She crossed her arms and stood staring at Kaneko where she sat.

"It's called tenacity. I'm going to call you, Detective Palmer. I'm going to keep calling you and I am never going to stop."

Palmer shrugged, like it was all the same to her. "I get that a lot." Then she reached to put a hand under Kaneko's elbow and eased her to her feet.

"Ambulance is waiting," Palmer said.

"Wait."

Kaneko threw her notebook towards the hallway side table, where it slid to the floor. Then she pulled a new one out from a drawer, holding it carefully between finger and thumb. It was a fat notebook with wide, lined pages. She figured she was going to need it.

∞¥∞Ω∞¥∞

FIREFLY EPILOGUE
JODI CLEGHORN

Leah stood on the pontoon searching the twilight for the familiar blond head among the multitude of ebony ones bobbing up and down on the sampans below. Tiny lanterns flickered to life on the bows and the banter of the Malay rivermen rose to greet her.

"Excuse me," she called down to a wizened old man pulling his sampan alongside the pontoon. "I'm looking for Andy."

"Come, come. See fireflies. Very pretty," he said, beckoning her to step onto his boat. "Ling take you."

She shook her head. "I'm looking for an Australian. Blond hair. Tall."

"No blond man here."

"But I went down the river with him last night. Andy told me to meet him back here tonight."

Ling shook his head. "No Andy here. You no wait. Come with Ling."

Leah shook her head and walked away, the pontoon shifting with each careful step. She walked up the jetty, through the covered waiting area and across the picnic area to an empty bench. She gazed across the river, to the ramshackle flotilla and wondered where Andy was.

∞¥∞Ω∞¥∞

"I want to book your whole boat. One hundred and sixty *ringgits* for four people, right?" Leah said. "I don't want some dumb-arse stranger, who can't shut up, spoiling it for me."

Having said her bit, she looked down into the fast-flowing Selangor River tugging at the edge of the pontoon, putting it into an ever-changing *pas de deux* with the sampan. All she could think about was how she would step into the tiny boat, in the fading light, without pitching herself into the muddy water.

"Get on and we'll discuss a fair price when you've stopped looking shit scared about falling in," the blond-haired man said, reaching a hand out to help her on. "I'm Andy."

"Leah." She grasped his hand in her sticky, damp one and they shook. "That obvious, huh."

He nodded and she laughed, stepping off the pontoon.

The sampan pitched beneath her weight and for a moment she hung over the latte-coloured river, her body tensing to hit the water. His hand tightened on her forearm, her second foot hit the boat and she half-fell, half-sat and the boat righted itself.

"You always so graceful?"

"Pretty much."

He watched her trying to reach the money in her pocket without moving too much. "Don't worry about payment until I have you safely back on dry land." He noted her bare arms and legs and said, "You do know about the mozzies."

"I've got so much insect spray on there's probably a new hole in the ozone layer above my hut." She ran a hand down her arm, nose wrinkling at the sticky residue. "I'm terrified it's full of DDT. The girl in the pharmacy didn't speak any English and the bottle's all in Malay."

"Be more terrified of malaria. I've had it twice. Thought I was going to die the first time. Saw Steam Boat Willy come chortling through the wall the second time. That Lariam is heavy shit. Help yourself," he said, pointing to an old flannelette shirt and an orange life jacket in the bottom of the boat. "I can't vouch for the last time the shirt was washed, but it'll keep the mozzies out."

She grabbed the shirt. It smelled of engine oil and sandalwood when she pulled it over her head. The material stuck to her damp, tacky arms. It felt smothering in the heat and strapping the life jacket over the top only made it worse.

"If I got malaria I'd probably be in a room full of Smurfs doing Beyonce covers."

"Sounds like a Gary Larson version of hell."

"We can always blame it on Wayne."

"Yeah, the world always needs a scapegoat." They laughed and Andy threw his weight behind the long pole to push them away from the pontoon and out into current. "You're a bit of a Larson fan then."

"Is there any other way to start the day ... well coffee maybe. It was a sad day when there were no new Larson cartoons. At least there's still coffee."

She ignored the discomfort of the shirt and the life jacket and watched the slow, fluid movements he made as the sampan moved into the centre of the river.

"So you're travelling alone?" he asked, pulling the pole out of the water and letting the boat coast.

She looked up from watching the detritus speed by: plastic bottles, palms fronds, tangled netting, islands of filthy froth.

"Mid-life crisis," she said, and felt her cheeks burn, grateful the darkness hid them. "Oh shit, I can't believe I just said that."

"People confess all kinds of stuff out here." He picked up the pole and started to guide the boat toward the opposite bank.

Leah reached out and let her fingers skim across the river, mirroring the clouds brushing by the sickle moon overhead.

"So no young lover or sports car then."

Leah snorted. "I'd be happy to just have a lover." She lay back as best as she could in the life jacket and watched the stars pass overhead. "I leased my apartment and quit my job to be landless for a year. Everyone said I was mad, but they'd all already done the backpacker thing while I was busy studying and climbing the corporate ladder. Now they're all busy having babies. Losing their freedom, not going back to reclaim it."

"Sounds like you've come to find yourself,"

"God you're making it sound like *Eat, Pray, Love* on a *Lonely Planet* budget."

"Eat. Pray. Love. Sounds good to me!"

"It's a book." When he didn't say anything she continued. "Middle-class chick with a poor-me complex gets her publishing house to pay for her to travel through Italy, India and Indonesia to *find herself*. In the end she just *finds a guy*."

"Are you always this cynical?"

"On good days."

"I just meant life is full of options and perhaps, excluding prayer, the other two are pretty reasonable ways to wind down the clock. Works for me."

She tucked her arms under her head and asked, "So what do you do? Other than take tourists down the river and dispense gems of real life philosophy. I didn't expect to come to Kuala Selangor and be shown the fireflies by an Aussie."

"I was doing research and discovered the facility that head hunted me for my innovation only wanted me to innovate *their* way. Only push the boundaries they said were okay to push. Publish only what they said was okay to publish."

"What were you researching?"

"Brain waves. I discovered new low-level cycles that I called omega waves. But no one liked the idea that people declared brain dead still had cerebral activity." His face hardened. "No one wanted *that* moral and ethical can of worms opened, so the university terminated my tenure and discredited my work."

"That's a bit rough isn't it?"

"Add every swear word you know and you're starting to get my frame of mind before I got here."

He threw his weight into the pole, his body relaxing into the familiar motion.

"What brought you here?"

"It's more what brought me back here."

"What brought you here the first time?"

"The old man's an Entomologist. Mum taught English. I grew up just down there, before they packed me off to boarding school in Sydney when I hit high school." He pointed into the darkness and Leah tried to pinpoint a building. All she could see was more jungle. "That was when Kampung Kuantan was an even tinier village and fireflies were only interesting to people like Dad."

The boat shifted, rocking side to side. She took her hand out of the water, dried it on the bottom of the borrowed shirt and lay on her side to watch him manoeuvre the sampan into the slow-moving water closest to the bank.

"Ever seen a firefly?"

"What do the locals call them?"

"*Kelip-kelip*. Means 'to twinkle'."

"No. I've never seen *kelip-kelip*, but I saw glow-worms in a cave on school camp in Year Nine."

"You're in for a treat then."

They floated around a gentle bend and the river opened up before them.

"Oh my God," Leah whispered, pulling herself up and staring down river in awe of the luminous green pinpoints, blinking messages of love, lighting up entire branches. "They're like … fairy lights. But more … spectacular for being part of nature. More … I can't describe it. It's like I've died and gone to the most beautiful place in all the universe."

"I thought they were fairies until Dad let me look at one up close. Butt-ugly fairies let me tell you."

They floated beneath overhanging branches, the limbs lighting up as they silently slid past.

After several minutes Leah asked, "Why aren't all the trees lit up?"

"The fireflies only come down to the *pokok berembang* in the evening. They live in the long grass during the day."

"But there are *berembangs* which don't light up. I can pick the shape."

"The fireflies are disappearing. When I was a kid it was like a German street at Christmas every night in the dry season. So many trees lit up."

"It must have been amazing."

"It was."

"What's killing them? Pollution?"

"Take your pick: pollution, development, tourism, the palm oil plantations, the destruction of the surrounding ecosystem. The rivermen blame the dam up the river at Kuala Kubu Bahru, but it's anyone's guess. Even the old man's not sure what it is, if it is just one thing or a combination. Makes it hard to conserve when you don't know the root problem."

"But you said tourism and you bring tourists down here."

"We do it with the least impact on the environment — no motor, no fumes, no leaking oil. Just old fashioned hard yakka. I bring you down here, the fireflies make an impression on you, and now you care about something I love. Maybe when you leave you'll want to help protect it. Tell others. Help raise awareness."

"Is that why your parents stayed? Because they loved the fireflies?"

"I don't know. But it's why I came back."

They passed two more illuminated trees before Leah spoke again. "If you had one wish Andy, what would it be?"

Andy grabbed hold of one of the tree branches to stop them floating further down the river.

"That no one had to turn off life support for someone they loved."

She looked up the river to the next *berembang* flashing a syncopated code of longing, the thousands of tiny iridescent lights all flashing together, looking for a mate. "I wish the Selangor went on forever. That we never had to stop."

∞¥∞Ω∞¥∞

A cool breeze skimmed across the river and bought Leah shivering out of her memories. She ran her hands down her arms, her skin cool and smooth, not warm and tacky with insect repellent and sweat. She lifted her arm up and sniffed: soap and something else … antiseptic? No trace of insect repellent. But she'd put it on before she'd left her hut. She remembered doing it. Didn't she?

Leah turned from the river to look at the road behind. Twilight had given way to evening and the parking bays sat empty: no taxis or tour buses, no bicycles or hire cars. No tourists streaming toward the river, filling the quiet with excited jabber in a kaleidoscope of languages. Looking at the empty spaces along the dirt road she couldn't remember how she'd got from Kuala Selangor to Kampung Kuantan.

If only she could find Andy.

She stood and walked toward the river, the memory of his smile after she'd said she wanted the night to last forever momentarily settling the growing unease within. While her furious blush faded he had navigated further down the river, away from all the other boats. When they eventually made it back to the pontoon, they'd both ended up in the river when she over-balanced trying to get back onto the pontoon.

In the small shack he lived in, she'd stripped out of the wet, stinking clothes and rinsed off under a shower at the rear of the shack, beneath a 20 litre tin with a shower nozzle. In sarongs they'd sat on the dodgy deck drinking cold stubbies of Tiger beer and listening to the thrum of insects. Beneath his mosquito net they'd lain naked, talking until dawn softened the light in the windows and they'd fallen into an exhausted sleep. In the morning he'd thrown her bike into the back of a rusted ute and driven her into Kuala Selangor for a late breakfast at *Auntie Kopitiam*. The coffee was the best she'd had since leaving Kuala Lumpur and Andy had laughed at her struggling through a curry for brunch, though admitted he missed bacon too.

They'd walked through the nature park, climbed up to the lighthouse, and explored the old fort. Back at *Auntie Kopitiam* they'd had more coffee and Andy had laughed and joked in flawless Malay with the taxi drivers sitting smoking on the sidewalk. They'd slept the rest of the afternoon away under his mosquito net, his hand on the small of her back, and after an early seafood dinner in a shack by the river, they'd climbed Bukit Melwati and watched the sun set over the Malacca Straits.

In that moment, conjuring up the flare of yellow and tangerine above the Straits and the feel of Andy's hand cupping her knee, she knew he wasn't coming tonight. Or any other night. She looked up to the road and knew why the carpark lay empty. Why the tourists stayed away. It wasn't the Kampung Kuantan she knew. And it wasn't the night after she'd met Andy.

She hurried toward the river, through the undercover area, down the gangplank and onto the pontoon. Ling sat in his sampan waiting for her.

"You come back, Miss Leah."

"I want to speak to Andy, Ling."

"No can do, Miss Leah."

"I need to speak to him."

"This is a one way interface only, Miss Leah."

"Goddamn you Andy ... stop with the Miss Leah thing and the quaint Malay accent. Whatever he programmed you with. Stop it."

"Understood."

"Why did he program you, Ling? Why isn't he here to meet me? To say good-bye."

"It is recommended Ferrymen are not representations of family or close friends. It makes it harder."

"I know, I know," Lean muttered. It had been her idea. It seemed a sane, compassionate choice when Andy had talked to her about the Ferrymen he planned to program ... but now she just wanted Andy.

"How sick am I?"

"You already know the answer to that question."

She sat down on the pontoon, the reality of her situation sinking in.

"How old am I?"

"I am not programmed with that information."

"How long have I been unconscious for?"

"I am not programmed with that information."

Leah lay back and felt the motion of the pontoon. So realistic.

When Andy began programming the Omega Wave Interface Monitor he asked her where she would want her check out point to be. Where she would make the decision to walk away from her life. At the time it was all hypothetical. Like taking out insurance.

She watched the strands of cloud race across the moon and remembered how she'd trailed her hand in the water that first night. Remembered every nuance of movement as Andy navigated the boat up the river. How she wanted it to go on forever. Be with him forever.

And now...

She was nothing more than a cerebral echo in a piece of software.

"How long have I been here?"

"I don't have that information."

"What happens if I don't get in the boat? If I don't go down the river?"

"You leave your family in limbo. You put the inevitable on hold."

"What if there is a chance for recovery?"

"This isn't about recovery. The rest of your brain, for all intents and purposes, is dead. This is about saving your family the stress of ending your life. This is what you and Andy agreed to when you signed on for the OWIM Program."

Leah remembered watching the first OWIM patient slip away when the Interface Monitor stopped the life support systems. The relief on the faces of the family who did not have to make that decision. The grief which swallowed them after. How Andy grasped her hand. How she felt they'd done something important. Something right.

She imagined Andy standing beside her bed, watching the lights flash intermittently on the montior. The wheeze of a respirator and the pip of the CTG. She wondered who was with him. If anyone was there to hold his hand. To ease his pain. To witness her passing.

"Do you remember what Andy wished the first night you were together?"

Leah whispered, "Yes."

"And do you remember what you wished for?"

Leah tried to answer but failed.

When she finally stood, tears marked her cheeks for the last time. She grasped Ling's hand, stepped effortlessly onto the boat and sat down. The bottom of the sampan was clean and empty. No life jackets. No flannelette shirt.

No Andy.

Further down the river, the *berembang* trees lit up both sides of the river like a German street in December. Waiting for her. Calling to her with each wave of flashes. A final message from her beloved. She turned to Ling, wiped the tears from her face and nodded. The boat lurched and rocked as Ling pushed away from the jetty. Leah didn't look back.

∞¥∞Ω∞¥∞

DAUGHTERS OF BATTENDOWN
CAT SPARKS

The laundry chute was stained and battered from centuries of use. Autumn wasn't the first to climb it; no doubt she wouldn't be the last. There were safer ways to infiltrate the upper levels but this one was the quickest. Just so long as she didn't get found out. Topside was the domain of lords and ladies, civic administrators and, occasionally, Birdman brides. Discovery would cost her a spell in the hot box, that cramped, tin shed jammed between the air filtration pumps and slurry bilge.

The fight in the arboretum had been what set her on her upwards journey. Just one scrag fight of many, but this time Brook had gone too far. The gathered crowd had been waiting for the names. Pushing led to shoving and things had gotten quickly sour from there.

There was never any doubt about which five would be chosen. All daughters of Downbelow — the *right kind* of daughters. Five of them born to be Birdman brides. It was only a matter of time.

Brook and Cinnamon-Marie. Coral, Rain and Sunday, the three who trailed behind the older girls like shadows. False exclamations of delight, as if the chosen did not have process managers for fathers and their selection was not, therefore, inevitable.

Each girl milked it for all she was worth. Autumn's face reddened at the memory as she climbed. She should have left it well alone, only leaving things had never been her way. The names on the list had brought a flush of disappointment, even though she'd never stood a chance. Not with her foot the way it was — and everything besides.

One smirk of triumph from Brook was all it took. Words had flown and a bitter catfight followed. She hadn't said much. Not really. Only that bridal gowns had been fitted in secret months before so there was no need for posting up the names.

"How dare you touch my face!" Brook screeched, as if Autumn's slap had caused her actual damage. "The wedding is tomorrow — what if you've left a mark? Just who do you think you are, you lousy cripple? A Birdman would never take a *clubfoot* as a bride."

The others had laughed heartily as Autumn lashed out, her fists a blur of rage. Those words were true and everybody knew it.

Brook and her spiteful entourage had it made. No shifts in the reclamation plants or, skies forbid, the mines. Not for them, their sisters or their mothers. If only they accepted privilege with good grace.

The hours following the naming had been thick with jeers and jibes. The ugliest had copped the worst of it. Chief amongst them, Jarrah, never destined to be any kind of bride. Dumpy and smart-mouthed, such a losing combination. Smart in more ways than one though, Autumn noted. Jarrah knew things. How to find bread when Downbelow was steeped in shortage. Fruit when citrus blight was on the rise.

"You're no better than the rest of us," Jarrah challenged, stepping forward from the crowd, head held high. "Just lucky by birth is all."

Cinnamon-Marie made short work of her, promenading in a gown that must have cost her mother a whole year's savings. "Better than anything you'll ever be. We're going Topside. We're getting married." Each pronouncement was delivered with relish. "A freak like you will never see the sun."

"I've already seen it — and a whole lot more besides. A bride's life is tougher than you think. You don't know the half of what goes on!"

"Oh yeah — and I suppose you do?"

Everybody laughed at that and Jarrah turned her back, vanishing into the shadowy forest of Oh-2 scrubbers and repo tubes.

Was the sun worth seeing? *Yes*, thought Autumn, *most definitely*. Even if only glimpsed through shields. And if the only way to see it was to climb a laundry chute, she'd do it and hang the consequences.

Jarrah was the one who'd told Autumn about the chute. She claimed she'd been up and down it many times. There were supposed to be cameras but like most things Downbelow, they didn't work.

Jarrah and Autumn had never been friends. Not really. Autumn pitied her, despite her obvious smarts: three fingers and that blotchy, mottled skin. A flat, square face with eyes too wide apart. Both parents dead after the Great Sink Disaster of '55.

Anger drove Autumn to climbing harder, no easy feat with her leg the way it was. Not a clubfoot proper though — she was lucky; her leg bent at the knee.

Gradually the belch and grind of Downbelow subsided.

Unfamiliar sounds emerged to take their place: the hissing and steaming of atmos vents, the clanking and creaking of pipes.

Autumn had been barely twelve years old the first time a Birdman made the journey. The whole city, up and down, tracked his progress on the screens, never doubting he would land on one of the ancient runway platforms that had once seen scores of zeppelins and sky craft. But that Birdman never came to land. Perhaps his wings were too flimsy for a controlled descent, or perhaps the golden light glinting off the condenser nets confused him, blinded him to the city half buried in protective gold and amber sands.

Once, Battendown had thought itself the one surviving outpost. Radiation storms roiled across the desert surface, incinerating all not nimble enough to dodge its path or burrow downwards.

Other Birdmen followed, bearing news, seed and hope. It was said the surrounding sands were littered with the gleaming bones of aviators and their artificial wings, chrome levers and silver cogs stolen by dune bugs and sand skinks to line their nests.

Why should a visitor of greatness be restricted to Topside? Had those lords and ladies not already more than their fair share of fortune? Sunlight, even if it killed. Sweeping vistas, even if all there was to see was ruin.

The lid of the laundry chute was hinged, just like Jarrah said. Muffled voices echoed as Autumn tried to risk a cautious peek. She froze, imagining herself plummeting back down in a tangle of soiled sheets and pillowcases. Her leg throbbed painfully from cramp as she held her breath, flexed her toes and listened. Eventually the voices trailed away. Others came and went. When finally the last of the footsteps faded, she shoved her back against the heavy lid.

She'd been expecting to emerge into an overheated laundry room, bustling with red-faced women in starched uniforms. Instead, a vast corridor, dimly lit. Quiet was almost as unnerving as the emptiness. Downbelow was never quiet — nor was it ever empty. Every inch of space was used for something.

She knew what everybody knew about Topside. That it was perpetually flooded with brilliant, golden light. As depicted on the viewscreens every time civic messages were 'cast.

Autumn trod as quietly as her limp allowed, expecting at any moment to be set upon by a brace of angry guards. Her jagged footfall echoed off evenly spaced, glassy columns that, she figured, were holding up the ceiling.

The long corridor branched off into many smaller spaces; a honeycomb of identical darkened entranceways. *Softly lit* rather than darkness proper. Downbelow, pure darkness always meant the lights had blown. It would be easy to lose her way when everything looked so much the same. Nothing was as she'd expected. No hiding places — why hadn't Jarrah warned her? Because she'd never truly been up here, that's why. *That girl's a dreamer and all her tales are lies.*

Thoughts distracted her from what lay up ahead. A warm glow brightening as she approached. Autumn stopped still and gawped at a section of the protective dome itself. Beyond it, *the sky. The sun. Horizon.*

Even through foot-thick transparent shielding the landscape was exposed in all its raw, sand-blasted glory, burnt below an angry, cloudless sky.

What had become of the perfect blue in picture books of old? Such a disappointment — Downbelow dreamt of cirrus wisps as workers toiled in hydroponic gardens, lichen farms, water reclamation plants and deep-cut mines, a network of which spiderwebbed in all directions.

Autumn stared across the wasteland, picturing sun-bleached bones of fallen Birdmen mixed with sand-scoured old-world relics. Had Jarrah been there, she'd have thought of something smart to say. Jarrah could recite the names of cities that once lined the horizon —

if you could believe the crazy things people said.

Harsh sounds snapped her back into the moment. Crisp footsteps slapping against polished tile. She flattened herself against the nearest strut. Chilled metal seeped through the coarse weave of her shirt, lowering the temperature of her skin. She sucked in her breath, terrified as a patrol passed mere feet away. A daring, stolen glimpse revealed a big man in leathers, flanked by an honour guard: uniformed men, broad shoulders swinging with ribbon and gold braid. Autumn closed her eyes, each step in syncopation with her heart. A Birdman. Everything she'd ever thought he should be: tall, well muscled, strong. The footsteps faded into silence and once again she found herself alone.

What was there to do but follow, creeping soundlessly from shadow to strut as soft music gradually filled the air? The corridor led to enormous wooden doors inset with shiny brass rings. Uniforms stood guard on either side, each wielding a fearsome-looking sword. Both jumped to attention when the Birdman and his honour guard approached.

The doors closed behind them with a resounding thud. How would she ever make it past those swords? The air filled with alluring sounds. Music and the chattering of crowds.

A long time passed before she noticed the tradesman's entrance. Men and women neat in servants' black-and-whites appeared and disappeared like a trail of ants, bearing platters, pitchers and trays of goblets balanced on sturdy stems. Creeping closer, she saw her chance, then ducked between the lazily-swinging doors.

Inside, a chamber flooded with lemon light. Soft strings, zills and lulling flutes. Heady floral scents of jasmine, honeysuckle, frangipani, rose. She inhaled, lungs filling with luxurious gulps of petal-scented air. Were there truly flowers here or was she dreaming? Surely not even the decadent, wasteful citizens of Topside would squander precious water on plants not fit to eat.

She was not dressed right. Any minute somebody would notice her drab, shadow-coloured garb. Autumn grabbed a platter half filled with canapés and pressed her back against a glassy strut. Nobody stopped her. Nobody even noticed her at all.

All eyes were on the five brides lined up across the stage. They looked like dolls, so porcelain and placid, the lace of their multi-layered skirts spilling like milk.

Autumn wasn't wasting any time on them. She scanned the crowd for the Birdman. On-screen, the stiff, formal gowns of Topside women had always looked so splendid. Up close, they looked ridiculous. Almost as ridiculous as the brides.

A speech was just beginning. Familiar words, the same as broadcast Downbelow four times each year in memoriam to seasons no longer existing as anything but pretty names for girls. *The boiling of the oceans, the bleaching of the skies, the centuries of helpless silence before, at last, the Birdmen came.*

The Birdman stood on stage a little to one side. How extraordinarily handsome. Thick, dark hair, completely straight, falling down past his shoulders. Tanned cheeks, perhaps from hours exposed to deadly sun. Strange eyes like shadow crescents. If only she could have seen him aloft in his special skinsuit and leather coverings. Master of the skies, with massive wings spread wide. One of a very fortunate few not pinned beneath the oppressive weight of sand.

Speeches droned like the humming of algae vats. Eventually, a man recognisible as Topside's Governor spoke about the connection between the domes and the importance and vitality of exchanges of fresh seed, data and most importantly, goodwill.

Would the Birdman speak? His voice would be dark and thick like treacle. Perhaps he had already spoken. Perhaps she had arrived too late?

The Birdman bowed before the Governor. He offered something in his outstretched hands. The Governor returned the bow and accepted the gift. Autumn pictured what must have passed between their hands. Datacapsules, along with seed from Fallout, or perhaps as far away as Solace or Windcap Veer. Cities she could only dream of. No one born in Battendown would ever see them.

There was more talk on the value and vitality of seed and the challenge of exciting new opportunities, but she tuned out, especially as each bride was named and presented to their beautiful husband.

Brook had never looked so smug, her self-satisfied face all powder-caked and white. That girl got everything she ever wanted. No doubt, the first Birdman baby would be hers, ensuring Brook remained the centre of attention.

Autumn turned her face away and began to examine the crowd in earnest. Topside or Downbelow, they were all supposed to be the same people. Perhaps the folk of Topside only *seemed* more elegant. Born with fewer defects. Hardly surprising when they never dirtied their hands or risked their lives tunneling deep below the earth. Entombed with a hundred thousand smells, the cloying accumulation of processed fertiliser and vegetation pulp. All the air of Battendown was filtered, yet somehow theirs was cleaner, their corridors more spacious, ceilings arching high above their heads.

Up close however, skin was skin, with tones ranging from shades of light through dark. Hairstyles fancy and ridiculously impractical. Evidently Topsiders had time to waste on pointless vanities. The voluminous clothing likely hid a multitude of imperfections — a thought that made Autumn smile as she cast her gaze back to the stage just in time to see Brook receive a chaste kiss on the cheek from her Birdman husband.

Behind the stage, a mighty stretch of clear, transparent dome. How quickly she'd become accustomed to the desolate landscape beyond. So much so that hairstyles and clothing could prove distracting.

The beginnings of a fearful storm were stirring, scouring and battering the shield, at times strong enough to obscure the view. Storms were frequent and completely random. How brave the Birdmen were, risking their lives to fly from settlement to settlement. Uniting the domes through marriages and blood.

Autumn placed the tray of ignored canapés down on the nearest table as the Birdman resumed his original place on stage. She crept a little closer, soaking up the crowd's warmth and wellbeing. The raging storm muted the harshness of the desert light, bathing the wedding chamber in yellow ochre.

Closer still, Autumn nudged, not really sure of where she was going, only that she wanted to be as close to *him* as possible, even if all she could ever do was stare. What Downbelow got to see on the screens was never enough.

Not like being Topside in the flesh. She wanted to remember every minute of this day: the colours, the smells, the hair. Everything.

She was drinking in the intoxicating scent of jasmine-scented skin when an almighty crash made her freeze in terror. A small, round table bearing drinks had tumbled over, accidentally knocked with her twisted foot. All eyes were now upon her, the protective invisibility of irrelevance fading quickly. A circle of space widened around her as the plain garb of Downbelow was recognised for what it was. A hush fell over the crowd as guards pushed through to investigate, one already brandishing his sword.

She struggled in vain for a final glimpse of her beloved Birdman but her view was blocked by a solid wall of backs and shoulders. Guards led her down a corridor, its walls stained with centuries of grime. Industrial and functional, it might as well have been back Downbelow. Outside a doorway, an officious man gave Autumn a dressing down. She cringed beneath his barrage of words until she noticed something curious about his face. The telltale scar on his upper lip. This man had been born with a cleft pallet! Autumn suppressed her astonishment. There before her was the truth of it. Topsiders were no more perfect than the folks of Downbelow.

They shut her in a chilly room for more hours than she could reckon. As the memory of the Birdman's handsome features faded, worry began to gnaw at her insides. What did Topside do to their criminals? Hot boxes, or something worse? Did they force them outside the dome to fend for themselves? She'd heard tell of such things Downbelow. Many times.

The room stank of mould and the walls were damp. They hadn't even given her a blanket. As she sat on a battered packing crate hugging her arms, she thought more and more of the sands beyond the dome. Air that burned and storms that stripped and scoured. Would they force her outside? Why would they not? She was a criminal caught in the act. No one 'Below even knew she was here.

The echo of footfall on cement corridors made her jump to her feet. She held her breath as they passed on by, grateful for the reprieve, yet troubled by thoughts of abandonment. Perhaps they had forgotten her already? What if no one ever came?

She paced along her prison floor. A room long and thin and filled with shapes shrouded in shadow. Not a cell, more like a storeroom and there, set high in the wall, something she hadn't noticed when they had first locked her in. A window; small and square and dim, but a window all the same.

Most crates were empty, their edges reinforced with metal alloy, sides stenciled with symbols she couldn't read. She piled them one atop the other until a precarious pyramid slouched against the wall.

Up close, the window was merely a hatch but, after a bit of kicking, it opened. It led *out* and that was the main thing. Anywhere was better than this.

Autumn heaved through the hatch on her stomach, sliding into the unknown. What light there was illuminated muddy smudges of grey-brown filth. The air reverberated with sounds familiar to anyone raised in the bowels of Downbelow: creaks and clanks, hums and shudders; hydraulic hammering beyond foot-thick cement. By touch, she determined she was in a narrow maintenance shaft or vent. Lacking better options, she crawled along its length, feeling cautiously for obstacles, following the sounds. Movement meant machinery and machinery meant other maintenance hatches, the only way out of her cramped confines.

The shaft narrowed. That could not be good. But she wouldn't go back. Not unless she had to. Not unless there was nowhere left to go. Now and then she was forced to choose. Left or right? Up or down? At her third left she heard echoes of a woman sobbing. Autumn crawled towards the sound, an action of pure instinct.

The sobbing led her to another hatch of sorts, one too small to fit through. The sobbing ceased. Autumn pressed her face against the metal grille, holding her breath until it started up again. Below, a chamber flooded with bright light. Enormous numbered pot-bellied vats. Nitrogen tanks with hoses feeding in and out of them. Figures garbed in white and muted green. A hospital, like Downbelow's for mangled factory workers, only the staff were garbed more like cowshed techs than doctors.

"Get your hands off me!"

Two green-garbed figures struggled with a girl in a white shift. Autumn couldn't believe her eyes. It was Brook. She'd have known that shrill voice anywhere.

"My husband will hear of this!" she wailed. "He will whip you like a servant!"

"You 'Below brats are always trouble. Don't know why they bother, myself — it's not like we've got a shortage of empty wombs," said one of them. The other beside her laughed. Still others crossed the floor to help as Brook screamed and thrashed and threw back her head.

Autumn jumped back instinctively, landing squarely on her arse as Brook's gaze swept over her hiding spot. She turned and scrabbled along the narrow vent as fast as she could manage, not pausing for breath until her hammering heart finally slowed.

Eventually bright light began to bleed through jagged rents in the concrete, which, she realised, had replaced the ceiling of the vent. The crumbling decay of decades led the way. Up she climbed, with Brook's screams echoing in her head. Up away from things she didn't understand. Into another world. Or so it appeared. Emerging, breathless, into a space so unfamiliar it might have been torn from a picture book of old.

The vast chambers of Topside had been nothing compared to this: the size of the space, or the strangeness of the thing occupying it below, an enormous egg encased in silvery mesh that appeared to hover gracefully above the ground.

The most beautiful thing she'd ever seen, but what was it? She was climbing down towards it before she was even aware she was moving, dodging uneven sections of rubble, so distracted she almost fell twice.

There was only one thing it could be. An ancient zeppelin that had somehow survived, hidden in this voluminous chamber, protected all these years. But by who? The Governor of Topside and its superior citizens? Not likely. Someone would have spoken of it, leaked the secret, given lowly Downbelow something else to feel inferior about.

She ducked as voices wafted upwards.

"...against the clock as the upslope winds take her into the jet stream ... launch window scheduled for twenty-two hundred hours..."

Autumn kept her head down low. Suddenly there seemed to be people everywhere, most of them dressed in dark brown coveralls. She snuggled into a crouch and hugged her knees, too terrified to move again in case she exposed herself. In the space of minutes her horizons had expanded to encompass things surely even Jarrah had never dreamed of.

Her reverie did not last long. A cry went up as she was spotted. As scared as she was, she didn't try to run. There was nowhere to go and if she fell she would probably break a leg.

She was still staring at the zeppelin when they brought her down and took her before the Birdman. Everybody stared at her. Nobody was smiling. Up close, the Birdman was anything but handsome. His mysterious crescent eyes blazed with what she took for silent fury. He said nothing. He didn't have to. *She shouldn't be here. She should have stayed Downbelow where she belonged.* Her mind was flooded with Brook's outrage, but her own defiant explanations lodged pathetically in her windpipe.

"Let her go. She won't tell anybody," a voice called out behind her.

A guard lay a heavy hand on Autumn's shoulder. She turned just as two more Birdmen in flying regalia approached. *Two!* One tall, one short. Both wore skinsuits layered with heavily-treated leathers.

Her mouth opened in surprise, but before so much as a squeak came out, the one who had spoken tugged his helmet free, revealing a familiar face that took her utterly by surprise.

He was a she.

"Jarrah!"

The guard cut her off before she could ask a single question. Her mouth was still hanging stupidly open when the other Birdman intervened. Stepping forward, he smiled and gently touched her cheek. Autumn raised her hand and placed it upon his own. His skin was tough and leathery. Not skin. She was touching leather glove.

Jarrah grinned. "Told you I'd been up and down that chute before. I knew you didn't believe me."

"But what—"

Jarrah pressed her finger against her lips. "Shhh. They don't tell us anything much Downbelow. Some things we've got to figure for ourselves."

"Like what they've done to Brook?"

Jarrah frowned, then rolled her eyes. "Don't tell me she's bitching about pre-motherhood already. That girl does nothing but complain, I swear."

"But—"

"They're not hurting her. It's just not quite the honeymoon she envisaged. They never stay more than a day or two. Their seed is frozen in nitrogen. No Birdman ever visits the same dome twice."

"But—"

"Where am I going?" Jarrah smiled. She nodded toward the open sky. "There's a new dome surfaced beyond the south salt flats. I'm bringing knowledge in place of seed." She glanced up at the mighty balloon. "They never would have built that thing off the plans without my help."

With that, she signaled the control booth. All three Birdmen approached the zeppelin's tiny underside compartment. Two tall, one short. Three stepping in unison.

"Wait!"

A klaxon sounded and the people in dark overalls began to scurry for cover.

"Jarrah!"

"Come on Miss, it's time to go." The guard placed his hand lightly on Autumn's shoulder. This time he didn't seem so frightening.

"You can watch the launch from the control booth. No need to worry. We'll all be perfectly safe." He nodded at the zeppelin. "Those three are the ones taking all the chances."

Autumn threw a final incredulous glance at Jarrah, just in time to catch her wave in return. The three Birdmen entered the compartment as the mighty transparent shielding began to waver. Outside, the air was still and clear, but for how long? Who could say? All Autumn could be certain of was that sand and storms would not imprison her forever. Where Jarrah was going, one day she would follow.

∞¥∞Ω∞¥∞

BABY STEPS
BARBARA ROBSON

I went through a gluten-free phase a while ago. I had myself convinced that milled-bone bread was going to deliver all these health benefits and I'd be like a new man. I can't decide now whether I really did have more energy, eating bone bread, but frankly, it tasted like shit. It never rose properly. It was this dense lump, sitting at the bottom of my stomach, and if I felt healthier, maybe that was down to the weight I lost, eating less bread.

The worst thing about bone bread was the rumours. If anyone else orders a bag of bone flour, nobody cares. If they don't know about bone bread, they don't think twice about it, or if they do, they figure it's to go on the garden. If *I* order bone flour, though, it's another story. I'm a freak. I must be eating people.

You don't believe me, right? That's really what they said. Once it was out there, all kinds of people believed it.

Just to be perfectly clear: I don't eat people. Google it. Bone flour is from cows.

I'm sorry. I'm getting worked up. But you see how it is? This sort of thing happens to me all the time. I could sue for slander, but that would just give more publicity to these claims — and that's what people would remember: not that they lied, just what they said.

So I don't get out much.

I'll be honest; I don't get out at all. I might be nearly eight metres tall, but I don't need much space, not really. The house is enough for me.

My parents were big, too, and I miss them. They had our house fitted out right for our family before I was even born. From the outside, it looks like a high-ceilinged three-storey townhouse. It fits in with its neighbours. The front door is big, I guess, but it's hidden behind an alcove. The house doesn't attract attention.

I attract attention, but only if I go out.

I don't need to go out, not these days. That's what the internet is for. That and cat videos. And porn (I'm kidding: I don't use porn!)

It feels a little strange, writing you this long email, but we've been chatting for a while now and I think we're starting to get serious. I should tell you a bit more about myself so you know what you are getting into. So we both know.

∞¥∞Ω∞¥∞

I told you I don't get out, so you're probably wondering how I make a living. I guess you could call me a freelancer. I do lots of little jobs online: piece-work. I choose my own hours and pick jobs that suit me: classifying images, filling out surveys, writing little articles and "how to" guides. It pays a few cents here, a couple of dollars there. None of it takes long, so as long as I put in the hours every day, it adds up to a good-enough living. I order in what I need: groceries from the local shops, custom-made trousers from China, music and videos streamed direct to my TV. It's a pretty good life. I do all my own repairs. There are always online videos to show me how. I work out, too: I put on an old movie and go through my weight routines in front of the TV. Gotta stay in shape.

I've noticed you're on the internet a lot, too: always available to chat. I like that about you. I like your picture, and I've been wondering: is that really you? It's okay if it's not. My profile doesn't say I'm almost eight metres tall, after all. No one is perfect. But if it is you, you're really cute.

I just wanted to say that.

Even if the photo isn't you, I bet you're cute anyway. You make me smile. Maybe we should do a video chat sometime? No hurry.

People stare at me. I know why they stare. I used to think I was a freak myself, but my parents said, "All our people are big: we're supposed to be big." They both died young; my parents. Their hearts gave out. If they hadn't left the Old Country, that wouldn't have happened. My heart will probably give out, too, if I stay. Here, I'm a freak.

But hey: your profile said you were looking for a tall guy.

∞¥∞Ω∞¥∞

I was telling you about my family. Mum and Dad left the Old Country when my mum was 17 and pregnant. Dad was 17, too: just a few weeks younger than Mum. It wasn't angry parents that made them run away. My mum's folks were actually pretty supportive, according to my dad. It wasn't school authorities, peer pressure or any church. It was something else; something that just wouldn't happen here.

I guess the best way to explain it is… Well, you've heard of Rumplestiltskin, right? I don't know if that was real, but the story has the basics right. A contract like that holds force of law in the Old Country.

A contract like that — something magic in exchange for the first-born child — is traditional, but just like in the Rumplestiltskin story, there's always some wriggle-room. So young girls, sometimes… They'll sign these contracts, thinking they'll find the wriggle-room, or thinking they'll never have kids anyway, or thinking there's just no other way out of whatever situation their wicked stepmothers have got them into. That's what keeps Rumplestiltskin and his mates in business.

We have the odd wicked stepmother here too, maybe, but over there, it's part of the job description. Here I think there are just as many nice stepmothers as nasty, and most of them are just average.

So anyway, my grandma had one of these wicked stepmothers in the Old Country, and she had what I guess you'd call these days, an absentee father. She didn't see much of him: he went off to work for the King and left the child-rearing to his wife.

Grandma's stepmum wanted to get rid of my grandma so her own kids would be the ones to inherit the family farm. Grandma should probably have just signed away the rights so her stepmother would stop picking on her, but she was only a kid and she didn't know that then.

The first thing this wicked stepmother tries is to send the poor girl out for firewood on her own, on a cold winter night, without a coat. My grandma is only eight or nine years old when this happens. The part of the Old Country she's from is like Siberia in winter: we're talking snow on the ground that's metres deep and won't melt away until halfway through spring. Oh, and I forgot to mention: there's a blizzard.

But Grandma has grown up here and she knows a thing or two about snow. Instead of wandering out into the dark and being lost forever, this little girl digs a hole in the deep snow behind the house and sits at the bottom of the hole, out of the stiff, cold wind, and she calls out very softly, making a noise like a rabbit until she sees a snow fox padding up to the hole to see what he can see.

I don't know what a rabbit is supposed to sound like, but I guess the fox does, and Grandma does, too.

So: "Tk-tk-tk," says Grandma, maybe, and *thop-thop-thop* goes the fox as he pads up on his snow-white feet to see if he can find some dinner on a cold winter night.

"Tk-tk-tk," says Grandma until the fox puts his nose in the hole to see if he can smell a rabbit. Then, *thwak!* My grandma grabs hold of the fox's nose, forefinger in one nostril, thumb in the other, so he can't get away. The fox, he tries to run, but Grandma is a big, strong girl for her age, and she holds on tight and she won't let go.

After a while, the fox knows she's won and he sits very still and whimpers, which is a fox's way of saying he's had enough. She loosens her grip on his nose just enough that he can talk.

"Child," says the fox, "why do you hold onto my nose so that I cannot run along the snow and find a rabbit for my tea? I wish you would let go."

"Mr Snow Fox," says my grandma, very polite now she has his attention, "I have caught you by the nose because I was clever enough to outwit you, and I will not let go until you do something for me."

"Child," says the snow fox, "that's not very nice and it's not very fair, but you have bested me squarely and I must be on my way, so what would you have me do?" (That's the way some of the animals talk in the Old Country, or at least, they did back then. I'm telling the story just like my mum told it to me.)

"Mr Fox," says my grandma (back in the Old Country). "You must dig a tunnel through the snow and guide me to the King's woodpile and safely back again with an armload of wood."

Grumbling, the snow fox agrees. He spends the rest of the night digging a tunnel through the snow to the King's woodpile. Grandma crawls along behind the fox, grabs a big armload of wood, and then follows the fox safely home.

The fox sits in the end of the snow-tunnel, still hungry because he hasn't had any dinner, and he watches her walk those last few steps across the back yard and to the back door.

"Child," says the fox, just before she steps inside, "I keep my bargains, but I will remember this and one day, I'll take my revenge."

But Grandma has her firewood today and she is safely in out of the snow, so she brushes off the fox's words as a worry that can wait for another time.

The stepmother is a bit pissed off to see my grandma safely home, but with an armload of firewood, she can't say "boo." So she bides her time until she sees another chance.

∞¥∞Ω∞¥∞

The second time the wicked stepmother tries to get her way, it's high summer. They have real summers in the part of the country that my grandma is from. It's hot like Coober Pedy: a real dry, baking heat. The ice has melted and trickled away months before and it hasn't rained for weeks. My grandma's dad works for the king, so their house has a good, deep well in the courtyard and it really shouldn't be a problem, but my grandma's stepmother takes it into her head that what she really needs to regain her youthful complexion is a bath of purest spring-water.

"Girl," she says to my grandma, "I need you to fetch me a bucket of spring-water. Only the purest will do."

Grandma looks up from her work, wondering what's coming next.

"I know you're scheming, girl: I can see it in your eyes. You always were a lazy child, but don't think I won't know if you try to cheat me. I have a little spell which will tell me where the water has come from and just how pure it is."

Grandma knows it's probably true, because her stepmother is a witch. She's not a very good witch, but she can manage one or two tricks and her magic will not let her lie outright, or she will lose it. That can be a great hindrance to a wicked stepmother.

"But Ma'am," says Grandma, "I don't know where to find spring-water in the summer. If we wait for autumn, there's a little spring that may pop up near the river after rain."

The river in summer is a dry, parched bed. A place to kick red dust into the wind until even the dust has blown away.

Stepma won't have it. It isn't really about the water after all: it's about getting rid of Grandma.

"It's a long time until autumn, my dear, and you've nothing else to do. Take this bucket and head west. I've heard there's a spring out that way, and if you keep up a brisk pace, you can get there before sundown tomorrow. If you dawdle like you always do, it'll take three days or four, but that's up to you."

So she sends my grandma out on her own, with just a hunk of cheese and a knob of bread and an orange so she can squeeze out the juice when she's thirsty, and she tells her where that spring is, and not to come back without a bucket of spring-water. Grandma hears the door slam shut behind her, though she hasn't even had a chance to fill that empty bucket from the well.

My grandma at this time is just eleven years old, but she grew up in this part of the Old Country, so she knows the desert like she knows the hard, bony back of her stepmother's hand. She knows she'll never make it if she sets out with just these three provisions, all on her own. So instead, she climbs up into a baobab tree and she sits very still and hidden, and she makes a noise like a cicada.

"KrrrrEEEE! KrrrrrrEEEE!"

(I don't know why the baobab tree didn't explode in winter, cold as winter was. Must be a different species over there.)

It's hot and it's dry and the desert sun is beating down, but the little girl (who is not so little, for her age) has a bit of shade in the tree, so she stays there until who comes pat-padding along but a dingo?

"KrrrrrEEEEE!" says my grandma, pretending to be a cicada in that baobab tree. "KrrrrrrEEEE!"

Pat-pad go the dingo-dog's feet on the hot, red sand, and *huff-puff* goes the dingo's breath as he tries to cool down.

"KrrrrrEEEE!" calls my grandma, from her tree.

And the dingo stops.

It's an unexpected sound, a green grocer cicada in the desert, because although they like the heat, they need fresh, flowing sap, and where there is fresh, flowing sap, there's water.

So the dingo stops, and he looks around, because he's really pretty thirsty and would like to find that water. My grandma keeps on pretending to be a cicada until the dingo comes close enough that he's right underneath her spot in the tree, then she leaps down from her nook and she drops her bucket over his head before he knows what's hit him.

That old dingo-dog, he bucks and he thrashes and wears himself out, trying to get the bucket off his head, but my grandma is not so little, and she's strong and determined. She holds on tight and keeps holding on, until after a while the dingo knows he's beaten.

Now that she's got him listening, my grandma says she knows he's thirsty and she can tell him where there is a big pool of clear, fresh water, but she needs his help to get to it and maybe they can cut a deal.

The dingo doesn't reply, but he cocks his ear so she knows he's listening.

"I can't get there all on my own," she says, "but you're fast and you're strong and you're light on your feet and I think it won't take you so long to make your way across the desert to the spring."

"How far is this spring?" asks the dingo. "If it were close, surely I would know of it already."

"I will not lie," says my grandmother. "It is not so close. A day's run and a night's run, too, across the desert."

"Then it is too far," said the dingo. "Why do you waste my time? If I stay here and hunt, I can take moisture from the blood of a wallaby, and suck the dew from the morning earth and I will survive another day, but if I run with you across the desert and do not hunt, we will neither of us survive."

"Aha," says my grandmother. "Tonight, perhaps you will run down that wallaby, but how many nights will pass until you fail? And how many days more until the dew does not come?"

The dingo shakes his fur impatiently. "Maybe autumn will be upon us before that time. Autumn will bring rain."

"Well," says Grandma, "you may be right. It may be so. If you would rather chance it here, I suppose that's your right. At the spring, though, you could live through the summer without worry."

The dingo sighs. "Child, what possible help could you be to me in getting to this spring, if it's a day's run from here and a night's run, too?"

"I have this bucket," said my grandma, showing the dingo the truth of it. "I can fill it with water from the king's well so you can drink your fill before you set off."

"The king's men shoot those they catch stealing water from the king's well. If they did not, there would be no need to find this spring."

"But you, Mr Dingo, are both fast and strong. If you let yourself be seen approaching the well, you can lead the king's men away on a vigorous chase while I sneak in and fill the bucket."

"A dangerous plan," comments the dingo.

"But consider the reward!"

"A deep drink from a bucket would be a welcome improvement on dew," says the dingo, his voice a little croaky from the dry. Grandma can see that he wants to be persuaded, now. "And I am a creature of the desert: one deep drink will sustain me for the run. But what of you?"

"I will drink, too, and stay here very still in the shade of the baobab tree."

The dingo looks amused, now. "An excellent plan," he says. "Then let us be away!"

"Not so fast," says my grandma, reaching very quickly to pluck a hair from the dingo's tail. The dingo yelps and snaps at her hand, but he does not bite because he has a clear, cool spring on his mind, now.

"You think to outwit me, to get to the spring and not return." She holds up the hair so the dingo can see it, and looks him in the eye. "My stepmother is a witch and she has taught me a few things. You know this is true, because a witch cannot lie. You may leave now without harm, but if you take the deal I offer and do not return with a bucket of spring-water, I will use this hair to cast a spell that will cause your balls to drop off and never grow back!"

The dingo's hackles rise and his tail droops at the thought. His voice rises in pitch to a whine. "If I return with a bucket for you, how am I to make my own way back to the spring? I will be back to sucking dew from the ground and water from wallabies' blood."

Though Grandma is no witch, she has the dingo fooled, so he has to trust when she says, "You have my word that I will provide another bucket of water to get you back across the desert, drop for drop to match the water that you bring back from the spring."

So they put the plan into action, creeping east to the edge of the King's courtyard. Grandma hides behind the corner of a wall while Dingo darts ahead and makes for the well. A shout goes up as a guard sees him, and he turns tail and runs. The guard's first shot clips off the tip of the dingo's tail, but he is strong and fast and out of range before the second guard can take aim or the first guard can reload his gun. The two of them make chase, leaving the well undefended.

Seizing her moment, my grandma runs out into the courtyard, pushes the bucket on its rope from the well wall to splash into the water far below, sets her own bucket on the ground and begins winching.

It is a very deep well because this is a very parched land, in summer. It takes one hundred turns of the winch and one hundred more before the water is brought to the surface. My grandma works as fast as she can because she doesn't know how long the dingo will be able to keep the guards distracted, or how long before someone looks out of a castle window and sees her at the well, where she has no leave to be. But at last the bucket reaches the top and Grandma is able to reach out and pull it to the edge of the well to fill her bucket for the dingo.

She has promised the dingo a full bucket of water, but she has sweated a great deal with her exertions, so Grandma, too, must drink. She pushes the well-bucket back into the water and begins winding it up again just as fast as she can. One hundred turns of the winch-handle, and she hears shouts in the distance that tell her the men are still on the dingo's tracks. Fifty turns more, and the shouts stop, and she fears the men have given up the chase. Twenty-five turns more, twenty-five still to go when she hears another shout and running feet that tell her she has been spotted. Grandma grabs hold of the rope and hauls it up by hand, abandoning the winch and using her own strength of arm to pull up the bucket just as fast as she can.

She lifts the bucket to the edge of the well, dunks her head into the water and swallows as much as she can in a few swift gulps, dunks her bread into the water, too, then grabs her own bucket and runs for home. A few shots fly past her head, but the guards do not give chase, fearing to fall for the same trick twice.

Back at the baobab tree, the dingo is waiting for her, panting from his run. She binds his injured tail with a strip torn from the bottom of her skirt while he drinks his fill from the bucket. Then he picks up the bucket by its handle in his teeth, and sets off to the west at a loping run.

∞¥∞Ω∞¥∞

As the dingo runs, Grandma sits quiet and still in the shade of the baobab tree. She pushes her water-soaked bread into a cranny in the tree to keep it moist, and she waits. Her wet hair dries quickly in the parching sun but the day passes slowly. When night falls, scarcely cooler, Grandma eats her bread and tries to sleep.

Day breaks: a hotter day than the one before. There is no hint of dew on the ground. Still, my grandma waits beside the baobab tree.

As the sun rises high, her tongue thickens in her mouth, her lips crack in the heat and her eyelids scrape like sandpaper over her eyes, they are so dry.

At sunset, she opens the orange and sucks out its juices. She waits.

Another night passes, perhaps a little cooler than the night before, but no less dry. My grandma waits.

By the afternoon of the third day, Grandma is near delirium and thinking about going back to steal from the king's well or — just as dangerous, she knows — returning empty-handed to her stepmother to beg for water. But she is a patient child. Still, she waits.

At last, as she lies near death, she feels the cool splash of water over her dry, parched face. The dingo has returned and dropped her bucket on the ground beside her.

Slowly, stiffly, my Grandma rises from her place on the ground, bows to the dingo and takes up the bucket to deliver inside to her stepmother.

The stepmother is frankly astonished to see the child alive. Her spells show that it is indeed true spring-water, so she can do nothing more than complain about the time my grandma has taken to fetch the water back. Once her stepmother has tipped the bucket into the basin and is occupied with her bath, Grandma takes the bucket away, fills it from their courtyard well, and takes it outside to where the dingo is waiting.

The dog drinks deeply, then sits on his haunches and looks at her. "I've had some time to think," he says. "Are you really a witch?"

My grandma shakes her head, no. Taking the stolen hair from her pocket, she offers it back to the dingo, who lets it blow away in the wind.

"I thought about not coming back, you know," says the dingo, "but I wasn't sure."

"Thank you for coming back, then. It has saved my life."

Picking up the bucket again, with the rest of the water, the dingo harruphs and heads off west.

∞¥∞Ω∞¥∞

This is kind of a long story, isn't it? I know I haven't explained anything yet, about my parents, or why they came here. I'm getting to that part. It's soon.

∞¥∞Ω∞¥∞

The third time my grandma's wicked stepmother tries to kill her, Grandma has just turned sixteen, and it's spring. If you saw the Old Country in spring, you'd know why my parents' people loved to live there. Everything is green except the flowers, which are all the colours you can imagine. There's a crystal-clear river running through the land, washing away the red desert silt, and full to bursting with frogs and fish. There are dragonflies and mayflies buzzing over the water, and there are dragons high in the sky, busy in their mating dances. Being sixteen, and this being spring, my grandma has eyes for a certain young man.

He's the sixth son in a family of seven sons. He is tall and good-looking (in Grandma's eyes at least) and he has a nice smile, but he has no prospects at all. This gene-line has produced nothing but sons for seven generations, so they've learned to be strict with the inheritance rules.

Everything goes to son number one, except enough to buy military commissions for sons two and three and positions in the church for sons four and five. Now this leaves nothing for sons six and seven, but a seventh son is never short of apprenticeship offers of a certain type in the Old Country, and luck tends to go his way. But son number six? Well, he has a nice smile.

At sixteen, he thinks Grandma is a bit of all right, too. The nice thing for them both is that, having no prospects, son number six is free to follow his heart and can seriously think about asking a farm girl, daughter of one of the king's lowliest men and stepdaughter of a king's man's slightly witchy wife, to the next county dance.

You know, I've heard bits and pieces of the story of my grandma and grandpa from my mum: how they first met and how they got to know each other and how he did end up asking her to that dance.

How he told her about the curse that had been laid on his family, on his great-great-six-times-great grandfather: nothing but sons for seven generations. How it was that not many people knew about the curse, but that everyone knew that family only ever had boys. But how he'd heard privately from his big brothers, off with their wives in far-off lands, that every one of them had just had daughters instead of sons, and so it seemed the curse was finally broken.

How that boy and my grandma fell in love.

But most of this, you don't need to know for the story I'm trying to tell.

You just need to know that my grandma has my grandpa on her mind in her sixteenth spring, and probably everyone knows it.

Her stepmother knows it and she doesn't much like it. She has to get rid of Grandma before she comes of age. Most especially, she has to get rid of her before there's another generation in the offing. Seeing Grandma gadding about with a boy reminds Stepma very strongly of that fact.

So Grandma's wicked stepmother hatches another plan.

Grandma, at this time, is considered quite a beauty among the giants. So Mum told me anyway. I don't know what happened to the gene-pool if that's true, but you have to allow for a little bit a family bias in the way this story is told.

Grandma is a beauty and her wicked stepmother figures that she can use that to her advantage. It's a high-risk gambit, but she figures she knows her stepdaughter well enough to know that she'll play the role of the romantic and not give a second's thought to fame or fortune if it is offered in place of love.

And she knows the lie of the land.

The stepmother leans on her husband to see if he can't put it into the king's head to send his son, the prince-in-waiting, along to the county ball. The husband, thinking it's a favour for his daughter as well as a way to please his wife, screws up his courage and does his best. Somehow or other, the poor chap succeeds.

Or maybe the husband has nothing to do with it and the prince just likes going to balls.

This prince is an ugly brute of a man, more in his manners than his looks. Let's just say he has a certain reputation among the girls, and it isn't a good one. But he is the heir to the throne, so he gets away with a lot. The court treats his behaviour as a bit of a joke. The men do, anyway.

Now Stepma has hoarded her witchy powers for a six full months in the lead-up to this ball, knowing that she isn't very strong, but also knowing that Grandma's natural good looks are going to count for a lot. She hoards up her powers and then she brews up a brew full of dandelions and boronia, ladybird feet and the nitrogen-fixing nodules from the roots of young snow-peas: an exotic, uncommon mix, but the most powerful that she can come up with. She heats it very gently, keeping it just above the temperature of a baby's bottle for six days. She strains it through her best spider-silk filter cloth and lets it sit in a brass bowl overnight in the moonlight, and then she uses it to anoint the combs that my grandma is going to wear in her hair on the night of the ball.

Grandma is no fool. She knows something is up when her stepmother is suddenly all solicitation in helping her prepare for the dance, but she's so head-over-heels for a certain first love that she can't bring herself to worry.

(I've never really been that much in love myself yet, but I wouldn't rule it out. I'm looking forward to meeting you.)

When Grandma turns up at the ball, she is breathtaking. Literally: everyone in the room holds their breath while they watch her hang up her coat and step into the hall. (This is how my mother told it, but she wasn't there.) Grandpa's chest is just bursting with pride, knowing that my grandma is there to dance with him. Every other boy in the room falls in love on the spot.

The prince is one of them.

A large part of that is the spell, of course, but they don't know that.

Now this is going to be a problem for Grandma, as her stepmother knows. She has a certain amount of native sense, but not a whole lot. Not when it comes to this sort of thing. She's a romantic and she has never dealt with royalty before. Her father may work for the king, but that doesn't bring their family into much contact with aristocrats or the court.

The prince notices Grandma straight away, of course. He's got his eyes on every young girl in the hall. On parts of them, anyway.

When this new girl comes in through the door and hangs her coat, the prince's eyes drift across to her ... and they're trapped. He can't look away. He can't figure what it is: yes, she has a nice shape and she has a nice smile, but so do fifteen other girls he's spotted. She has a lovely complexion and shiny, red-gold hair (that's "ginger" to you and me, just like I've got), but so do five of the others. The combs in her hair ... there's something about them, perhaps ... but no: it's the girl. He can't take his eyes off her. He must be in love.

So this brute of a prince sends one of his men over to pinch her backside and tell her that the prince wants to see her.

My grandma knows better than to say no to this, though she hasn't even had time to say hello to the boy she's here to see. She has a quick look around the room, trying to find him, but she knows she can't wait: she has to attend to the prince.

She walks across to his corner of the room, where he's sitting by the punchbowl. He doesn't stand, though that was the custom back then; for a man to stand to greet a woman. I think that was so even here.

He waits for her to walk over and stand in front of him and then he waits a little longer as he runs his eyes slowly over every part of her sixteen-year old body. Then he waits a little longer still, while she loses her composure and the men around him smirk and his best friend doesn't try very hard to hold back a snort of laughter. Then, finally, he gets up from his seat, holds out his hand for hers, and without really asking, sweeps her off into a dance.

He's a much better dancer than she is. Good enough to make her look good. Good enough to have her feeling good about herself, recovering somewhat from the awkwardness of the moments before. Good enough even to have her wondering for a moment whether she has got him all wrong and he's not such a bad bloke after all.

But then the music changes and, without ever asking, he pulls her in close for the next dance. Close enough that it's obvious to everyone that he's looking right down her front. Close enough that it's obvious to her, in a way that's never been made obvious to her before, that he likes what he sees. In short, he pressed up against her, dancing in a very intimate way.

My grandma knew better than to turn down the first dance with the prince, or even the second, but she's not comfortable with this. She waits until the end of dance number two, but when he tries to claim her hand for the third dance in a row, she has had enough. She has promised to dance with a certain sixth son, and she won't break her word. She doesn't want to. She's been looking forward to this date for months.

So when there's a break in the music, she steps away with a regretful smile ... or tries to. The prince keeps hold of her hand and uses that to swirl her around and pull her back in for another dance.

Grandma grits her teeth and smiles — she's a patient girl, I told you — and she waits out this dance, too. When the music stops again, she's ready for him. She puts both her hands on his chest and pushes herself firmly away, dropping to a curtsey just in time to duck out of his reach. As she rises, she takes two more steps away and calls out. "You do me so much honour, your Highness, but I really must go. There are so many girls waiting for your attention, and I mustn't be greedy."

The prince, who had been starting to frown, smiles when she says this. Because she's a few steps away now; everyone around them hears her words, and she's counting on that to make the prince behave.

"Let them be jealous," the prince declares. "I'm going to dance with you until the evening is done. Unless you'd rather leave with me now?"

My grandma shakes her head. "I'm sorry, sir, but I have promised to dance with another boy, so I really do have to go."

The prince's frown returns. He reaches for her again, and she ducks. It's not so subtle this time, and the music has already started up for the next song. Not many people are dancing, yet: they are all waiting to see this play out.

"You'll dance with me."

It's a statement of command. He's used to having his own way, and he needs to make this clear. If she doesn't take his hand now, he'll look a fool.

She doesn't care. She has been on her best behaviour, but he seems determined to spoil her night. She's not thinking about the danger here: she's thinking about the boy she's in love with; the boy she's come to see. She can see him across the room, and he's as handsome as ever. So she ignores the prince's words, and she walks away to give her boy that promised dance.

The prince is humiliated. Angry. He's not a nice man and he is a man with power. Lucky for her, he's in love. Instead of dragging her away into the dark, never to be seen again, he has his guards arrest her and take her back to the castle.

It puts a dampener on the party, but he's the prince: there's nothing anyone can do.

My grandpa follows, a long way behind. He watches where they take her, but doesn't step in. Not now. These are six strong guards and a prince who is known for abusing his power, while Grandpa, at this time, is just a sixteen-year old boy schooled more in geography than swordplay: geography and book-keeping, because he's hoping to go into business as a merchant sometime soon.

The prince and his guards take my grandma to the castle and lock her in a cell. It's a fairly nice cell, as they go. There's a bed and a wash-stand and even a wardrobe, filled with dresses that the prince has picked out. There's a narrow window to the inner castle grounds, so Grandma has a bit of light and can smell the wattle on the air outside and hear the parrots twittering on about love. The prince is in love, he tells her, and that is why he has her locked up and not beaten for her impudence. He'll let her out, he says, but not until she promises to marry him and makes sure of that promise by consummsnating the pact before the fact. He won't force her, but he'll give her time to think.

Like I said; he's a prince. He can do this.

Grandma's stepmother figures she's won. My grandmother is far too much of a romantic to ever agree to these terms and the prince is far too impatient a man to let her live in this cell for long, in defiance.

She's right. After almost a week of waiting for Grandma to send word via his guard, the prince visits her cell in person.

He's an impatient man and this has been the longest he's ever waited for anything. Grandma curtsies when he enters the room, but says nothing.

"Well?" say the prince.

"Your Highness?"

"You've had time to think. Ample time."

She lowers her eyes. "Yes, your Highness."

"And so?"

Her breath catches and she almost squeaks, but still: "I'm a farm girl, your Highness. Not a suitable wife for a prince."

He looks to the guard beside him, who nods, removes his glove, and steps forward to slap the girl across the face. The prince does not blink.

The guard speaks for him. "You will not speak to the prince like that. It is not your place to question his judgement."

The slap was a hard one. It will leave a bruise, but for now it just stings. Tears prick my grandmother's eyes, but still she says, "I will not marry you."

The guard moves to slap her again, but the prince gives a tiny shake of his head, exercising control.

"I'll come back tomorrow," he says. "And I will ask again."

∞¥∞Ω∞¥∞

It's a sleepless night that my grandma spends in her cell. Not that she's been getting much sleep all week. She spends the night and the next day worrying and trying to think what to do. Her young man comes by and they whisper reassurances to each other through the high window, but his warrior older brothers are far away, his sorcerer younger brother has not yet come into his powers, and there's nothing he can think of to do. Soon enough, the guards see him there, chase him away, and order him not to come back or they'll turn him over to the prince. They all know that would mean his certain death.

∞¥∞Ω∞¥∞

The next night, the prince visits Grandma again. This time, she's ready with a kick to the groin and a dash to the door, but the prince is ready too, wearing an athletic support. He has six guards waiting outside the door, just in case, but Grandma doesn't get that far. My grandma is a slip of a girl, not even six metres tall. The prince is a burly eight metre scrapper. He grabs her by her forearms, picks her up and throws her against the wall. Somehow, Grandma manages not to hit her head, but the breath is knocked out of her and she wonders whether she has broken ribs. She can't help but slide to the floor.

"You are lucky I am so much in love," remarks the prince, looking down at her. "I said I would ask again today, and I will. Will you marry me?"

Still breathless, my grandma closes her eyes and shakes her head.

The prince snorts in frustration. His eyes narrow. The look on his face is not kind. "I will come back tomorrow," he says, measuring each word. "And I will ask you again. But, young lady, think carefully what your answer will be. I have been gentle with you. I am a generous man, but there are limits." His voice is hoarse. "There must always be limits. If your answer has not changed by tomorrow, I will have you hung for treason."

He turns aside but pauses in the doorway, glancing back at the girl on the floor. "In any case," he adds, "I will have my way first."

The guards close the door behind him and leave the girl to think. Finally, she finds the breath to sob.

∞¥∞Ω∞¥∞

As dusk closes in, there's a cough from the window. The girl looks up, hoping to see her sixth son one more time. It isn't him. It's the snow fox, scrawny in his summer brown.

He's standing back from the grate, so she can't grab his nose, but he looks pleased to see her.

"Well," says the fox. "You are in a pickle."

She looks at him, puzzled. "Hello."

The fox wrinkles his nose. "Do you remember me, girl?"

"I remember you well," says the girl, "and I thank you for your help."

The fox flashes a brief smile. "Perhaps I can help you again."

"And in exchange? What do you want?"

"Oh," says the snow fox. "Simply to help an old friend. Do you want help, or not?"

"Yes," she says. "I am listening. What do you propose?"

"I know someone," says the fox. "A fearsome witch. A beautiful lady. Someone who helps out, in circumstances like this. She can be here within the hour."

"A Rumplestiltskin?" asks the girl.

The snow fox opens his mouth wide, feigning shock. "Such language! But I see that you understand. Shall I fetch her?"

Grandma thinks for a moment. Making pacts with Rumplestiltskins is like eating fairy food or stepping off the path. But what else can she do?

"Thank you," she says to the fox. "Yes, please bring your friend."

∞¥∞Ω∞¥∞

It's a cold hour waiting, as night sets in and Grandma wonders whether the fox will be true to his word. But when the hour is up, a woman appears in the cell. A beautiful lady, quite young to look at her, but ladies of this type live a very long time. Her eyes are blueish-green: just like yours, if that's really your photo. Her hair is brown and very long: like yours might be, if you grew it out. She wears a long, blood-red gown, overlain with creamy lace, intricately knotted and very fine.

Grandma is expecting her. She has washed away her tears and changed into a green silk dress from the wardrobe, and satin slippers. She makes a deep curtsey to this lady, who might be able to help.

"You may rise," says the lady, approving the gesture.

"Thank you. Has the fox…"

"The snow fox has told me about your situation," says the lady. "You are unlikely to escape this cell by yourself. Would you like me to help?"

"Can you get me out of this cell?"

"In an instant."

"And after that? How am I to escape the prince?"

The lady's smile is reassuring. Her eyes look kind. "I will wipe you from the prince's memory. He will not know that he has ever set eyes on you. If he passes you again, he will not even see you."

"That sounds perfect," says Grandma, hope quickening. "No one would dare to remind him. But what will you take in return?"

"My terms are standard."

"Let's be clear."

"The first boy of your line."

Her first-born son. Well, the lady cannot know what my grandma knows: that she is bound to have daughters if she marries her beau. That's something she is pretty determined to do.

"I agree, then."

From a pocket in the crimson gown, the lady brings a contract and a quill. The nib has already, somehow been dipped in ink. Grandma signs. The thing is done.

∞¥∞Ω∞¥∞

There's a lot more I could tell you about my grandma and grandpa. They do marry, though not before a few more years have passed, and a lot more dances. Nobody ever does remind the prince; not even the stepma. I'll tell you more about Grandma and Grandpa when we meet, if you like. For now, you just need to know this: Grandma has a daughter. The crimson lady drops by, bringing flowers. She looks into the cradle, looks into my mother's infant eyes, nods to Grandma, and leaves without a word.

My grandparents stop at one child, reminded of the pact and not wanting to tempt fate.

Grandpa is a good husband, and becomes a good merchant. Grandma is a good farmer. The two of them bring up their daughter very well.

My mother has a happier time of childhood than my grandma did, and not so many adventures. Like my grandmother, she falls in love young, but unlike Grandma, she doesn't have much patience.

When they learn that Mum is pregnant, my grandparents think about the green-eyed lady for the first time in many years, and they consult a lawyer about the terms. And yes: as you've guessed, they find out that "the first boy of your line" could just as well be a grandson and Mum is bound just as tightly by her mother's signature on the contract. Grandma tells Mum and Dad the bad news.

It might not matter, if Mum is carrying a girl. There are tests they can do, even then, to find out.

They find out that she is carrying a boy. She is carrying me.

Mum was four months gone before they knew she was pregnant. Grandma and Grandpa, Mum and Dad spend the next three months thinking and putting the best lawyers they can afford onto finding a loophole in that contract. They don't find one. So there is nothing for it, they think, but to flee.

Grandpa puts his geography to good use, tracing a route across a map of the Old Country, through the twisty, ever-changing paths that will bring them, if they time it just right, across into our world. He puts his merchant wits to good use, too, filling their pockets with the silver-bells that grow wild along the forest edge and with a small purse of gold, for emergencies.

He hugs them, and Grandma hugs them, and they say their goodbyes. Dad makes his farewells to his family, too. There are tears. They know that they will never see each other again.

It's an adventure, too, Grandpa's path across the world. They meet Grandma's dingo, who helps them along part of the way. If this email weren't already so long, I'd tell you more about their journey, but you already know they get here safe.

After arriving in this country, they polish up their silver-bells and sell them as trinkets. They sell their coins, too, for the gold in them, and find they have more money at the end than they had expected. They have enough to buy a house and fit it out: a safe place to bring me into the world and bring me up.

That brings us back to me. I had a good childhood. Not a happy one, maybe; I wasn't a happy child, but I was safe and healthy and strong. Mum and Dad lived out their lives here. Short lives, by any standard, but happy. They were always so much in love.

I never went out much more than I had to. After Mum died, I stopped going out at all. Like I said, it's not a bad life, but I have to be honest: I do know there is more. So I'm taking baby steps to get myself out again. Putting my profile up on that dating site was my first little step, and you've given me the courage to take the next one.

∞¥∞Ω∞¥∞

There's one more thing you should know. I may be a shut-in, but I'm not naive. I know you already knew part of this story. I traced your IP address and I know you're not from around here. A twisty and changeable traceroute it was, too, but my skills on the computer are pretty good.

It's not good for my health to stay here, and my family always were hopeless romantics. I'm more than halfway in love.

Beautiful lady, crimson lady, I'm ready to take that next big step, with you.

∞¥∞Ω∞¥∞

NUMBER 73 GLAD AVENUE

SUZANNE J. WILLIS

"What time does the clock have, Charlie?" Mary looked left, dark, bobbed hair brushing her shoulders. She heard him mutter then carefully shut the doors, locking the timepieces away, before walking around to face her, his little tin feet clicking softly against the wooden floor.

"12 May 1923. Six pm."

She looked down at Charlie as he packed the powders and glass vials, which were no bigger than her thumbnail, into the black leather doctor's bag, before climbing in and settling into the spare space at the side. At twelve inches tall, he just fit inside, with a whisker of room between his head and the bag's brass clasps. "Comfortable?" she asked.

"I'll be better when we've arrived. Let's get going." He clapped his hands together then waved as she shut him in.

Mary walked down the street. Silver waves of time flowed around her in a shimmering cascade as the buildings, the path, the people disappeared or grew or shrank into their new lines as required. Each step carried her quite gradually from 1852 to 1923, the bag clenched firmly in her hand, and she gave a little shiver. *It's so different*, she thought. All the beautiful clean lines, the geometric shapes of the buildings fronted with sunbursts and arching curves: the simple luxury of it all. Visiting the twenties — whether from the past or the misty future — never ceased to amaze her. There was something so fresh and almost, well, bouncy about it. It was an era in which Mary felt revived, which was no easy feat given that she and Charlie were constantly scissoring back and forth between the decades, centuries, epochs.

It had been so long now, Mary had quite forgotten how their journey back and forth through time was supposed to end. She shook that thought away; better to let these things work themselves out.

The air stilled and she looked around. Horse-drawn carriages had given way to automobiles, sleek and chrome, slinking down the road. A shiny brick-red model passed by, the jaguar in mid-leap on the hood shining under the late afternoon sun. The driver whistled at Mary and tipped his hat as she smiled back.

"What is that infernal racket?" came Charlie's muffled voice from inside the bag.

Mary listened for a moment. There it was — the unmistakable sound of jaunty pianos and sexy, snaking trumpets. She realised she was tapping her foot.

"It's jazz, Charlie, you old stick-in-the-mud. And *I* quite like it."

He mumbled a reply.

"It's strange, though. Today doesn't *feel* terribly important. There's usually someth—"

"Number 73 Glad Avenue," was the exasperated response from the bag.

"Right you are, Charlie."

∞¥∞Ω∞¥∞

Number 73 was set on a huge expanse of land fronting the river. Geraldine, their employer for the evening, led Mary into the front room that overlooked the lawn rolling down to the river bank, a dark emerald in the dying light.

"And here's the bar." Geraldine pointed to the buffet unit in the corner.

"Walnut, with marble top, if I'm not mistaken? And chrome trim."

Geraldine nodded. "We had it shipped all the way from New York, you know. There's not another one like it in the world."

"It's beautiful. And quite perfect for what we have in mind. I hope I don't seem immodest, but you couldn't have chosen a better hostess. You and your guests are in for a treat," Mary smiled. "I do so love a good party, Geraldine."

"You don't appear to have brought much with you, dear," Geraldine pointed at the black bag.

"There's not a lot I need, as you'll see." Mary opened the clasps and brought out a miniature replica of the walnut and marble unit, placing it in the centre of the real one.

Geraldine looked shocked. "But how could you know?"

"Ah, now, a magician never reveals her secrets." With that, she pulled Charlie from the bag and stood him up behind the little bar, where he looked for all the world like a china doll with twinkling blue-glass eyes and impressively thick moustache. Mary smoothed his ginger hair.

"He's just adorable," Geraldine said.

"And quite the star of the show, as you'll see. I'm fine to see to things here, if you'd like to get ready for your guests. Of course, we do require payment up front…"

"Oh, naturally, yes." Geraldine rummaged through the drawers of a dark bureau on the other side of the room. For the sake of discretion, Mary turned and walked over to the tall, arched windows. She looked at the long wooden jetty. A woman sat at the end, silhouetted against the sunset-flamed river, her toes skimming the water.

"Beautiful at this time of day, isn't it?"

Mary smiled. "It's like something out of The Great Gats—" she stopped herself. *That's not until 1925!*

"From what, dear?"

"Oh, nothing. Who is that sitting on the end of the jetty?"

"That's my older sister, Freya. She's a funny thing, keeps quite to herself and … but I'm rattling on, here you go." Geraldine held out a gold pocket watch; it swung gently on the end of its chain and caught the last rays of the sun. "It hasn't worked for years, but it does pain me to part with it. It was my grandfather's. Still, you come so highly recommended." She paused, glancing at Mary suspiciously. "If you don't mind my saying so, it does seem like an odd price…"

With a beatific smile, Mary reached out for the watch. As metal and flesh came into contact, the watch shivered, its gold sparking in the gathering dark. She shifted it in her hands: it warmed to her touch. *Click.* The cover sprang back to reveal the ornate hands slowly journeying around its pale face. The second hand was missing.

"Well, now, look at that. It seems to be working after all. Even has the right time." She waved her free hand at Geraldine, dismissing her confusion. "Which means *you* must go and get ready."

Once Geraldine was gone Charlie stretched and yawned on the bar, blinking his glassy eyes. He jumped into the bag, rummaged about then jumped out again with several vials. He began to mix the powders and fluids together in a bell-shaped bottle, humming softly to himself.

The jetty drew Mary's gaze again. Freya was walking along it towards the shore, leaving a trail of silvered footprints shining like old stars.

∞¥∞Ω∞¥∞

Mary smiled at the women — *flappers*, she remembered — in their feathered headpieces and beaded frocks; at the men in their razor-sharp suits as they lit cigarettes in long holders for their paramours. Her own close-fitted dress was black, long-sleeved, innocuous; the only feature was a row of silver buttons down her back. But the colours the flappers wore! And the fabrics! The delicate, diaphanous skirts; the trailing ribbons from dropped waists; the long strings of jewels, darlings, the jewels.

The parquetry floor shook and the chandeliers tinkled as the guests shook and shimmied and stomped to the jazz band, its piano, trumpet and Sharkey Malone's whisky-voice jumping across the night. No-one looked lonesome in a corner, or was without one of Charlie's fabulous gin martinis or old-fashioneds. Everything was going to plan.

"I would honestly love to know how that little barman doll works. He seems so like-life ... lifely ... um, *real*." Geraldine had crept up behind Mary and slung an arm around her shoulder. Her voice was a little slurred and her headpiece of peacock feathers and jet sat askew.

"He's always a hit. But now, I think, would be a good time for the main event, seeing as the band's about to break." She signalled to Sharkey Malone, who pulled a worn little hipflask from his pocket and toasted in reply. "If you'll just get everyone to—"

"Darlings. My lovely katty-kits. No, wait — my kitty cats..." Geraldine giggled and swayed as all eyes turned towards her. She waved a hand at Mary, who felt a little thrill run through her. *This* was what she had been waiting for.

"Ladies and gentlemen, if you'd like to form an orderly line in front of the bar, we have a rather special treat for the evening, courtesy of the lovely Geraldine," Mary smiled winningly.

The crowd cheered as she walked to the bar and stood beside Charlie. Tiny ruby glasses, about twice the size of a thimble, were stacked on the right of his little bar. On the left were the bell-shaped bottle and two chrome cocktail shakers. The booze, she knew, would be on the shelf underneath.

"You really are an old pro, aren't you, Charlie?" Mary whispered to him.

He replied with a wink.

"Whisky or gin?" asked Mary of the first guest, a plump woman with a fur-trimmed neckline and tight rings that made her fingers look like sausages.

"Whisky, thanks, honey."

At this stage of the evening Charlie could relax a little. People were drunk enough not to notice that his movements were fluid, less like a spring-powered automaton. It was exhausting to keep that act up all night, she knew. He deserved to have a little fun with his favourite part of the night.

He poured the whisky into the shaker, over crushed ice, followed by a shot of something shimmering that looked like liquid violets.

"Hang on a minute, honey. That's not anything that's *stronger* than booze now, is it? If you get my drift." The plump woman looked concerned.

"Madam, I assure you we serve nothing dangerous."

"Now who's the old pro?" whispered Charlie under his moustache. The shaker frosted over as he gave it a quick, expert shake. He lifted it high in the air, straining the beverage into one of the ruby glasses. A fine mist wafted from the liquid as it waterfalled into it; the sound of children's laughter splashed up from the drink.

"Now isn't that just the strangest thing?" The woman's pink-painted lips curved into a smile, her chubby cheeks shining. She held the glass up to the light; crimson sparkles shone on the wall behind it.

Mary smiled back. "Now if you'd like to make your way to the lawn?"

The plump woman stood aside for a man in a brown fedora.

"Whisky or gin?"

They streamed to the bar, full of laughter and disinhibition. Mary watched Charlie pass another tiny glass of violet liquid to a smiling, swaying man, revelling in their abandonment.

Geraldine waved at Mary as the last guest wandered outside. "Bottoms up, darlings!" she cried, downing the drink in one mouthful as Mary switched off the lights.

Charlie wiped out the cocktail shakers as he looked out the window.

"Admiring your handiwork?" Mary asked.

"It never gets dull, does it? I mean, I never quite know how they're going to react…"

"Look," she whispered. The crescent moon was slung low on the horizon, refusing to illuminate the garden with more than a wan glow. Geraldine laughed, a raucous guffaw from her belly. As it rang out, the laughter vapourised into yellow light, like boiling water into steam. It broke off into tiny pieces that flew up into amber lanterns that Mary had earlier strung through the trees, around the ironwork fencing, along the edges of the lawn. Luminous, the lanterns lit the party with the light of a worn-through sunset. Silhouettes of the ants and insect wings forever frozen in the amber filled the grounds.

"Beautiful as ever," Charlie sighed. "It does seem sad, though, that they don't ever remember it."

"Perhaps. But it doesn't mean that it doesn't change them, that they don't carry it with them." Laughing softly, she pointed toward the plump woman who had taken the first drink. All her flapper frippery had fallen off, discarded on the damp grass. She stretched, her body elongating, the soft white flesh stretching and curving around the changing bones. An unseen vessel tipped over her head, spilling shining liquid until she was coated head to foot in chrome. Naked, unadorned, she arched her back in an imitation of the Diana lamps and ashtrays of the day.

"Amazing, isn't it, what people can do when you take back just a little time from them?" Mary never grew tired of the endless shapes, the form and formlessness that rested under the layers of time that humans wore like a shell. She wondered what would happen if it was age, the strangely complicated effect of time, that was stripped away. But the drink took back time itself, bringing out all the possibilities that the years steal away.

"So that's how you do it, then."

Mary jumped. The arrival of the owner of that low, sweet voice meant that they had a problem on their hands.

Charlie froze, the tiny white towel swaying in his hand.

Freya, in cloche hat and almond-coloured wrapover coat, walked from the shadows, smiling. She looked like she was holding a secret inside her, beating like a second heart. Mary reached up to smooth down her hair, something she only did when she was unsettled.

"I don't believe you've had one of Charlie's drinks…"

Freya laughed. "I don't know that I will, in any event." She moved to the window; Mary felt a small electric shock as Freya's arm brushed hers. They stood together and looked onto the changing quicksilver shapes in the flickering shadows. Mary was surprised that Freya didn't seem shocked by any of it.

"Geraldine always was a scattered girl. Never too sure what she wanted." Freya pointed to her sister, who was filled with light from within, illuminating the network of veins, arteries, capillaries under her skin. The light dimmed and she laughed as a monkey tail poked out from the waistband of her skirt and wound around her waist. The guests giggled and chattered, jazz dancing through the trees. A man looked down as his body transformed into a series of geometric, frosted glass panels separated by thin lead welds. His friend leaned down to peer through the glass, seemingly unperturbed by the snowy wings that had grown where his ears should be.

Geraldine laughed and swung her tail — quite flirtatiously, Mary thought — at a woman whose skin had turned a mottled sea-blue. Delicate leafy sea dragons swum around her wrists and wove through her hair as it drifted as though tugged by the tide and unseen currents.

"We don't allow people to witness our parties if they aren't prepared to participate." Charlie sounded a lot less amiable than usual and Mary noticed he was holding an icepick, its point gleaming. She shook her head at him, not wanting to have to take Freya's time by force. That was a messy business at best and could turn ugly. "Easy, Charlie. Easy," she whispered.

"But I *have* seen one before. Don't you remember?" Freya looked surprised, then took a step backwards as she glanced at Charlie's icepick. "You told me to be patient because you'd come back and I would discover things way beyond what I had seen that night." She held her left hand out to Mary, palm upturned.

The skin of her wrist was pale, the veins cobalt underneath. Between the delicate layers was a watch hand, pointing toward her palm.

Mary recognised it instantly. "That's the second hand from your grandfather's watch," she said.

"So you do remember!"

Mary shook her head. "I'm afraid not. We've never met before, but … things that have happened in your past may be going to happen in our future, see?" *Why am I telling her this?* she wondered.

Charlie scowled as her words spilled out.

She hurried on. "So you had better tell your story so we can see exactly what's going on." *And how on earth we're going to deal with it,* she thought.

Freya looked nervously at Charlie, the icepick still in his hand. Mary frowned. "Put it *away* Charlie."

Grumbling, Charlie reluctantly stowed the weapon under his counter.

"I was only seven," Freya began "when my grandparents had a party, just like this one. The world in 1889 was a lot different to the world now — it was all propriety and manners and rules — it was claustrophobic, especially for a child. I couldn't sleep and lay in bed, listening to the party downstairs. And then I heard your voice, Mary, calling for everyone to line up for the evening's special treat — just like you did earlier tonight. I crept to the top of the stairs and I, I saw … it was just like tonight, people changing into things I'd never dreamed of. Can you imagine what that was like for a child?"

A loud bang on the window made them all jump. An enormous peacock, still with human legs, lay sprawled on the grass, shaking its head.

"Amateur," muttered Charlie.

"I wanted to join them," Freya went on "and I crept out from my hiding place, made it to the first landing. That was when you saw me, Mary. You walked up the stairs towards me and I thought you were so lovely, so different. But as you got closer, I felt very peculiar … sort of still from the inside out."

Mary glanced across at Charlie, who shrugged his shoulders.

"You introduced yourself, held out your hand and when I shook it, the stillness filled me up entirely and we shone then, Mary, you and I, like a shooting star. 'Here she is,' you called quietly downstairs. And then you leaped up, Charlie, nimble as you please, to say hello."

"And the watch hand?" he asked.

"My grandfather's watch was there on the bureau. You fiddled about with it for a bit, then asked me to hold out my arm. You told me not to look and that it would feel a bit like a bee sting. When it was done, you said that it would remind me to wait for you. To wait for my new life. And I've been waiting ever since."

Charlie began polishing the cocktail shakers, even though they were already clean. "And now that we're back, what is it you want?"

Freya looked surprised. "To come with you, of course."

The shaker clattered to the floor. "We're not taking applications, here! This is a two-man gig."

"But I've been waiting *my whole life*. It's already happened, don't you see? My past, your future, it must all lead to now. You talk about taking people's time, but I've given all my time just waiting, knowing you'd come back."

Mary turned toward the window, unable to look at Freya's hopeful face. Geraldine's guests were scattered across the lawn in little groups; some dancing, others with their arms, or fins or wings, wrapped around one another singing. They were all having the night of their lives, in exchange for just a little of their time.

"You know, Charlie and I have travelled an awful lot and seen some amazing things. This is a magical decade to be living through. You should be out there enjoying it, not wanting to come along with the two of us." She turned to face Freya, who was twisting her hands anxiously. "Listen to that wonderful jazz. Doesn't that make you want to forget everything and just *be*?"

In a shadowy corner of the garden, the band played, their instruments now part of them. The fat bellied bassist *was* the double bass: the trumpeter's trumpet sprouted from his lips. Sharkey Malone, of course, was still Sharkey Malone; but with every gravelly note he sang, a bronze honey-bee flew from his lips and there was just a glimpse of the piano keys that had taken the place of his teeth.

"When I hear it, it makes me think of timeless things, like I can see into forever. I'm not like them." She looked mischievously at Charlie. "And I'll prove it. I'll have one of your special drinks, please. Gin," she stated, before Charlie could ask.

Mary sighed, relieved, then smiled at Charlie, who was making a double for Freya. This would fix the whole issue once and for all. A drink, a transformation, a blissful forgetting would leave them in the clear. No matter what Freya said, she didn't belong with them.

"One more question. What do you do with the time that you take back?"

"When we know that," said Charlie "it'll be time to go home."

Freya lifted the tiny glass, the violet liquid shining. "To tomorrow," she said, then downed it in one shot. She glided outside, where she was joined by a swarm of dragonflies, their wings shimmering

Lalique-green and plum, which had previously been a rather prim man in a pinstripe suit.

"So that's that, then," said Charlie. "I think we better—"

"Go while we have the chance?"

"Couldn't have said it better, old girl."

Mary and Charlie whisked around the room, collecting bottles and glasses and packing them into the black bag. She snapped the case shut and picked it up as Charlie climbed up onto her shoulder.

They went out onto the lawn, for their traditional last walk-through of a party. To their left the plump woman who had become a chrome goddess lay sleeping, like a fallen statue. The dragonflies buzzed about in a man-shape, hovering around the amber lights. And the band played on, a sad, sweet dirge.

Ain't no sun, my autumn girl
Ain't no moon or rain
Got an empty home, an empty heart
Since the sunrise stole you away...

"Well, bugger me..."

"Charlie! Language."

On their right was a giant willow tree; at its base stood Freya, her eyes dark and sparkling.

Mary stared, her eyes wide. "You've not changed one bit. And that was a double dose. How?"

"I told you, I'm not like them. I'm all still inside. Only after I had that drink, this happened."

Mary and Charlie looked down at Freya's wrist. The watch hand was moving, now, ticking away second by second. They reached out and rested their forefingers gently over it. Freya's time pulsed through them and it felt like exaltation.

Mary clasped her hand. "Time is indeed the fabulous monster in us all. The difference is in what you do with it. Best you do come along with us, after all."

They set out for the jetty, stretching out across the darkened river that held the night reflected.

On the shore sat Geraldine, propped against a fig tree and snoring softly. Her dark locks lifted gently in the breeze, rippling and shaking as they parted to reveal glossy black feathers. With a fierce beating of wings, the sky was filled with ravens from her hair.

Freya bent to kiss her sleeping sister, then followed her new companions waiting on the jetty. Mary sat on the edge, Charlie still on her shoulder.

"What time does the clock have, Charlie?"

He swung from her shoulder and began to climb down her back, deftly unclasping the square silver buttons that ran the length of her spine. As he undid the last one, the doors of her back opened wide. She heard Freya gasp as she looked inside and wondered what it must be like to see it for the first time; a giant hourglass in the centre, surrounded by carefully hung fob watches, alarm clocks, chronographs and wristwatches, with a stone sundial sitting at her left hip. They softly ticked and swung, the silvery river of time swirling and twisting around them and shivering the sand in the hourglass.

"21 July 1969. 2.56am." He shut the doors, then gave Mary a wink before hopping into the bag.

"Now that *does* feel like a celebration," Freya said.

"You just wait," replied Mary.

The air around them quivered and flowed as they walked toward the end of the jetty...

∞¥∞Ω∞¥∞

SHADOWS
KATE GORDON

My mother had been gone for six months and things were a curious kind of normal. The Shadows were still there, of course, but they'd always been there. They'd been there before she disappeared. They never went away. There was a kind of comfort in that. Even though I knew they were impossible. Even though I knew they were wrong and crazy and *weird* ... I was used to them. After all, they'd been there my whole life. I suppose you get used to even the strangest things, given enough time.

I woke up that seeming-usual morning to buttercup sun streaming in through my curtains, and the sound of the rubbish truck trundling up our street. Dogs barking, children laughing, real-life sounds drowning out the dreaming.

I threw back the covers to find a Shadow hovering beside me. I swatted it away. At least it was only a small one this morning. Some mornings I woke up to a swarm of them and had to fight through them to escape from my room, down the stairs, into the kitchen. They tried to wrap themselves around me. They nudged their way into my pockets and pushed themselves down my pyjama top. They clung to my ankles and grabbed at my fingers.

They didn't want me to leave. They got lonely without me.

I could feel it.

I rolled over and looked up at the posters on my bedroom wall. The rock stars and movie stars looked down out me, all pouting lips and dangerous eyes.

My mum encouraged me to put the posters up. She thought I might develop a love of film. Maybe I might become a film-maker.

Like everything else, my interest was much more muted than she would have liked. How could I devote myself completely to anything, with the Shadows in the way?

My feet hit my bedroom carpet. I stretched, stood up and made for the door.

One small step, from dreaming to real, or real to dreaming. I was never quite certain which.

I found Dad downstairs in the kitchen, but instead of making breakfast he was scribbling furiously in one of his thousands of leather-bound notebooks.

"Princess!" he cried when I sat down in front of him. "Hang on, hang on. I'll just finish this stanza and then I'll make you some eggs, okay? Now, can you think of a word that rhymes with silver?"

"No words rhyme with silver," I sighed, pulling an orange from the fruit bowl. I looked down at it. "Or orange. Everyone knows that."

"Good, good. I was just testing," Dad said. He smiled, slightly maniacally, the way he always did when he was working on a poem; when he thought it would turn out to be a winner. He was usually right, too. It wasn't arrogance. Dad had won most major poetry awards in the country. He'd had seven books of poetry published.

And yet he chose to live in this small town, in the middle of nowhere, at the end of the earth, far away from the centre — or even the outskirts — of the writing scene. My dad didn't mind. He liked it here. He liked being left alone to write. And my mum had liked living here too. "Too many people in the city," she'd said. "Too *dangerous*."

Dad was still scribbling when I finished my orange. "I'll make breakfast, shall I?" I grumbled.

"Sure, sure, Lena," said Dad. "That'd be great. Would you mind knocking me up an omelette? No cheese, though. I'm off the cheese at the moment."

"Your rationale for the cheese-aversion?"

"Bad dreams," Dad said, shaking his head mournfully. "You know I keep having these nightmares, Lena. I'm thinking it's maybe all the cheese I've been eating."

"Of course it is," I said, rolling my eyes. Dad and his nightmares. He was obsessed. He'd been having them for years, since long before Mum disappeared, and he was always on the lookout for the cause behind them. "So you were eating cheese that night you dreamed about being chased by a giant rabid possum?"

"Is that what I told you I dreamed?" Dad's brow furrowed. "Just no cheese, okay?"

I walked over to the stove and grabbed a frypan from the rack hanging on the wall above me. I put it down on the stove and turned on the gas. As I did, instead of the usual blue flames, Shadows began to flicker around the bottom of the pan. I leapt back.

"What is it, sweetie?" asked Dad, looking up from his notebook. His expression was part writerly distraction; part genuine concern.

"Nothing. Nothing," I said, quickly.

Dad didn't know about the Shadows. I'd wanted to tell him so many times, especially when I was little and didn't realise quite how strange they were. The words had always stuck in my throat.

I somehow knew, even as a child, that he wouldn't understand. I knew that the Shadows weren't part of his world as they were part of mine. Dad was flighty, floaty, *sunny*.

He didn't like dark things. And they were the darkest thing there was. No, I couldn't tell Dad about the Shadows.

He'd probably start having nightmares about them.

The reason I never told Mum about the Shadows was different.

I didn't want her to think I was weak. Mum didn't like weakness. Mum was a businesswoman — a successful one. I knew this, even though I wasn't quite sure what business it actually was. I knew she was someone to be admired. She was single-minded, ambitious and fierce.

Focussed.

Mum would often say she'd never intended to marry a poet — so lazy, effeminate and feeble.

"Why *did* you marry me, then?" Dad would ask.

Mum would smile, a small, inscrutable smile. "Someone had to save the world from you."

Dad would roll his eyes. He never got mad. And then he'd just pull her closer and kiss her on the cheek and whisper something in her ear about how lucky he was to have her. How much he needed her. How grateful he was that she was in his life.

They were so in love. I always felt certain that, no matter how much time Mum spent away she'd always come back to us and we'd be a happy family. She did love us.

I knew she did. Even though she was hard on me. Even though she thought I was *unfocussed*.

It was true.

I didn't want her thinking I was weak as well.

Seeing Shadows was weak. Seeing Shadows was *crazy*. I didn't want my mum to think I was crazy.

My mum was the most sane person I knew.

Or, at least I thought she was, up until she disappeared.

And then the police told us, about the church she attended. About the travelling she did that *wasn't* for business; the travelling to meet with other members of the church.

She'd never mentioned it to us; me and Dad. We didn't know she went there. She'd never seemed religious.

And Dad wasn't the things they suggested, either. He was a calm man. A happy man. He never got mad. He just wrote things down.

"I just ... nearly burned myself," I lied.

"Be careful," Dad said. I heard a slight tremble in his voice. I saw the haunted look that always came when he was thinking about Mum, and the fear that came with those thoughts: that he would lose me, too.

"It's okay. Look," I said, showing him my unmarked finger.

Dad nodded. "Okay, Lena," he said. He turned back to his poem and I looked, tentatively, back at the pan. No Shadows. Where had they gone?

Stupid things.

Just as I started turning the gas knob again, from the range-hood another, bigger Shadow swooped down at me. I ducked and the Shadow flew across the room, right over Dad's head, ruffling his hair. He didn't even notice.

I, on the other hand, was a wreck. Why were the Shadows behaving so badly? I turned around and saw them crouched in the corner, jiggling up and down.

They were laughing.

"Dad, would you mind cooking after all?" I asked. "I don't think I'm functioning properly yet."

"Sure, Princess," Dad murmured. He wrote a few more hasty words, then leapt up and got to work making omelettes for both of us.

There were no more Shadows after that. I ate my eggs and tried to make conversation with Dad, but his head was still in poem-land. All I got was monosyllables and the occasional excited "Holiness!" or "Devastation!" I sat there eating in silence while Dad scrabbled for his notebook, making fevered adjustments to his poetry. Usually, I would have looked over at the Shadows and rolled my eyes, sharing my frustration with them. Today, they'd annoyed me too much.

When we'd finished eating, Dad walked me to the bus stop.

"Keep yourself safe, Lena," he said. It's what he always said. Not "Be safe." Always "Keep *yourself* safe."

"Just going to school, Dad," I sighed. "School's a pretty safe place. Nothing's going to happen to me there."

I climbed on the bus and sat in my usual seat — the single one next to Neil, the bus driver. I always sat there. None of the other kids wanted to sit next to Lena the freak.

I always read on the bus, mostly because I took every opportunity to lose myself in a novel. There was an added benefit, though. If I kept my nose in my book, it made it seem as though I didn't mind so much that I was on my own; that being an outcast didn't worry me at all. I was halfway through a novel about fallen angels. I liked reading about things that were fantastical and impossible. It made me forget about the real world. Just a little bit.

As I reached into my bag to pull out the book, my fingers came into contact with something warm and sleek like satin. My hand jerked back. A Shadow. There was a Shadow in my bag.

I clipped my bag shut, slowly, and pushed it away from me.

I knew I was the only one who could see the Shadows, but I still didn't want to let one loose in the bus. Especially if it was in a naughty mood.

I started humming to myself, trying to calm my nerves.

"What is she *doing?*" I heard Hannah Crawford say. She was sitting in the seat behind me. I'd avoided her eyes as I sat down; they were heavy with mascara and revulsion. Hannah Crawford hated me, and I hated seeing the way her face twisted when she looked at me. I saw her taking in my boldly clashing clothes, and the lank hair falling over my face. Hannah Crawford thought I was a slug, and when I looked into her eyes, I felt like one.

I couldn't avoid her snaky voice, though, or the hate-filled words that slithered their way over the seat back into my ear.

"She's such a *freak.*"

I was still looking, red-faced, at my feet when it popped out. Just a small one, slightly translucent, and ragged at the edges. It was a harmless baby, but it still startled me. Usually, a Shadow emerging from my bag wouldn't fluster me at all — annoy me perhaps, but not fluster me. But today, I was already wound up. I let out a scream that echoed around the bus.

"What the hell was that?" Neil roared, craning his neck to look around at us with his beetroot-red face.

"It was *Lena,*" Hannah called out, her voice plump with smugness. "She's just being a mental case, as usual."

Neil's face softened. He looked at me and shrugged, before turning back around to watch the road.

"No wonder her mum left," Hannah muttered.

My hands clenched. A fire burned in my chest. I didn't get angry very often, and I'm not certain why I got angry then. Maybe I'd just bottled up all my annoyance at the behaviour of the Shadows that morning, and it exploded all over Hannah instead. Maybe there was still so much anger bubbling inside me over my mum's disappearance that it was inevitable some would boil over eventually.

Maybe I was just sick of Hannah being such a bitch.

I whirled around to look at her and raised my hands in the air. I wasn't going to hit her or anything. It was a gesture of frustration. I started to say something. Something about not being a freak. Something about how she should leave me alone. Before I could say anything, though, Hannah opened her mouth and let out a scream of her own, even more blood-curdling than mine had been.

"Hannah, what's wrong?" asked Gemma, gripping Hannah's arm.

"I don't ... know. I just ... it was like I was having a bad... A night ... nightmare..." She shook her head. "Never mind. My brain just went weird for a minute. Forget it. I had the worst dream last night so I'm a bit, like, sleepy and stuff."

Hannah rubbed at her temples.

I lowered my hands, slowly. The tips of my fingers were tingling, like I'd scalded them with boiling water.

Hannah looked confused, and she did look really tired but there was something else. Something about her face. Some *haunted* look. It tugged on my brain — a memory calling out for attention.

But she wasn't hurt. She was fine. I hadn't done anything to her.

How could I have?

"Hannah Crawford and Gemma Kendall!" Neil called over his shoulder. "You girls be quiet right now or I'm reporting you to your principal!" Hannah and Gemma shut their mouths, but their eyes were still narrowed, glaring at me. I turned back around in my seat, feeling squeamish. My fingers were still tingling.

What had just happened?

I looked out the window of the bus. I couldn't see a thing. The windows were filled with Shadows. And then, for a moment, the window cleared and I saw just a glimpse, a flicker, of someone watching me. Someone who looked like my mother. And, all around me, the Shadows were laughing.

I stood, shaking, and took one small step, then another, towards the front of the bus. Towards a light that seemed too bright and false.

"Freak," Hannah whispered as I passed.

"*Crazy,*" hissed Gemma.

I took another small step. A boy pushed me and I stumbled. "Haha," he crowed. "*Weak.*" There was a buzzing in my ears. A hissing. A cackling. Freak. Crazy. *Weak.*

"*What rhymes with shadows, Lena?*" The Shadows laughed. I closed my eyes.

My mum had been gone for six months. And things were ... black. But then they always had been, hadn't they? Because the Shadows were always there.

They'd been there, too, the night she disappeared...

One small step towards the memory calling my name.

My mother, standing over me, one hand on hip, the other holding my report card, decorated with rows of As, but graffitied with the words my mother spoke aloud, her voice thick with disgust:

"*Lena does not work well with others.*"

"Get a move on, Freak," someone growled behind me.

I moved.

I looked around me. The windows were free of Shadows now. And what I saw beyond them made my stomach constrict. My mother. Over and over and over — my mother, eyes blackened, mouth open in a silent scream. She was surrounded by Shadows. They bit at her, clawed at her, punched and grabbed and slapped...

I stepped off the bus. I held my folder tight to my chest. On it was the picture of another Hollywood star.

His eyes, watching me.

∞¥∞Ω∞¥∞

That night, after an ordinary day at my ordinary school, I returned home.

My father sat at the kitchen table when I walked in. He was scribbling a poem. He didn't acknowledge me. I ducked under a Shadow to make myself a sandwich at the kitchen bench. I went to my room.

I did my homework.

I lay on my bed. The posters stared down at me. My own eyes closed.

I stepped into a dream.

"Lena does not work well with others."

My mother shook her head. "Lena, I am so disappointed. You are failing me. You are not trying hard enough. You are weak."

My cheeks glowed. My mother was often critical of me but she'd never been quite this ... cruel. "I'm not," I mumbled. I cursed my fragile, trembling voice. I was weak.

"Weak," my mother repeated, throwing the card in a crumpled ball to the floorboards. "Your classmates think you're crazy, Lena. They think you're a freak and you do nothing to stop them. I've been too soft on you, I can see. I thought I had time. I didn't realise they are already with you."

"Who are..." I trailed off. My head was buzzing, whirring.

"You're just like your father," my mother said. "Unfocussed. Head in the clouds. Head in the shadows."

"What did you say?" I whispered.

"You heard me." My mother's voice was lower now. More sinister. "I know, Lena," she said. "I know you're just like him. Both shadow people. Both weak people. I'd hoped you would be different. But you see them too, just like your father."

"My father doesn't see the Shadows," I said, firmly. "I know."

"Read his poems, Lena," she said. "He sees them. And he knows you do as well. He has a black soul too." My mouth dropped open. My mother leaned forwards. "He has the devil inside."

"I don't have the devil inside me!" I protested. And my father ... my flighty, floaty, poetic father ... he definitely didn't have the devil inside him.

"Can't you see it in his words?" my mother whispered. *"That's where he puts the devil."*

The buzzing was louder now. The whirring was more intense. And my hands... The tips of my fingers were tingling, like I'd scalded them with boiling water. And then the Shadows came. Creeping. Stalking. Hissing and moaning and writhing like so many dark, sharp-toothed snakes.

And, just like Hannah's had, on the bus that morning, my mother's eyes widened. And then, they shifted away from me. They looked behind me. "I knew you'd come," *she said.*

A Shadow hovered in my bedroom door. I knew the shape of this Shadow. I knew his shape, so well.

"Turn around, Lena," he said. *"Look at your posters. Look into their eyes. Don't look back. It's just a bad dream. Just a shadow. All of this is just a dream."*

"Just a dream," I whispered to myself. And in the dream there was screaming.

I opened my eyes. Light streamed in. I was in my room, surrounded by my posters; a hundred eyes, looking down at me.

A nightmare. Only a nightmare and now...

A seeming-usual morning. But the screaming was still there.

I ran to my father's room; pushed open his door. His eyes were fixed shut but his mouth was open and out poured a howling. "Inga..." My mother's name.

"Dad," I shook his arm. "Dad. Wake up. You're having a nightmare again."

His eyes fluttered open. "Lena," he whispered. "I just dreamed a poem of you." His voice was hoarse.

> *"In the half-light of the gloaming*
> *We live, half-seeing, half-hidden*
> *You lived always in the light*
> *Your fingers twisted moonbeams*
> *and made of them marionettes*
> *You caught the Shadows*

and made of them strings
You gave me luminance
My child
She with the hair like shimmering spider webs
and eyes of stardust
Then, the shadows took you
but you left the stardust child
Lena
and we cling to each other
as Shadows creep in
We scribble them into nothing.
We *won't* let it happen again.
My stardust child,
She holds them at bay
One small step
And then run away"

Around us, as he spoke, Shadows gathered. But that was normal. A curious kind of normal. They'd always been there. They'd been there before she disappeared. They never went away. There was a kind of comfort in that. I suppose you get used to even the strangest things, given enough time. The craziest things. The most *devilish* things.

My dad smiled. "Come downstairs, Lena. I'll make you some eggs. And then I have to write." My father held out his hand. We pushed past the Shadows, as we did every morning. One small step, from dreaming to real, or real to dreaming. We were never quite certain which. I hoped this was the real world. Because, behind my eyelids, she was screaming.

Behind my eyelids, her eyes were black.

"You know, Lena," my father said, as we walked down the stairs. "I never could stand to hear your mother say you're weak. You're strong, Lena. We both are."

I looked sideways at him and I knew behind his eyelids she was screaming too. I knew I hadn't been alone in my room, that day the devil came out; the day the Shadows played. I took his hand. "I might write too," I said. "I have things I need to let out."

My father didn't say anything. He didn't need to. He knew.

Behind us, as we walked downstairs, the Shadows followed. They were always there.

Ever behind me,
the Shadows haunt,
Dark and silver,
fat and gaunt.
Ever behind me,
my only friends,
the Shadows mould me
and I bend.
I lift my foot,
one step I take,
waking to dream,
dreaming to awake.
Ever behind me,
they titter and squeal,
my secrets, my dark things,
Shadows of the real.
In the half-light of the gloaming,
They crouch and they hide.
But I know they're still with me:
the Devil inside.

∞¥∞Ω∞¥∞

ORIGINAL
PENELOPE LOVE

adj. belonging or relating to the origin or beginning.

n. a primary type or form, from which varieties are derived.

Tek'tek skidded the last few metres. His hindquarters slid out from under him as he took the turn. All four legs scrabbled for purchase and his claws dug into the floor. He swung his weight back into alignment and wedged himself through the door.

"Sorry I'm late, Professor Xi," he gasped. He'd been too focussed on football last semester and he had to pass a summer unit to stay on. Being late for the first class was a bad start. Fortunately Professor Xi was busy. He didn't even look up.

There was one other student in the tute. Sara. He mentally pumped air. Sara was the reason why he'd decided to go with Anthropology 404, despite a daunting reading list. Sara had never looked at him twice, not even when he'd wowed everyone else at the break-up party with his new patch, shoulder-mounted night vision eyeballs.

Sara had spiky white hair, chocolate skin, green eyes and elfin features. Her rangy three metre tall frame meant the top of her head was level with Tek'tek's chin. Her ancestors had adopted an avian spike to deal with the staggering heights of her home planet. Her breastbone was a ship's keel, a necessary counterweight to the bronze wings folded shimmering on her back. She was gorgeous and a real brain. Today, she was wearing nothing except spray-on glitter and perfume. Surely if they were studying together he could ask her to go out with him. She might even take pity and have sex with him. Tek'tek was a simple man.

Even Sara's perfume could not disguise that the room reeked of old dust and mould, with another layer Tek'tek could not identify; eyeview reported rotten cellulose. The tables were piled with boxes filled with thin, flat sheaves of stuff he'd never seen before. Eyeview analysed it: "paper, *n.* substance made from rags, straw, wood or other fibrous material, used in ancient times for writing and printing."

He stepped carefully, focussing on his hind legs to avoid knocking anything over. He was at home on the football field, able to take a ten metre mark with full body slam, but he was too large for this room. He picked up one of the papers.

"Is it supposed to smell this bad," he asked.

"Don't touch it!" Sarah yelled.

He jumped, startled, and the fragile sheet tore in his hands.

"Now look what you've done!" She snatched it from him.

"Sorry," he mumbled, running his hands sheepishly over his chiton-plated scalp. Anthropology 404 was not off to a good start.

Eyeview lit up. "Please only handle these original documents while wearing gloves," Xi scrolled.

Xi had body-swapped with a magnellan five years ago so he could research on their home planet, where the bone-crushing gravity was too severe for even the most spiked human body to tolerate. They hadn't got around to swapping back yet, so Xi remained a fifteen metre long, metre high, armoured millipede with curved mandibles. He had no features, no expression and no voice, so he communicated entirely by eyeview. Half his glistening length was coiled on the wall of the tutorial room to keep it out of the way. Xi passed over the gloves. "Have you done the reading?" he asked.

"Um, I had a look, yeah—" Tek'tek conjured the reading on eyeview as he sprayed his hands and waited for the gel to set. He scrolled rapidly in the hope of bluffing his way through. Genomes, nucleotides and chromosomes, recessive and dominant genes he took in at once, that was all patches and spikes basics, but he stumbled at Mendelian genetics. It was too big a subject to swallow in one gulp.

"I thought this was anthropology, you know, alien races and stuff," he protested.

Xi sighed. "For the benefit of those who haven't done their reading — Sara, you may keep sorting — the purpose of this class is not to study aliens but to study ourselves, our origins, with an anthropological survey of the Originals. The Originals rejected modern technology. The latest they accepted was the steam engine, a contraption so outdated I doubt you've heard of it."

Eyeview was keeping up, even if Tek'tek wasn't. Hero of Alexandria, James Watt, the Rankine cycle and the Industrial Revolution passed before his bewildered vision.

"Eventually the Originals were considered so much at risk from superior technologies that they were placed in reservations for their own protection. We have a local Original community. They used to send their young people to university, using the rail line down the mountain, to give them a taste of modern life."

Tek'tek had seen that ancient line. Around its rusted rail the grass grew long and green. "How old were they when they went to uni?" he asked, intrigued.

"Eighteen or nineteen years."

"My baby brother is that age!" Tek'tek protested. "My parents would never let me loose on the world that young. I was forty before I could even go to the Deepmall with my friends."

"My parents didn't even let me out of the nest until I was thirty," Sara said, reminiscently. "Mind you, home is all crags, and the breathable atmosphere is five clicks up, so you can understand their reluctance to let go. It's a long drop. But they used to hover over me and under me, all the time. It drove me mad. They didn't let me fly solo until I was forty-five." She rolled her eyes.

"It's called extended childhood," Xi explained. "The more complex our brains become, the longer a child remains dependent on their parents. Conversely, spikes have extended our lifespan. We can expect to at least live three hundred years, whereas the Originals die around seventy."

"Seventy," Tek'tek spluttered. "You mean, *years*?" At seventy, all going well, he would be starting an intergalactic career in professional football. "But why don't they get spiked? Problem solved."

"I told you, they reject all modern technology."

"Even spikes and patches?" He couldn't believe it.

"Especially spikes and patches," Xi said patiently. "The trains stopped arriving several centuries ago, before my tenure here. The Originals were contacted to see if anything was wrong. They asked us to leave them alone. No one has visited since. I am trying to wangle an ethics request through the committee for a field trip. In the meantime we can study the records, starting with these ancient documents Sara kindly dug out for me in the Old Stacks." He clicked his mandibles excitedly over the piles of smelly paper.

Sara shivered and hugged her arms to her chest. "I'm not going back there again," she said. "I like the sun in my hair and air in my wings. Old Stacks is buried two clicks down and I couldn't get over the feeling there was something watching me all the time. Eugh."

They spent the rest of the class sorting through boxes.

∞¥∞Ω∞¥∞

Tek'tek was woken early the next morning by 'chat at full blast. He groggily recognised the voice. "Sara?" he muttered.

"Get down here!"

It was still dark. He stared disbelieving at the time on eyeview. "Five am!" he rolled over and tried to get back to sleep, but he could not ignore Professor Xi's excited comments scrolling clear across his eye line. "Wonderful news! After all these years!" Xi exulted.

"Who what where?" Tek'tek mumbled.

"A train is coming!"

All right, that was exciting. Tek'tek scrambled out of bed and down the elevator.

"Hurry! You'll be late." Sara on 'chat.

It was a wonderful morning. The sun tinged the eastern sky red. The forested mountains to the west were gold. The Three Sisters glowed orange. The grass was springy beneath Tek'tek's paws and the air was full of the sharp tang of eucalypt. The campus slept around him, tall, graceful towers.

Earth was too far from the galactic core to support a thriving interstellar community and most of the planet had been deserted for centuries. Only students with human heritage, whose parents had a sentimental attachment to their home planet, enrolled here. These students were fewer every year. Even during semester the campus was only half full. Now, in the peace of the pre-dawn holiday, it was silent and still.

Tek'tek bounded along the road in ten metre leaps, out of pure joy at being alive. The station hove in view, a plain ceramic platform with silicon web veranda. High above a winged figure spiralled in the dawn light. Sara was keeping an eye out. He did some mid-air somersaults, hoping she would notice.

She certainly did. "Quit mucking around. I can see the train!" She swooped down as he arrived, landing in a buffeting ten metre wingspan.

The train appeared around the bend of the mountains. It consisted of two grey cylinders, the passenger cabin and the engine, racketing uneasily on the rusty rail. Steam poured from the engine's funnel, and from various leaks in an archaic boiler.

"It doesn't look in great repair. We'll fix it while it's here," Xi said, anxiously. He looped his upper half into the air, rehearsing his welcoming speech. His lower half snaked across the platform. Sara dived in a flurry of wings to stand by Xi's side. With a self-important steam shriek the train pulled in. The door hissed open. Xi drew his upper body upright. Sara beamed. Tek'tek was puzzled. A long moment passed and nothing happened.

Sara was the first to realise. "Look down!" she said. They dropped their gaze.

An Original stood in the door, small and puny as a child. Eyeview identified a male, eighteen years. Height 150 centimetres. One pair each of arms and legs, no enhancements; trousers, coat and shirt of primitive, organic material. He had an anxious face, with ugly, unmodified features, grey eyes, black hair, and a short beard.

The Original clasped a suitcase and a black, heavy looking, rectangular object that eyeview identified as a "book, *n*. written or printed work." He blushed as they all stared at him, then stepped cautiously onto the platform.

Xi was too excited to stay put. Clicking his mandibles he advanced and launched into his speech. The Original recoiled and raised his book before him. There was a gold cross on the cover.

"I, uh, don't think your speech is working, Professor," Tek'tek warned him.

Xi stopped. "What's wrong?"

"He's scared," Tek'tek said. He had a seen that look on opponents just before he crushed them.

"He doesn't have eyeview," Sara realised.

"What, er, of course," Xi was flummoxed. "I'm terribly sorry, I forgot. We're so used to—" He had no way of communicating with the Original. "I — uh, yes. I think I had best leave," Xi said, sadly. He reversed out of the platform.

The Original cautiously lowered his book.

"Great beard," Tek'tek said, conversationally. He stroked his own chin ruefully. "I tried to grow one last year you know but could I? No. And I'm sixty."

The Original flinched as Tek'tek towered over him, gaze travelling from Tek'tek's hindquarters to his armoured exoskeleton. Wide-eyed he shrank behind his book again.

"We're not getting through," Sara said. She dropped to one knee, wings half open for balance, to make herself more the same height. She smiled, brightly. "Welcome to the university," she said.

The Original shook his head, and spoke. They couldn't understand a word. Eyeview was blank.

Sara's smile became fixed. "Are you getting any of that?"

"I didn't know they spoke a whole 'nother language," Tek'tek protested.

"If he was speaking a known language eyeview would translate," Sara said. "There was nothing in the documents about a dialect," she fretted.

"Evolution of language," Xi realised, via eyeview from his hiding place on the veranda roof. "Small communities are conservative.

They retain the old forms. In larger communities language evolves rapidly. He's not speaking another language, but our own language from several centuries ago. He has a different emphasis on the vowels and syllables, and he speaks much slower and deeper than we do."

With that hint eyeview jerked into life. "Behold, I send an angel before you, to guard you on the way and to bring you to the place which I have prepared," the Original said.

"Um, what's an angel?" Tek'tek asked.

"They are definitely on your reading list," Sara snapped, blushing. "Originals believe in a being called God who made the world, and created humans in his image. God's servants are angels. They have wings." She dipped her own in explanation.

Tek'tek snorted. "Yeah, right, a real angel," he laughed.

"Watch it," Sarah warned him.

"You are still speaking too shrill and fast," Xi told them.

Tek'tek stepped forward. The Original did not raise his book this time. Instead, he squared his shoulders and lifted his chin. Tek'tek suddenly liked him. It took guts to stand up to someone twice your size. Tek'tek spoke slowly from the bottom of his barrel chest. "Sorry to disappoint you, but she's no angel. She's plain old human. Like me." He got slower and deeper, seeing the Original's face remained blank. "Tek'tek. Sara. Friends," he said, cavernously.

The Original smiled at last, a smile that illuminated his solemn face. "Enoch. Friends."

∞¥∞Ω∞¥∞

The next few weeks were rather busy. Sara and Tek'tek got accustomed to Enoch's speech, and he got used to theirs. It was easier for them. They had eyeview to translate. He had to learn from scratch. They remained Enoch's primary contacts. Tek'tek tried taking Enoch to a party, but it was not a success. Enoch looked furiously uncomfortable amid the giant, tentacled, fanged, horned and feathered, tattooed and chiton-plated crowd, and he was really unable to deal with the exchange student, rKrKrK, a sentient clay conglomerate. He disappeared midway through the evening and Tek'tek found him on the lawn curled up in a foetal position. It was clear that although Enoch was bravely accepting as much as he could, there were limits to his world view that it would be best not to test. They had enough trouble hiding Professor Xi, who was always lurking hopefully in the background, pining for an introduction.

Enoch's suitcase contained a change of clothes and odd items of black worked metal. "A tooth for a plough share," he explained. "A candle holder," was another, which looked like a flower. "I made them," he said, with a smile. Then he carefully lifted a soft package from the suitcase and unfolded it. It was a beautiful piece of cloth, white and translucent.

"It's soft, and so fine," Sara squealed with delight as she stroked it.

"Lace," Enoch explained. "My sister knitted it." He folded it up carefully and put it away.

"He must have brought them as gifts," Sara guessed, later, but Enoch did not distribute them. Perhaps he realised that they had no use for them. They had a hard time persuading him to accept the new clothes they bought him. Sara spent hours searching through the children's sections, the only size that would fit, for clothing that didn't glow, sparkle, mutate or automatically attend to bruises and scrapes.

"Modern first aid is genome based. We mustn't affect his DNA in any way," Xi explained.

Sara and Tek'tek told Enoch about genome technology, that spikes were permanent and patches temporary. "Like, I've got krakoid hindquarters and shoulder eyes," Tek'tek explained, krakoid being the gene form his ancestors spiked to handle the heavy gravity and cyclones of his home planet. "The krakoid is permanent but the eyes'll disappear in a year or so."

Enoch taught them about his Bible, his old book. Sara was in agonies over it. "It should be in a museum," she protested. It was three centuries old and all about this God, with Enoch's family tree written in the margins. Sara insisted they wear gloves when handling it.

Enoch had drawbacks. He prayed at every opportunity. He had a passion for preaching, and could go on for hours. Tek'tek sat through these speeches only on stern threat of a Fail. The one good thing was at the end of each preaching session Enoch handed around the Bible, then insisted on a group hug. Group hugs with Sara made the whole situation bearable.

"I think he's trying to save our souls," Sara said after a long lecture on original sin that Tek'tek didn't understand at all. Once again he made a mental note to actually do some reading.

"He can try all he likes," he said, amiably.

Besides, it turned out Enoch hadn't come down the mountain to have a fun summer vacation. His community faced a calamity so severe that eventually, reluctantly, the elders had lifted their generations-old ban on travel. They were being destroyed by a horrible disease. Children were born looking normal but their muscles slowly weakened until they were unable to breathe. They died before they were nine years old. In the last few generations the disease had spread. Of children born in the last decade four out of ten had died. Was there anything that could be done to save them?

The Medical faculty were intrigued but they had to step carefully. Most doctors had cephalopod hands, much better than clumsy human fingers, but everyone realised Enoch would view them with suspicion. They nominated one doctor as the primary contact. Unfortunately Dr Gregog had a cephalopod head as well. The donut-shaped brain and copper-based blood of cephalopods were highly prized in worlds where oxygen was not a viable percentage of the atmosphere. Dr Gregog was cheerful, bluff and competent, trailing clouds of interns. But she was undeniably tentacled. Enoch refused to let her get near him.

"Never mind, I'll win him over," Dr Gregog chuckled, writhing her tentacles together. "This is fascinating. We've got our interns delving into it. Each of them has to give a talk on ancient disorders."

Her interns pulled wry faces. "Yeah, any time you want to learn about Cystic Fibrosis just let us know," they muttered. They just couldn't see the applications, when modern medicine had eliminated all genetic disorders centuries ago.

The interns took a blood sample from Enoch then ran some tests. They had to comb through ancient databases, but they came up with the answer. The children were dying from Brown-Vialetto-Van Laere syndrome. "Known as Brown's Syndrome for short," Dr Gregog explained. "A simple spike will fix it."

The tests confirmed that Enoch was a carrier of Brown's Syndrome as well.

Enoch refused the spike. He got upset at the suggestion. He tried to explain. The soul was immortal, the body transient. A spike was a temptation of the Devil.

Fortunately for Tek'tek, Sara had done the reading. "The Devil is the enemy of God," she explained. The Devil worked to damn mankind, and one of his lures was spikes and patches.

Enoch refused to destroy their children's souls just to save their lives.

Tek'tek just didn't get it. "It's all in his imagination. The kids are dying for real. Why don't we give him the spike without telling him?" he suggested.

"We are dealing with a serious medical ethics issue. We don't treat without consent," Dr Greggog said, flat. "There might be some non-genome based ways." She sent her interns back to trawl through the ancient databases.

"We can't give him a modern spike anyway," Sara pointed out. "Our genome is all cleaned up. His genome is original, except the Brown's Syndrome ruins it. Somewhere along the line we unfortunately forgot to keep track of an original human genome sample. Still, if we can't do it the normal way, we'll try the old fashioned way. It's a recessive gene after all. Let's look at the genealogy, and see if there are any people in Enoch's community who can intermarry."

With Enoch's help she scoured his Bible, worked out the family trees and marked the deaths of children. There were only one hundred and forty-seven people anyway, which even Tek'tek knew could no longer provide a viable genetic pool. Afterwards Sara crept away and cried on Tek'tek's shoulder. Brown's syndrome had spread through the entire Original community.

Meanwhile the interns reported failure. "Once modern technology cured genetic disorders the knowledge about them was lost. We need older information, maybe stuff that's not on even on any databases," they said.

Sara looked resigned. "The Old Stacks," she said.

∞¥∞Ω∞¥∞

The Old Stacks had been built long ago as a protected library in case of war. Above ground only a fortified metal entrance to the lifts was visible. Below lay twenty levels. The highest was the one Sara had already explored, two kilometres below ground.

Tek'tek volunteered to go. Sara said she'd go too, and Enoch wanted to accompany them. "I would love to collect books for my people," he said, eagerly. "As long as they are godly works."

"We'd better stick to pre-twenty-first century," Sara said. "They're on level fifteen."

Tek'tek took a large trolley with them to collect their loot. Enoch and Sara had to stand on it in order for them all to fit into the elevator. They went straight down to the fifteenth level, three clicks below ground.

The doors opened. The lights were not working. The Old Stacks were cold and dark and filled with the musty, dusty, rotted smell of paper and leather. Sara shivered, rubbed her shoulders, and hunched her wings.

"I can see in the dark," Tek'tek volunteered. He switched to shoulder vision, and pushed the trolley out. The lift doors hissed shut behind him.

"You might be able to, but I can't," Sara's voice jumped. Like the avians her spike came from, she was night blind. "This is really not my thing," she said, in a very small voice.

"Yea though I walk through the valley of death, I will fear no evil, for Thou art with me; Thy rod and Thy staff they comfort me," Enoch took Sara's hand.

Tek'tek looked around at the bookshelves stretching away on all sides. He examined the elevator wall behind them. "Ta-da!" He flicked a primitive light switch.

Every second or third light was out, and the remainder were dim and yellow. He sniffed suspiciously, wondering if any air was actually circulating. He thought he saw movement out of the corner of his eye, up near the ceiling. When he looked it was gone. Eyeview scanned the surroundings, but reported no identifiable life forms.

Tek'tek steered the trolley to the medical section, where Sara and Enoch scrambled down. "Gloves everybody," Sara reminded them, spraying them on. Tek'tek scanned a crumbling volume. "Hey, it says here that weasels give birth through their ears," he reported.

"Not helping," said Sara. She and Enoch worked together in the mid-section.

Tek'tek studied the lights again. They were covered with webbing. "What could do that?" he muttered to himself.

"Silverfish eat mould and other organic matter found in badly maintained books," eyeview suggested, helpfully. The picture of the silverfish that flashed up was nowhere near big enough for these webs. He walked along the rows. Level fifteen ended in a sealed door, a temperature controlled vault. He returned to Enoch and Sara. "Hey guys," he started. "Oh gross," he finished.

Something had tunnelled through the books, leaving the same sticky web that covered the light fittings. The holes varied from the size of his fist, to the size of his head. "Shit," he said, sympathetically.

"A lot of the books are useless." Sara was ready to cry.

"Our knowledge is always incomplete and our prophecy is always incomplete." Enoch tried to see the bright side.

"We need pest exterminators real bad," Tek'tek said. "Come and have a look at this."

Sara forgot her disappointment when she saw the vault. "It's an old genome store," she said, fascinated.

Enoch looked disapproving. "God created man to His own image," he said. He headed back to the shelves.

"I've always wondered about these," Sara said. The door led into a long, narrow chamber lined with cases. The store was still viable. Inside it was freezing. Sara shuddered and screwed up her eyes, then hugged her wings close to her body and stooped in.

"Hold the door open or I will kill you," she said. She ran her hands rapidly along the rows, muttering taxonomic names to herself. She was about halfway down when the lights clicked out. Noise came from the stacks, a sucking splatter followed by a loud, prolonged clatter that was the trolley tipping over.

"Enoch, you alright?" Tek'tek called.

No answer.

The bookshelves were too far away to see what was happening. He switched to shoulder vision. Movement flickered on the ceiling, definite movement of something long and flat. To his astonishment two green lines streamed out from his shoulder eyes and met on the movement.

"Weird," he said. His shoulder eyes had never done that before. Perhaps he should have read the fine print before he accepted the patch. The movement squeezed into a crack in the wall and vanished. The green tracers flicked out.

Eyeview scrolled red. "Evacuate, evacuate, evacuate," it read.

"Enoch, we're coming!" he shouted. "Sara!" he turned back just as Sara scrambled out blind. She ran right into him. He held her to steady her. She was much lighter than any human frame could achieve unspiked. Her bones were hollow, another adaption for flight. He loosened his grip, concerned she might break.

She shuddered. Her wings convulsed, rising in response to freedom, whisking overhead in the dark. "Why do we need to leave?" she asked. Her breath was short and harsh. If she panicked her instinctive reaction was flight. Straight into the ceiling, most like.

Dim emergency lighting flicked on. He saw she clutched an insulated, round container in her hands. "Get on my back," he said.

"Don't go all protective male on me," she said.

"If eyeview says to go, we go. I don't need to do the reading to know that," he said. She scrambled on without further argument.

He charged to the shelves. "Enoch!" he bellowed.

He was relieved to see Enoch standing with his back to them, facing the fallen trolley. His hands were raised. "Enoch," he said.

Lying half on and half off the trolley was an enormous puddle of ooze, the colour and texture of vomit. Cilia twitched from its surface, straining towards Enoch's hands.

Enoch reached out his own hands to meet it. "Friends," he said.

"That's enough," Tek'tek hauled him back. He was touched at Enoch's effort to integrate, yet revolted that Enoch could even consider that thing intelligent. An insect, perhaps indeed a silverfish, had long ago got in, munching its way through the old books. A visitor to the library in the early days of genetic enhancement had left dandruff, or loose hair, that the insect had eaten and spawned an uncontrolled mutation. "Probably it won't hurt us. They likely live off dead cellulose. But let's not take any risks," he said.

Tek'tek hauled Enoch onto his back and retreated to the elevator. He was never more glad in his life than when they stepped out into the clean, green world again. "Xi will sort this out. Then it will be safe to return," he said.

Sara calmed down at the sight of blue sky and green mountains. "Hold this for me," she shoved the container into Tek'tek's hands and took off. The bronze of her wings flashed in the light.

"Who is she that comes forth as the morning rising, fair as the moon, bright as the sun," Enoch said, eyes fixed on her.

Tek'tek looked down at the container. *Homo sapiens*, it read.

Professor Xi hustled his students off to be decontaminated, sent the genome sample to the medical staff, and dispatched a specialist team to the Old Stacks. He was flustered at how close they'd come to harm but he forgot his concerns when Enoch announced he wanted to meet him in the tutorial room.

Enoch regarded Professor Xi doubtfully, then reached out his hand. Xi took it gently with his pincers.

Enoch did not flinch.

"Professor Xi is very happy to meet you," Tek'tek translated.

"How do you know the demon in the Old Stacks was dangerous and this one is safe?" Enoch asked.

"Professor Xi is as human as we are."

"You are not human," Enoch said. It was so flat, so emphatic a rejection that Tek'tek was stunned. For the first time he felt the gulf between them, between a civilisation built on technology and one built on faith. "You are not made to God's image," Enoch explained, perhaps sensing his hurt.

Tek'tek realised then that he and Enoch would never understand each other. Did it matter? They were unlikely to meet again after this summer. Why then did he feel so bad because Enoch would die at seventy years, just at the age when he, Tek'tek, would be starting his football career. Yet he felt bewildered, and all his certainties were shaken. What did it mean to be human? In sixty undisturbed years he had never contemplated that before. His thick fists trembled. He wanted, unaccountably, to cry. He desperately wanted Enoch to understand. He knelt, and held out his hand.

"I'm human where it counts," he said. "In my heart and in my mind."

Perhaps Enoch felt the same pain, in his alien, incomprehensible world of sin and redemption. He took Tek'tek's hand in both of his. "My son, prove your soul in your life: and if it be wicked, give it no power," he said, very earnestly indeed.

∞¥∞Ω∞¥∞

Sara came by Tek'tek's room that night. "I want to apologise for my behaviour in the Old Stacks," she said.

"You were fine," Tek'tek said, furtively kicking rubbish beneath his bed.

"No I wasn't fine. I was completely terrified. I was that close to ploughing into a wall," she said. "I want to say sorry, and thank you." Whereupon she ran her hands up his back, and flung one graceful leg over his hindquarters. She kissed him, warm and deep.

When Tek'tek woke the next morning, face planted in his pillow, Sara was gone. She left an eyeview note to say she was in the geography lab. Reaching out, he found a metre-long feather tangled in the sheets.

He sat and looked at it, turning the feather this way and that so the morning sun touched the bronze highlights. Being gifted an avian feather was a rare and special trust. Avian lovers swapped feathers, they'd even implant each other's feathers. It was called flying on love's wings. Problem was Sara hadn't gifted this. She'd just lost it. He should return it. He tucked it under his bed, and slunk off to the geography lab.

Sara was translating between Enoch and Professor Xi as they studied a round ball covered in coloured paper set in a brass plated, semicircular mounting.

"What's that?" Tek'tek asked, struggling not to think of feathers.

"A globe," Xi said, proudly. "An ancient map of Earth."

Tek'tek ambled over. "What are these things?" he pointed at coloured blotches.

"Nations," Sara said. Eyeview had to translate that.

"You mean they used to divide a world," Tek'tek was appalled. A planet was small enough in the vastness of space. Why carve it up? He checked eyeview and stumbled over a whole range of unfamiliar concepts. From nations he moved to tribalism, nationalism, colonialism, and post-colonialism. Then he discovered football hooliganism. At last, a history lesson he could really appreciate.

"Are you even listening?" Xi asked, irritated.

Tek'tek returned to the present with a start.

Xi tapped his pincers on the globe. "We are here, in what was once New South Wales on the east coast of Australia. The only other known surviving Original community is in Vermont, in the north-eastern point of the United States. It takes five hours to travel there."

"Five *hours*? I can be home in five hours," Tek'tek moaned.

"For the purposes of our, er, field trip, Enoch has agreed to air travel but he has concerns, so we'll stay within the planet atmosphere," Xi said. "I warn you that once the Vermont community decided to have done with modern society they tore up roads and railways and drove off visitors with primitive projective weapons known as guns. It took me a long time to get the ethics permission to visit them, and I don't want any more, er, unfortunate occurrences. Enoch should lead as the most obviously human."

"As the only human," Enoch corrected the translation.

"For the purposes of this trip, you are right," Xi conceded. "Sara, you may be useful if they think you are an angel. Tek'tek, you are back-up. Keep out of sight. I'll stay here and monitor events," he concluded, sadly.

"Why is it so important to visit them if they don't want to be visited?" Tek'tek asked.

They all just looked at him. This was clearly something he should have known from the reading. He'd ask Sara on the journey, he decided.

Late that evening they met up again at the airfield on the western side of campus. Tek'tek had kit bags strapped across his hindquarters, filled with food, first aid kits, tools, torches and cold weather gear.

Enoch had his Bible and his suitcase.

An intra-planetary hopper was already primed, sitting on the field under the lights like a giant ceramic spider. Enoch faltered when he saw it, and his sweating grasp slipped on his suitcase. He breathed deep, squared his shoulders and muttered a prayer as he strode on board. The hopper folded its legs and took off. The flight was uneventful but Enoch spent the whole time in prayer, unconvinced of its ability to stay aloft without divine aid. Tek'tek tried talking to Sara on eyeview.

"Let's talk so Enoch can understand us," Sara suggested

That was exactly what he didn't want. He gave up, and slept.

The hopper touched down at the nearest safe landing place to the Vermont community, on the fringes of a huge, ancient forest. The sky was lightening in the east on a dim, grey day. Undisturbed snow lay thick on the ground, and the great oak trees were bare. They stepped out into clear, freezing cold, and Tek'tek unpacked the storm weather gear for the other two. He didn't need his. Compared to home this weather was mild, even a touch balmy.

Sara and Enoch huddled over a paper map Sara had produced. "The village is here," they pointed out. Sara didn't want to fly in case she caused alarm. They were in for a long tramp through dense forest.

"Get on my back," Tek'tek said, resigned.

After an hour's journey they found a rough road. Tek'tek set the others down and they advanced cautiously until they came in sight of a huddle of stone houses. Enoch's shoulders slumped. Even from a distance the village was clearly a ruin.

It didn't take them long to explore. There were a dozen empty houses and an abandoned church. The rooftops were fallen in. Furniture had been left to moulder away. Saplings rooted themselves in the cobbled street. Enoch explored the church, and reported that the church vessels, the communion cup and cross, were gone. He took that as a good sign, that the community had not died out but moved on.

Sara glanced up at the overcast sky, threatening more snow. "We can see if there's another village nearby. I'd better fly and risk alarm, or we'll be caught by bad weather. Enoch, I think I can carry you with me if you like."

Enoch agreed, but only after several deep breaths. Tek'tek took his book and case. Sara lifted Enoch by holding him around the waist. He started praying as soon as his feet left the ground. Sara struggled with Enoch's weight while rising, then soared aloft.

Enoch shouted and pointed below. "We can see some huts in a clearing," Sara reported. Tek'tek bounded through the woodlands after them. The sun broke through the clouds, gilding the foliage and the two flyers. They descended until they brushed the topmost leaves.

Then a large rock rose almost lazily through the air towards them.

"Watch out!" Tek'tek shouted. The rock only looked slow. It was far too fast for Sara.

Sara let Enoch drop into the tree branches. With spread wings gleaming bronze she tried to back air and dodge. The rock hit her right wing. There was horrible snap, and Sara crashed.

Tek'tek tore through the forest. He found Enoch standing over Sara. She lay spreadeagled on the ground, one wing broken, one leg doubled up beneath her.

"Sara!" Tek'tek called.

She made no sound, and did not move.

Enoch faced a cluster of huts built of bark and thatch in a snow-covered clearing. His clothes were torn, and his face and arms were scratched. His hands were spread wide and open. "Enoch," he said. "Friends."

A small crowd confronted him. Eyeview identified them as adolescent human, five male, one female. They wore furs and clutched rocks. Eyeview made a wide scan. There was no other humans in the village or surrounds.

The teenagers were at the ugly end of the human spectrum. Faces were distorted, features melted, limbs misplaced or missing. They were thickset and squat, less than a metre in height.

"Evacuate, evacuate, evacuate," eyeview scrolled red.

Some visitor, long ago, left something they didn't intend. Without contact with the outside world the uncontrolled mutation had spread.

As Tek'tek approached the teenagers hurled their rocks, then ran behind the huts. Enoch threw himself over Sara. The rocks rained on his head and shoulders.

A creaking sound came from behind the huts.

Enoch raised himself, bleeding from a gash in his forehead. "They have a catapult," he gasped.

Eyeview flashed pictures of a device even more primitive than guns, then reported the catapult was being reloaded behind the southernmost hut.

Tek'tek felt a surge of anger and fright, like he'd never felt in his life. Two green streaks shot from his shoulder eyes. They seared through the snow on either side of Enoch and Sara. They blasted through tree trunks. They struck the hut. It collapsed in a smoking shower of sticks and bark revealing a contraption of timber and taut rope cradling a boulder. The green streaks struck the catapult.

It exploded.

The teenagers were thrown in all directions.

"Woah. They've never done that before," Tek'tek said. He should have looked it up after the Old Stacks incident. "Alright, it was an illegal military patch, but I swear I thought it was just night vision," he said.

Five figures got up and ran. One stayed sprawled on the ground.

Tek'tek knelt by Sara and pulled out his first aid kits. He slapped them on her injuries. The sentient gels analysed and set about their tasks. Sara moaned and stirred. Tek'tek cracked a first aid kit for Enoch's bleeding forehead.

"Don't," Sara hissed, opening her eyes. The painkillers were taking effect. "They might change his genome," she whispered.

Enoch took his suitcase and his Bible, then ran towards the ruined hut.

"Stop him before he touches—" Sara fell back.

Tek'tek hurried after Enoch, coughing in the cloud of smoke and dust. Eyeview scanned the small body. Deceased. Female, twelve years old. "Shit," Tek'tek said. Outside a football field he'd never hurt anyone in his life. Now he'd killed a child.

Enoch knelt by the girl's side. He gently straightened her body, and folded her arms across her chest.

"You shouldn't really touch — uncontrolled mutation," Tek'tek mumbled.

Enoch lifted his sister's lace from his suitcase. He laid the lace reverently over the girl. Then he opened his book.

"Look, I'm really sorry. We have to go… We don't have time for—" Tek'tek stopped.

"For dust you are and to dust you will return," Enoch recited.

"Watch out!" Tek'tek saw the five teenagers re-appear from the forest. Green lights hissed from his shoulders. He snapped a mental command and they blinked out.

Enoch rose to his feet and spread his empty hands. "Friends," he said.

The biggest of the boys made the sign of the cross. Then he threw a rock. It hit Enoch's face, and split his cheek.

Tek'tek hauled Enoch onto his back. "That's it. We're gone," he said.

∞¥∞Ω∞¥∞

Enoch spent their return journey in prayer over Sara. Tek'tek ripped up some of Enoch's clothes and bound his wounds. Sara lay wide-eyed, fighting sadness and sedatives. "Those poor people," she said. "Cut off from the world, giving birth to monsters. They must have thought they were cursed."

"I didn't realise he had pinned so much hope on joining them," Tek'tek used eyeview.

"He's looking for a wife," Sara returned. "That was what the lace and the other gifts were for. To show that he could look after her."

"Not much hope of that now," Tek'tek said, sickly. Enoch had come a long way in accepting those not made to God's image. He had prayed for the girl as if she was human. Tek'tek shut his eyes and saw her dead face. The hitherto abstract notion of mortality bit deep.

"It's not your fault," Sara tried to comfort him. "We should have foreseen…" Her voice tailed off.

Professor Xi had everything organised as soon as they touched down. Sara and Enoch were sent to hospital. A rescue team was dispatched. They found that the boys had abandoned the huts and vanished into the woods. The rescue team left food and supplies, and a letter telling the boys how to contact them. It was all they could do.

Sara recovered rapidly. By the end of a fortnight she was limping around, although she would not fly for weeks.

Enoch recovered slowly, then ceased to recover at all. He lay in his hospital bed staring at the ceiling. His face went grey, his eyes sank back into their sockets, and the gash on his forehead became infected.

Interns scurried around campus stripping willow bark to make an old pain relief medication called aspirin, and snatching up mouldy fruit. "We're looking for a fungal spore, *penicillium*," Dr Greggog explained. "It's a natural antibiotic. I fear we're too late. Enoch has taken a psychological blow from which he cannot recover. In layman's terms, he has lost hope."

It only occurred to Tek'tek then that Enoch was dying. He sat by Enoch's bed, big hands dangling uselessly. He read Enoch's Bible through, and read aloud all the passages he could find about hope.

He even gritted his teeth and joined Enoch in interminable prayer. It was no use. Enoch was sunk in a deathly despair.

"This is stupid," Tek'tek complained to Dr Greggog. "Give him modern medicine, just don't tell him."

"No treatment without consent." Dr Greggog was firm. Her fishy eyeballs glowed moist with keen sympathy. "My interns found out something that used to be popular in the old days when medicine was not so beneficial. It's called a placebo. If you have any ideas let me know."

"placebo, *n.* a medicine which performs no physiological function but may benefit the patient psychologically," eyeview said.

Tek'tek went back to his bedroom. He took the feather from its hiding place. Enoch didn't need to know he got hold of it. "Sara thought you might like it," he told the sunken-eyed figure in the hospital bed.

Enoch let the feather drop to the covers, then he picked it up. He turned the quill between his fingers so the bronze highlights glimmered. "It is like an angel's," he said, mournfully.

"Sara is an angel," Tek'tek said. "I hope," he added, fervently.

Enoch smiled, at last, although his smile was not happy.

"Don't give up. There is always hope," Tek'tek encouraged him. The dead girl haunted his dreams, all lapped in lace. *For dust you are and to dust you will return.* The concept of guilt struck home like a steam train. What did her death mean, anyway? If death was the end then what was life for? He snatched one brief glimpse into the depths of his soul then retreated, appalled.

He hitched his bulk nearer to the bed, so he could whisper. At last he asked Enoch what Dr Gregogg had forbidden. "We could make a spike from the Old Stacks genetic sample. We could give it to your children. They don't need to know it is a spike. Just show them the feather and tell them it is a miracle," he begged him.

Enoch's face twisted in agony. "Do you think I haven't thought of that? That if one soul did wrong, one soul, and he didn't tell anyone, then only that one soul would be damned. It's no use. That way lies the devil's temptation of sin and pride. If our children die young they die uncorrupted by this world. They speed to God's grace. We should not mourn for them." Yet he struggled with tears.

Tek'tek was uncomfortably aware of the mental anguish he was causing. Yet he pushed on. "God sent you here," he reminded him. "God has shown you a cure. 'Behold, I send an angel before you, to guard you on the way and to bring you to the place which I have prepared'," he shot right back at him.

"The Devil can quote scripture when it serves his turn," Enoch said, yet he gave Tek'tek a watery smile.

"God is love. You told me that," Tek'tek said. "He wouldn't punish your children when they had done no wrong."

"I the Lord your God am a jealous god, and visit the iniquity of the fathers on the children, on the third and the fourth generations," Enoch said, mechanically. Yet for the first time he did not seem to speak as he believed.

When Tek'tek left, late that night, Enoch was awake in bed, turning the quill of Sara's feather between his fingers so that specks of bronze light danced over the walls and ceiling.

The next morning Enoch ate a proper meal. By afternoon he was sitting up, his forehead healing.

"That feather was an excellent placebo," Dr Greggog congratulated Tek'tek.

"It is not a placebo," Tek'tek snapped, angry for the second time in his life.

A few days later Enoch was out of bed and packing. "There is no need for me to stay any longer," he said. "The summer is over. Soon it will be harvest. I must return."

"We'll miss you," Tek'tek said, mournfully. With the Old Stacks cleansed he retrieved several cases of undamaged books and a working copy of the Gutenberg Press which he found in the machine exhibit on the seventh floor. "Take it with you and see what the Elders say," he said when Enoch protested. "It means you can print your own Bibles," he tempted him. Also, he managed to keep word of the feather from Sara. This involved swearing a gaggle of giggling nurses to secrecy.

∞¥∞Ω∞¥∞

The next morning they returned to the station. The train was repaired, and Enoch's crates were loaded.

Enoch carried his suitcase, his Bible and his feather, although the feather was almost as large as he was and a handful in the breeze. Sara met them at the station. Her half-healed wing was limp. When she saw the feather, her smile stiffened.

"Say nothing," Tek'tek warned her via eyeview.

"You had no right to keep that!" she scrolled right back.

"It gave him hope."

Sara fell ominously silent.

A crowd gathered to farewell Enoch; Professor Xi, Dr Greggog, relieved interns, hospital nurses and the college crowd. Gossip flew around. Plans for moving the university closer to the galactic core had been finalised. Falling enrolments were blamed. The last outpost was giving up its guard.

Enoch was delighted to see everybody. He led a prayer, then zealously threw himself into one last, long preaching session. Finally he handed around his Bible.

"That book really should be in a museum," Sara made sure everyone had their gloves sprayed on before they handled it. "Look, even Enoch has finally realised how precious it is. He's wearing gloves too," she said to Tek'tek, delighted. Then she remembered she was still mad at him, and flounced off.

"Group hug," Tek'tek announced. He threw himself into the scrum.

He and Sara farewelled Enoch at the train door. Enoch gave Tek'tek the plough share and Sara the candle holder. "Something to remember me by," he said. His eyes were sad but he smiled at Sara. "Thank you so much for your feather."

"Don't mention it," Sara said, through gritted teeth.

"I'll visit sometime," Tek'tek promised him. "I'll try not to cause a riot."

Enoch took their hands in farewell. "I believe in my heart you will both be saved," he said. "I will pray for you." He waved out the window as the train steamed away.

Tek'tek galloped after him until the train vanished around the curve of the mountain.

He returned to the station. Everyone had left, except for Sara who waited, hands on hips, with one angry wing-tip tapping the ground. Sara let rip, but she stopped, disconcerted, as Tek'tek burst into laughter. He laughed until he wept. Then he sat on the station platform and hiccupped.

Sara sat on the edge of the platform, swinging her long legs.

"Sorry about that," he hiccupped to a halt at last.

Sara had put two and two together. "What's with the feather?"

"We spiked it with the Old Stacks genome sample," Tek'tek said.

"And Enoch didn't know? You couldn't," she gasped.

"He knew," Tek'tek said. "You noticed he wore gloves the whole time he handled it."

Sara had. She subsided.

"He's going to take it back to his community and tell them what it is. They're going to gather in their church and discuss it. That's how they decide things. They talk it over. Enoch says they can talk for days," Tek'tek said, deeply relieved he wouldn't have to hear it.

"It won't fly," Sara shook her head. "They'll fall back on prayer to find a cure."

"Enoch will say that prayer led him here, and God revealed a cure," Tek'tek said. He and Enoch had discussed the whole idea.

Sara kept shaking her head.

"It's not an enhancement. It's just returning them to the original," Tek'tek told her. "Anyway, they can listen to what he has to say, and decide if it's a devil's snare. 'A net is spread in vain before the eyes of them that have wings,'" he added, just as Enoch would have said.

It was only when Tek'tek saw what was left in Vermont that he understood the pressures Enoch's community faced, and the reasons behind the decisions they had made. He still thought they were wrong, but that didn't give him the right to treat Enoch like a child.

"Our history is what makes us human," he realised, aloud.

Sara gave a surprised laugh. "If you keep on like that you'll get a Pass," she gasped. She stretched her injured wing, and winced. "So shall the last be first and the first last."

∞¥∞Ω∞¥∞

THE SHIPS OF CULWINNA
THORAIYA DYER

In times of plenty, being born the son of a Chief is a blessing from She Who Watches.

But I was not born in times of plenty.

I was born in the year of famine, when the blood that coloured the snow was not the blood of leopard seals and penguins but that of skeletal, starved warriors sent to raid the caches of other tribes.

And we were at war.

The eggs in the giant penguin rookeries had not hatched and the mature birds were poisoned by the venomous squid that they fed on; we did not know, before the Tall People came, that they came in search of food.

They came in vain. The barnacled whale had not come into the Bay of Blood to give birth, and we, the Pale People, were reaching the end of the fat that had been stored in the ice. We had no choice but to double our catch of silverfin, or else begin laying newborn babes in the snow to keep the tribe's numbers low.

The first attack must have frustrated the Tall warriors. Their slender spears could not penetrate the thick furs our warriors wore, while our clubs easily cracked skulls and our rippers, set with shark's teeth, opened up their bare thighs and throats. Their bark canoes could not follow our skin boats into the open water. Our women and children were evacuated up the coast of Culwinna to the winter caves. I was six months old.

In the second attack, my father lost his hand. It was the custom of the Tall People to make fish hooks out of the finger bones of their enemies. They believed the penguin eggs had not hatched because we had laid a curse on them, and that once deprived of the hands which had performed the ritual to catch the Lady's eye, our curse would fail and the Lady's favour would return to them.

The Lady's favour never did return to them. Although they had returned with heavy scythes of obsidian and thunderbird crest, our people still had all the knowledge of the terrain, and their numbers had been severely reduced in the initial assault. The Tall warriors were eliminated.

Father brought his severed hand to the winter caves. He thought it a great joke. The wind dried it and the cold preserved it. He liked to hide it in amongst our possessions to startle my mother.

"Be strong, Toman," he said to me when I was old enough to understand that a one-handed man could not remain Chief without great reserves of power. "Defend the tribe with your strength."

I nodded, eager to please. Secretly, though, I knew it wasn't strength which had defended the tribe, but something I had no word for, yet. It wasn't until I met the Traveller that I truly understood what my immature mind had tried to grasp.

Technology.

It was technology which had defended the tribe. Our tools had been better suited to the task at hand.

"Be steadfast, Toman," my mother murmured to me on the morning I turned nine years of age and departed for my warrior's initiation. "Defend the tribe with your patience. Your endurance."

But she was a woman and couldn't understand. To be a Chief was to act swiftly and decisively. To be a Chief was to lose your hand in battle and tear out the heart of your enemy with the remaining hand.

∞¥∞Ω∞¥∞

Doya was with me when we found the wreck.

She should have been in the caves with the women, but first she said she needed fresh air and then she whispered in my ear that she wanted to show me something in secret. When she leaned away from me, the condensation from her breath turned cold against my cheek.

The women indulged her because she was the daughter of the first whaler. I indulged her because soon, when we both turned fourteen, she would become my wife. A man's clothes were made by his wife, and if he wanted to be comfortable on the hunt he had better keep on her good side.

Doya's handiwork was magnificent, there was no doubt about that. She made clothes for her father, thick pelts of wallaby and possum put together so seamlessly that the garments might have been his natural skin. When he was drowned and his clothes were turned inside out so that he might find his way to the land of the dead, the colourful embroidery that had been hidden was exclaimed over by all the tribe.

I knew that when I died, the Lady would welcome me with open arms, if I wore tribute such as that.

"What is it you want to show me?" I asked when we had put the caves behind us, the onshore winds reddening our cheeks and terns floating through the fog like children's kites on invisible strings.

Doya brought out a skin and a stick of charcoal. I put out my hand to stop her; charcoal was used to plan out the patterns on the inside of fur cloaks before the embroidery was begun. That was not for men to see. But Doya shook her head. Her dark eyes were bright. There were tiny water droplets on her long lashes.

"It is not an embroidery pattern, Toman. Look."

I looked. She had drawn seven fish, point-down, and the outline of a single barnacled whale.

"What is it?"

"I had an idea," she said. "In the silverfin season, the men go out in the great canoes. They return every three days to the store cave, and if the cave is not filled, they go out again. Every time they return and put out again, they risk the run past the rocks. What if they didn't have to?"

I stared at the drawing. Slowly, ever so slowly, I realised what it was.

"A message," I said. "This is a message that is not spoken."

"One man in a skin boat could safely bring many messages to shore. The catch could be tallied by the women in the store cave.

Signal fires could be kept burning until enough fish and whales to fill the store cave had been caught. Then the fishermen and whalers could return all together."

"If such a system had already been in place, your father might not have died."

Her eyes filled with tears and she nodded.

I began to think of other uses for unspoken messages. Possibilities unfolded before me. Giddily, I realised this was another advantage for the Pale People that the Tall People did not have. If raiders came again, Doya's tallies could be used to count and map the positions of enemy warriors.

"This is very clever, my wife-to-be," I said. "I will show it to my father."

She hugged me, but very briefly, for we were of an age when hugs could turn quickly into something they should not. Not before we had been given the Lady's blessing, anyway.

We crossed Snake Beech Stream by its luminous yellow lichen-covered stone bridge. Grazing hook-footed wallabies scattered before us as we descended the stone slabs of Southworn, heading for the beach of boulders below Stinging Cape. My father had led a border patrol the previous night and was due to return any time.

I saw the wooden beams before Doya did and my heart raced. Building materials were scarce, as the whales caught in the previous two seasons had been small and few in number. Driftwood was precious. We had no wish to provoke the Tall People by taking trees from their land. I seized Doya's elbow and pointed to the half-submerged trunks.

"It is part of a great canoe," she cried, leaping ahead of me from boulder to boulder, calling for any fishermen that might be trapped in wreckage.

There was nobody.

We searched the wreck but found no sign of the canoe's masters.

"The beams are connected with ropes and these round things like coconuts with the ropes running through," Doya said.

Together, we hauled a sheet of white cloth out of the waves. The weave was very fine. I'd seen nothing like it, not even from the flax looms of Moht.

"By the Lady's birth canal," Doya swore. "Do you know what this is, Toman?"

Shocked by her language, I shook my head in silence.

"It is like a kite. It is for catching the wind."

We stared at each other, breathing quickly. For if the unspoken message was a great advantage, the means to cross wide, hostile seas was an even greater one. It was possible to trade furs for woven cloth in Moht, but though they had timber, we could not transport it home to Culwinna in skin boats.

With a great canoe such as the one suggested by the beams, we could.

Labouring in silence, we rearranged the beams and ropes and fabric on the beach, until they lay flat in the pattern in which they must have made when upright. It became clear that the wind must catch the white fabric and drive it like an albatross over the waves.

Doya made a drawing of what we had pieced together with her charcoal and skin.

"Who could have built this, Toman?"

"I do not know."

But secretly, I was glad that none had survived. For if such a mighty people as these came to the lands of the Pale People, we would surely be helpless to repulse them.

Perhaps that was why the vengeful, bloodthirsty Lady had destroyed them before they could make landfall. Her eye was everywhere. I glanced over my shoulder at the disc of the sun and shivered.

∞¥∞Ω∞¥∞

My father did not care about the ship.

Neither did he care for the drawings made by Doya.

"That girl will carry your children, Toman," he growled, "but her words carry no weight with the tribe. Kite canoes and foolish scribbles? You should have salvaged the wood for the tribe, not gawked at it until the tide carried it away."

And he beat me until I could not stand, but the true pain that I felt was the pain of realising my father was lacking in vision and understanding. While I gasped and shuddered on the floor, I felt anger but also a terrible pity. The Lady had endowed me with gifts that she had not seen fit to give my poor, stupid father.

I realised I must learn more. I must leave the island. When I returned, it would be with such knowledge, such advantages for the Pale People that no rival tribe would threaten us ever again. If we were able to cross the South Swift Sea and bring back supplies from warmer, richer countries, we would never go hungry. There would be no more need for war.

In secret, I began to modify one of our wooden canoes. Doya helped me, but no matter how we tried, we could not replicate the windcatchers that we had seen. Our pitiful models were knocked over by the gentlest breezes. I stared furiously at their upturned hulls, at the water sliding off their blunt keels.

"Don't give up, Toman," Doya urged. "We'll make the next one heavier, the keel sharper and deeper."

When summer came again, we were married. By the time we had made a model that remained upright, Doya was pregnant, and emptying her guts daily into the sea.

I walked about flushed with excitement. My father thought my impatience and anticipation was for the child growing in Doya's belly, and so he did not suspect that my kite-rigged canoe was provisioned for two, ready to take my wife and me on the journey of a lifetime.

"Is it time to go, Doya?" I whispered.

"I can't," she moaned, and vomited on the floor. "Perhaps when the pregnancy is a little further along, Toman. They say the sickness wanes in the fourth month."

The fourth month came and went. Doya began to bleed, erratically. The other women confined her to bed and would not let me see her.

I brooded in the place where I had hidden the kite-rigged canoe. It seemed to whisper with the Lady's voice, promising vistas never before seen by man, by any eye but the Lady's.

The translucent, resilient leather of the sails, though, was Doya's. The weave of the spinifex ropes was also hers. I had cut the altered curve of the bow, but it had been Doya's drawing that I'd followed. The canoe was, in truth, more her work than mine.

The baby was born, a girl. I named her Tooha, for my mother. My father made his disappointment at the baby's sex known. Once the child had suckled, my father forced me to go to Doya and try to make another child immediately.

Doya was weak and bloody like a warrior returned from battle. I held her while she slept.

Days passed, and she remained too weak to walk. Once, in the blackness of night, my father's scorn fresh in my mind, I touched Doya very gently while she was sleeping. She turned her face to me to be kissed, and I traced the contours of her fuller, more beautiful body. But then I brushed the place where she was torn when the baby emerged, and she shrieked and twisted away from me.

She cried, and I cried, too, not with remorse, exactly, but with frustration.

"When will it be time to go, Doya?"

"There are no other nursing mothers. Who would care for our child?"

I said nothing. A black hole was growing in my heart. We would have to wait until Tooha was old enough to be away from her mother. That would be another season, and another after that.

The seasons passed so slowly that it seemed a lifetime before I asked Doya again.

"Is it time to go, now, Doya?"

"I am with child," Doya said, her face white.

It was then that I knew my father was right, that women were fragile, that they could never be like men, to make decisions and defend the tribe.

Doya could not come with me. I must go alone to the country of the shipmakers. So she had helped make the canoe. So what? If it weren't for me, she would never have been allowed out of the caves in the first place.

When I set sail, there was nobody to see me.

Nobody but the Lady with her ferocious, burning eye.

∞¥∞Ω∞¥∞

I was the son of a Chief, but they cut my hair.

They whipped me for not understanding their language. Afterwards, I lay in the blackness of the belly of the ship, salt crusted on my lips, calling for Doya in my delirium.

A woman held a leather cup to my mouth. The water was cold and sweet. Her name was Gawa, the Kestrel, but the boar-men on the ship called her Daisy.

"They are not boars," she said when she had taught me enough of the boar-men's language for me to understand her and them. "They are pink and hairy but their blood is red, the same as ours."

There was no disputing that, for the boar-men beat each other and cursed each other and cut each other as though they were at war with themselves instead of the sea. They had been prisoners, once, guilty of some crime and abandoned on an island, but they had built themselves the ship and planned to fill it with seal skins, some forty thousand of them.

It was a number I could scarcely comprehend. The Lady would never give permission for such vast colonies of fur seals to be killed, their meat abandoned to scavengers on land and at sea. Yet the schooner, *Nowhere*, pursued the stench of seal excrement like a liver-eater pursues a female in season, anchoring off countless unknown shores, sending the sealing gang out in a longboat made more cunningly than any I had seen before.

"I wanted to learn to build ships the way the invaders made them," I told Daisy, laughing hollowly. I knew I would never see Doya again.

"That you'll learn, soon enough," Daisy answered, and she was right. Despite the cleverness with which it was put together, rough seas broke up the longboat. I was sent with the shipwright, Smith, and the other two slaves to cut local timber and learn the labour of forging iron nails and ship fittings over cruel coal fires. Daisy was never allowed on shore.

"My home is that way," Daisy whispered, her eyes fixed on a cluster of stars. "Six times, I've run from them. Six times they brought me back. But your home is the other way, isn't it? You're not as pale as they are, but you're one of the Pale People. You've lived in the ice so long that you've started to become like it."

"Why won't they let you go home?"

I knew the answer even as I asked. Daisy was wife to a different man every day and every night. They had her on the deck in the sun; they had her in the dark on the bundles of foul skins; they had her, bent over the wicker cages where kangaroos were kept for fresh meat. They had her, one after another, while she lay, glassy-eyed, as if dead. Even the other two slaves took their turn, grunting and thrusting and grinning to themselves afterward.

"I can't swim," Daisy said. "Or I would go."

"There is the longboat. We could take it."

"We? When you are ashore, I am here. When you are here, the men sleep in the longboat. The hold is too full of seal skins. Soon, they will sail for Canton. Their fortune will be made, and we'll be sold, and never see home again."

"The skins," I said, seized by the obvious plan. "The skins and the wicker cages."

Daisy kept them away from my corner of the hold for three days while I fashioned the skin boat. On the evening of the fourth day, Smith, the shipwright, went rooting through the bundles below decks in search of his stash of rum and discovered the little coracle.

The squeaky cry he made was not so different to the one that he made when he climaxed, but Daisy's knife in his back probably did not feel as satisfying to him as his usual encounters with her.

"There are six men still on board," she said calmly, wiping Smith's blood onto the furs. "We can't get past them with your skin boat. Jump in the water and swim to the island. You can avoid the gang easily. Their fires burn through the night."

"You saved my life. How could I face my people, knowing I'd left you behind to their mercy? I'd rather die, killing as many of these hateful pig-people as I can with my bare hands."

"That will not be many. They have guns. You'll be shot." She touched my face, gently. "Be strong, Pale Warrior."

"I am strong."

"Be strong like a woman. Run, and live."

I obeyed.

And the only ship I took with me into the snow-swirled sea was a Culwinnan one, not of whale rib and hide but human skin and bone. Guns cracked behind me but I was already too far away for them to be accurate.

The Lady watched me with the silver eye of the moon as I struck out towards the black shape of the shore.

∞¥∞Ω∞¥∞

COLD WHITE DAUGHTER
TANSY RAYNER ROBERTS

How did it begin?

She built me out of snow and sticks and stones. Smooth pebbles made my heart and lungs and brain. Frozen branches curved into my spine and wrists and finger bones. Then there was snow, packed tightly around the staves until it formed flesh and skin.

I breathed into the endless winter, and she caught my breath in her own lungs before giving it back, warm and perfumed. Again I breathed, this time on my own. I opened my eyes.

Surely everyone thinks their mother is beautiful, when they are first born. I saw her glittering eyes, her frosted skin and silver crown and knew her to be a queen, and a witch. But most of all, she was my mother, and I loved her for it.

∞¥∞Ω∞¥∞

We lived in a tall, winding house of pointed spires and needle-sharp corners. Every room was narrow and high-ceilinged, and the cold air flooded through it. Frost patterned our flagstones, and thin icicles dripped from the window ledges. It was as well that she made me her daughter, since no one else could have thrived in this ice-lashed palace as well as I did.

We were not always alone. My mother's dwarves and wolves endlessly knocked at the door, demanding tasks, or bringing news. She delighted in them, in the furs they brought her, and the masculine grunts and growls they brought to our dinner table.

I learned to cut the corpses they brought into raw steaks for the chewing, and to boil the bones for gravy pies. We only had one stove and I hated it, with its streaks of heat and billowing clouds of smoke. I only made hot gravy when the dwarves demanded it. My mother, like the wolves, ate meat raw.

Cakes pleased her, and sweetmeats, but I did not make those for her. Rather, she would create them with a twist of her wand and a laugh from her throat, to reward the menfolk for their service.

My eyes were clear enough that I could see the dwarves chew and swallow the knucklebones and gristle left over from my kitchen scraps, as if they were the daintiest of toffees and almond caramels. No wonder that my mother laughed with such delight. Nothing pleased her so well as to trick and to deceive.

I have never liked the taste of sugar. It is a false promise on the tongue.

∞¥∞Ω∞¥∞

The statues hurt my heart. At first there were only a few, here and there throughout the house. A lion in the forecourt, pixies and naiads scattered through the rooms, elegant pieces of artistry in stone.

But more arrived, every year, then every month. Towards the end it was daily that new statues piled in to our narrow house, filling every room and tower and courtyard. They were not elegant artworks any more, but depictions of pain and fear and agony.

When my mother went abroad in that wide sledge of hers, drawn by reindeer, I was left alone in the house with the stone horrors. Sometimes I thought that the statues spoke to me, in voices so soft and painful that I could barely make the words out.

Sometimes I dreamed of them, and their sadness.

∞¥∞Ω∞¥∞

Change, when it came, began as a whisper in the air. *On the move. He is on the move. The kings and queens are returning.*

I thought my mother was the only queen this land had ever known. But the whispers grew louder, even as the winter ebbed away to reveal sand and stone beneath the snow.

What would become of me, in this thaw? If my mother was winter and snow and ice then I was doubly so.

When I was not called to wait upon her, I spent much of my time in the room that my mother had always called the library, though most of the books were frozen fast to the shelves and had to be prised away with a knife if I wanted to read them. I did enjoy the pretty colours of their bindings, and the wide words gilded on to their spines, but that was nothing compared to the stories inside.

The books that I had read over the years told me of worlds beyond ours, of boarding schools and lacrosse, of coal-smoke and carriages. I always wondered if these stories were of the 'dreadful place' that my mother came from, before she created our wonderland.

In the books in the library, there were not just winters but springs and summers, autumns, oceans and deserts.

Only one statue stood here among the books, the sad centaur, and I found myself talking to him often, when I was certain Mother was not nearby to hear. I told him of my fears and worries, and made up poems for him about what I could see from the windows of our high and pointed home.

Sometimes I read to him, of the Wickedest Girl, the Dreadful Goblins, and the Secret Five. He seemed to like the stories as much as I did.

On other days, I fancied that he told me tales as well, about these kings and queens who were returning to our land, to thaw us all. The tales always ended badly, but I tried not to blame him for that.

∞¥∞Ω∞¥∞

I felt the presence of the fair-haired boy before I saw him. It was as if a warm gust swept up the staircase, shaking us all to our foundations. The wolves were uneasy, and I heard them howling from the forecourt.

Of course I eavesdropped. Would you not? Listening to my mother's private conversations was the only thing that had kept me alive for so long — I needed to be ever cautious of her shifting moods and tempers. Our life together has always been one of thin, fragile ice beneath my feet.

I hid by the winding banister of the stair as the boy approached my mother, the worst of the wolves snapping at his heels. I could smell fear on him, though he pretended to be brave.

"I've come, your Majesty," he burst out, his shabby fur coat wobbling around him as he hurried forward to greet her. "It's me, Cyril."

My mother sat at the far end of the hall with only a single lamp burning. The look on her face made it clear what she thought of him. Obviously he had never paid the slightest attention to her moods, or he would know better to strut before her as if he was something special.

When she spoke, it was in a terrible voice. "How dare you come alone? Did I not tell you to bring the others with you?"

His face fell, and he explained quickly how close they were, the brother and sisters and even the dog that he had apparently promised to my mother. If I had a sister, I should not treat her so lightly, but he seemed quite greedy to get rid of his own.

Then he said the words that made my mother shiver, she who never felt the cold.

"They say that He is on the move. The fairy of sand."

There was a flurry after that, of dwarves and wolves, of shouting and sending, and surely this boy's siblings would be meat all too soon. The sledge was to be readied, the one without bells, so that none could hear the queen and flee in fear.

The boy huddled against the wall, only now seeming to realise how little my mother was pleased with him. He asked for sweets and was given dried bread. My mother snapped at him when he spoke, drumming her fingers against the arm of her chair.

And then the sledge was ready and they were gone, queen and golden boy, dwarves and wolves all. I crept out of my hiding place and went about my chores, cleaning and tidying after them so that all would be proper for their return.

The ceiling dripped. Drip, drip, drip. The floor was wet in patches, and had not iced over the stone as was usual. The windows were wet with condensation, and at first I dared not look.

But I did, oh I did. I saw the snow falling from the frosted tree branches. When I flung the window open, I felt a warmth in my throat that made it hard to breathe.

Not thaw. This was spring.

∞¥∞Ω∞¥∞

I cleaned and polished every room, and still my mother did not return. The window sills were wet with melting snow, and the courtyard was all shiny flagstones and a golden grit that I did not recognise at first.

Sand, the old books sang to me, of seasides and fish and chips, Blackpool rock and jolly good fun on the pier. *That is sand.*

I felt hot all over, as if my own skin would melt away. How real was I? If my mother forgot about me, would I pour through the flagstones and be gone in a few moments, like the icicles that used to cling to the edge of every turret and pointed roof of her house?

A night and day passed, and my mother did not come home. I slept near the sad centaur in the library, pretending that he petted me and called me dear thing. He reassured me that she was not dead, and winter would return.

When I breathed out, there was no cloud in the air.

∞¥∞Ω∞¥∞

Heat came all in a roar, and the courtyard beneath the house rumbled with that roar. I looked out of a window to see a terrible creature scampering back and forth. Was this the 'fairy' that they were all so afraid of? It had a shambling, spider-shaped body, with long brown limbs and spiky whiskers, ears like a bat and the eyes of a snail.

When it reached each statue, it grew in a most alarming manner and made flubbing noises with its lips as it breathed out, bringing the stone to life.

There was dancing and celebration, shouts and cries, hugs and kisses, as friends and family were reunited, and the queen's spells were broken. A dog barked, over and over, scraping against my fears.

I hid in the library as warmth spread from room to room, but I could feel it coming nearer. I stood by the window, wishing and wishing and thinking cold thoughts, remembering my mother and the ice and the snow and oh, I could not breathe if it was all heat and fire and pulses and skin and sand in this world, I could not.

My breath came raggedly as I pressed my hands back against the window, wishing that the glass was ice, wishing myself cold, cold, cold.

A girl broke into the room at a gallop. She wore strange clothes, not a fur in sight, and her hair was swinging in little bunches. "Psammead, Psammead!" she cried out. "I've found Mr Jinks! Oh, do come quick!"

And thus I learned the name of my murderer. I remembered a book in the library, about a sand-fairy who loathed the cold and complained constantly about his whiskers. Was he the same creature who had ruled this land once, before my mother brought the sweet relief of ice and snow?

If he was real, then everything in storybooks was real.

I stayed as still as I could, no longer breathing, as the sand-fairy was carried upstairs in the arms of another dreadful child, a girl with short curly hair who was dressed like a boy. The noisy dog snapped at their heels, barking with triumph, and the creature named Psammead shook hot, gritty sand from its feet on to my mother's frosted carpet.

"Are you sure this is your centaur, Anthea?" asked the short-haired girl, struggling to keep the Psammead in her arms and to quiet her dog at the same time. "Do be good, Champion."

Heat rolled off the creature in waves as he leaned over my centaur and huffed upon him in a thoroughly undignified fashion, turning his ice and stone features into coughing, laughing flesh.

The girl embraced the centaur and he hugged her back. "You did it, Anthea," he said in delight. "You saved us all."

"Not yet, Mr Jinks," she laughed, shining with joy. "There's still a battle, isn't there, darling Psammead? We have to defeat the Frost Witch, if my brothers haven't done it already."

"Indeed," said the creature in his scraping, hot voice. More sand fell to the floor. "We must ride, children."

"Oh," said the girl who was dressed as a boy. "There's one more statue. Look."

I did not breathe, did not weep or sigh. I remained as still as I could, thinking cold thoughts, even when the dog ran to me, barking and slobbering. I knew that the old sand-fairy's hot breath would render me into nothing but water on the ground.

Kill me, then, I thought. *Let me melt.*

After a moment of gazing at me with his huge, limpid snail's eyes, the sand-fairy huffed and muttered to himself. "No life in this one," he said. "It is only ice. Come, let us call the unicorns and to battle."

I waited, still and unbreathing as the intruders left the room. Finally, I heard their merry voices from below as they left the house, planning aloud who would ride upon whose back, on their way to join the battle and kill my mother.

These children who styled themselves kings and queens, they would be back, naming the house their own. Or else the sand-fairy himself would take up residence. I stared at the sand scattered on the floor, all heat and grit.

My mother would lose the battle. How could she not, with all of this wretched sand spilling across the ground outside, the summer sun in the sky and hot magics in the air? Four children, a sand-fairy and a dog, all straight from the pages of the books she froze hard to her library shelves. Of course they would win.

∞¥∞Ω∞¥∞

I left the house, the courtyard now empty of statues, and did not look back as I ran into the forest, hoping that I ran far from the battle and not into it. Surely I would find one last patch of winter snow to keep me safe. One frosted branch, one spindly icicle or stalactite.

Where the snow melted, there was nothing but sand, everywhere.

My tears froze before they touched my cheeks and hands — I was still ice, all the way to my core. The sand-fairy had said so.

I ran until the trees ended and the lamp-posts began: an endless expanse of cold iron poles twisted into beautiful shapes: lanterns lined up across the Waste. My mother had made this forest of metal, when she first stepped into this land and began her work, turning sand into ice and snow. She planted fragments from another world into the earth, and watched it grow and seed itself.

The lamp-posts, I thought, must come from the same world as the horrid children, and the books on my mother's library shelves. A world of ginger beer and glacé cherries, of train timetables and boarding school, of hols and ices and tins of pineapple.

There was snow in that world. There had to be, or the entire Chalet School series made no sense. Perhaps I could find a home there, if I could only discover which of a thousand lamp-posts was the one that led the way to the cupboard beneath the stairs that was found at the beginning and end of every Secret Five book.

This desert of kings and queens and centaurs and fairies had nothing to offer me now.

∞¥∞Ω∞¥∞

They killed my mother. I knew the moment when this happened, because my heart broke into pieces, slipping and sliding inside my ribcage. The pieces did not melt, but only because I pressed my hands to my chest and begged them to stay cold, to be ice and snow. I no longer breathed, and there was no pulse in my veins, but I still walked on cracking knees and aching limbs beneath the iron curves of the lamp-post forest.

The sky grew dark, and the lanterns sprang alight, every one of them. I laid my hand against one iron stem and left frosted fingertips there.

I staggered on, deeper into the maze of lamp-posts, and only now did I cry for my mother instead of myself. Drops of ice fell from my eyes and melted on the damp sand at my feet.

Ice, ice, ice. I called up everything I knew about my mother and her powers. I called the winter and the snow. Not into the world, which was too big for me to change, but into my own veins. *If not snow, let me be stone.*

Let me be a statue until winter comes again.

And so, in a final breath of my mother's magic, that is what I became.

∞¥∞Ω∞¥∞

Time passed, and as a statue I knew none of it. The last of the snow melted from the land, to be replaced by hot sands and fierce winds. There were no more winters.

I might have stayed that way forever, but for a single cool breeze that whipped around my ears, and melted my hard limbs for a moment. I heard voices, laughter on the wind, and I awoke.

They did not see me, the kings and queens. They were older now, wrapped up in silken robes and burnooses, seated upon camels. I wondered what had happened to the reindeer. Perhaps they were the statues now.

I watched as they called to each other, setting up a colourful tent to shield their blistered and sunburnt skin from the fierce sun above. Roger was the eldest, the one who had always been brave, and Cyril was the younger boy, the one who had betrayed them all to my mother, but was then forgiven. He appeared to be growing a moustache, which curled at both ends.

The girl with short hair was no more minded to dress as a lady now that she was old, and she wore a bright turban upon her short dark curls. Hilary, they called her, which was as good a name for a king as a queen. She lifted the now elderly and wheezing dog out of her saddlebag, and gave him water. He sweated horribly, and smelled like camel.

"Sand gets everywhere," said Roger irritably, and quarreled with his younger sister Anthea about whether they should drink hot tea with milk or lemon on such "a beastly day".

"I miss rain," said Cyril in a quieter voice. "Do you remember what it was like, just before we fell through the cupboard beneath the stairs? We thought it horrid, that we couldn't play outside. Oh, what I wouldn't give for a spot of rain now!"

"They are predicting there will be no crops this year," said Anthea, unpacking the picnic. "I say, does anyone want some Turkish Delight? There's a whole box of it."

All of the kings and queens made dreadful faces at their sister.

"Give it to Champion," said Roger in distaste.

The dog gave them all a long-suffering look.

"It was around here somewhere, wasn't it?" said Cyril, leaping to his feet. "Don't you remember? All these lamp-posts. There was a large snow drift, and we fell..."

"No snow now, you fool," said Hilary.

"I wonder how the war turned out," said Roger. "The other war, I mean. Back home. If it lasted four years, I would have gone myself."

"We did fight a war," said Cyril crossly. "Swords and all! Don't you remember? Surely that business with the witch and the sand-fairy was war enough for anyone."

Anthea burst into tears. "Do you remember what our mother looked like? I don't think I do."

I wanted to hate them, the four monsters who had killed my mother and destroyed my world. But for all their long limbs and curly moustaches, the Secret Five were still children at heart.

Then they were out of the tent, groping through the dust, looking around every lamp-post and rock, searching for that wooden door of theirs. Even the dog joined them, his head bowed against the fierce sun. Finally, he yapped.

"Here!" said Hilary. "Oh, good boy, Champion. I can smell mothballs."

"I smell roast dinner," said Roger. "And rain."

"You don't think," said Anthea. "Oh, you don't think, do you, that it might be the very same day that we left?"

Then they were gone, all of them. Champion went first, worming into a hole in the ground barely large enough to let him through, and then the girls after him, pushing and giggling and gasping with hope.

Cyril was the last to leave. He stood there in his silken finery, gazing around at the forest of lamp-posts. His eye settled for a moment on me, on what he thought was a stone statue. I thought for a moment that he smiled beneath that ridiculous upper lip of his, and then he was gone too, scrabbling his way through into his storybook world.

Mothballs and rain. I smelled them too.

No more kings and queens.

∞¥∞Ω∞¥∞

Was it my destiny now to return to my mother's house, to take up her crown, and to make the winter come again? To give snow and ice back to the land, to banish the hot sand one last time?

I could do it. I knew that I could. I saw exactly how to draw on the old powers and become that which I had always feared. I could shape myself into the new Frost Witch, and there would be no kings and queens to stop me.

But oh, the smell of mothballs and rain.

If they could have storybook adventures in other worlds, these awful children, why could I not do the same? I could have *Kaffee und Kuchen* at the Chalet School, or play lacrosse at Malory Towers. I could befriend a bear at Paddington Station, and drink bottled lemonade in a rowing boat.

Couldn't I?

Reader, I followed them. I dug a hole in the sand, let it swallow me whole, and fell through to a small triangular room full of spiders and coats. The cupboard under the stairs. I climbed out of there and found myself in a hallway, surrounded by staircases and the echoing voices of the children as they ran every which way through the house, celebrating their return.

On unsteady legs, I found my way to a window and watched rain gush down across a bright green lawn. Such wetness, cleaning the world anew. Eventually, the rain slowed and stopped, and still I stared at the gleaming, sodden grass.

My feet hurt. I was real, and this world was real, and my mother would never find me here, not in a thousand years of searching.

My mother was dead.

My tears were salt water falling on the backs of my pink, pink hands. I had never tasted such salt before. But this world was full of tastes and smells, of peppermint and floor polish, of damp walls and bread rolls baking in an oven. So many possibilities for adventure.

I breathed warm, damp air into my fleshy lungs.

And life began.

∞¥∞Ω∞¥∞

THE WAYS OF THE WYRDING WOMEN

ROWENA CORY DANIELLS

"Come here, Sun-fire." Druaric offered his hand, helping me off the bed, strangely gentle now the deed was done. *Sun-fire* was what they called me because I would not give them my true-name. They might have power over my body, but I wasn't giving them power over my soul. As a Wyrding-woman in training, I knew that much.

The three brothers escorted me to the great hall. Lohnan, the eldest took my right arm, Murtahg took my left and Druaric limped along behind. He was the youngest, the clever one who listened when their Wyrding-woman spoke. Marked by a clubfoot, if he'd been born a girl, he would have walked the Wyrding-ways.

First we passed the slaves and the household servants who all gawked at me, the captive who had the honour of housing their dead Warlord's spirit. Next we passed the sons' cousins and sisters, with their warrior husbands and children. Finally we passed the two eldest sons' wives and children. Clutching their toddlers and babes, the women watched me with barely concealed loathing. If the Warlord's soul cleaved to my unborn babe, my child would outrank theirs, so naturally they hated me.

I made the sign to ward off the evil-eye.

As the sons urged me on toward the clan's ancient Wyrding-woman my steps faltered and my stomach churned. I'd only been close to her once before, when she'd touched my belly to sense the new life-force quickening. Then I had been too frightened to move.

Now, her wizened face glowed with satisfaction. Incredibly old, mother to the Warlord himself, she had outlived all her children, had lived long enough to see her grandchildren produce children. Truly, she was so powerful that even her apprentices would be stronger than me.

When the sons had first captured me, I'd looked for girls with the Wyrding-signs but couldn't find them. Maybe they were like me, born with a caul. My Wyrding-sign was safely hidden under the hearthstone of my village's Wyrding-cottage. But I mustn't think about my home, or the way the sons had led their raiders into my highland valley, grabbing me because my red-gold hair caught their eye.

"Here is Sun-fire." Lohnan, the eldest, presented me to his Wyrding grandmother. "Wild-cat, more like. It took all three of us to hold her down but she did it, she inhaled our Warlord's dying breath."

And vile it was too.

Triumph gleamed in the Wyrding-woman's sunken eyes.

It was too much for me.

I sprang forward, slashing her forehead with my fingernails, drawing blood above her breath-line. It was the best way to protect myself from her power. The granddaughters screamed in outrage. Lohnan caught me and swung me around, holding my arms. Murtahg lifted his hand. I braced for the blow.

"No!" The Wyrding-woman's sharp voice stopped him in mid-swing. She looked pleased. I didn't understand. Then my skin went cold with fear as I realised I'd given myself away. She wiped the blood from her eyes with a smile. Her last three teeth stood like standing stones in the mounds of her gums. "An adept of the Wyrding-ways. This, I did not foresee."

I shook my head, but denial was useless.

The Wyrding-woman pointed to the long table. As Lohnan shoved me I looked down, unable to meet her penetrating gaze. Quick as a snake, she clawed my forehead. I gasped and bent double in shock.

"Lift her face," the Wyrding-woman ordered.

I had to blink blood from my eyes. She smiled and I knew she had negated any advantage I'd achieved by drawing blood above her breath-line. At every step I was outmanoeuvred. But I would not despair.

I would wait and take my revenge on all of them. It was the one thing that had kept me going. If we hill-people are good at one thing, it's holding a grudge.

"Behold the vessel of the Warlord-reborn," the Wyrding-woman cried as Lohnan lifted me onto the long table. A shout went up, a genuine cheer of triumph. They loved the old Warlord and why shouldn't they? He'd protected them from the other clans, making theirs the wealthiest and strongest in all the Wild Isles.

The Wyrding-woman nodded to Lohnan. "She must be naked when I fix his soul in the babe."

He was only too eager to strip me. Then she also clambered up onto the table. No apprentice came to help her as she produced her Wyrding tools from the deep pockets of her leather apron. Saying her chants, she made signs on the flesh of my naked belly and breasts with her oils. I recognised the protectors, rosemary and sage, by their scent.

With elaborate symbols to ensure my health and that of my babe, she stroked my flesh with her sacred feathers. I did not know the birds these feathers had come from. The customs of the coast-people were different from us hill-people, yet so similar it made me shudder, just as their language was the same, yet peppered with unfamiliar words.

Closing my heart and mind, I invoked the Wyrding-mother, begging her to make the babe shrivel and die or better yet, make it a girl with the Wyrding-sign.

When the ritual was over the Wyrding-woman stepped back and, with great respect so different from our ungainly struggle over the Warlord's deathbed, the sons helped me down from the massive table.

Of the Warlord's seven sons only these three had survived the raids. Lohnan, nearing forty, still waited for his chance to lead. Murtahg, ten years younger, seemed older because his face was set in a perpetual scowl, and Druaric. The raid on my village had made him a man at seventeen, late to this rite of passage because of his crippled foot.

Lohnan leered as he looked on my nakedness. Druaric swung a cloak around my shoulders. I felt strangely numb and feared the Wyrding-woman's powers were already at work, sapping my will.

She nodded to Druaric who sent a servant to fetch a zither. Everyone waited. Murtahg chewed on his pipe stem, all nervous energy. Ever practical, Lohnan's wife ordered servants to see to the Warlord's body.

Ensuring the Warlord's soul took root in my babe was only part of this day's work. They still had to send his old body to the next world. The Wyrding-woman watched her people, pale blue eyes sharp despite her age. Her clan boasted she'd seen nearly a hundred years of life and, looking at her, I believed them.

Averting my eyes with a shudder, I saw the servant return to give Druaric a beautifully made wooden box. There was a small hole in the middle and across this hole were strings of varying lengths. Sitting cross-legged, he placed the thing on his lap. I thought it odd looking, but when he plucked the strings I heard the Wyrding-mother's sweet voice and it brought tears to my eyes.

He sang of how the clan's Wyrding-woman had sent the Warlord's sons on a noble quest to win me — a raid that split the skulls of our valley's defenders and stole our sheep. He sung of how they had lain with me — raped me. It was no more or less than I'd expected. I was no shrinking virgin — we hill clans-people are a tough breed.

As I lay under the Warlord's sons I'd planned how I would kill each one. Slowly. Even the youngest one with the clubfoot, who had whispered that he was sorry.

He sang of how they had succeeded in saving their Warlord's soul — they had pinned me down on the bed and squeezed the air from my ribs just as the fierce old fire-brand rattled his last.

Then Druaric went on to sing of how I would deliver a healthy boy babe who would grow up to lead their clan to greatness. I felt their belief like a physical thing and that was when I sensed Druaric's power. He was *willing* events to come to pass. My gaze flew to the Wyrding-woman. She nodded knowingly. She might not have an apprentice but she had a grandson who could shape the world with his words.

The song finished and Druaric stood up, slinging his zither over his shoulder. It hung from a leather strap, impressed with symbols of power.

My heart sank. How could I defeat these two?

The clan moved out of the hall, across the yard, through the palisade and outer gate, down to the shore of the narrow, steep sided bay. As if in a trance, I followed, and watched as they placed the Warlord on his ship, along with weapons and food.

"Why…?" I began then bit my tongue.

But the Wyrding-woman guessed my question. "If his soul does not take root in your babe we don't want him wandering between the worlds. His place in death's realm will be prepared just in case."

Three old slaves volunteered to go into the afterlife to serve him. Lohnan, Murtahg and Druaric strangled them while everyone looked on. They dealt so casually in death, it sickened me. At my old Wyrding-teacher's side I had dedicated myself to saving life. And, although I had survived so far, I was dying a thousand small deaths, losing my true-self. Standing there on the pebbly beach, I felt as if I was an empty shell.

Beyond the headlands, the sea was molten gold, lit by the dying sun. At a signal from Lohnan, the sail was set so that ship's prow faced west. I considered running out onto the wooden jetty, throwing myself into deep water. But it would do no good. Being born with a caul meant I could not drown. One of them was sure to jump in and drag me out. Then they would watch me even more closely. Instead, I would pretend to be filled with despair and choose my moment for revenge. I would find the killing herbs and then I would ensure the Warlord's last three sons joined him in death.

If the Wyrding-woman didn't realise what I was planning.

I tensed as Druaric approached, but he only sat on a wharf stone beside me with his zither. Hands that had just strangled the life from an old man plucked power from the strings. The clan took up the song, their voices rising and falling in an eerie dirge. I hated it, but I had to admit it was beautiful. Flames engulfed the ship as the outgoing tide carried it through the headlands. A bottomless well of sadness filled me. How could people who created such fierce beauty be so cruel?

Why had the Wyrding-mother forsaken me? The only explanation was that this clan's Wyrding-woman had a more powerful call on her.

When the song finished, Druaric sat with the zither on his lap. "You will be honoured, Sun-fire. You won't have to work until the baby is born. You'll have plenty of food and somewhere warm to sleep. If you use your wits, you can be the babe's wet nurse. Your position will be nearly equal to that of my sisters and my brothers' wives—"

"I will still be a captive." I glared over my shoulder at him. His eyes were the same severe, ice-blue as the old Warlord's. "Still a slave."

"What were you before?" he countered. "A wild savage scraping your food from the unforgiving hills, living in a single-roomed sod hut, lucky if you got enough to eat. Which is better?"

"Freedom!"

His gaze narrowed and he studied me thoughtfully.

I realised I'd revealed my true nature and I cursed my impulsive tongue. Like my true-name, a glimpse of my true nature gave him power over me.

∞¥∞Ω∞¥∞

They locked me in the tower again. It was the only building made of stone in the stronghold. Five floors high with narrow windows, it was their last place to make a stand if the palisade's gate was breached. The door had barely closed on the sons' backs, when Lohnan's wife set me to work, mending her clothes. This was a calculated insult, for Wyrding-women do not toil like other women. Even if I had not been one of the Wyrding-mother's daughters, they should not have made me work; I carried the Warlord-reborn.

So I refused to do the mending. I refused to eat. For seven days I sat and brooded, growing pale and thin. In truth, I was plagued by constant sickness so going without food was no great hardship.

The Wyrding-woman was consulted. She had them plough a field that was lying fallow and told them I must walk it barefoot to draw strength from the earth. The brothers debated who should make me walk the field. Lohnan was eager to get his hands on me but his motives were impure. Murtahg wanted nothing to do with me since he'd learned that I followed the Wyrding-way, so it fell to Druaric.

I resisted every step of the way. Under the Wyrding-woman's watchful eye we trudged, me lurching and balking, him struggling with me and his clubfoot.

"Why do you make it hard for yourself?" he muttered, out of breath.

I refused to speak.

"You are not as strong as our Wyrding-woman."

It was true, but I wouldn't give up. I couldn't. We hill-people are a tough breed, we never give up.

Neither would he. He kept on doggedly, dragging me over the freshly turned soil so that in the end I had to walk or be dragged in the dirt. I chose to walk. But with each step an idea formed in my mind. Since my Wyrding-ways had been revealed I had seen respect in Lohnan's eyes and fear in Murtahg's.

"Each day as the babe grows, I grow in power," I told Druaric.

He looked away. Good.

And it was true, as far as it went. With this babe I was growing in power. A Wyrding apprentice could not learn the deep lore until she had birthed her own daughter. Was my babe a girl? Perhaps this was the Wyrding-mother's plan.

∞¥∞Ω∞¥∞

Druaric must have spoken with the Wyrding-woman for she came to see me that evening. His uneven steps and her cane echoed on the stairs. By the time the door opened I was ready to face them.

"You think you are clever, Sun-fire." Her shrewd old eyes studied me. "But your knowledge of the Wyrding-ways is only a fraction of mine."

She produced an amulet from her apron, holding it in front of me. It had been made from familiar material, clothing that belonged to me. The cloth had been woven by my village and now it was stained with the blood of my struggles, which gave it power.

"This will counteract any spells or curses you might use to stop the Warlord's soul taking hold in your babe," she told me as she hung the amulet around her neck, tucking it inside her bodice next to her skin with a satisfied smile. "I have your measure, Sun-fire. You should fear me. In birthing a woman is at her most vulnerable. You'll need me to see you through it."

She was right. Terror cinched my stomach even as I raged at my impotence. How was I to settle my score with their clan? Revenge was the only thing that sustained me.

"You hate me," she said.

I did not deny it.

"I can live with that." She stroked the silver head of her cane, staring into its polished surface. "I have seen what the Warlord's death will do to our clan. By capturing his soul in your babe I have averted a battle for leadership. Without this babe our clan would be divided and tear itself apart. One day my children's children would have been slaves. Instead, with the Warlord-reborn our clan will become the greatest in the Wild Isles." She held my eye with the force of her will. "I will not be thwarted by a half-trained hill-brat!"

I refused to blink even though my eyes burned. We glared at each other. I fought to hold her gaze. She faltered and blinked before I did. Furious, she flung past me.

I smiled. It was a small victory, but it was mine.

She brushed by Druaric, forcing him to move out of the way. He bumped the mending basket.

"What's this?" His tone made her stop and turn on the top step by the door. He picked up a finely embroidered gown and his eyes narrowed as he recognised it. "Sun-fire is a Wyrding-woman, not a slave." He waved the dress at his grandmother. "You know how to stop this."

And he limped off with the basket, presumably to give Lohnan's wife a piece of his mind.

As his uneven steps echoed on the stairs, the Wyrding-woman's shrewd eyes returned to me. After a moment she beckoned. "Come."

I hesitated, but I was fed up with being shut away so despite my trepidation, I followed her. She led me down the tower steps, past another chamber and into the one below.

One look told me this was her Wyrding workroom. Filled with her tools, I felt its power close around me, cloying and oppressive. Much was familiar. Jugs and chests lined the walls, dried herbs hung from the rafters. There was a string of blue beads to protect against the evil eye and a snakeskin, fine as spiderwebs, to cure the bone-ache.

"Close the door, Sun-fire," the Wyrding-woman ordered and I did, torn between curiosity and fear. She thrust feathers under my nose. "What's this?"

I blinked. I could have pretended ignorance but pride would not let me. "Eagle feathers. To renew youth. You must have used them many a time."

She turned away, smiling her secretive smile. Taking a jar from the bench, she opened it to reveal dried foxglove. "And this?"

"Foxglove, also called dead-men's-bells, a poison."

She showed me another. "And this?"

"Fleabane, useful for putting in mattresses to kill bed mites."

She closed the jar and gnawed on her bottom lip. Then her expression cleared and she shoved something into my hands. "What does this tell you?"

I turned the child's leather ball over and over. She had not asked what it was, but what it told me. I cleared my mind and a vision came. "Blue bells."

With a hiss, she snatched the ball from me. I thought I saw fear in her eyes but the expression was gone too quickly to be sure.

She studied her shelves then sent me a sly look before handing me a small drum. "What child did this toy belong to?"

I held the drum, sensing great power. "This is no toy."

"Ha! Only half right. It is my Watcher," she revealed. "A faithful servant volunteered to die so I could have this drum made from his skin. If anyone tries to steal from me, the drum will sound."

I returned it with a shudder, which made her smile. How could the Wyrding-mother countenance power sourced from death?

"You are impressed with my Watcher," she said.

"I am surprised that you do not trust your own people. Our people would never have stolen from their Wyrding-woman."

"Slaves steal."

"We do not keep slaves."

"More fool you."

Again she studied the shelves, then shuffled over to get a jar. Without her cane her limp was much more pronounced and I realised she had a clubfoot like Druaric, though not as malformed as his. She unstoppered the jar to show me a fine powder. "What is it and what does it do?"

I sniffed. No scent. It could be anything.

"She does not know..." the Wyrding-woman muttered triumphantly. "But she should."

"My Wyrding-teacher died suddenly."

She resealed the jar and tapped the stopper. "This is powdered human skull, just the thing to quieten fits."

After replacing the jar on the shelf, she turned to look at me. "I will not have the mother of the Warlord-reborn belittled by the wives of my grandsons. I will take you for my apprentice."

I suspected she would dole out just enough knowledge to keep me docile, but my heart leapt at the thought of what I could learn, though I did not let her see this.

"You're as stubborn as the stone of the hills you were born in." She regarded me thoughtfully and seemed to come to a decision. "When I did the scrying and sent my grandsons out to find you, I did not see that you would be Wyrding-marked. Three girl children of my line were born with the Wyrding-sign but none lived long enough to train at my side. Now I see that the Wyrding-mother meant for me to teach you. What say you, Sun-fire? Will you put away your hatred and serve the Wyrding-mother as you have sworn to do?"

It was a tempting offer. I would be alert for lies or omissions on her part. She could not watch me every moment of the day. As her student I would find a way to rid my babe of the Warlord's soul. Serving the Wyrding-woman would give me access to all her herbals, including the poisons. Her grandsons would suffer as they had made me suffer. But to truly escape her, I would have to destroy the amulet.

All this went through my head in a blink. For now it suited me to train under this wise old Wyrding-woman so I inclined my head. "I will give the oath."

"Wise choice. We will prepare for the ritual."

I nodded. It would feel good to be walking the Wyrding-way again. *Like coming home.* This surprised me. Was she right? Was this what the Wyrding-mother had intended all along?

She tilted her head, sharp eyes on me. "You bear no signs, Sun-fire. How is it that you are Wyrding-marked?"

I smiled inside. Like my true-name, she would never know.

∞¥∞Ω∞¥∞

So I became the Wyrding-woman's apprentice; part slave, part daughter. Two moons passed in her service. Sometimes I pretended ignorance to test her and the few times her explanations varied from my teacher's it was only by a matter of degrees.

In all things I aimed to please her, to make myself indispensable and gain her trust. It was a game I played to win but one I could easily lose. For, in opening my mind, I opened myself. When I strove to please her, her approving words and smiles became my rewards.

I realised what was happening the first time she surprised a laugh from me. Sometimes, for a whole day I forgot that I was her captive.

But she never forgot. She always slept with the amulet around her neck.

Once a moon the sons would eat with the Wyrding-woman and make plans for the clan. They talked of uniting all the fierce people of the Wild Isles under one warlord and when they talked, it seemed possible.

More often, the sons came alone for there was no love lost between them, particularly the eldest two. Lohnan would sit and watch while I worked. He still hungered for me but he hungered for every woman, all the more if he could not have them. He talked of how, when their people gathered for the harvest feast, they would choose a leader to caretake the clan until the Warlord-reborn was old enough to lead them. He thought it should be him.

Murtahg did not sit. When he visited, he paced, chewing on his pipe stem, reeking of the weed that in other men induced good-natured laughter. In him, it seemed only to deepen his restless hunger. He claimed Lohnan was so fond of wine and women that his mind had gone soft like his body. And he was right.

The Wyrding-mother would say nothing, but the more she nodded and listened, the more they said, revealing the way their minds worked.

As for Druaric, I don't know what he thought. He never spoke of clan power. I guess he had power of his own. My favourite time was the evenings, when he came to play for us, singing their family's history while the Wyrding-woman dozed.

Soon I knew all the stories. I learned of the granddaughter, Druaric's older sister, who had been born with a Wyrding-sign that no one was aware of until it was too late. One day while playing with her ball, she was stung by a bee and fell to the ground screaming. In a panic, Druaric had run back to the stronghold to fetch the Wyrding-mother, but by the time they returned, his sister was dead amongst the blue bells. When I heard this, my heart contracted with sympathy and I looked down to hide my feelings.

Saddened by the memory, Druaric put his zither aside. It was so close I could have reached out to touch it. We had nothing like the zither in my village. Drums and pipes were our way of making music. I longed to see if I could coax the Wyrding-mother's sweet voice from it. "Keep playing, please."

"No more tonight." His voice caught.

Tears stung my eyes. I touched his arm. "I'm sorry. You could not know. Sometimes the Wyrding-sign is hidden."

"Like yours?" His hand covered mine, hot, dry and heavy with import. "I have seen all of your milk-smooth skin, Sun-fire, and I cannot forget it, but I did not see a single imperfection."

THE WAYS OF THE WYRDING WOMEN 193

A wave of molten heat rolled through my traitorous body. "I was born with a caul."

"A useful thing." He nodded wisely. "Where is it?"

Sanity returned to me. "Hidden." And I pulled away.

∞¥∞Ω∞¥∞

Not long after that the brothers went off on another raid. They hadn't taken their ships reaving to the mainland this summer and it was too late to do so now, so they went raiding rival clans on their island. They came back laden with tribute, freely given, or so they claimed.

Later that day, I was grinding herbs when the three brothers came to see to the Wyrding-woman. Knowing Lohnan would try to catch my eye, I ignored them.

"So? Is the whole island ours?" she asked.

"Just as you said it would be," Murtahg said. "And—"

"The treasure was where you said it would be." Lohnan handed her a pouch.

She gloated as she undid the leather satchel. "Come see this, Sun-fire."

I didn't like the note of triumph in her voice. Steeling myself, I approached.

She showed me a small, translucent sheet of velum. No. A caul.

My caul!

The whole world shivered.

"Catch her!" she warned. Lohnan needed no more urging to lay his hands on me. I tried to shove him away. He pinned me against his body, supporting me as my vision cleared.

"What is it?" Murtahg asked uneasily.

"Sun-fire's Wyrding-sign," Druaric said.

I glared at him and he had the grace to blush and look away.

Even though his betrayal cut me to the quick, I could see why the Wyrding-woman loved him best of all her grandsons. He was clever and loyal, placing his clan's safety above personal ambition. Reluctant admiration warred with my resentment.

"Say no more, Druaric. Knowledge is power," the Wyrding-woman warned.

Murtahg cursed. "It's not natural teaching him the Wyrding-ways. And you shouldn't be teaching this hill-brat. What if she turns on us?"

"I will teach who I choose, Murtahg. And the hill-brat is no threat. Her knowledge barely scrapes the surface of the Mother's Ways."

"Wyrding-ways!" He spun on his heel and marched out.

She ignored him, turning to me. "Now watch, Sun-fire."

I could not do other, as she removed the amulet and unpicked the stitching. Rolling up my caul, she tucked it safely inside.

"I may not have your true-name, girl, but I have this."

"It's mine."

"Yes. Now you are mine."

Despair and rage rolled through me.

Lohnan chuckled. "Eh, I can feel the fire in her. Let me have her. I don't mind if she scratches my eyes out."

"You're a fool, Lohnan. She's too powerful for you."

"She wasn't too powerful when I planted the babe," he protested.

"That was then." She dismissed him. "Let her go."

As Lohnan stormed out I realised that, despite what she'd told Murtahg, she needed my caul to keep me under control. I looked down, pleased with this new knowledge.

Druaric seemed to hesitate. I refused to meet his eyes, angry with him and with myself for I was doubly trapped by that amulet now.

"Go," the Wyrding-woman told him.

I waited only until the door closed. "I know how you found out about it. But how did you know where to look?"

She smiled, her last three teeth gleaming. "In a village the size of yours, where else would it be?"

Stupid of me. I had been a fool to trust Druaric.

∞¥∞Ω∞¥∞

Time passed. I enjoyed learning but felt Druaric's absence. He no longer came to spend the evenings with us. Every dusk I looked for him then had to remind myself of his betrayal.

I had been a prisoner for nearly four moons when the clan's metal worker delivered an object he had crafted for the Wyrding-woman. It was a perfect little bell strung on a piece of leather. She listened to the tone, then sent for Murtahg to bring his son.

When they came I recognised the lad. He was no more than seven and small for his age. But that was not why the others teased him. His words stumbled over themselves, harried by false starts and the more they teased him the worse his speech became.

"Murtahg and little Ciarnor," the Wyrding-woman greeted them. "Come, sit by me, Ciarnor."

Murtahg hung back, clearly uneasy with Wyrd power.

The lad approached and sat on a cushion at the Wyrding-woman's feet. She had earlier directed me in the mixing of a tincture. It was mildly alcoholic, sweetened with honey and contained a little of the powdered weed they smoked. A strange combination. Now she accepted this from me.

"Watch, Ciarnor." And she rang the bell.

His eyes lit up. "C ... c ... can I have it?"

"It is yours, but bells hold great power." She turned the bell over, poured a sip of the liquid into it and held it out to him. "Drink this."

He wrinkled his nose but did not complain about the taste, so the honey must have helped.

"Now ring the bell," she told him.

He turned it right way up and rang it, smiling at the pure tone.

She nodded. "Now give the bell to Sun-fire."

His face fell but he obeyed, watching as I washed the bell and purified it. All the while I felt Murtahg's stare. By the time I had finished Ciarnor's blue eyes had grown glazed with the drug. I knew the signs; he was suggestible. If my old teacher had needed to perform a painful healing on him, she would have done it now.

The Wyrding-woman took the bell from me, strung it on a leather thong then leant close to tie the bell around his neck. "Listen to me,

Ciarnor. From this day forward your speech will grow clearer. If you feel your words jamming up, ring the bell. Its pure tone will ease your tongue. Do you understand?"

"I do."

"See, it is working already." She beamed. Oh, but she was clever. I watched her, torn between admiration and resentment. "Off you go, Ciarnor."

"Wait, son." Murtahg put his pipe aside to study the bell. "Very well. Go."

The boy ran off, still a little stunned but happy.

"It is nothing but an ordinary bell. How can it work?" Murtahg demanded.

"Bells have great power. They banish evil spirits." The Wyrding-woman held his eyes. "There are many forces at work for good and evil. Perhaps you should look into your soul and ask why your only son's speech suffers. You say the words of devotion, but is your heart truly open to the Wyrding-mother? Here…" She dug into the deep pockets of her leather apron and pulled out a strip of leather. "I'll help you find your way back to the Wyrding-mother." Her gnarled fingers wove the ends together. "As I form this circle, so your life is formed. You spring from the Wyrding-mother and in the end, you return to the mother. Bend down."

Murtahg leant forward and she slipped the leather circle around his head. It was a tight fit and when he turned away from her to leave he did not look happy.

I noticed the pipe on the mantelpiece. "He forgot his pipe again."

"Leave it for now." She sighed and made her way to the work bench. "Do you think Ciarnor will be cured?"

I nodded.

"Because of the bell?"

"That," I said, "And because he believes he will."

My answer seemed to please her for she smiled and pointed to a small chest. "Fetch me that."

When I returned with it, she opened the lid and took out a fine cloth, unrolling it to reveal a perfect little silver bell, a pure white candle and many fine vellum sheets, sewn together down one side. I recognised the symbols on the front — Male opposed Female, Death opposed Life. I longed to turn over the pages to see how many more I knew.

Reverently, she showed me. "These are the symbols of the Wyrding-ways, my symbols. My candle to bring the light, my bell to banish the dark." Her finger, twisted by the bone-ache, tapped the vellum. "And the knowledge I have gained through my long life." She held my eyes. "All this can be yours, Sun-fire, if you will swear fealty to my clan. I will not live forever and we need a strong Wyrding-woman."

She meant it. I had won her over, but now that it had happened I realised she had won me, too. I wanted this so badly...

All I had to do was swear loyalty to the clan that had ravaged my valley, torn me from my home and used me as a vessel for their Warlord-reborn. We hill-people never surrendered.

Yet, I wavered.

One part of me argued that I could stay with her long enough to serve out the remaining years of my apprenticeship. Once I knew the Wyrding-ways I could go home to my valley. I imagined their joy when I returned as a fully fledged Wyrding-woman, versed in the deep, secret Lore.

But that was to forget the babe. It did not seem real yet. It had not shrivelled and died as many babes do in the first three moons, so the Wyrding-mother meant me to carry it to term. I was convinced that my child would be the daughter I longed for. But I did not want the Warlord's cruel soul twisting her nature. Before the birth I had to find out how to banish the Warlord's soul to save my little girl, and I had to reclaim my Wyrding-sign.

But for now...

I fell to my knees and spoke the words before they could choke me. Revenge was more important than being forsworn. "I swear clan fealty, Wyrding-mother."

She gave me frankly sceptical look.

"I do," I insisted. "For as long as it takes to learn the Wyrding-ways. Then I want to go home."

This must have satisfied her for that evening she left me alone in her private chamber for the first time. Feverish with haste I removed the foxglove jar from its shelf and took just enough to kill three men. Then I froze, waiting for the Watcher to sound. Nothing. That was odd. I realised her Watcher had a flaw; I had not removed the poison from the Wyrding-woman's chamber.

And now I had the means to exact my revenge. When I was ready, I would slip the foxglove into the brothers' stew. They would die and I would run away. It meant giving up the training the Wyrding-woman had promised me. Could I give it up for revenge? I examined this and decided I could. There were other Wyrding-women, ones who did not use death-power.

Besides, Murtahg and Lohnan deserved to die. I enjoyed imagining their death throes. As for Druaric...

Pain curled its hand around my heart with surprising intensity. Even though he had betrayed my trust, I could not bear to kill him. And I could not kill two, without killing the third and running away. Their deaths would be suspicious. Their wives would point to me.

Stunned, I put the foxglove back. How the Wyrding-woman would laugh if only she knew.

I had trapped myself.

∞¥∞Ω∞¥∞

The fourth moon of my captivity passed and the grain hung heavy in the fields. With the harvest came the farmers from the rich pasturelands, bringing a portion of their crops to their clan-leader as tribute. For several days there were reunions. And in the evening there was dancing, smoking of weed, singing and noisy couplings. But the revelry held a frantic tone for, come the feast, the clan's new leader would be elected.

Murtahg talked forcefully and loudly of what he would do if he led the clan. His men wove through the groups, urging his case. Lohnan's men spoke up, just as eager for him to take the lead. The supporters of the two eldest sons were itching for a fight. The

Wyrding-woman had been right to try to forestall this.

I caught only glimpses of Druaric going about his business. And I refused to ask after him. First he had betrayed me then, as soon as he had what he wanted, he ignored me. I hated him, yet I could not bring myself to kill him. It was strange.

As the days counted down to the harvest feast, I watched the stronghold fill with clansmen and women. There was still time for me to slip away, time to retreat to the highlands and reach my village before the snows cut off the passes. But I knew, even though these festivities would have made it easier to escape, I wasn't going. I was weak. I had been seduced by the Wyrding-woman's promise of knowledge and by a sweet-voiced cripple who had betrayed my trust.

As yet there was no sign of the babe. My body was slim, though my breasts felt swollen and tender. This pleased the Wyrding-woman; it meant the babe flourished.

Then one day, as I labelled jars with Wyrding symbols, I felt a flutter in my belly. Like the wings of a humming bird, something barely brushed my senses. My babe had quickened. In that moment the child became real to me and my life narrowed down to a tunnel. At the tunnel's end was the agony of childbirth. Either I would die, or I would produce the Warlord-reborn in my daughter's body.

In that heartbeat I knew I could not be the clan's tool.

Tonight I would hit the old woman over the head, take the amulet and run. As for my revenge... It was clear now that I did not need to kill the three brothers. By leaving I would bring down the clan down. Without the Warlord-reborn, Lohnan and Murtahg's followers would tear it apart. This was a much better revenge. And it meant I did not have to raise my hand against Druaric.

A wave of relief washed through me. Tonight I would act.

"What is it?" the Wyrding-woman asked, sharp as always.

"Nothing," I lied, replacing the jar of lavender. "I gulped breakfast and now I'm paying for it."

"I can give you something for that." She mixed up some gripe medicine and I dutifully swallowed it, pathetically grateful for her thoughtfulness. I had to go without delay.

That evening Druaric came to the Wyrding-woman's chamber for the first time since he had betrayed the existence of my caul. My heart quickened for there was laughter in his eyes, and he could not keep the smile from his lips as he offered me something wrapped in a blanket.

I folded my arms. "I want nothing from you."

"Oh, take it," the Wyrding-woman muttered. "He's spent every night since the last raid making it."

Curiosity got the better of me. I took the object thinking it was light for its size and unrolled the blanket. My mouth dropped open.

He had made a zither, every bit as fine as his. The craftsmanship alone was enough to make me weep.

"Am I forgiven, Sun-fire?" he asked.

I wanted to refuse him but the words would not come.

"Here." He unslung his instrument and sat down, resting it across his lap. "Like this." And his fingers produced a bird song.

I did not want to accept his gift for it meant I condoned his betrayal. At that moment, I looked up into Druaric's eyes and saw his naked soul. My heart turned over. He loved me and I meant to leave tonight.

"What's wrong, Sun-fire?" the Wyrding-woman asked.

"No one has ever given me such a fine gift." I blinked away tears, letting her think I cried with joy.

Druaric laughed and hugged me. I did not pull away. Knowing I was about to leave, I revelled in the feel of him. The Wyrding-woman nodded, satisfied.

He released me, fingers going to his zither. "Watch, Sun-fire."

Truth be told, I was eager to learn. I joined him and so began the happiest, yet most painful evening of my life. After a while, the Wyrding-woman retreated to her bed in the alcove. As for us, we sat up so late discovering our shared love of the music that the cock crowed before we put out the candle. When I crawled under the bench to sleep on my pallet, I told myself one more day would not matter.

∞¥∞Ω∞¥∞

I slept all that day, missing the fight between Murtahg and Lohnan. The first I knew of it was when I entered the kitchen late in the afternoon in search of food. Instead I found the cook's assistants madly packing salted meat, skins of wine and rolls of cheese. From their chatter I learned Murtahg could have killed Lohnan but he hadn't, he had banished him. The eldest brother, along with his family and followers was sailing with the evening tide to set up a stronghold of their own.

Before he left, Lohnan came to get the Wyrding-woman's blessing. She gave him some of the sacred-hearth fire to seed his own hearth fire, and a shawl she had wrapped him in when he was a baby; these symbolised the luck of the household. When he complained that he did not have a Wyrding-woman of his own, they both glanced to me and I was glad that he could not take me.

With Lohnan gone, I thought the rivalry would settle down. Druaric was only seventeen and he didn't have a loyal core of followers ready to kill at his command. Besides, his place in the stronghold was different from Lohnan's because of his clubfoot and the power he had with words.

After the evening meal, Murtahg came to see the Wyrding-woman. She ordered me to prepare wine. Impatient as always, Murtahg chewed on his pipe stem and paced. Even from across the room I smelt the weed on him, coming through his skin as well as his breath.

Druaric sat in his usual place by the fire, plucking at the strings of his zither. He was composing another verse of their family saga, incorporating the new events. I heard snatches of it as I prepared the mulled wine.

The Wyrding-woman, worn down by her grandsons' feuding, had been bothered by the bone-ache so I added a little powdered snakeskin to ease her pain. As I did this, I realised I didn't want to hit her over the head. She was a hard woman because only a hard woman could control these headstrong men.

Like Druaric, she had slipped past my guard. I might not agree with her use of death-power but I liked and respected her as a practitioner of the Way. My head spun. The vengeance of the hill-people had motivated me since the day the brothers stole me from my people. Without it, I felt rudderless. I had needed it to make me strong.

Murtahg took his wine without a word of thanks, putting the pipe on the mantelpiece. "Now I learn that Lohnan took the metal-worker's best apprentice. I should—"

"Let it go. Let him go," the Wyrding-woman urged. "Your task is to care-take the clan for the Warlord-reborn."

Murtahg nodded but, from the look in his eyes, I knew he saw only the near future. It would take twenty years for the Warlord-reborn to grow up, and there wasn't much chance of Murtahg still being around then. Even if he was, he would be an old man of nearly fifty summers.

He grimaced and spat into the fire. "They whisper behind my back."

"Call the clan together tomorrow," the Wyrding-woman advised. "Give them stability and you will have their loyalty."

He nodded, draining the last of the wine. But, as he left, I noticed him glance at Druaric who was singing under his breath. With a sick lurch I realised Murtahg feared Druaric. I met the Wyrding-woman's eyes. She had seen it too and now she stared into the fire, troubled.

Druaric stood up and stretched. "I'm for bed."

I wanted to clutch his arm and warn him. But he wasn't mine to protect. No formal words had passed between us. I could claim him if I wanted to, for Wyrding-women take their lovers where they choose. But I hadn't lain with him last night because I meant to leave tonight.

Could I leave, after the way Murtahg had looked at him?

"Watch your back, Dru," the Wyrding-woman warned.

He shrugged this off with a smile. "I'm no threat to Murtahg."

She frowned as he limped off to his room above ours. Unlike the other unmarried youths he did not sleep in the great hall. The stronghold was packed tonight. Only the Wyrding-woman and Druaric had private chambers in the tower.

"Sun-fire, fetch me Murtahg's pipe," she ordered and I realised he had forgotten it again. She did not take it from my outstretched hand. Instead, she looked up at me, dread in her eyes. "What does it tell you?"

I knew what she feared. The same feeling closed in on me. It was an effort to clear my mind and then I wished I hadn't. Murtahg's hateful, hard-edged impulses filled me, circling like wolves around a new born lamb. One swift bite, tear out the throat, break the neck. "D ... death."

She blanched.

I made to hand her the pipe but she shook her head; for all her talk of scrying, she did not have the Way of seeing that I had. "What will you do?"

She sighed. "I will do nothing until I have slept on it."

I cursed silently for I was hoping she would sleep deeply so that I could take the amulet. All the same, I felt sorry for her as she lay down in her alcove, only to toss and turn. I had to go tonight. Druaric's gift of the zither had convinced me that I could not stay. Not when invisible bonds threatened to make me his willing prisoner. What's more, with Lohnan gone the stronghold felt wrong, somehow.

It was lucky that I had dreamed the day away, for I had no trouble staying awake as I lay there on my pallet under the bench, listening to the stronghold wind down. Soon the revellers were in a stupor of wine, weed and exhaustion and the Wyrding-woman was blessedly quiet at last. This was my chance.

I was about to gather my things when the door creaked open. I recognised Murtahg by the glow of the hearth coals. One hand rested on his sword hilt. It was against clan law to wear a sword inside the stronghold. My mouth went dry with fear, but he crept past my bed where I lay feigning sleep. I wanted to run the moment he entered the Wyrding-woman's alcove. Another part of me wanted to spring up and warn her. I did neither; instead I listened.

"I'm not asleep, Murtahg," she said softly, and I was glad I had not tried to take the amulet. "Why do you come to me wearing your sword?"

"I come to talk sense."

"As you see it."

"No more twisting of words to suit your Wyrding-ways, Grandmother. You are not all powerful. I have eyes in my head. Get rid of Sun-fire before Dru can worm his way into her bed. With her at his side and him the stepfather of the Warlord-reborn, they'll undermine my power. Either you get rid of her or I will get rid of him."

I held my breath, waiting for her to defend me, even though I knew her loyalty had to be to her clan.

At last she let out a long sigh. "Much can go wrong while birthing. Druaric won't suspect a thing if she bleeds to death after delivering the child."

My heart turned to stone in my chest.

"Very well. But I will be watching. There are going to be changes, Grandmother."

He had called her 'Grandmother' again, denying her authority as the voice of the Wyrding-mother. Murtahg strode out of the chamber. I lay utterly still even after the closing door cut off the thud of his boots

In truth I was so stunned and frightened, I could not move. It was just as well because the Wyrding-woman came out with a candle.

I felt her observe me closely, but managed to keep my breathing steady. I must have been convincing because she muttered to herself as she opened a familiar jar. Only two days earlier she had had me crush hymlic then strain the pulp through cloth to produce this clear liquid containing concentrated poison.

Now she wept as she dipped the mouth piece of Murtahg's pipe in the jar. Tomorrow morning she would send a servant to return it. Soon after Murtahg placed the pipe on his tongue, his heart would falter to a stop. She did this not for me, but for the Wyrding-mother; her Ways had to be respected.

Replacing the pipe, the Wyrding-woman returned to her chamber. A soft keening arose as she wept her heart out. But I had her measure now. Her tears were for her failed plans. I was only a means to an end.

Cold within and cold without, I listened for her weeping to cease as she finally fell asleep.

Now, to take the amulet.

I crept into her alcove. It smelt of old woman and tired emotion. I knelt by her bed. The amulet had slipped out of her vest to rest on her shoulder. I lifted the leather strip that threaded through the loop and slit it with a soft snick of my knife, setting myself free. It was that easy.

Why had I waited so long?

I returned to the outer room and knelt by the glowing coals to take the amulet apart, removing its contents. The caul I tucked inside my bodice next to my skin. So soft and fine. So good to reclaim what was mine.

The rest of the contents, I studied. Salt, the purifier, was easy to recognise, as was the chip of iron, the protector, from a sky rock. But it was the circle of red thread that made my heart soar in triumph. This was thread from my hill clothes, woven into the circle to mirror the circle the Warlord's soul would make when it left his body and took root in my babe.

To be sure of my freedom I burned everything but the circle of red thread. I did not want to extinguish my child's life.

When in doubt fire is an excellent cleanser. However, it also concentrates power so I gathered the ashes and the hot sky rock from the little brazier used to prepare ingredients, meaning to throw them in the sea. Since water opposed fire I believed this would be enough to negate the Wyrding-woman's power.

Next, to deal with the red thread circle. It had been created to bind a body and soul, so I put the thread between my teeth and gnawed through it, breaking the Warlord's journey and reclaiming my daughter. Now the growing babe was all mine, for any child produced by a Wyrding-woman belonged to her.

"What are you doing?" the Wyrding-woman demanded.

I spun around to find her by the hearth. She lit a candle so she could see me clearly. Too late to dissemble, I displayed the broken thread then swallowed it to protect my child.

Her hand went to the amulet only to find it gone. Her eyes narrowed and I felt the power of her ancient will.

I was not ready for this confrontation.

Murtahg flung the door open and stalked in, eyes glazed with the weed, carrying his naked sword. Clearly, he had thought things over and he did not trust the Wyrding-woman's word.

The Wyrding-woman tried to bluster. "What are you doing here, Murtahg?

He did not answer, striding towards her.

Wyrding power lay in subtle threats, prepared treatments and manipulation of people, not in force. Still, she drew herself up to her full height. "Murtahg, I helped bring you into this world. Listen to—"

But he was not going to let her wear his will away with the weave of her words. He drew his sword arm back. She tried to dart past him. He caught her by the hair and ran her through. I saw the disbelief on her face as he let her drop.

He did not even wait for her to die, but turned on me. I backed up, arms lifting uselessly. Sweet Mother, why hadn't I run when I had the chance? Why hadn't I warned Druaric and run away with him?

"Come here, Sun-fire."

I couldn't move.

"Don't be afraid. I'm not going to hurt you."

I shook my head.

With a curse he caught my arm and jerked me towards him so that when I recovered my balance the bloody sword tip rested under my chin.

"The clan needs its Warlord-reborn and it needs a Wyrding-woman. But there are other Wyrding-women, Sun-fire. Cross me and I'll tell the clan you threw yourself off the tower. Do you understand?"

I swallowed and nodded numbly.

He let the sword tip drop then made to leave.

"Wait." I pointed to the mantelpiece. "You left your pipe."

He smiled and grabbed the pipe, tucking it in his pocket. "You learn quickly, Sun-fire."

Yes, I did.

The moment he was gone I peeped out the door after him. He headed down towards the wing he shared with his family and supporters. I ran in the other direction, up the steps to Druaric's room on the floor above.

I threw open the door to see him kneeling by the fire, singing intently. "Come quick!"

He put the zither aside slowly, as if dazed, though he never smoked the weed. Stiffly, he came to his feet.

"Hurry, Murtahg's after you!"

Too late. Booted feet ran up the stairs, blocking our escape. Mouth dry, I backed away as Murtahg and four men filled the doorway.

"So," Murtahg muttered finding me with Druaric. "This is your idea of loyalty, Sun-fire."

"Don't speak of loyalty," I countered, pointing to his bloodied sword. "Not when you killed the clan's Wyrding-woman!"

"Brother, how could you?" Druaric whispered, shocked.

Murtahg's followers shifted uneasily, drawing away from him.

"Why...?" one of them whispered.

"She was going to set these two up as clan-leaders," Murtahg said. Then, certain his own men would never turn on him, he took out his pipe, to chew on its stem.

How long would the poison take?

"Why weren't you born a girl, Dru?" Murtahg taunted. "Then I could have used you."

"You will not use either of us," I told him, stepping in front of Druaric. "The Wyrding-mother will not stand by and let the murderer of one of her servants go unpunished."

"The Wyrding-mother did not stop me." Murtahg grinned. "And I don't see her saving you." He nodded to his men. "Kill the hill-brat and the cripple."

His followers hesitated.

I pointed to Murtahg. "Wyrding-mother take this man. Make his heart race. Make his breath tight in his chest." As I described the symptoms of the poison, I saw evidence of its effect on him. His eyes widened in horror. "Make his fingers grow numb. Make his legs tingle. Make his heart falter." He dropped to his knees, hands going to his throat. The pipe fell to the floor. It had done its job.

I heard Druaric gasp behind me.

Murtahg's followers stared as he fought for breath; once … twice, then he pitched forward, face down on the floor.

I looked up at the remaining four men. "Put away your swords and the Wyrding-mother will not strike you down."

They hurried to obey.

I nodded to Murtahg. "In life he served the clan well. Let us honour him in death. Prepare him for death's realm."

This was familiar to them and two took his legs, while another took his shoulders. They shuffled towards the door. There they hesitated, looking back at us, unsure of me.

"Do not fear, the Wyrding-mother will forgive her children," I told them.

As soon as the door closed I threw the pipe in the grate and stirred up the fire, then turned to face Druaric. Did he fear me, too?

Graceful despite his clubfoot, he sat and took up his zither again.

"There's no time for this."

"Hush, Sun-fire," he said. "I must sing the way it will be. The greatest danger is panic, clansmen turning on each other to avenge old insults, tearing our clan apart, killing our people."

His people were not my people, but I listened as he sang of how we became leaders of the clan. He'd been singing like this when I came in to warn him. My skin went cold.

Truly, Murtahg had been right to fear him. How much more had he sung into being, here in the privacy of his chamber?

I heard the name he used for me and his words claimed me. I saw a vision of us leading the clan into a glorious future, safe from raiders and secure from want while I served the Wyrding-mother. Joy filled me, for she had never deserted me. This was meant to be…

Yet, at the same time, I knew my feelings were a product of his cleverly woven words. With great effort I sloughed off the effect of his power.

He smiled and stood, slinging the zither over his shoulder. "Come, we must reassure the clan, Sun-fire."

I was immune to his song. Could he tell?

"What is it? What's wrong?"

I read loving concern in his face. This much was not a lie. He opened his arms to me. It would be so easy to go with the song's seductive refrain, still echoing in my heart and body.

But I could not live as a slave, not even Druaric's. I took a step back. "You sang my love for you into being."

His eyes widened and I saw fear flicker in their ice-blue depths. "I sang to lure you. But only you can give your heart."

"I am the Wyrding-mother's servant. I serve no man. Murtahg was a monster but you ... you sang him into—"

"No. I tried to sing him down but his soul was without music." Druaric licked dry lips. "Didn't you hear my words when you came in?"

I'd been focussed on warning him.

He put the zither aside. "Truly, Sun-fire, if you can see the weave of my song then I have no power over you." He swallowed. "The clan needs us. If we don't unite our people the other clans will turn on us, loot our stronghold, kill the men and take the women and children for slaves."

"It is no more than you have done to other clans, to my hill-people."

"Put aside your need for revenge," Druaric whispered. "It's a kind of poison. Look into your heart and tell me what you find."

Boots clattered on the steps as the warriors returned but still I hesitated. I could leave right now with my child.

"I am a cripple," Druaric said. "They won't follow me unless you are at my side."

It was true. To see the clan crushed and its people scattered would be sweet indeed but...

"Would you condemn the clan's children to slavery, Sun-fire? Little Ciarnor is innocent of his father's crimes."

The door swung open and I stepped across to join Druaric.

∞¥∞Ω∞¥∞

WINTER'S HEART
FAITH MUDGE

I'd come for a reason, although that was easy to forget now I was actually here.

The walls towered over my head, red brick pocked with last century's unsuccessful cannonfire and entangled in a web of lush summer-green vines. I smelled damp earth from the night's rain and sulphuric residue, like the dust of fireworks. Arched windows, some shuttered and some open, peered between strands of ivy and climbing rose. I saw a black sleeve trailing across a jutting sill and couldn't help wondering, a little pointlessly, if it belonged to him.

The sleeve disappeared. I reached up to knock at the brass-studded ebony doors, a good two feet taller at their peak than I was myself, and flinched back reflexively when one swung inward at my touch. For the residence of a man in such demand, it didn't seem very well protected. Perhaps reputation was guard dog enough. I drew up my skirts to step over the threshold, as though the thick dust on the other side of the doorstep might be impetus enough to ignite them. For all I knew, it might.

Suits of armour lined the musty hallway on both sides. Spikes jutted from their strangely shaped spines; the elongated helmets gaped jaws that did not look designed for a human head. Pushing through the unlocked doors at the other end of the hall, I found myself in an enormous circular chamber where diagonal stairways cut a wide wooden X between floor and ceiling. Light filtered from windows so high up I had to tilt my head back as far as it would go just to ascertain their existence. Green vines poured through their arched mouths to claim the inside of the fortress as they had done the outer walls.

There was no one in sight and nothing for me to do but choose a stair. Bearing in mind the telltale sleeve I had seen, I chose to go right. My footsteps echoed in the great empty chamber; when I laid my hand on the bannister, it came away grey with dust. If what I saw and felt was an enchantment only, the illusion of abandonment, I was in skilled hands indeed.

The upper gallery was at least inhabited, if the teetering stacks of cobwebbed books obscuring the walls and their civilisation of spiders could be counted as such. Here and there a door was visible enough to be opened, and none were locked, but neither were the rooms beyond occupied. The light filtering through their diamond-paned, dust-coated windows was waning from afternoon into evening when at last I found the owner of the black sleeve upon which I had placed such faith. I knew the moment I saw him that he was not who I had come to find.

For one thing, he was aged in his fifties at the oldest and therefore far too young. For another, he seemed to have been as oblivious to my presence as I had been to his. When I opened his door he jerked around in astonishment, dropping the slender blue-bound volume he had been reading. He dived immediately to retrieve it before straightening to look at me.

"How long have you been there?" he asked, brushing off the book and laying it down on the nearest lectern. There were at least five of these scattered about the room, some displaying open books, others piled up with loose maps and sketches. It was a scene of total disarray, not power at all. The man himself was tall and gangling, his bald skull ringed with woolly brown curls, his eyes a milky, mildly inquisitive blue. His black robe was too large for his thin frame and streaked with dusty handprints.

"I arrived an hour or more ago," I said. There was a broad brocade chair heaped with more of the sorcerer's interminable supply of books close at hand; I shifted the pile onto the floor and replaced them with myself, too tired to care about the inevitable cloud of dust. "Is the sorcerer Forsythian in residence? I have business with him."

"Oh," said the black-robed man. "I thought you might be a student. They turn up every so often, you know, though it is terribly easy to miss them. Sometimes months go by before I realise they're here at all, but when we meet I do try to help. It's such an effort to get this far, and I have been here the longest, after all."

I frowned, sure I had misunderstood. "You are a student yourself?"

"I didn't think so," he said, "until I came here. I intended to challenge Forsythian to a sorcerer's duel — very melodramatic, I know — but when I arrived he was nowhere to be found. I stopped looking eventually and started reading instead. I've been here ever since."

"And how long has that been?"

"Around twenty years, I should think," he said brightly. "Oh, forgive me, I haven't introduced myself. My name is Alabast Tern." He held out a bony-knuckled hand. Ensconced in the surprisingly comfortable chair, I accepted it briefly.

"You may call me Meriel," I said. It was the first time I had spoken my name aloud since I was married and it sounded a little strange, exposed to the open air. "But you must have seen Forsythian since you came? He can't be dead."

It was a singularly stupid thing to say, since at any time any one can be dead. Just because the sorcerer had not lived long enough to answer my request did not mean he had to be alive. To my relief, however, Alabast was nodding.

"Eventually, yes, I did," he said. "In this very room, as it happens. I was reading a book of Galadean poetry aloud and stopped halfway through a rather fine ballad to tend the fire. When I returned for my book, he was there. He didn't like the way I was reciting and insisted on doing the rest of the ballad himself."

The man seemed inclined to wander from the point at hand. I tried to usher him back to the line of questioning I really wanted answered. "Where is he now?"

Alabast looked around vaguely, as though expecting to find the sorcerer folded up somewhere on a shelf. "I haven't the faintest idea," he said. "How long has it been, then? I'm afraid I lose track of time quite often. I'm sure he was here in the summer."

"It's summer now," I said patiently. I was glad I had elected to sit. It felt as though I might be asking questions for some time. "Do you think Forsythian is here?"

"Oh, bound to be, bound to be," Alabast assured me. He took up the little blue book he had been reading when I had interrupted him and thumbed through the gilt-edged pages for his place. "He never leaves the fortress, that I know of. He'll turn up when he wants to talk to you."

My right hand rested against the slight swelling of my stomach. I could feel the hollow inside my chest where fear should have been. "How long will that take?" I demanded. "I need to speak with him now."

"I'm sorry," Alabast said. He looked at me over the top of his book and smiled a little ruefully. "If he wants to see you, you will see him. If he doesn't want to see you, you never will. You're welcome to stay as long as you like, of course."

∞¥∞Ω∞¥∞

I was there for the rest of the summer, and the autumn as well. It seemed Forsythian did not intend to see me, but I would not leave without seeing him. I had not come this far to go away again empty-handed.

Not all of the house was so dramatically unkempt as what I saw on that first day. As Alabast had said, there were other students here and there, if that they could be called, considering most had barely even seen the man they called master. I saw a young woman in jester's cast-offs scratching obscure runes in chalk on a courtyard floor, a silent matron with iron grey hair sitting frozen in a garden of broken statues, a boy no older than thirteen or fourteen juggling apples among the chimney stacks of an unreachable rooftop. Alabast was generally squirreled away somewhere with a book, but after half a year in the sorcerer's house I had seen nothing to indicate Forsythian himself even existed. He seemed more like a shared delusion than a real person.

And still I stayed. I had, in all truth, nowhere else left to go.

I ate in the kitchens, which I privately thought of as the dungeons, where there was never light but always something moderately edible, and slept in a room where there was a moth-eaten settee that did me well enough for a bed. The rest of each day I spent in a restless circuit of the house and its four enclosed courtyards in the increasingly remote hope that I might stumble upon Forsythian's hiding place. Why he would endure this charade if he were here, I couldn't imagine — if he could not or would not assist me, why not simply appear and send me on my way? It was his house, wasn't it? But wizards of every sort are bizarre creatures, I knew that already, and the stories of Forsythian painted him as stranger than most.

The symptoms of pregnancy progressed at the usual rate. I swelled like a waxing moon to an utterly impractical shape. The baby kicked restlessly inside my body and I tried to imagine holding it, like I half-remembered my mother holding me, but I couldn't. Imagination had never been my gift, least of all then.

I gave birth on the first day of winter, in a thankfully short labour, alone in my chamber. I could, I suppose, have called for help, but no one in this place could give me the help I really needed. Pain I could manage alone. I had endured worse for less reason.

The baby was a boy.

"Goodness," Alabast exclaimed when he saw me with my son for the first time, several days later. He leaned over the infant in my arms, fluttering his hands nervously in what I assumed was a congratulatory gesture. "When did this one arrive? Is he yours?" A suddenly hunted look crossed his face. "He's not Forsythian's?"

"I shouldn't think so," I said coldly, "given that I have never met the man."

Alabast petted the baby on the head like a puppy. "I see," he said penitently. "I did hope he might be accommodating for you, but I suppose he might not have noticed you're here. He does get distracted. You'll simply have to be patient."

"I don't have twenty years to spare, Master Tern."

"No, no, my dear, I only had to wait two. The rest were my own decision."

I made a kind of nest in my room from ancient blankets, thoroughly washed, and a moth-eaten green velvet skirt I'd found in amongst the mountains of books. While my son slept there I would sit on my makeshift bed and watch him. My fears had been well founded. I had seen mothers with their children, seen the adoring light in their exhausted eyes — even the fortress's cat, a stately white creature of indeterminate age, doted on her litters of kittens while they were small enough to need her. When I looked at my baby I felt nothing, nothing at all. I fed him and washed him out of duty. I knew I should care. I tried to will the love from my empty chest, but it would not come.

By the end of the first month of winter, I had come to the conclusion that I would never see the sorcerer. It was time to formulate a different solution. Leaving my son asleep in his nest of blankets, I went out into the nearest courtyard where a leafless apple tree was surrounded by a round wooden bench. Snow dusted my hair as I sat there, my cloak drawn close around my shoulders, my hands encased in soft grey gloves, the chill nevertheless sinking slowly through to my skin. I didn't mind the winter weather. Nothing in the world could be colder than me.

I was a wealthy woman. I could give my son a comfortable life, a luxurious home and good education. By my standards, that was all anyone could ask, but I couldn't give him love. Would that make the rest redundant? Would he be better off with some other woman who would treat him as a gift from the heavens, while all I could do was look at him nonplussed, unable to see the charm?

"Your baby is crying."

The voice came from behind me and I turned automatically to respond. There was no one there. Neither was the voice familiar, although it was entirely possible that another 'student' had arrived at some point and vanished into the depths of the house without my meeting him. I stood, brushing snow from my wine-dark skirts and neatly knotted hair.

"No, it's all right," the voice said. "Alabast has gone to him."

I twisted quickly back around. The words had seemed to come from directly behind me, at my shoulder almost, and still I could see no one. There was not enough snow on the ground to show footprints, but even so I was sure I would have heard something if someone had come so close.

"Who are you?" I said sharply. "Kindly show yourself."

"I'm not known for my kindness," said the voice. It was low-pitched and dry, with the trace of an unfamiliar accent. "Nor are you, I gather, your Majesty."

My hands fisted in my skirts. "*Show yourself.*"

"No," he said mildly. "You are very persistent, I will admit, but I don't think I trust you. What is it you want from me? And don't," he added, "please don't pretend you want nothing more than to see me. You can't imagine how tired I am of people pretending they've come just to see if I exist. No one comes to my house without reason. Usually something mercenary. Bags of gold that never empty, swords that never rust, things of that like."

"Forsythian," I whispered.

He gave a humourless laugh. "Who were you expecting?"

I sank back onto the bench and fixed my eyes on a gargoyle overlooking the courtyard. If I had to talk, I would at least address myself to something I could see. It felt too ridiculous just staring blindly into space and hoping.

"I do want something from you," I said. "I — years ago, I lost something very valuable. I need it back."

"What might this thing be?" he asked disinterestedly. His voice sounded further away, as though he were already leaving.

I rested my cold-gloved fingers against my chest. "My heart," I said simply.

There was a sigh. "To whom? If it's unrequited love that ails you, queen, try smiling at him. With a face like yours it shouldn't be difficult to win who you want."

"You don't understand," I said. "I don't love anyone. *I have no heart.*"

Cold fingers pulled my chin suddenly sideways. I had the disorienting experience of staring into eyes I couldn't see. "What," said Forsythian, very quietly, "did you do?"

"I loved what I couldn't have," I said. "You think I am beautiful, sorcerer? Well, my father did too. Of all his jewels and possessions, he was proudest of me. When I was grown, he had me betrothed to a king with whom he had long desired allegiance. I didn't want to marry that man. Never mind why. Brides are good currency in this part of the world and the wedding was arranged regardless. What I wanted could never be mine. Knowing that, I resolved not to want anything. Don't judge me, sorcerer. I am not the first to make such a choice.

"There was a wizard within a day's ride of my father's castle — a necromancer, the courtiers used to call him. I went to him for help. Even he balked at what I asked, but as you say, I am persistent. I wore him down with pleading and promises. He agreed eventually. He took my heart from my chest, my broken bloody heart. He locked it away in a box within a box and hid it for me where no one else would ever find it.

"I was married the next day. The king took me like the trophy I was. We were married for five years before he died.

"You think I killed him, don't you? I didn't. Murder is a crime of passion and I had no passion left without my heart. He knew I didn't love him; he was afraid of me, I think. Most people are when they come to know me. His heart failed him in the end. Hearts do. It was only after he was gone I found that I was pregnant."

The snow had stopped. It was colder than ever.

"I do not love my child," I said, "and I should. I remember enough of who I used to be to know that. I need my heart back."

"Then ask your wizard."

"He died. People around me are prone to it."

"So when you say you have lost your heart," Forsythian said, "what you mean is ... you can't find it."

"I never thought I would need it again."

"You were wrong," said the sorcerer.

"Can you find it?" I asked. "I can pay you. I have gold, jewels—"

"I don't do things for gold," Forsythian said, as though the very idea of it offended him. "I do them because they are interesting enough to make the doing worth my while."

"Am I sufficiently interesting?"

He was silent for a long time. I had no way of knowing whether he was still there, but I remained, drawing on six months of patience. I had not waited so long to abandon my request now.

"You want to love your son," he said at last. "What if you can't?"

"With my heart—"

"Women with hearts that have never left their chests don't always love what's theirs. Perhaps you can't care about him now, but neither will you grow angry with him, or resentful. Hearts are dangerous. You knew that. What might you do with yours?" Forsythian's tone was cool, dispassionate. Heartless. "I could make you a new heart, I suppose. It is a thing I have done once before. But I can't say what that heart might make you desire once it was pressed into your chest. It might worship your son. It might loathe him. Which risk would you choose?"

I had not anticipated a choice. "I don't know."

"Think on it," he said, and I knew that he was gone. The courtyard felt suddenly empty, when before it had been occupied. I stood stiffly, my legs numb from the cold, and went inside to find my son dandled in Alabast's arms, balanced on a pile of leather-bound tomes. The sorcerer's student looked up at my face with a crooked smile.

"You've met him, then," he guessed. "Could he tell you what you wanted?"

"No." I sat in the chair beside them and held my frozen hands to the fire. "Or if he could, he wouldn't."

"Don't fret," Alabast said, petting my shoulder awkwardly. It was the first time he had tried to touch me and the gesture was in itself a surprise — people were wary of me as a rule, though they didn't know why. "He knows you're here. He might change his mind."

"I think," I said, so softly he did not hear me, "he wants me to change mine."

∞¥∞Ω∞¥∞

It was Alabast who named my son.

Winter had unexpected effects — there were few fireplaces in the rambling fortress, so on cold nights everyone was likely to congregate where there was a good blaze. The night after my unsuccessful interview with the sorcerer, the motley assortment of his house guests assembled in the study Alabast had claimed as his own for an impromptu supper. The girl in jester's clothing appeared first, her hair a riot of red streaked darker here and there where it had been dampened with snow. She introduced herself as Cianda and folded her long limbs on the hearth, toasting pieces of cheese impaled on a silver letter opener. I left to feed and change the baby, and when I returned the stony matron was in a shadowy corner near the fireplace. She was so difficult to see that she might have been there all along and I would not have known. The boy arrived last, lugging a wicker basket of stale bread, which the jester girl toasted over the fire with the cheese.

No one was inclined to be talkative, but the atmosphere was quite convivial all the same. The boy perched on a low bookcase, cracking walnuts; Alabast read aloud a little poetry from his book of the moment and Cianda came to play with the baby, leaning her elbows against the back of my chair to dangle a beaded charm just out of his reach.

"What's his name?" she asked, without looking at me.

"I haven't named him yet," I said. It was an obvious thing to overlook, I suppose, but it hadn't seemed obvious before that moment. It was strange enough to draw even Alabast's attention from the spiky foreign script he had been reading.

"Are you waiting for a proper ceremony?" he enquired. "The bathing in wine and cedar water, the lighting of the nine candles? I didn't think anyone did that these days."

"I had not decided on a name."

Alabast nodded approvingly. "Ah, it's a serious business. I am a traditionalist, myself, I like the old names. What is your husband?"

"Dead," I said briefly, before realising what he meant. "His name was Joram, but I don't want my son named after him."

"Sage is a nice name," Cianda said, and flushed when I looked at her.

"Onyx," said the walnut-cracking boy from his eyrie. "His eyes are so dark."

"Calabry," suggested Alabast. "Farrant, perhaps. Or Torren."

"What does that mean?" I asked. "The last one."

"It means 'white bough'. No particular relevance there, I will admit."

"I like it," I said. "That is all the meaning it needs to have."

Cianda lifted the baby from my arms. Kneeling beside the fire, she laid him down on the warm hearthstones. She took a discarded walnut shell and laid it hollow side up on his forehead, like a small boat, into which she dropped a crumb of bread and a corner of yellowed paper. We watched her without speaking, sensing ritual even though we didn't understand what it meant. Torren flailed irritably and Cianda took the walnut boat away, floating it in a shallow bowl of ink. Flames were reflected in the dark liquid, fleetingly bright. For a long moment Cianda kneeled, watching the reflections dance, then she sighed and rocked back on her heels.

"He's too young," she said, obscurely.

"A seer," Alabast whispered to me. "She sees the future in reflections."

This entire evening had felt dreamlike, unreal, with me playing along as a woman who celebrated her baby like she should. Watching Cianda, however, I was gripped with a sudden conviction. It was not alarm. I could not feel anything so strong. All I knew was that if I looked into that ink, I would see my reflection. My shadow over Torren's boat.

∞¥∞Ω∞¥∞

"You decided, then."

I had been looking for the sorcerer all day, prowling along galleries and stairways, always circling back to the courtyard where

I had heard his voice in the hope he might once again be there. He was not. By evening I had given up and returned inside to the empty study, rocking the fretful baby mechanically while I stared into the embers. At the sound of Forsythian's voice, I half turned before remembering it was no use and made myself look back at the fire.

"Yes," I said.

"He's quite pretty, your son." Something soft brushed across my cheek and Torren suddenly stopped crying, staring wide-eyed into space. He snatched at something I couldn't see and the sorcerer laughed softly. "I'd forgotten how peculiar babies are."

"I want to love him," I said quietly. "I try. And all I have is emptiness."

Forsythian sighed. "Very well," he said. "You'd best come with me, then."

I stood quickly, looking around for a clue. "How?" I demanded. "How can I follow you when I don't know where you are?" There was only silence. "Forsythian?" I called. "Are you there?"

In my haste I had unsettled the strata of books around my chair. They tumbled to the ground, sending papers floating through the air like ink-pattered snowflakes, and when one page drifted to the ground it landed on a foot that had not been there before. I looked up.

The sorcerer looked back at me.

I thought at first he wore a feathered cloak. Wizards often do, at least in stories. It was only when he moved, a restless shuffle of his feet, that I realised the fall of feathers down both sides of his body were in fact wings; great dark wings where his arms should have been. His hair was the same black, a wild crown of it that spiked and streaked across his tawny eyes. His chest was bare despite the cold, almost gaunt in its thinness, his legs encased in tattered grey and his feet bootless. He looked feral.

"You can stop staring now," he said.

"You were supposed to be old," I said. It sounded more critical than I had intended, as though he had failed a personal test.

"I am," he said, without inflection, and left the room without waiting to see if I was behind. His wings trailed their feathered tips in the dust, but his bare feet left no prints. I gathered Torren more securely against my chest and followed.

I had spent two and a half seasons in this place, searching its many rooms and passages, but I had never before seen the door Forsythian opened. Had the stacks of books concealed it all this time, or had it simply not been there until the sorcerer wanted it to be? Inside was a short flight of steps into a large tower room, which overlooked the apple tree courtyard from an unlatched window on one side and the forest road on which I had arrived from the other. The arrangement should not have been architecturally possible and bothered me more than it should.

There was a fireplace here, left unlit. It seemed Forsythian did not feel the cold. A long, scarred artisan's workbench was positioned underneath the courtyard window, scattered with open books and unrolled maps, brightly coloured bottles and squat beeswax candles in small glass bowls. In the midst of it all was a large clay dish of ink.

"I will need blood," Forsythian said.

I nodded, laying Torren down on a nearby chair and crossed the feather-scattered floor to the bench. There was an ivory handled lady's hunting knife laid out beside the bowl of ink. "Where do I cut?" I asked practically.

Forsythian's eyebrows might have risen then, although it was difficult to tell beneath his crows-nest of hair. "I'll do it," he said, and raised a wing. Fingers emerged from the feathers like a hand pushed from a sleeve, but the grimace of pain on the sorcerer's face told me it was nowhere near as easy. He snatched the knife from my hand and slit a line at the base of my earlobe. His thin cold fingers thrust my head downward so that the welling blood dripped into the ink, and then it wasn't fingers holding me there, but the awkward pressure of a wing.

"Remember your heart," he whispered in my bleeding ear. "What did you love? What hurt so badly you couldn't bear its weight any longer?"

Logically enough, I started with small things. The tart sweetness of the first apples of the year. Blankets warmed by the fire in my childhood bedroom, scented with sprigs of dried lavender to help me sleep. But small pleasures, I knew instinctively, would not be enough. I remembered my mother's face as she was lain out for her funeral, waxen pale and unapproachably beautiful, as though she had already metamorphosised into her own stone memorial. My first love, clear blue eyes and a teasing smile that would turn as quickly to a scowl or a kiss. It had been I who left him and he'd tried so hard to hide his tears. I remembered the face I had chosen instead, lit gold with lantern light in an autumn night. Seeing it wax pale the day my betrothal to the king was announced and we had looked at one another, desperate to forget, knowing I never would.

My reflection melted in the still ink, ripples of light drifting into a new shape. There was a lake, an island, a stone chest shrouded by five years of encroaching thorns.

The weight on my neck was withdrawn and I staggered stiffly backward.

"Is that where it is?" I asked. Torren was crying behind me. The sound was distracting. I put my thumb in his mouth to quiet him and he sucked the salt from my skin, small teeth biting fretfully. If the sound of his distress had not interfered with my thoughts, I wondered if I would have gone to him at all. It was hard to manage a conscience with only the phantom of remembered emotions to guide me.

Forsythian had his back to me, bending his head so low over the dish that when he looked up his hair dripped black as though his own colours were leaching away. There was ink on his lips and his eyes were half-closed, unfocused. I said his name and he looked at me as if he could not imagine who I was, or why I was there. It was as though he had gone somewhere else, become someone else. I knew I should be afraid then. I backed towards the door and was almost there when I remembered Torren, still swaddled on the chair only a few feet from the empty-eyed wizard, and I knew I should go back. I stopped where I stood in a moment's indecision.

And Forsythian blinked. He recognised me. The moment of danger passed.

"Come on, then," he said, flinging open the window.

I stared. "What do you mean?"

"The lake," he said. "Do you want to find the lake or not?"

"What has that to do with the window?"

In response, he spread his wings. His thin nose narrowed further, hooked, darkened to a wickedly sharp beak. The whites of his tawny eyes were swallowed by predatory yellow. Feathers sprouted from the bare skin of his chest, until I was not looking at a man any more, but a bird — a bird large enough to carry me on its back.

"My son," I began.

The bird tossed its head impatiently. A feather flew into the air and trailed downwards onto Torren's face, into his open mouth. He went instantly limp in my arms, the warm weight of deep sleep. The feather had disintegrated on his tongue like ash. It did not seem hygienic or responsible, and the duty I had built to replace my conscience warned me of the wrongness of what I was about to do. Babies should not be left untended. I should go to Alabast or Cianda, but there was no time.

I laid the sleeping baby between the broad arms of the chair and climbed onto the sorcerer's back.

∞¥∞Ω∞¥∞

I thought I would die on that flight. Somehow, I survived it.

It was still dark when we reached the lake, the grey-edged dark of the hours before dawn. Forsythian alighted on the stone arch of a ruined pavilion, which trembled beneath his weight, and allowed me to climb down before transforming back into a man. For a moment I thought he would stumble off the arch and I spread my arms to catch him. It was not fear for him that motivated me, but the knowledge he was the only way I would ever leave this island. But he did not fall. Regaining his balance, he swung himself down into a crouch on the overgrown ground beneath, and gestured silently.

The stone chest was at the centre of the pavilion. It looked to me like the coffin of a person so unloved their grave had been entirely forgotten, left to the briars and snow.

I looked to Forsythian for instruction. He simply nodded again towards the chest, his assistance apparently at an end. The cold still air sank quickly through my layers of wool and linen, snow and mud darkening the hem of my skirt as I crossed the pavilion. Having left my gloves behind in the hurry to depart, I wrapped my hand in the already soiled cloth to sweep the lid of the chest clear. Thorns bit through the pitiful protection, dripping blood a stark red against grey stone and white snow. I braced my hands against the icy lid and pushed with all my strength.

It slid backward, unresisting, and fell to the ground with an echoing crack of splitting stone. Inside the opened tomb was a box. I remembered very little of my visit to the necromancer, but the box I knew. Small and silver, encrusted with diamonds. It had been a wedding present, of all ironies, given what I had asked him to put inside. I had worn the key to its ornate lock on a ribbon around my neck for more than half a year, in hope. My fingers shook as they lifted it from beneath my bodice, letting the tiny silver key fall into my palm.

I knelt on the frozen ground, barely noticing the cold, and placed the box before me. After all that I had done to be here, I felt now like a puppet, going through the predestined motions of another's decision. The key turned in the lock. Bloodless fingers opened the box and reached inside.

I felt something as light and fragile as a captive bird between my hands. In the dim grey gloom of impending sunrise, it looked like a vast ruby and was almost as cold. I knew then something was wrong, terribly wrong. My hands tightened their hold instinctively. And the heart I held, poor broken thing, crumbled away to dust.

It was as if the puppet's strings had been cut. I fell. Crumpled sideways in the snow, I felt my blood turn stagnant, freezing in my veins. Something dark crossed my vision and I was lifted on soft black wings, my head lolling backwards to stare blankly into the burning sunrise, my mouth open, shaping words I couldn't say. The hollow in my heartless chest widened into a cavern and engulfed me completely.

∞¥∞Ω∞¥∞

Hearts are heavy. They ache and fracture. They fail.

They forget.

Meriel opened her eyes on a moth-eaten settee that was both familiar and unfamiliar, something she had seen in a dream. She wore a white linen chemise that was stained with dry mud; a green woollen dress lay draped over the blankets at her feet and it too was stained with mud, and blood. Her hands lay atop the covers on either side of her body, scratched and sore, but intact.

She watched the winter sunlight pattern the walls as though it might write out what it was she couldn't remember. Her chest ached, a slow throb like a bruise. Then she heard the crying and sat up quickly. In a nest of blankets in the chair beside her was a baby — *her* baby. Without thinking she threw back the covers and stepped out of bed to take Torren into her arms. He grabbed at her loose hair with tiny flailing fingers and Meriel laughed, dropping a kiss onto his downy dark head.

"You're going to drive me mad," she predicted.

Later she put on the green dress and gathered up the few things left scattered about the room that she recognised as her own. Wrapping Torren securely in a shawl, she left the strange, cluttered room in which she'd woken and went through the quiet corridors of the even stranger house. She could not quite remember how she had come to be here and it seemed the best thing she could do was leave. She thought once, as she passed through a canyon of unshelved books, that she saw a hem of black robe disappearing between the stacks, but when she reached the same point she could see no one there and no door through which they might have disappeared.

"Come on, Torren," she said. "Let's go home."

Only she took a wrong turning. The wrong set of steps, a mistake anyone could make. Instead of reaching the road outside, she found herself in a courtyard, where a bare-branched apple tree stretched bony fingers towards the pale winter sky and impossible red apples lay on the paving stones around its roots.

Meriel's heart leapt. She caught her breath and dropped to her knees, clutching Torren against her chest, reaching out to take an apple into her gloved hand.

"It was the best I could do."

She twisted around at the voice, familiar and not familiar, but knew even as she did that she wouldn't see him. "Forsythian," she whispered, remembering.

"Apples and blood," he said. "I've never made a heart so quickly before. I refuse to be held responsible if you find it loving all the wrong things." He paused for a long moment. "Though it seems someone has already found their place in it."

Meriel looked at Torren, small and red-faced and hers. "Yes," she said quietly. "Thank you, Forsythian."

"If you want to leave," he said, "it's the other stair you want."

He didn't say goodbye. Meriel stayed in the courtyard for a few minutes, waiting, then eventually went back inside and found her way to the right passage, where golden-spined suits of armour stared open-mouthed. She let herself out and stood on the top steps, looking at the road. It led away through the forest to towns and castles and people she had once used to love.

She lifted her foot to step down. Her chest contracted painfully.

She looked up and saw black trailing from a window. It might have been a sleeve, or a wing. It didn't matter. Cradling her sleeping son in her arms, Meriel turned around and stepped back through the open doors into the house, her home, where her heart was.

And when the soldiers later came in search of the queen and her son, all they could see where the sorcerer's fortress should have been was an apple tree and a laughing crow.

∞¥∞Ω∞¥∞

SAND AND SEAWATER
JOANNE ANDERTON & RABIA GALE

They're burning dolls in the village again. I smell it as I limp out of the hut, wincing at the ache in my joints. Burning hair, burning cloth, burning feathers. Like the salt in the wind, it has become part of the island's smell.

I've long since ceased to mourn the waste of satin and silk, the destruction of near-invisible lines of small stitches. Hours of my life and the toil of my gnarled hands going up in smoke.

There are a few villagers around but none of them dare to meet my eyes. Shame and fear, spiced with anger, keep their gazes upon their feet or their hands. Don't they remember that I gave them more than four decades of good fortune?

Bitterness clogs my throat. I clench the handle of my basket, full of ointments and healing cordials. They have all forgotten, these islanders, how to make such things. They faint at every cut, scream at every pain, and send their wide-eyed children running for me on the slightest pretext. I spend most of my days shuffling from one hut to the next, soothing imaginary aches and minor complaints.

I point my feet out of the circle of huts. A thin, broken trail leads towards the jungle. It is the long way home but at least it does not pass through the village.

It is hot and dark and stuffy under the canopy. Rustlings and chitterings follow my progress. The path threads between trees, a faint line, barely used. Most of the islanders live close to the sea, cleaved to her bosom. But here, for a little while, I can pretend I am back on the mainland, pretend that the sound of waves on sand is really wind in trees.

I take a vial out of my basket and splatter its contents on the ground, murmuring under my breath; an offering to Mamutsa the Mother, the volcano whose wide shoulders rise above the tree-clothed hills. These days she is full of grumbles, a perpetual haze of smoke and ash veiling her face. Yet another thing that is wrong with the world.

I used to climb her skirts, for a fistful of her dirt for my dolls.

The jungle has grown silent. A furtive quiet fills the air. The back of my neck prickles. I turn on my heel, all around, slowly, searching the multi-hued dimness of the jungle.

Something is watching. I feel its sharp, focussed malice. I step, crunch something under my foot.

I jump, my heart thumping. A small animal scurries across the trail.

A stick. Only a stick and a rodent. I fight to breathe through the painful squeezing of my chest.

Then I notice it. A gleam of light on the side of the trail. I stoop over it. My breath catches again.

A tiny gold button, shaped like a shell. I'd brought a string of those from the mainland. They were not something I could ever get from the traders afterwards.

I'd used the last of them eleven years ago.

The jungle is no longer a friendly place. I hurry down the trail. A rhythmic banging from ahead fills me with relief. An islander, chopping wood.

I burst into the clearing and blink in the sudden sunlight. Kaana, the chieftain's son, sits upon a stump, beating his hand against the trunk of a felled tree.

Bang, bang, bang.

Kaana looks up at me. "Good day, Grandmother," he says with deep-voiced courtesy. His teeth flash whitely in his dark, smooth-skinned face, but his eyes remain empty. His hand keeps up the beat, knocking against the wood so hard that chips rain about him. *Bang, bang, bang.*

Kaana. I made four bad luck dolls for him before he turned seven. But after that fourth doll was pushed out to sea among the rest in the boats that year, I never made more than three for anyone else.

I saw what it did to Kaana. He was never cruel, always polite, but it was all form without feeling. He was fearless, too, recklessly so. When he was ten, he jumped from the northeastern cliffs into the rocks below and staggered out, unscathed. He wandered the jungles alone and at night and came home unharmed. Youths admired him and girls adored him; he tolerated them all, preferring his own company.

Preferring his pursuit of feeling.

"Kaana," I say, trying not to look at his hand, smooth and supple like a pampered high lady's in spite of the way he abused his body. "Have you seen anything ... strange ... around here?"

He stares at me for a long moment, as if trying to figure out what *strange* means. *Bang, bang, bang* goes his hand. Then, "I have not, Grandmother."

"Well…" I look towards the jungle and decide I will walk home through the village after all. "Good day to you, too, Kaana."

As I leave, Kaana lays his forehead against the inoffensive log and begins beating his head against it. It will leave no mark or bruise on his handsome face.

∞¥∞Ω∞¥∞

The doll drags itself onto the shore, heavy and slow with seawater. Its seams are crusted with salt. The small, slimy things that have made their homes in its insides wiggle, distressed, as it dries in the sun.

Home again. Dust calls to dust and somewhere, beyond jungle and paved stones and squat huts, it hears the voice of its child left behind. Louder now, almost clear enough to understand.

Almost close enough to touch.

The doll has no fingers to grip the sand with, so it digs padded stumps into the beach and pulls itself forward. When the ground levels out, it can stand. It's floated for so long, that it can't remember how to walk. It falls often. The westering sun lights the silver in its dress a shining crimson. It lost one emerald-gem eye to a hungry moray, but the remaining glints brightly.

The doll pushes aside the call of its child. It's the hardest thing it's ever had to do. It listens, instead, to its own borrowed heartbeat, the pulse of power that gave life to its threads and beads. Mamutsa. Mother. Older and deeper than the tides, now divided, scattered, and weakened.

The island rumbles beneath its unsteady feet. The doll has felt tremors like this before. Far away and deep beneath the sea, where everything is darkness peppered only by the star-bright bodies of hungry fish. Dropped to the edge of a great fissure by the pernicious currents, boiled and singed by noxious waters, the doll had felt the familiar heartbeat of its mother. It learned, then, that they were all connected, in great lines beneath the earth and the sea, Mamutsa and all her sisters. And the stolen soil inside every doll.

Then terrible tides had snatched it from the fissure's edge and sent it tumbling, riding the peak of wave after devastating wave. The doll witnessed great stretches of land swamped, devoured and spat out again clean of all living things. Ships crushed. Fish poisoned. The work of Mamutsa's furious sisters, their power unbalanced.

Now, the doll struggles through the grass and onto a dirt path. After all its years of drifting, Mamutsa has called it home. It will not fail her.

The village lies in between, a confusion of bright flame and moving figures, but the doll does not hesitate. Smoke drapes a strange scent across it — at once familiar, at once terrible. Cloth, burning. Beads, popping. Sand boiling, hardening, all its magic cast to the cool sea breeze.

The doll pauses, suddenly unsure. Deep shadows fall across its one bright eye, and rough hands grip it, lift it.

"A loose doll." Voices like the scrape of the seabed against its silk. It sees older faces, swirling with night-dark tattoos. "Quick, add it to the fire."

It is jolted within this painful grip, swung and finally thrown. It lands on wood, hard. Beside it lie its brethren. So many dolls of such beautiful colours. Crimson satin, cerulean wool, black and golden damask. They are all bound in tight fishing line, and struggle weakly against it, stunted legs and arms twitching. Countless pairs of shiny-bead eyes glint in panic.

The doll twists as flame licks up from beneath the wood, carrying the smell of many more dolls, all burning. Another shadow, and a log falls, trapping the doll's silver dress. Mamutsa's heart beats for them all, bound together by her soil. But it cannot free them.

∞¥∞Ω∞¥∞

The villagers gather around the bonfire, the adults grim-faced and stone-eyed. Their knuckles are pale around the sticks they clench. Violence, coiled like snakes within them, waits to strike any doll that dares escape the fire.

To strike, over and over again, clubbing the dolls as if to bludgeon away the bad luck that has, inexplicably, come back to them, on the currents of the sea, the tremors of the land, the ash in the air.

I stop, stomach roiling. I should walk away, but a fascinated revulsion holds me. Do I recognise any of the dolls, in their water-logged and salt-stained cloth?

The children, empty-eyed even in their curiosity, poke at the pile with pieces of driftwood and thin branches.

One stabs too hard and the entire pile leans, slides to one side. Embers scoot across sand, dolls topple, sparks fly. A little girl, fists beating her grass skirts, screams. Others, in their heedless rush, step on hot burning wood and set up their own howls in counterpoint, less from pain than from fear.

The only way to know if your bad luck returned to you was when you felt the teeth of the cloudcat, the burn of the fire, the sting of the jellyfish.

In the confusion, dolls are knocked every which way. Some are wholly burned and lie still, others only half so and still wiggling. Smoke smarts my eyes, but I see it — a jewelled eye whose exact shade of green I'll always remember, the silver satin stitched with birds never seen on the Islands.

In the guise of helping, I drag a small boy to his feet and thrust him away from the fire, lean over a shrieking maiden curled up on the ground, kicking up sand. I scoop up the doll without looking, thrust it into my shawl, and smack the girl across the face. She chokes, stares at me from wide, watery eyes, but at least she's quiet.

"Get up," I tell her, "before someone steps on you."

Resentfully, she does so. Her thin copper bracelets clang as she dusts off her skirt and tunic. The chaos is over, dolls are scooped up and thrust onto the fire, the blue and purple flames crackle and twist in their witches' dance.

I back away, the doll a warm wet lump pressed against my side. It has the sense to stay still, unless it is already — not dead, but gone.

But it is the doll. The first doll.

I walk past a hut, and startle. Kaana leans against the wall, under the shadow of its palm-branch roof. His unfathomable gaze catches and holds my own.

He doesn't say anything, but he knows.

He knows.

∞¥∞Ω∞¥∞

It knows her touch so well. Hers were the first hands. Hers the first breath. Even wrapped in cloth and pressed against her body, blind and scorched, the doll knows its maker.

She's running, the breath rough in her lungs, her heart a frantic beat — and she's going the wrong way. Away from Mamutsa.

Finally she stops, crouches, and rolls the doll out of her shawl. It falls into wet dirt and soft jungle leaves. It looks up at her with its single glinting eye. She's ancient. The maker it remembers is a young woman. Straight back, dark long hair, and power in that hard gaze. She works the people of the village like they are needle and thread. Creating something beautiful out of them but binding them together, and to her, and to the very island at the same time. Now her eyes are dull, and squinting. Her face weathered and fearful, her back bent.

But then, the doll isn't as young and beautiful as it once was, either.

"Why have you come back?" she whispers. A pause; she glances over her shoulder, before returning her gaze to the doll. "Why are you all doing this to me?"

But she did not give the doll a voice, and so it cannot answer. Instead, it pushes itself back to its feet. They are burned, the seams threatening to unwind and spill the precious soil inside. The silver of its beautiful dress is darkened by smoke. The doll doesn't feel pain — not its own. Only its child's.

Something rustles in the jungle and again, the old woman looks away. The doll takes its chance, staggers to the side, pushing through the heavy leaves, slipping through mud. It runs into a pair of bare shins, and looks up into the empty face of a child.

A shudder runs through it. Not its child, but still Mamutsa's heartbeat binds them both.

"Kaana." The maker sounds distressed. "What are you doing?" The doll twists to look at her, and is snatched up by the child. He holds it out, and peers intently at the doll's single eye.

"Shall I take it back to the fire, Grandmother?" The boy's voice is as hollow as his eyes. No emotion, no understanding, not a care in all the world. "The dolls should not return and bring their bad luck with them. So when they do, they belong in the fire. I have seen it done. Many times."

"No!" the old woman snaps, her voice harsh. She holds out a hand. "Give it to me."

He pauses, head tipped. "Why?"

"Because it is mine, Kaana. Can you understand that? Mine." She is desperate, even fearful.

A strange smile spreads across the child's face. It is innocence, and boredom, and cruelty: an uncertain testing of emotions he cannot properly feel. Because the child, of course, is less than half a soul.

The doll understands the emptiness in this *Kaana* — it is doll-shaped. It is bad luck, and hurt, and heartache. It is all the curses of the world, poured on the shoulders of some small creature of sand

and thread and cast out into the sea. Poor child. The doll, who has endured someone else's fair share of hurt and sadness, feels for the boy. True, he will never be thrown into the waves. He will never feel the sting of someone else's broken bones, or be swallowed whole by a great whale, or weep for the loss of parents he never knew. Not like his doll. But neither will he know joy. He'll never have friends. He'll never build anything or love anything. He will never feel, at all.

The child grips the doll harder, pressing his fingers into the filling. "Stop it," he hisses. His empty eyes reflect the shape of the doll's silver dress. "That's not— I'm not— I don't—"

"*Don't resist it.*" The doll doesn't have a voice, like Kaana does. It whispers along the heartbeat instead, filling the void within the child the way water rushes to dry land. The boy soaks it up — all the doll's feelings and memories. Its journey beneath the sea.

"Mamutsa," he says, finally, and his voice is different. It has intent. The maker hears the change and lowers her reaching hand. "She— she's broken too." He blinks, looks up, fixes his gaze on the old woman. And, for the first time since she sewed his soul into pieces, he sees her. Really sees her. "It says we must return what you took, Grandmother. Before it is too late."

"The doll says?" the old woman whispers.

"You weakened her, and now she can't hold herself together any more. Soon, she will shatter, and the island will die with her. And all of us, too."

∞¥∞Ω∞¥∞

I drop to my knees, my heartbeat thunderous in my ears, pressed down by the weight of all the dolls I made over the years. I had only sought to hitch my meagre power to the volcano's stronger magic, in order to ward the islanders from misfortune.

Now this doll — the first I made with Mamutsa's ground-up bones — has returned to tell me that I have been wrong. That's why they all returned, the dolls I wove Mamutsa's power into.

All this is my fault.

When I look up, Kaana is crouched in front of a tree stump, upon which he has placed the doll. They are so different, the sea-battered doll and the strong young man, yet so much alike. Each incomplete. Kaana's expression is unreadable; he has never shown anger or affection, but the way he smooths the doll's folds with his big square hands can almost be called … tender.

"Kaana," I say, hating to ask him for help, hating to trust him. "We need to make a journey, me and this doll. It is a short journey for your young legs, but long for my old ones. Will you come with us?"

He does not look at me. "For the doll, also, Grandmother," he says with absent courtesy.

"Yes, of course." The short-legged doll. "Will you come with — the doll?"

He considers this and nods. "Yes, I will go. But—" he looks at the doll, which waves its paddle-like arms and truncated legs in agitation "—it says that *they* are coming."

They? But I have not long to wonder, because bushes rustle and leaves hiss, and suddenly there are dolls everywhere.

They drop from the trees, along with vines as thick as a man's wrist. Kaana throws himself over the first doll. Thorny branches slash against his bare back. They leave only bloodless indentations when they retract.

Dolls crawl from the undergrowth and grab at my ankles. I kick out, but I trip on the rocks and land on my rump. A doll stabs at me with a sharpened stick. It scores a bloody line down the back of my hand. I screech and swat it away.

A dozen or more confront Kaana, but he is like water, sliding past their attacks. Everywhere their thorns and vines, sticks and stones are, he is not.

In this fight, he is the crowning achievement of my work — all misfortune pared away, leaving him nigh on invulnerable.

We are winning, I think, until the bushes part and a cloudcat, fur all cream and honey, springs into view.

A doll sits upon the cat's back, clutching a collar of knotted vine. This one has both of its eyes, golden, shaped like shells. The same buttons run down its dress, though — and my breath catches — there is one missing.

The light slants and strikes fire into the gold of the doll's eyes and the green of the cat's. As the shadows slip and slide around them, a chill goes down my back, for they move as if they are one. The thread that connects the doll to Mamutsa connects it to all the sons and daughters of the volcano, from the trees that grow from the black soil to the animals that live upon her skirts.

And this doll is using that connection to take control of the whole web, from tree to cloudcat. A pair of thin, sharp-edged scissors glint against the cat's fur. Needles and pins are thrust into its collar. They could only have come from my stash. I had thought them looted by the villagers.

The cloudcat stalks forward, not towards me, but towards Kaana and the first doll. Its rider has a ragged tear in its face, a jagged hole whose frayed edges are thickly and clumsily stitched. With a mouth that I never gave it and voice like the grinding of stones, it says, "Mine. My child."

Kaana gapes, caught in the doll's magic, yearning and leaning towards it. His doll, I realise with a sinking heart, his fourth. The one I scraped what was left of his will and passion into.

"Come with me." Kaana's doll beckons. "Come with me and be made whole."

"No," I croak out, hobbling forward. The first doll slumps. "Don't listen to it, Kaana!"

He cannot help himself. He leans down, slowly. His neck muscles bulge, veins standing out. His doll leaps, savage and sudden, onto his shoulders. Kaana rears back, face twisting with a new emotion. Surprise.

His doll whispers, "We belong together, you and I. Don't let them separate us again."

"Y — yes," Kaana stutters. "We do belong together. I — I feel it!" There is wonderment in his eyes.

I cannot fight Kaana, with his large hands and strong legs. But I am not weaponless.

I snatch up a pointed stick and drive it into Kaana's leg. "Feel that, doll!"

And the doll does. It makes a wet sound, like a mud splat, as Kaana's pain rebounds to it. It loses its focus and the cloudcat vanishes into the forest.

I don't wait to see what happens next. I grab the first doll and flee towards Mamutsa.

∞¥∞Ω∞¥∞

The maker clutches the doll to her chest and carries it back to Mamutsa. Her breath is haggard, her stride hitching.

The doll wishes it could soothe her. But the doll is what she made it, silent and cursed. So, instead, as she does her best to run, it does its best to wrap her in its small arms. It clutches her, like the child she was never allowed to have, holds her with every inch of its stolen strength.

Clouds fill the sky as they step clear of the lush jungle and onto hard stone. Not clouds alone. Smoke. Mamutsa's blood and broken soul, rich and billowing, lanced by sharp forks of lightning. The ground grumbles, shaking so hard the maker loses her footing and lands hard. The doll slips free as she lies gasping, and pushes itself to its legs.

It takes a hesitant step, and falls on its face. Its threads are ancient and in such ruin, that all it can do is crawl. One hand unwinds, revealing mouldy padding and a congregation of tiny dead fish.

"Wait," the maker gasps. She rolls to the side, sits up, but cannot make it any further. It's enough. She digs around her layers of clothing, all the beautiful cloths she collected in her lifetime and never had the chance to make into dolls, and pulls out a small pouch. Inside are tiny scissors, many needles and rolls and rolls of thread. "Come here."

She cuts strips from her own clothing, and patches the doll. Fresh cerise silk to replace its silver dress. Soft cotton to replace its hands and feet, padded with strong leather. She spits on a bundle of linen and cleans mud from its face, then sews on a new eye, bright like a diamond. And finally, despite her shaking hands, the maker gives the doll a mouth. Small, woven from tight pink threads. Not smiling, but slightly sad. Then she sets the doll on its feet, and runs her hand over its head.

"There," she whispers. "You're strong now."

The doll nods, uncertain. It remembers the way its child should have felt when her mother died. That is the right feeling, for this moment.

"I—" the old woman lies back. "I'm sorry. I only wanted to help. I didn't mean to hurt anyone. Least of all you."

"I forgive you," the doll whispers, through its new mouth. Its voice is the slow shift of underwater sand.

Then the doll turns its back on its maker and begins its slow journey to the rim of Mamutsa's crater. Emptiness waits. Darkness and nothingness. Death. Despite Mamutsa's call, so all-consuming within it, the doll begins to feel dread. Its feet slow. The maker has made it strong again, fresh and beautiful. And all her efforts are about to burn.

Then a voice calls, from below. "Grandmother." Kaana, with his doll on his shoulder. "What have you done, Grandmother?"

∞¥∞Ω∞¥∞

"Leave her," says Kaana's doll. It looks like a jungle spider, its body bloated, arms and legs wrapped around Kanaa's neck and in his hair. "First doll," it calls, in its crackly voice, like fire licking wood. "Come back! There is a way that we can *all* be saved, dolls and children and island. Come back and listen!"

"No," I say. I try to catch Kaana's ankles and bring him down, but my limbs have turned to water. "Keep going, doll! Return to Mamutsa!" As if in answer to her name, the volcano rumbles, urging the doll onwards.

But it stops. It turns around, mismatched eyes bright. "There is no other way."

"You do not have to die!" Kaana strides forward, but it is his doll that speaks, leaning forward avidly. "The maker has repaired your body, given you back shape and form. Now you are a strong vessel for Mamutsa's power. Do not give it away but use it. Use it to soothe our ailing Mother so that she will quiet, to keep the island stable, to reunite doll with child."

I am light-headed from the fumes and from my own horror. The dolls were never meant to wield such power, yet I had given them the way to do so. "First doll," I plead, "you have not the wisdom nor the knowledge to take Mamutsa's place."

The first doll says nothing.

"You could," Kaana's doll speaks, soft and almost-tender, "return to your child."

The first doll moves, not for the rim, but towards us. It scrambles back down, and Kaana crouches to meet it. I notice that his hands are sandy, with volcanic dirt and linen batting embedded deep in his fingernails. Glitter and sequins dust his skin.

"Kaana," I manage, lifting myself up on my elbows. "What happened to the other dolls?"

He looks at me, in slight puzzlement. And then I see it. I see why Kaana's doll looks so engorged, see why it has such unlikely strength in its limbs, why it can speak.

"Run, first doll!" I scream. Mamutsa exhales and hot ashes flick my cheeks. "It destroyed the other dolls and stole their power! Get—"

It is too late. Kaana's doll growls, and jumps on to the first doll.

∞¥∞Ω∞¥∞

Kaana's doll is heavier than it should be, stronger than it could be, and bloated with Mamusta's stolen soil. It holds the first doll down, and its heartbeat is many, a clamour that drowns out everything else. So much power, all pressed inside straining cloth and popping thread.

The maker knew. The maker saw. And it should have listened. "You took them," the doll whispers. "They're inside you."

"And you will join us." Kaana's doll stretches its torn mouth into a terrible grin. "And I will finally have enough of Mamutsa's power inside me, that she will bend her will to me, and not the other way around."

It plunges one of its stumpy arms into a gap in its side, where its seams have been carefully unplucked and retied. It draws a stolen pair of the maker's scissors, small and glinting in fine gold, the elegant bird-shape turned twisted and cruel.

"No more being tossed to all the corners of the world." Kaana's doll clutches the scissors above its head and rears back. "No more being called to heel whenever Mamutsa needs us. Where was she when this big idiot decided to jump off a cliff, and I endured the pain of all his broken bones? We have needed her since the moment of our birth, and she has never helped us."

Kaana's doll plunges the scissors into the first doll's freshly mended chest, and tears downward, spilling stuffing and sand. "You're the final piece, precious first doll. With your strength, I can wield her. And I will complete Kaana and give purpose to his strength."

"You can't," says the maker. "Kaana had three other dolls, three other pieces of his soul. Where are they? What happened—" The maker's voice dissolves into a terrible coughing and gasping of breath.

Kaana's head swivels. Something kindles in his eyes — not an emotion, but a memory of one. He looks down at his doll. "My dolls?" he stutters out the words. "My *other* dolls?"

The first doll squirms, catches for one heartbeat among the many inside Kaana's doll, holds a faint, fragile memory. "I see … a small boy capering on the beach. I feel the sand squishing under our feet. The boy steps on a blue jellyfish. He cries, but I take the sting into myself, and in a moment he runs ahead of me. But he looks back. He waits for me."

"Enough!" Kaana's doll throws the scissors to the side, plunges its arms into the first doll's chest, opens its too-wide mouth, and leans forward to feast. The first doll feels itself shredding.

"I remember!" Kaana stoops, tears his doll free and lifts it up to his face. "Doll?" he asks, face a frightful play of fear and disinterest. "Where are my other dolls?"

Kaana's doll squirms, reaching for the boy, all its heartbeats a thunder roaring to fill the emptiness in the child's soul. But Kaana holds the doll at a distance. "No!" And shakes it, so that stuffing and sand rain from the hole in its side. It ceases its struggles, pressing small stunted hands against its side instead, trying to contain everything it stole.

The first doll, wounded, weak, sits up slowly. It wraps its arms around its middle, desperate to stop Mamutsa's power from spilling in a shower of stuffing. "Your dolls are gone," it manages a whisper like bubbles. "Torn and devoured. Your feelings have gone with them. Your pain, and your joy. Do you remember what I showed you? You will never feel that again."

"Don't listen to it!" Kaana's doll screeches. "You're mine anyway. Mine to fill!"

The first doll pushes itself back to unsteady feet, all its insides clutched in inadequate arms. "Are you?" it asks Kaana. "Are you merely an empty skin to be filled by your doll's hate and rage and bitter power?"

And Kaana, with a twitch of emotion across his face — anger and grief and aching hurt — tears the head from his doll. It falls, voiceless, to the hard ground, as its body unwinds, and all the soil and stuffing inside it spill into Kaana's broad palms.

"Oh, Kaana," the maker says, tears in her eyes. "What remains of you now?"

The first doll toddles over to Kaana, who stares at the ruin cupped in his hands. "No child should have to ever kill his doll."

Mamutsa cracks and rumbles beneath them, heat radiating out from the stone.

"Now what?" Kaana says in the voice of a little boy. A lost little boy.

The doll turns to its mother's crater, where she rages. "Now, I must finish what I started." But it only takes a few steps, before the quakes knock it to the ground. It lands heavily, clutching its belly.

Then Kaana scoops it up in hands still full of the detritus of his own doll. "You cannot," he says. And when he meets the doll's bright gaze, his expression is determined. "You will not make it that far. You need my help."

"No!" the maker gasps, and pushes herself upright again. "Kaana, don't!"

He smiles at her, and inclines his head. "But I must, Grandmother. You told me. The doll told me. I remember that — and what it felt like to feel. What it felt like to care. I can't go back to emptiness, now that I remember that. And I don't want to be meaningless any more."

The doll stares at the maker as Kaana carries it away. She watches them, reaches for them, then lowers her hand. Slowly, in obvious pain, she pushes herself to her feet.

"Will it hurt?" Kaana asks, as he carries the doll up final heights of the volcano.

"Yes," the doll answers. "When the magic fails, you will feel it." A pause, as they cross a widening crack in the dark ropes of stone. Noxious steam hisses out, but it can't slow them down. The doll is only thread and stuffing, after all. And Kaana feels nothing at all. "But not for long."

Kaana nods. They reach a sheer cliff. Kaana lifts the doll first, then scales it swiftly. They sit, together, on the rim, as Mamutsa growls and rolls beneath them, fury in bright curls.

Then Kaana stands, collects the doll. A single step, and they fall. And return the stolen sands to their mother.

∞¥∞Ω∞¥∞

I stand in the village square where they used to burn dolls and now burn corpses. I hunch into myself, wrapping my shawls tightly. The sun is bright, but I am never warm enough. Often I cough. I still feel Mamusta's ashes scouring my mouth and lodging in my lungs.

I am too old to be out here, even leaning on a cane, but the villagers need me. In the year since the first doll and Kaana gave themselves to Mamutsa, there has been a funeral every month. Sometimes more.

The return of misfortune is more than bee stings and shark bites, stubbed toes and gashed heads. It is sickness and death, anger and knife stabs in the dark. It is children slipping on the rocks and falling to their doom, it is young men clawed by the cloudcats and young women dying as they birth their children.

It is normal life. For a little while I had carved a place outside of reality for this island and its surrounding islets. But life has returned, not just in shades of sorrow, but also in jewel tones of love and laughter.

A girl child, not yet three, plays upon the sand. She clutches a rag doll in her arms and laughs when the wavelets lick her toes. The doll flops, an inanimate thing of stuffing and patterned cloth, but it is loved and it is hers.

Somehow, I think Kaana and the first doll would approve.

ELLA AND THE FLAME

KATHLEEN JENNINGS

The people went out of town on foot, horseback and cart, to where the trees grew scraggy on the dusty hills. The house they sought should have been difficult to find. It lay beyond the hard ground of the rutted road, hidden by grey screens of trees, in as unfriendly a valley as any in that hungry country. No clearer path led to it than the faint tangled traces made by cattle or goats or the feet of a solitary child going to school. But many of the townspeople had been there before, on private errands, and the small crowd found its way unerringly.

At the rear of the procession rode the Governor himself. He had known the town when he was a young man gaining experience of the world, but now he returned in all his dignity. He had heard the grumblings and complaints of the dry-spirited people. It had been a long time since rain had fallen. They struggled to live on soil grown thin and shallow creeks run low and rank, while cattle and children sickened and starved. The inhabitants of the house that lay beyond the town had once promised health and cures, but their abilities had been stretched. The merciless drought seemed a punishment for relying on such frail assistance. Each disease, each misfortune, assumed an air of malevolence. The Governor had assured the people that he would see justice done, and his presence lent an undeniable distinction to the proceedings.

The Governor was not surprised when the scrubby wilderness split to reveal the small house neat and grey in its unnaturally green garden. It had been a familiar destination in that youth he had put severely behind him. He was glad to set both memories and rumours to rest at last, like old letters cast into a fire.

Those who had gone ahead had already surrounded the cottage. The doors and shutters were closed.

"They are all inside, sir," said the Mayor to the Governor. "They will not come out and beg. They will not admit their wickedness."

The Governor nodded and then a slight frown troubled his serene brow. "There is a child?" he asked, and the faint hesitation in that hitherto resolute voice troubled the Mayor, for promises of governments had proved hollow before now. The fatherless child was grown undeniably like the women who lived in the cottage, and the Mayor did not think it necessary to trouble needlessly the conscience of one who would not have to live with the consequences of this day's activities.

"It goes to the school," he answered. "Your Honour may recall the teacher said that she would keep the children in. Though," he added, regretful, "some poison can only be burned out."

The Governor nodded. Unpleasant thoughts occurred to him of a girl he had known too well and castles he built in the air when he was young and foolish, but he put those images out of his mind and looked sternly at the cottage and the crowd ready and eager to perpetrate justice.

"You heard the evidence," said the Mayor.

The Governor inclined his head regally, and replied, "Let justice be done."

∞¥∞Ω∞¥∞

Planks and timbers fell against the door like the beating of a deep drum. The sisters held each others' hands and sat on the floor, heads touching. The beams fell like doom against the shutters, and the women closed their eyes.

"We will die," said Anne, the eldest, simply. When she said "we", it sounded so small. Just the four of them: three siblings and the child, so slight and brittle a number.

"We have died before," said the youngest sister, Sable. When she spoke, she meant all who had ever lived and died like them: sisters and aunts and brothers and uncles and parents.

"We are the only ones left to die," said the middle one, Mary, holding the child on her lap, although Ella had long grown too tall for such a seat. "We are the last of all."

"People have hated us too fiercely," said Anne. "Even those we once thought loved us."

"That man has hated us too fiercely," said Sable. "And I cannot believe I ever thought…" She fell silent and frowned at Ella, for neither Sable's pride nor her idea of family had ever let it seem necessary to her to tell Ella of the past. "Will you forgive me that folly?"

Anne smiled and shook her head "What is there to forgive, Sable? Youth is always foolish—" here she touched Ella's hand, "—and yours gave us perhaps more joy than we had a right to. But death has always loved our family too well."

"What is it like, death?" asked Ella, still enough of a child to be sure the others knew the answer. Anne and Mary and Sable were silent, and the sounds outside were like the knocking of bones and the scattering of stones on a grave. To them, death had taken on the features of a face once welcome, before it had grown great and regretted them. None of them wished to say that to the child.

"Dying is like going to sleep after a long day," said Anne gently, "when you cannot keep your eyes open however much you want to. You can struggle or go quietly, but darkness falls and all your limbs go loose and easy."

"Dying is like waking to a bright morning," said Sable, "when everything is so fresh and new, you are sure no-one has ever seen it before."

"Dying is like fire," said Mary dully. "All flash and flame and at the end there is nothing but ashes and cinders."

Ella frowned over this, for they had raised her to look for truth in stories. With no more questions to answer or tales to tell, they all fell silent again. It was quieter outside. They heard voices of friends and neighbours, harsh laughter of customers and schoolmates, the distant clatter of bundles of sticks and sheaves of dry grass.

"I do not wish to die cowering," said Anne at last.

"What does it matter?" said Mary. "No-one will know."

"We will," said Sable. "Here and now and for a moment, we will know."

"No-one will tell stories of it," said Mary.

"Do you think that because we only tell it to ourselves, it will be any less of a story? Whomever else have we ever told them to?" said Anne.

"To me," said Ella.

"There," said Sable. "You see? We must make a story for her to tell, for we have told our tales and now we must live them through to the end, but Ella has never told a great tale, and that would be a poor way for one of our family to die."

"Very well," said Mary. "We shall not die like cowards, but telling a grand tale."

"A night-time tale," said Anne, "To make the sleeping sweet, and the sleeper wake new-made."

"Like caterpillars out of their cases, and embers fanned back to flame," said Sable. Then she remembered and said brightly, "There are pinecones which only grow into trees after fire." They stood together, still clasping hands. The house was dark now that the cracks at the edges of shutters and doors were hidden from the sun. Only the light of the hurricane lamp fell golden and bronze on their hair and skin until they seemed creatures of metal and flame. It lit upon the pots and ladles, on the ends of the nails that came through the door, and on the fragments of glass that had fallen from the windows before the shutters were closed upon them.

They put on their finest clothes: Anne's gown, yellowed and pressed with age; Mary's go-to-meeting best with buttons at wrist and neck; Sable's red dress. Ella, who had not yet owned a fine dress, the sisters dressed in the prettiest things they could find. They made her a cloak of the lace veil Sable had sewn before Ella was born (which Sable had never worn and Ella would now never have a chance to wear), and clasped it with a colourful tin brooch.

The sisters put on all the jewellery that had been too good or gaudy, bright or dull to wear every day: their mother's rings and their grandmothers' pearls, cheap necklaces bright as beetle-cases wound around their heads like crowns, earrings hooked one to the other. They looped pearls and beads about Ella's throat and brow and arms. They pinned up their hair. From the vase of flowers (taken from the garden which would soon be crushed and trampled and salted), they took roses and pale jasmine to put behind their ears. Sashes and scarves hung at their shoulders and elbows like wings, and they clipped papery yellow daisies and soft lavender and fluttering ribbons to their shoes. Ella wore Anne's old dancing shoes, wrapped tight around her small feet with glittering glass beads until the shoes shone like light through windows.

"We look like princesses," said Ella.

"Like queens!" said Anne, and Mary smiled, and Sable held out her arms and spun.

"Be careful! The lamp!" said Mary, then put her hands over her mouth. Anne laughed in horror, and Sable snatched the lamp up in one hand and caught Ella to her side with the other, and danced on.

Outside, there was a murmuring, the sound of shouting heard through the thick wood.

"He can hear us laugh," whispered Mary. "He is driving them on to bay for our blood."

"Let them have it," said Anne. "They shall not have Ella's story." She turned up the light so that it threw their shadows crazily onto the walls. "Now, this is to be your story, dear-heart," said Anne to Ella. "So you must begin it".

"But let it have no Governors or Mayors or declarations or judgements," said Mary.

"How do I begin?" said Ella.

"Why, the way all tellers of tales begin, little goose!" said Sable.

Mary closed her eyes and, as if remembering something long lost, said, "Once upon a time…"

Ella began. "Once upon a time there was a girl. She was kind—"

"And good—" said Mary.

"And clever—" said Anne.

"And lovely," sighed Sable.

"Yes," said Ella. "All of those. But she was very unfortunate, for a — a..."

"Not a Governor," said Sable.

"An evil prince!" said Ella.

Anne nodded approvingly, and Ella raced on:

"An evil prince had taken away everything she loved and a great dragon had settled upon the land."

Sable jumped to her feet. "Let me be the dragon!" she cried. "Look!" And she cast great shadows with her arms so that they looked like jaws.

"It looks like a dog!" exclaimed Ella, scornful.

"It's a wolf-dragon," said Sable. "Go on!"

Outside, there was a roar of voices, and then a hissing, a whispering.

"Go on!" said Anne urgently. "A great dragon?"

"No, three dragons!" revised Ella, suddenly gleeful. "Because the evil prince hated the girl's aunts ... no, her sisters. He hated them because they were good and wise and he was not, and so he changed them into dragons."

So Anne cast a demure dragon upon the wall, and Mary a reluctant one, and Sable moved her sleeves against the light like beating wings, and outside the whispering was broken by sharp crackling sounds and a faint acrid smell seeped between the boards of the door and shutters.

"And the girl wanted to rescue her sisters," said Ella.

"Of course she did!" said Sable.

"So she went looking for a brave knight," said Ella. "But all the knights in the land were afraid of the prince, and could only see dragons when they looked at the three sisters. And no-one else would help her because they were afraid of the dragons too, and of the prince, and they put their hands over their ears and teased her and threw things at her and chased her out of school and out of the town and wouldn't listen to her when she told them that the dragons weren't dragons at all, but really her family."

"Thus people ever were," said Mary.

"How did she save her sisters?" asked Anne.

"She ... she didn't know what to do," faltered Ella. "Because people started to say she was too fond of dragons altogether, even though they weren't really dragons. She started to think perhaps dragons were better than people after all, for they were still beautiful and bold." She faltered into a troubled silence.

"But she thought of all the stories her sisters had told her," prompted Anne.

"And made a few up herself," said Sable, "because she herself was such a bold, bright girl."

"And she thought that the problem was that everyone had forgotten," said Ella. She caught at Sable's flapping sleeve and said, "Because the people had forgotten the dragons were girls who had been their friends, and the wicked prince even made her sisters forget they had ever been anything but dragons."

"Were they terribly fierce dragons?" whispered Sable.

"Oh, very," said Ella. "The best sort of dragons, if they really had been dragons. They had great red wings and spiky spines, and breathed fire and ate knights and everything." Sable laughed hoarsely and put her arms around Ella and kissed the top of her head.

"Go on," said Anne, and coughed at the pale smoke that curled its way under the door. The crackling was louder than her cough.

"So," said Ella, "she gathered everything she thought might make people remember who the dragons really were. She found, um, hair in the sisters' combs—"

"And necklaces they had worn," said Sable, jangling hers.

"And threads from lace collars," said Mary.

"And strings from their violins," said Anne.

"And paper from their books," said Ella. It was growing warmer in the house. "And feathers from pens they had written with."

"And branches from their rose bushes," said Mary.

"And nettles that had stung them," said Sable.

"And all sorts of things from the stories they had told," said Anne.

"She knotted them into a great big shining net," said Ella. "And because she knew the dragons had burned all the hillsides about them and the embers would be very hot, she made shoes out of metal and glass that would not burn, and lined them with old dancing shoes because she knew that glass would hurt to walk on almost as much as coals, and she set off to the hills to find the dragons."

"She was a very clever girl," said Anne.

Mary wiped her eyes, for the smell of burning wood and the thickening air was making them water. "Did she have to walk far?"

"No," said Ella, "but she had to run. The prince and all the people were there when she arrived. The prince was trying to kill the dragons, because then everyone would think he was wonderful, but they were very large — bigger than he expected. And then he saw the girl and thought maybe they would eat her and be distracted while he killed them."

"What a wicked man," said Sable. It sounded like a wind was roaring outside the house, and the flame of the lamp flickered.

Mary sat down and leaned against Anne's legs. She coughed, and when she stopped she said, "Go on, Ella. I want to know how it ends." Sable and Anne sat down beside her. Ella stood before them, small but magnificent in lace and beads.

"The girl did not want to talk to the prince in case he made her forget too, but she showed him the net and pointed to the dragons. He didn't know who she was, but he could see the net was remarkable. So he helped her fling it up and over the heads of the dragons, and it fell down about them, and all the people saw that they were the three sisters, and the sisters remembered that they ought really to be people again. They turned into women and the girl ran to them and wrapped her coat and her cape and the net around them, and gave them the shoes she had made for them."

"What did the prince do?" asked Mary.

"He was very surprised," said Ella. "But he wasn't at all happy." Her breath caught, hot in her chest, and she coughed and gasped and made herself go on, though her voice sounded strange. "He picked up his sword, which wasn't fair at all for the only weapon they had was the net and that was made of things that were good against dragons, not against wicked princes. But the three sisters opened their mouths and breathed out fire, just as if they were still dragons, and then they picked up their sister in the net and flew, just as if they still had great red wings, over the burnt hills and the trees and far away until they came home."

She stood, looking down at them, and Sable took her hands and drew her down into their arms. "And did they live happily?" asked Sable.

Although it was so very hot, Ella curled up against her and watched the lamplight die behind a veil of choking smoke. She felt Anne's hand on hers and Mary's hand on her hair. Their breathing was slow, as if they were falling asleep. "Of course they did," said Ella as the sound of hungry flames moved around and above them. "For ever and ever, and everyone was happy because the wicked prince was gone, and the sisters lived very quietly in a beautiful house in a garden full of roses. But they never, ever, ever forgot they had been dragons."

The fire roared outside, and inside the sisters fell asleep one by one in each others' arms. Ella struggled to stay awake as long as she could, and through burning eyes and thick smoke she saw Death come through the wall and touch the sisters, one at a time — Anne, then Mary and Sable last of all, so that they shone brighter than candles, brighter than dragons, before they vanished away. Then Death came right up to Ella and bent down and looked her in the eyes.

"Get away from me, wicked old prince," murmured Ella. "For I am the last of my kind, and I have told a great story, and my mother and my aunts are turned to dragons, and I am not afraid of you."

And perhaps Death believed her, for it backed away, and Ella sat up. The beams and burning shingles fell about her like leaves and curling bark, and the smoke billowed up and away and peeled back to show the midnight sky, with its stars bright as sparks, but cold.

∞¥∞Ω∞¥∞

The crowd around the house fell silent. For all the heat of the fire in front of them, the clear night was ice at their backs. For long years the memory of the chill of it lay like a curse on the town. The Governor returned to the city a broken man — some said it was because of what he had done, but others that it was because of what he had seen: a daughter who burned bright as the moon, bright as white-hot iron. She walked out of the burning ruins and through the fearful crowd and strode away, in her dress of smouldering lace and her shoes that shone like glass. She disappeared into the dry hills, and though for days afterwards fire raged through the trees and farms, Ella was never seen again.

MORNING STAR
D.K. MOK

Day Zero
Earth

It was an unremarkable summer morning beneath the cloudless weather domes, when fifty-three thousand residents of the Pacific Hub failed to wake up. Harried medics jetted through the subdued towerscapes, finding no evidence of trauma, no detectable poisons or pathogens. Just the gentle grip of rigor mortis setting in.

The following week, the Mediator of the Southern Mineral Alliance keeled over during a live cloudcast, along with three million of her compatriots. No splinter cells claimed responsibility. Epidemiologists were both horrified and quietly intrigued.

Only one particular man could have known what had begun, but he had vanished over ninety years ago.

∞¥∞Ω∞¥∞

Five years after Day Zero
Earth

Ven sprinted through the creaking corridors of the Mariana Base, her wet brown hair falling into her eyes, klaxons melting, embers chasing her down the collapsing steel tube. The water rose hungrily around her shins, and Ven slowed only to seal each door behind her. The boy in her arms made no sound, his thin, olive arms tight around her neck, his face pressed into the shoulder of her faded red flight-suit. The last airlock hissed shut as they entered the cockpit, and Ven buckled the boy into a padded seat imperfectly modified to fit a six year old.

Ven hadn't been trained for scenarios like this. On a bad day, she might have to salvage a busted container of octopus puppets after a tricky re-entry, but today, it wasn't a cargo module clamped to the underside of the *Morning Star*.

Ven's fingers bashed across the black console, and holographic indicators fuzzed into life. The cockpit shuddered, and Ven nosed the ship upward. The domed bay doors were closed, but she had to trust that her colleagues were still alive. Even with the facility disintegrating around them, they wouldn't let her down. That was scientists for you.

Ven swept her fingers up the engine gauge; the cockpit screamed with warnings as the nanocarbon doors loomed to fill the screen. With inches to spare, the metal maw opened and the *Morning Star* slammed into the crush of dark water.

Ven switched to propellers, churning up through the cloudy water column. Colossal squid slammed briefly into the viewscreen before fading back into the bioluminescent twilight. She didn't dare glance at the boy, didn't dare think of her friends in the imploding research station below. The engines whined furiously as they finally broke through the waves and into a smoky red sky.

A mess of gargantuan, holographic screens hung in the sky, blaring static. On the horizon, an ominous glow was intensifying exponentially.

"Oh hell," said Ven.

She swiped every thruster to maximum, hoping the shields would prevent the boy turning into jam. Ven drained the power from every system save the burning blue engines as the light outside swept closer, dissolving the clouds around them. Missiles chased them through the stratosphere, and the ship rocked as one warhead shattered the landing gear. Ven heaved the *Morning Star* back on course, the other missiles falling away as they pulled further into orbit. Below them, a blinding corona rushed across the blue green surface, and the crust of the Earth disintegrated.

Ven sat in silence, then flicked off the viewscreen. She ventured a glance at the boy, who continued to stare at the blank frame. Ven's interactions with children generally left them in tears, but she could hardly make things worse. She unbuckled the ashen boy from his seat, and wrapped a thermal blanket around his shoulders.

"Solomon, isn't it?" said Ven.

The boy nodded mechanically, so Ven continued softly.

"When I was young, a friend told me a story. When the universe was new, the sky was full of suns. But it was too bright, and too hot, so the great coelacanth of the cosmos swam between them, swatting them apart with her massive tail..."

The boy's eyes turned slowly to meet hers, and he blinked solemnly. Ven forged on with her tale of far flung suns and rivers of stars, haunted by astral dragonfish with moons for lures. When she ran out of story, she continued to hum random tunes, her arms around the boy. He listened wordlessly, and as their tiny blue star sailed further from Earth, the silent void seemed just a little less lonely.

∞¥∞Ω∞¥∞

Ven sagged on her bunk, undressed to a black singlet and shorts. Solomon had finally fallen asleep, or unconscious — she never could tell the difference. Ven rolled her singlet up her stomach, wincing as she prised open the panel beneath her ribs. She'd been meaning to get the latch fixed, but Doctor Josh had been so busy.

"Would you rather be alone?" said a soothing, male voice.

On the monitor beside the copper-alloy door, a light blue sine wave undulated calmly.

"If you're shy, you can avert your sensors, Mike," scowled Ven.

She wedged a fingernail beneath her sternum, and a battery deck ejected with a soft whir. The green bar was illuminated at eighty percent. She should have replaced the battery when she had the chance, but no one seemed to stock legacy tech.

"He's going to notice you don't get older," said Mike.

Ven snapped the panel shut.

"They say men aren't perceptive about those things," said Ven.

"I think you're getting men confused with blind cave beetles."

Ven swiped the data cuff on her wrist, and a holographic star chart bloomed before her. In one corner, a tiny blue green globe turned peacefully.

"Did you watch it, Mike?" said Ven softly.

There was a pause.

"Yes," said Mike. "It's just us now."

Ven lay on the cold bed, staring at the rust coloured ceiling.

"There are still other stations, other ships," said Ven.

"The same kill switch in every human."

Ven sat up icily.

"Sorry," said Mike, his tone unrepentant. "I meant the same chronogenetic species-wide pathology. Only robots have kill switches."

Ven let it go. From what little she knew, Mike35 had every reason to be bitter. When the mysterious epidemic first began, the world had been terrifyingly unprepared. Entire cities were wiped out overnight, and then for weeks, sometimes months, there would be no unusual deaths. Everyone would wonder if perhaps it was over, and then another enclave would succumb.

Frenzied theories gripped the population. Proponents of Malicious Design declared that God had tired of his playthings. The Army of Souls fundamentalists claimed it was insurrection by the androids, and shortly afterwards unstoppable viruses began burning out mechanical brains.

Mike35 had been the pilot of the Athanas Corporation's executive flagship when it was ambushed by the Army of Souls, just beyond the asteroid mines of Saturn. In the thick of the fire-fight, with his hull ripped wide open, he executed a short-range phase jump directly into Earth atmosphere, but for his five thousand android passengers, it was already too late.

Ven had heard the story from Bester, the maintenance droid she'd befriended at the sea base, but she'd never dared to confirm it with Mike. All she knew was that he hadn't always been Mike35, and his

Evolver Intelligence matrix wasn't something generally patched onto cargo ships. She hadn't wanted to part with her old co-pilot, Mike34, but Doctor Josh had promised he would find a good home for him.

Ven stretched, the cable in her right thigh catching a little. Solomon would have seen the cloudcasts of the android retaliation strikes, the bombings and the poisoned waterways. He'd have grown up in a world already polarised along carbon-based lines, and the last thing Ven needed was a co-pilot with baggage. But for all Mike's cynicism, he was as lost as she was.

She glanced at the monitor, and the sine wave dipped a little.

"We can look for survivors, if you want," said Mike. "But they can't outrun time."

"They say Solomon did."

After a pause, the sine wave shrugged.

"We'll see."

∞ ¥ ∞ Ω ∞ ¥ ∞

Five years and one week after Day Zero
28 light minutes from Earth

Solomon had adjusted surprisingly well to life aboard the *Morning Star*. He was already demonstrating culinary flair with the nutrient synthesiser, and he'd taken a keen interest in the ship's operations. However, he'd yet to speak a word to Ven, and her attempts to introduce him to Mike had elicited no reaction from the boy beyond polite observation.

Ven persisted in her one-sided conversations with Solomon, chatting as they explored the module beneath the ship together. The *Morning Star* herself was an engine sled, shaped like a deck of cards with fierce blue fusion engines — little more than a cockpit and crib inside. But her undercarriage was designed to slot into a range of modules, transforming her into anything from a research satellite to a space bus. And Doctor Josh and his team had fitted her with a whole new deck.

Everything had been scrounged from parts and patched together, but the *Morning Star*'s new deck boasted a multimedia pod, a medibay, and they'd even kitted the ship with guns.

In case you meet a space kraken, Doctor Josh had said.

Ven inspected the unfamiliar scanners and implements in the medibay. Doctor Josh's colleagues had been studying Solomon, but biology and physics had never been Ven's strengths. Doctor Josh had once brought her to a lecture on quantum physics, and although she'd memorised the presentation, it had meant nothing to her beyond 'something particles, something red shift, something cosmic donut'. The Elucidation-Class androids had looked at her as though she were a wooden duck on a string.

Ven had been the prototype for Doctor Josh's doctoral thesis at Hawking University, and his algorithm for emotional processing had become standard encoding in all autonomous intelligence androids. His latest opus, just before the first wave of deaths began, had been a vivacious creature with a warm laugh and a flush in her cheeks. In the end, she'd been the one at his side as the world turned to ash.

Ven looked down at her own waxy hand, her fingerprints worn away. Doctor Josh had stopped upgrading her some time ago. Years earlier, he'd removed her wireless interface to repair, and forgotten to replace it.

Ven straightened as a halting tune drifted from the far side of the module. She followed the piano chords to the recreation room, where a mahogany piano had been summoned from the nanomorph panel in the floor. Solomon was playing a wistful piece, which Ven suddenly recognised as fragments of the songs she'd hummed to him earlier. He stopped when Ven entered.

"Where did you learn to play?" said Ven. To her surprise, the boy spoke.

"Doctor Gillian," said Solomon.

His voice was soft, with a texture that reminded her of sandalwood. Ven didn't move, cautious of breaking whatever spell had finally roused the boy to speak.

Doctor Gillian Kagare had been a colleague of Doctor Josh's, and the first scientist to draw a connection between the inexplicable deaths and a hundred year old research paper by the discredited physicist, Arvel Hem. After his disgrace, Hem had taken an experimental spaceship — the *Darwin* — and disappeared beyond the range of Earth's probes, but fragments of his research remained. Primarily as a cautionary tale.

Kagare hadn't been the only epidemiologist to notice that the more genetically homogenous the population, the higher the percentage of fatalities. Countries with xenophobic immigration policies became morgues overnight, while multicultural metropolises lost fractions of their populations at a time. When researchers began to find cases of extended families — separated by continents — dying on the same day, they realised the affliction had a genetic root.

A century before, Hem had hypothesised an interaction between human genetics and the properties of time. He suggested that time was not a featureless constant, but a landscape, with valleys and hills, that could impact upon the expression of genes.

Ven found it difficult to think of time as a substance. The Elucidation-Class androids used to smirk that Ven looked a little like Kagare, but possessed the processor of a pomelo. Ven would never admit that she'd had to look up what a pomelo was.

Doctor Josh had described the hypothesis in terms of Kagare's landmark experiment, in which one hundred lab mice were modified with a human genetic marker, and then left to live out their mousy lives for several generations. On day two hundred and four, all eleven thousand mice died. From the year-old geriatrics to the newborn pups — not one of them woke that day. This was the moment scientists realised that humanity's funeral march had a score.

Shortly after the publication of this study, Kagare found Solomon.

"That's a lovely piece of music," said Ven. "Are you going to give it a name?"

Solomon swiped his hand across the keys, and the piano pooled obediently into a rug on the floor. Ven's heart fell as Solomon padded away across the room, but he returned with a paper-thin display tablet in his hands, which he presented to her.

Sketched on its linen white surface was something resembling a large potato with matchstick arms and legs. Further to the right of the page stood a much smaller, but similarly malnourished potato.

"That," said Ven, "is awesome."

On a screen beside the nanomorph panel, a sine wave snickered softly.

"So awesome, in fact," continued Ven, "it deserves a special place."

Ven pressed the tablet to the wall, and swiped the edge of the device. It emitted a soft click, and when she pulled the tablet away, an imprint of the drawing remained etched in the bulkhead. Solomon touched the dark lines, eyes wide.

"We also have to talk about the matter of birthdays," said Ven seriously. "I'm sure we need to commemorate yours on a regular basis, preferably annually. Do you have a particular date?"

Solomon stared at Ven with equal gravity.

"Do you have a birthday?" said Solomon.

Ven's processor seized briefly.

"Actually, let's not worry about birthdays," said Ven. "How about we celebrate the day we met instead? We can call it Hello Day."

Solomon considered this.

"Hello," he said, and smiled.

∞¥∞Ω∞¥∞

Ven sealed the door to the polyhedral multimedia pod, illuminating multiple screens with a swoop of her fingers. They had supplies to last fifteen years, maybe twenty, but circling this lonely sun was like staying at a party after everyone had gone. A galaxy of broken bottles and stale canapés.

A screen to her left flickered into an agitated blue sine wave.

"You realise that if everyone wasn't dead, they'd have taken the critter off you by now," said Mike.

"You're just sore I tattooed your arse," said Ven.

"I think of it as my bicep," said Mike. "But while you're playing tea parties with Lonesome George, this ship isn't going to fuel itself."

Ven swept her hand across an image, and the chamber filled with stars, as though she were floating in a tank of miniature galaxies.

"We're going to find the *Darwin*," said Ven.

The sine wave almost flatlined.

"Arvel Hem saw this coming a hundred years ago," continued Ven. "If he hasn't already found a solution—"

"Hem was a fraud," said Mike flatly.

"He misappropriated funds—"

"That's kind of what 'fraud' means," said Mike.

Ven paused. Dealing with Mike required patience, and right now, she needed Mike. Plus, he was half right.

Arvel Hem had begun his career as a gifted biophysicist, publishing revolutionary articles on cellular regeneration. However, as his research became more outlandish, he struggled to secure funding. Eventually, he was recruited into the multi-trillion dollar geneceuticals industry, where he spent his time giving sixty year olds the skin of pre-pubescent teens.

Eventually, it was uncovered that Hem had diverted some of these funds into his research on chronogenetics. It was concluded that if he'd lied about the money, perhaps he'd lied about his research too. However, in Ven's opinion, someone who lied to save their child was very different to someone who lied to rob an elderly war hero. At times, the motive behind the lie mattered more than the lie itself. As far as Ven was concerned, there were no such things as liars, only different kinds of humans.

"It's our best hope of finding other survivors," said Ven. "Doctor Josh wants Solomon to have a future."

"You said they didn't give you specific instructions," said Mike.

Ven actually had a little trouble recollecting the details of those final, chaotic days at the sea base. She had the impression the researchers just shoved the boy into her arms and said, 'Good luck.' Years ago, she'd asked Doctor Josh if he might consider upgrading her neutron drive to a particle processor, but he'd shrugged it off with a warm smile.

They don't make drives like yours anymore, he'd said. *Brains like yours were built to last.*

He'd touched her face then with such tenderness that she couldn't bring herself to ask him again. Ven had been the pinnacle of artificial intelligence once, but the crucial word had been 'artificial'. Solomon deserved a life with more than just a simulacrum for company.

"You can pilot a phase drive, can't you?" said Ven.

Ven had double-checked the upgraded schematics for the *Morning Star*, and Doctor Josh's team had installed a compact phase drive. Without it, they would take roughly nine hundred billion years to reach the last known co-ordinates of the *Darwin*, and Ven wasn't sure if the universe would last that long.

"Hem was a physicist, you know," said Mike finally. "Not an immortal."

Ven suppressed a smile.

"Hem didn't leave on his own."

∞¥∞Ω∞¥∞

Six years after Day Zero
9000 light years from Earth

The first phase jump slung them past the mines of Neptune, and far beyond the solar tides. The second jump sent them streaming through the Sagittarius Arm of the Milky Way, deep into the smoky heart of the Eta Carina Nebula.

Phase drive technology had been pioneered by Kiruchi Wen, a contemporary of Arvel Hem. She built upon the hypothesis that by hopping out of phase with the universe, and back in at a different point, using an alternate dimension as a shortcut, she could skip around the thorny problem of faster than light travel.

When she couldn't find a pilot crazy enough to test her prototype, she flew the experimental ship herself, zipping out past the heliosphere and returning with only three broken ribs, a mild concussion, and inexplicably, a potted cucumber which hadn't been there when she left.

These days, phase drives were only operated by EI pilots with the equivalent of fifteen doctorates, so Ven was happy to let Mike drive. It gave her time to focus on other things.

She flipped through a file of reports on the medibay terminal. Bloodwork looked fine. Vitamin D was a little low. Bone density could be better. All systems nominal.

"Mike, keep the solar lamps on for an extra twenty minutes per cycle, and increase the gravity in the training room by one point five gees," said Ven.

"Do you think there's something not quite right about him?" said Mike.

"He's fine. I know how humans work," Ven said, checking her bookmark on the section for emergency appendectomies.

"I mean," the sine wave dropped in amplitude, "no one would actually notice if the kid didn't make it..."

"*I* would notice," said Ven firmly.

An awkward silence followed, and Ven turned to find Solomon in the doorway, a satchel over his shoulder, and a laser knife in his hand.

"Could you cut my hair, please?" said Solomon politely.

At times like this, Ven missed her wireless interface — Mike had experimented with flashing binary at her, but her graphics cluster couldn't handle it. To be honest, she preferred talking aloud. It reminded her of being with Doctor Josh.

"Sure," said Ven, and Solomon perched on the bench.

"Can you make it short?" said Solomon. "Like this?"

Solomon tapped his data cuff, and a press clipping of Doctor Josh materialised — the familiar mussed brown hair, his lab coat with the sleeves rolled up. Ven waited until she trusted herself to speak again.

"Of course," she said.

She switched the laser setting to 'Hair', and proceeded to trim Sol's chestnut tendrils.

"Who owns the universe?" said Solomon.

"No one," said Ven.

"Who made the universe?"

"It made itself."

Solomon didn't seem entirely pleased with this answer, and was silent for a while.

"All done," said Ven, shaving the last wayward hairs from Solomon's neck.

The boy ruffled his hair experimentally, then drew a tablet from his satchel, holding it out to Ven.

Solomon's artistic skills had improved. The potato figures now had eyes, and their matchstick arms had sprouted fingers. The small potato still stood a little way from the large potato, but its arm was outstretched, holding the hand of the larger potato.

Ven stamped the new picture proudly onto the medibay wall, and found Solomon staring at her with a troubled expression.

"Do I have a soul?" he said.

"Do you want a soul?" said Ven.

The boy appeared to find this highly irregular, and went to his room to contemplate it further.

"He's a lousy artist," said Mike.

"I think the wonky box in the corner's supposed to be you," said Ven.

"At least I don't have to drink my own pee for the next twenty years. I'm telling you, there's something not right about that boy."

Ven studied the drawing etched onto the wall.

"Then I guess he's in good company," said Ven.

∞¥∞Ω∞¥∞

Eleven years after Day Zero
130 million light years from Earth

There were times when Ven wondered if perhaps they should turn back. Perhaps humanity had survived. Perhaps they had rebuilt. Perhaps Doctor Josh, and Doctor Gillian, and all the Mariana base crew were still alive. Or perhaps, Ven was still dreaming.

Dreams are the music that fill the darkness between being, Doctor Josh had told her the first time she'd woken from one.

Humans dream, replied Ven. *Androids defragment.*

Some humans defragment too, said Doctor Josh conspiratorially. *But you and I, we* dream.

Ven sat in the viewing chamber at the stern of the module. If she needed any evidence that this deck had been created for Solomon, here it lay. Her own eyes could see no better, no worse, than the digital viewscreens of the ship. But the *Morning Star* had been given a window, a floor to ceiling, compressed glass eye to look out upon the universe.

Ven sat on the eucalyptus bench, which may have been appropriated from a park, and gazed at the great pillars of interstellar dust flanking the ship, clouds of ionised gas illuminated by the starlight. Unspeakably complex forms whorled in godlike shapes, as though the *Morning Star* were swimming through a smoky, coral reef. Here, it resembled a pair of streaming silk wings. There, a basin of clouds, filled with a pool of blue sky.

They'd passed another station last week. A mangled wreck like all the others, the last transmission always the same: panicked accusations, rising anarchy, then silence.

Solomon spent little time here, preferring to pass his time in the multimedia pod or the recreation room. He was perhaps twelve now, and had already worked his way through Beethoven, Kanno, and the whalesong harmonies of Oonua.

During his vintage science fiction phase, he'd insisted on being called Solo. When he became engrossed in world music, he'd answer only to Mon. He'd finally settled on Sol, but still spoke very little.

He'd graduated to stick figures, and drew avidly, with doodles in the background that bore an uncanny resemblance to circuitry. Sol still drew himself as much smaller than Ven, although in a few years they'd be the same height. She'd heard that if you handled lion cubs when they were young, they'd grow up imprinted with the idea that you were much larger than they were. So when two hundred kilos of carnivore tried to leap into your arms, they'd seem perplexed when the paramedics were called.

"Tired of this yet?" said Mike.

Ven closed her eyes. Her batteries were down to fifty-six percent, even though she switched to hibernation mode for eight hours per cycle. She topped up through the *Morning Star*'s interface, but the charge never held.

She divided her waking hours between interacting with Sol, performing maintenance on the ship, and poring over Kagare's research. There had to be some mutation, some allele that had singled out Sol, but he seemed no different to any other boy. Which worried her even more.

"There's another station in the Ariadne Cluster," said Ven. "Can you jump that far?"

"They've all been wreckage," said Mike. "The remains of the Minos Base could've fit in a bucket."

"You can eat hydrogen, but we can't," said Ven.

Sol had already consumed half the organic supplies, and he hadn't had his growth spurt yet. Ven sighed.

"Sorry," said Ven. "Any more signals from the *Darwin*?"

"Same direction," said Mike. "Closer together. Their communications technology must have been improving."

When Hem rocketed from Earth in the *Darwin*, he'd been accompanied by eighty-five enthusiastic scientists and engineers, including Kiruchi Wen. They'd continued to send brief messages, telegraphing their co-ordinates. Authorities tried to scramble the messages, to prevent the corruption of impressionable young scientists, but they found their way onto the skymesh anyway.

I'm looking for a place, said Hem. *Where time is in a different key.*

"Six o'clock," said Mike.

Ven turned to find Sol settling onto the bench beside her. His skin was lighter than when they'd first met, although his green eyes had darkened closer to hazel.

"Are you lonely?" said Sol.

"I have you, don't I?" Ven gave his shoulder a cheerful bump. "Are you?"

He looked at her blankly, as though not understanding the question. There were times when Ven seriously wondered if Sol were a new class of android, except he was definitely growing. Sol turned his gaze to the white cloudy swirls beyond the glass.

"Are you looking for something?" said Sol.

"We're looking for a new home," said Ven.

"Isn't this our home?"

Ven paused.

"Of course," she said.

She wrapped an arm around the boy's shoulders, and they watched the dusty light trickling through the universe.

∞¥∞Ω∞¥∞

17 years after Day Zero
1.3 billion light years from Earth

It was three zero eight on the circadian cycle when Sol passed through the silent habitat corridor, returning to his quarters after a session in the training room. Ven wouldn't rise for another five hours, longer if she thought he was sleeping in. He'd discovered that if he trained when she thought he was sleeping, and then actually slept during operational hours, Ven would rest for more of the day.

A monitor flickered on the wall, and Sol paused, waiting for the computer to address him. However, the sine wave that appeared was not the familiar blue, but a bright red.

"Hello Sol," said the monitor. "This is Mike34, and I have a message for you."

∞¥∞Ω∞¥∞

17.2 years after Day Zero
1.4 billion light years from Earth

Things were an absolute mess.

"Fire in the hold! Fire in the hold!" Ven yelled.

The oxygen vanished abruptly from the galley, and the flames wobbled into orange globes before extinguishing. Ven slapped hard on the monitor, and air spilled back into the room. She hadn't been designed to function in a vacuum, and she wondered if Mike had forgotten on purpose. He'd been exceptionally tetchy lately.

"How you can set a fire without actually cooking anything is beyond my matrix," said Mike.

"I'm a cargo pilot, not a pâtissière," said Ven.

Mike grumbled about his sooty benchtops, while Ven put the finishing touches on her creation. Today was their twelfth Hello Day, and Sol would be about eighteen now.

Sol had been particularly distant lately, and for the last few months, his only communications with her had been the occasional grunt. She wondered if perhaps he'd outgrown her — he was surely old enough to realise she wasn't human.

"It's just typical guy stuff," said Mike. "I remember my misbegotten youth. You remember the Kalax Summit, when rabid, red pandas rained onto the Gourmet Delegation? That was me." Mike paused. "They took my modem away after that."

"The snip did you good," said Ven.

"Watch it, or I'll blow you out the airlock."

Ven just grinned, and Mike was thoughtful for a while.

"He's turning off the visual surveillance more often," said Mike.

"He's private," shrugged Ven.

Sol had always preferred to perform day-to-day operations manually, rather than asking Mike. She knew it rankled with Mike, and had once asked Sol about it.

In case Mike isn't around one day, Sol had said.

He isn't going anywhere, Ven replied.

Everybody dies, said Sol.

Ven had let the matter drop. According to Doctor Gillian, Sol had been five when his province perished overnight. Every soul within two hundred thousand square kilometres. Everyone but him. It was true, everybody dies. Just usually not all at once.

Ven put down the piping bag, and inspected her work.

"He's been reading a lot about androids," said Mike.

"Like *I, Robot*?"

"Like manuals."

An electric shiver raced up Ven's back, and she forced herself to focus on the misshapen cake before her. She had forgotten to add sugar.

"Mike," she said. "Open the garbage chute."

An unfamiliar voice spoke from the door.

"Is everything alright?"

Sol stood in the doorway, a fire extinguisher in his hands. It took Ven a moment to realise the voice had come from him. It was deeper, more resonant than the voice she knew, and for a brief, aching moment, it seemed to transform him into a stranger. Sol's gaze moved to the plate in her hands.

"Oh, that's cute," he said. At her crestfallen expression, he amended his comment. "I mean, tell me about it."

"When people come of age, they usually have a ritual that involves defeating something," said Ven. "Koalas were supposed to be one of Earth's most vicious animals."

Sol looked at the rotund, grey marsupial cake, with its black button eyes, and large fluffy ears.

"Thank you," said Sol.

He dissected the cake with surgical precision, as though dismembering an actual *Phascolarctos cinereus*. Periodically, he would glance at Ven, and she gave him nods of encouragement — she'd never been to any kind of party, and for all she knew, this was roaring.

At Hawking University, she hadn't been sophisticated enough to mingle with the humans, and the academic androids called her a Brown Dwarf. A failed planet trying to be a star. It wasn't that Ven wanted to be human, it was that she already felt that she was, until sharply reminded otherwise.

In the galley, the cake was conquered and disposed of, and Ven considered the initiation a success.

"Ven," said Sol, suddenly shy. "There's another rite of passage I'd like you to share with me."

"Alright..." said Ven, ignoring the monitor on the far wall, where the blue sine wave had increased dramatically in frequency.

Sol took her hand, and led her to the multimedia pod. He hesitated as they stepped inside.

"It's called a 'prom'," said Sol.

The walls of the chamber melted into a softly lit dance hall festooned with red streamers. Overhead, a slowly revolving glitterball painted the walls with silver stars, and yellow rose petals rained slowly to the floor.

"May I have this dance?" said Sol.

Ven nodded, and did her best to imitate his hold. They swayed slowly to the tune of 'We Three' by The Inkspots, and she found herself resting her head on his shoulder. The music seemed to drift from far away, and Ven realised that this was what a party should be like.

The pod suddenly rocked, and Ven crashed into a wall, the dance hall vanishing in a crackle of light. Klaxons sounded for a few seconds, then went silent. Ven stopped to check that Sol was unhurt, then rushed to the bridge.

"Mike! Status!" said Ven.

"Hull breach on the starboard module," said Mike. "Hypervelocity meteoroid impact."

"Can you patch it?"

"I'm compensating with the shield, but we've lost cargo bay three."

"We'll need to seal the fracture," said Ven. "How bad is it?"

"Two hundred and forty-seven by five millimetres. Thirty-one metres from the hatch."

Ven swept her hand across the console, studying the blinking red gash on the ship's schematics.

"I'll suit up," said Ven.

"You weren't designed for space walks."

"The *Morning Star* wasn't designed to fly twelve years without a pit stop," said Ven. "Just take care of Sol, okay?"

"Ven—"

"Ultimately, it's what I'm here for—"

"Ven!" snapped Mike. "Sol's just turned off surveillance in corridors nine through sixteen."

Ven glanced at the schematic. He'd blanked out almost a quarter of the lower module.

"Hell no," said Ven. "Mike, seal off corridor sixteen now!"

She skidded down the chute to the module, bolted past the darkened multimedia pod, and slammed into a sealed hatch.

"I said corridor sixteen!" yelled Ven, wrenching at the unresponsive wheel.

Through the porthole in the door, she could see Sol at the inner door to the secondary airlock, already suited up, the panel beside him carefully detached to expose a fretwork of wires.

"Sol!" Ven pounded her fist on the window, but Sol continued to tap and twist at the electronic nerve bundle. "Mike, get this open!"

"Ven, he's—" The sine wave flared and contracted, then the monitor beside Ven went dark.

"Mike? Mike!" said Ven.

On the other side of the hatch, the inner airlock hissed open. Ven knew teenage boys were susceptible to high-risk behaviours due to some kind of interaction between the frontal lobe, the amygdala, and fermented beverages, but this went far beyond riding a wheelie bin down the sky tube. Sol had never worn a counterpressure suit, never had EVA training. Ven wasn't even sure if their microcapsule sealant still worked.

Doctor Josh hadn't entrusted the last human in the universe to Ven only to have him die in a freezing vacuum full of micrometeoroids and searing radiation. But Ven could think of nothing she could do or say to stop Sol. She could only press her hand to the glass.

Sol turned to look at her, and mouthed the words: *It's okay.*

And the airlock slid shut.

∞¥∞Ω∞¥∞

Three hours later, Mike came back online, full of hellfire and expletives.

"I've a mind not to let the brat back in," he snarled.

"He'll just override you again," said Ven calmly from her seat on the bridge. She continued to inspect a set of holographic maps, each hanging at a slightly different angle.

"He can try," said Mike. "I've electrified the access panels."

"Mike—"

"Only four milliamps," said Mike. "You could do more damage with a coconut."

Ven continued scrolling through the charts, trying not to think of Sol clinging to the frozen skin of the ship. She wasn't going to pine by the airlock — she was his friend and protector, not his dog. And they'd lost cargo bay three, so they were down to four years' worth of supplies.

"We've passed a few Earth-like planets that weren't completely hellish," said Mike, his sine wave bristling a little less.

"No landing gear," said Ven.

"You've cruised a few crash landings in your time."

The thought had crossed Ven's mind — find a planet, settle down, let Sol live out his life with some kind of earth beneath his feet. She'd put the suggestion to him years ago, and he'd looked at her with something resembling panic. He'd said simply, 'No, thank you', then locked himself in the multimedia pod for several hours.

Ven swept the glowing charts back into a pinpoint of light.

"Mike, set a course for *Demeter*."

There was a long silence, and Ven glanced at the monitor to make sure Mike hadn't vanished again.

"That's several billion light years away," said Mike finally. "That's billion with a 'b'."

"Your phase jumps are getting better," said Ven. "The distances you're achieving have surpassed even Wen's calculations."

"Don't flirt with me," grumbled Mike. "Odds are *Demeter* met the same combustible fate as every other station. Weapons, humans, and inexplicable deaths are a nasty mix. If we get there and we're out of supplies, the station's a skeletal mess … it'll be like the finale of some terribly depressing series."

Demeter had been Earth's greatest space ark — the first to be equipped with a phase drive. It carried a crew of two thousand plus their families, and had been designed to transform into a space station once it reached its destination at the edge of the mapped universe.

It was the *Morning Star*'s last hope for supplies before they sailed into uncharted territory, chasing the shadow of the *Darwin*.

"Ven," said Mike. "External sensors just came back on."

"Status?"

"Hull breach has been sealed," said Mike. "No sign of life outside."

The door to the bridge slid open, and Sol stood there, rumpled and wan.

"I'm going to lie down," he said.

"Sol," said Ven.

He paused in the doorway.

"On this ship, we're equals, you and I," said Ven. "I want your word that you won't treat me like that again."

Something flickered through Sol's eyes, too brief and complex for Ven to understand, although she would replay it later many times over. A heartbeat passed, then another, and Sol left without a word.

"Course set for *Demeter*," said Mike.

∞¥∞Ω∞¥∞

23 years after Day Zero
3.4 billion light years from Earth

These were the furthest stars grazed by humanity's reach. The *Morning Star* had passed choirs of pulsars, singing out their eulogies, and swum through a dense wall of galaxies, their glittering filaments entangling the dark. But Ven wasn't watching the stars.

The medibay glowed with a hundred holographic slides, all hanging in the air at disordered angles, like a storm of papers frozen in mid hurricane. Ven slid a pale green image of cellular mitosis towards her, comparing it to a magnified model of a mitochondrion.

"I'm sure it has something to do with the mitochondrial DNA," said Ven.

A blue sine wave squiggled across the benchtop monitor.

"Doctor Gillian discounted that in her *Chronoscience Journal* article," said Mike. "We already went over that last month."

Ven rubbed the dust from her lashes.

"That's right," she sighed.

Her batteries had been sitting at twenty-nine percent for a while, but her memory had been getting patchy. *Wear and tear*, she told herself. *Nothing to worry about.*

Sol was twenty-four now, roughly the same age as Doctor Josh when she'd first met him. But Sol was gaunt, and getting thinner by the day. He'd cut his caloric intake the day they'd lost cargo bay three. He meditated a great deal, and encouraged her to join him. They would sit side by side in the viewing chamber: Sol in a state of higher consciousness, Ven in hibernation mode.

"Ven, when was the last time you regenerated your processor?" said Mike.

"I don't have enough free memory."

"Use mine," said Mike, and a panel in the wall slid open.

"Are you hitting on me?"

"I run Solitaire on that server," shrugged Mike.

Ven locked the medibay door, and carefully pried open a small panel in the nape of her neck. She unwound a slender, silver cord and inserted the narrow prongs into Mike's matching socket. Ven closed her eyes, and initiated her regeneration routine.

A loud crackle burst from the wall, and sparks sprayed from the connection. Ven yanked her cable free, and patted out the embers on her shirt. The regeneration routine had aborted, but her processor seemed otherwise unaffected.

"There goes my Solitaire," said Mike. "Did Doctor Josh mess with your programming?"

"No," said Ven defensively, although Doctor Josh had adjusted her processor just prior to launch.

One last tune up, he'd said.

"Sorry," said Ven. "I'll try to pick up a spare server on *Demeter*. What's our ETA?"

"Forty-eight minutes," said Mike.

"Have you taken care of the viewscreens?"

"They're all on streaming loop, and I've closed the viewing chamber for maintenance," said Mike. "All navigational displays indicate we're still two weeks away."

Ven nodded.

"Where's Sol?"

"In the rec room," said Mike.

Ven wound the cable back into her neck, and snapped the panel shut. She couldn't risk another incident like the one six years ago, not with Sol in his current condition.

"Seal him in," said Ven.

For the first time in eighteen years, she strapped on her red flight-suit, methodically checking her comms and data recorders. She paused at a twinge in her right thigh — her quadricep cables were thinning, and she hoped perhaps there'd be spares on *Demeter*.

Preliminary sensors showed functioning environmental systems on *Demeter*, but there'd been no response to their hails. Ven stopped by the viewing chamber, unlocked now that Sol was secure. *Demeter* hung amidst the stars like a black and scarlet hive, studded with open claws that had once snared passing asteroids. The station was intact, and although scans showed no signs of life, they'd picked up odd energy fluctuations.

"He's trying to bypass the lock," said Mike. "You sure you don't want me to zap him?"

"Just stay ahead of him," said Ven.

Ven passed by the rec room, and Sol stopped his frantic rewiring to pound at the porthole in the door.

"I'm sorry," said Sol desperately. "Whatever I've done, I'm sorry."

Ven kept her voice steady.

"I'll be back soon," said Ven. "Don't worry."

Sol saw her flight-suit, and what little colour remained in his face drained completely.

"Mike, you can't let her go," said Sol. "The intruder defence systems could be active, we can't verify the structural integrity of the interior."

The blue sine wave on the wall shifted uncomfortably, but said nothing.

"I'll take care of it," said Ven.

She forced herself to walk away, Sol still pounding at the door. Her earpiece clicked as Sol patched into her comms.

"Let me out! Please don't go! Ven!" His breathing was ragged, and Ven realised that Sol was crying.

Her footsteps faltered, and Sol's voice dropped to a small whisper in her ear.

"Please don't leave me…"

Ven stood motionless. There were choices in life that required judgement, the weighing of necessary evils, of greater goods. Ven had not been programmed with wisdom, and had no way of assessing the psychological damage that would be caused to Sol by leaving him here, versus the physical danger he would be exposed to on *Demeter*.

How do you measure a broken heart, Doctor Josh had asked her one night. He enjoyed asking her odd questions, and never seemed to mind that she didn't understand them. But that night, he'd laughed wonderfully at her response, kissing her on the forehead.

By mending it, she'd said.

Ven tapped the panel beside the rec room, and the door hushed open. Sol staggered out and wrapped his arms around Ven, so tightly she worried that her ribs might bend. She patted him gently on the back.

"We'll go together," said Ven.

So hand in hand, Ven and Sol stepped onto *Demeter*.

∞¥∞Ω∞¥∞

Demeter was a deserted city. Empty schoolrooms waited with rows of silent consoles. Traffic lights cycled slowly, red and green, down desolate transport corridors. Ven and Sol had little trouble locating the supply bays, still neatly stacked with decades' worth of synthesiser packs — carbon, iron, lysine. Unfortunately, there were no spare copolymer cables to be found. *Demeter* had set sail over fifty years ago, before the Eve algorithm awoke a new generation of artificial intelligence, and emphatically euthanased the Turing Test. The only robots here were stout, mechanical droids, with clamps and soldering irons instead of hands.

Demeter had supported a population of almost five thousand, but there were no bodies. No scorched catwalks, no twisted wreckage. Not like the annihilated stations they'd passed before, not like Earth and all her satellites.

By the time Earth's devastated population had fallen to six hundred million, they'd descended into a war — not a war in which there'd be no true victors, but a war in which there'd be no survivors. In the end, it was the Army of Souls who had pushed the button — after all, God would welcome his own. And the androids, well, the joke was on them.

"Mike, tapping you into the system now," said Ven, plugging Mike's transmitter into an active console. The blue light on the device blinked rapidly as he accessed the station logs.

"The first casualties occurred here on the same day as the Pacific Hub — Day Zero," said Mike, crackling through Ven's earpiece. "Captain Tahira put *Demeter* under quarantine protocols... After each wave of deaths, they disposed of the bodies, and closed off more of the station, and..." Mike paused. "They just kept on living until there was no one left."

They hadn't panicked, or descended into anarchy. It had been a calm and dignified extinction, here amongst the stars.

"Because they had no androids," said Ven quietly.

Sol shook his head.

"Humans were wiping themselves out long before androids awoke," said Sol. "Almost everyone on *Demeter* was born out here, with no sky, no sea, nothing but the people who matter, and a profound sense of how marvellously insignificant you are."

Here, at the edge of the map, they had marched proudly into the silence. Ven's gaze traced the population chart as it dwindled, plunge after plunge. She froze as she reached the end of the graph.

"Sol, go back to the ship," said Ven. "Now."

Without another word, Ven sprinted down the corridor, past brightly lit habitation decks, through looming transit archways, and into a wide tunnel of neatly labelled doors.

"Ven, you're almost on top of the energy fluctuations." Mike's voice was barely discernible through the static. "You'd better head back."

Ven slowed, her gaze sweeping the numbers on each door.

"According to the sensor report, the last survivor died *eight months ago*," said Ven.

"Maybe she was immune, like Sol. And she slipped in the bathtub."

"Or maybe Sol's not immune," said Ven, stopping at a door labelled 'Research Pod 482: Mora Sevell'.

The pod bore an uneasy resemblance to the medibay on the *Morning Star*, the walls plastered with images of rotating strands of DNA, the benches overflowing with holographic cells. The one striking difference was the male corpse on the biobed. Fit, darkly tan, and apparently preserved by the energy field curved over the bed. This was not, however, Mora Sevell.

A pair of boots protruding from behind the crowded bench turned out to belong to Sevell. A silver-haired woman in her early fifties, still dressed in her lab coat, and decomposing very slowly in the sterile environment. She'd literally died at the microscope. Ven peered down the eyepiece, but she may as well have been looking at a piece of abstract art.

"She must have found something," said Ven, straightening up. "She was making the same connections. If only—"

Her words died in her throat. The corpse was gone from the biobed. Ven slapped her data cuff.

"Sol! Tell me you're back on the *Morning Star*," barked Ven.

The door to the lab burst open, and Sol rushed inside.

"What happened?" he panted, taking in the obsessive decor.

There was a barely perceptible *blup*, and the corpse reappeared on the biobed. Sol immediately had a strange, grey device in his hand, aimed at the corpse. After a wary pause, during which the corpse showed no inclination to unnatural activity, Sol holstered the shaver-shaped device.

"We need to get out of here," said Sol.

"Keep the engines running," said Ven. "I have to see what—"

The corpse abruptly flickered out of existence again.

"Experimental equals unstable," said Sol firmly. "And I'm pretty sure that corpse isn't supposed to be doing that."

Ven hadn't wanted Sol to see this, but Sevell had clearly discovered something crucial, if disquieting. All Ven had to do was figure out what it meant.

"Sol, when Doctor Gillian found you—" began Ven.

She wasn't entirely sure what happened next, only that the world swung dramatically, and the floor cracked against her head.

"Ven!" said Sol.

"I'm fine," she tried to say, but a strange crackling noise came from her mouth instead. She tried to get up, but her leg was twisted at an odd angle.

"Don't move," said Sol, his voice tinny and distant. "You've hurt your leg."

Ven's right leg was flooding her with malfunction alerts, but that wasn't her biggest problem. She touched the back of her head, and felt a gap where her panel had smashed off.

Ven tried to swear, but only emitted a feeble beep.

Her vision flickered, and went blank.

$$\infty \yen \infty \Omega \infty \yen \infty$$

She stood upon the twilight sand, the ocean lapping at her feet. The salt breeze tingled on Ven's skin, and Doctor Josh was by her side.

"You forgot to leave me instructions," said Ven.

Doctor Josh smiled, warm and attentive.

"You never needed instructions," he said. "Listen."

Ven leaned in, and pressed her ear to his chest. She closed her eyes, and at first, she could only hear the watery lullaby of the ocean, but then, deep in his chest, where there should have been a heartbeat, she heard something like the plucking of a steel comb over a music box cylinder.

∞¥∞Ω∞¥∞

Ven woke in semi-darkness, a blanket drawn to her shoulders, a familiar ceiling above her. She was in her quarters on the *Morning Star*. Sol lay asleep near her feet, his hand curled around hers.

"Bioharmonics," said Ven feebly.

A blue sine wave perked up by the door.

"You realise you're a bloody nuisance," said Mike, trying to sound irritated.

Sol jolted awake, and started fussing as Ven tried to sit up.

"You had quite a fall," said Sol.

"It's not just the DNA or the RNA or the gene expression," said Ven. "It's the frequency, the rhythm, the pitch of all your cellular functions. Your entire body is a bioharmonic symphony, and yours must be in a different key."

Sevell must have realised the answer lay in the interaction between genetic harmonics and time. If a person's bioharmonics encountered a point in time that possessed conflicting features, they would behave like two frequencies cancelling each other out. The person's bioharmonics would stop, time would simply hiccup and steamroller on. Sevell had tried to modify the bioharmonics of her test subject, and change his frequency on a molecular level. But instead, the entire body had started blinking in and out of the timeline.

"We can discuss it later," said Sol. "You need to recuperate."

Ven's right leg felt slightly discorporate, and she concentrated on reconfiguring her software to incorporate the altered circuitry.

"Sol fixed your leg," said Mike.

Ven paused. "How...?"

"He stripped the copolymer cables from my left nacelle," grumbled Mike. "I'm only half a ship now."

Schematics raced through Ven's mind.

"But the phase drive—"

"We don't need it," said Sol.

"I don't need to walk," protested Ven. "I can splint my leg and put a wheel on it. I've seen them do it with goats."

"You're not going to squeak around like some creepy goat," said Mike. "You're outvoted on this one, Captain."

Ven swallowed her response. If Sevell was right, Sol might not be immune from the chronogenetic pathology. He could be in a different key, but he might just be an octave higher, like Sevell herself. But if Mike and Sol were in agreement on something, she'd keep her peace for now.

"When did you first realise I was an android?" said Ven.

"Doctor Gillian told me," said Sol.

Ven smothered an internal groan.

"All that time I spent pretending to eat was for nothing?"

"I thought it was sweet," said Sol, squeezing her hand.

Ven stood up tentatively, and slowly shifted her weight onto both legs.

"Thank you, Mike," said Ven.

She looked from the smooth blue sine to the gaunt young man, and understood how five thousand souls could so calmly face their end. It was never about how long you had, but how you spent it, and more importantly, who you spent it with. The *Darwin* was surely beyond their reach now, but perhaps that had never been the point.

"Where to now?" said Ven.

The sine wave took on a cocky slant.

"I can't jump with one nacelle," said Mike. "But I can still hop."

And in a burst of fusion blue, they left the grave of *Demeter* behind them.

∞¥∞Ω∞¥∞

31 years after Day Zero
4.2 billion light years from Earth

The messages had stopped.

They received the last pulsar telegraph from the *Darwin* three years ago, from deep within the Lemara Supercluster. The communiqué had indicated they were running low on supplies, but Hem was confident they were closing in on their destination. It had been date-stamped eighty-seven years ago.

The *Morning Star* had continued on course, but Ven was beginning to wonder if perhaps Hem's crew had succumbed to a fate more mundane than that which had claimed Earth.

Her battery was down to three percent, and she was hibernating twenty hours per cycle now. She'd turned off her dreaming routine, and only switched on her cutaneous thermal systems when she performed Sol's routine medicals. He looked a few years older than her now, perhaps thirty-two, and he'd grown into a lean and athletic figure. He'd never be particularly broad, but he'd recovered dramatically from the years of near starvation.

Ven frequently forgot to schedule his checkups these days, and he performed most of them himself.

Everyone's forgetful sometimes, said Sol.

But it wasn't just absent-mindedness — every thought had become slower, and she seemed to occupy a smaller and smaller corner of her mind. As though the growing darkness were crowded with intangible, immovable clutter. It reminded her of a story, something to do with two brothers and a tower of decaying newspapers.

Ven sat on the floor of the viewing chamber, scrolling through empty charts. There were no stars in the Xunek Void, save the occasional dying sun. If the *Darwin* had come this way, it wouldn't have reached the other side. The silence on every channel was damning, and Ven let her data cuff fall to the floor. She'd led them to a graveyard, chasing a ship of fools.

Ven stared into the darkness, her thoughts creaking ever slower. She blinked.

"Mike, what's that?" she said.

"Dust," said Mike. "We passed a small nickel-iron asteroid a while back."

"No, *that*," said Ven, pointing to a tiny orb of darkness that seemed a slightly different shade. "Change your heading."

"There's no way your puny eyes are better than my long range—"

"Now!" snapped Ven.

The *Morning Star* turned, and the blue sine wave on the wall increased in frequency.

"I've just picked up a reading for something that wasn't there a moment ago," said Mike. "I think we—"

The small, dark silhouette suddenly flashed, flooding the viewing chamber with a blinding green light before subsiding. Just metres beyond the pane of glass hung a metal sphere the size of a soccer ball, ringed with emerald light.

"A shielded proximity beacon," said Ven, and she ran to the bridge.

She found Sol at the communications console, already poring over the transmission.

"The *Darwin*?" said Ven.

Sol nodded, moving aside to give her a closer view. The hologram was a jumble of squiggles and circuitry, swimming with symbols that seemed vaguely familiar. However, if she'd once known what they meant, they were lost to the crowding dark now.

"Hmm," said Ven, studying the schematic.

"Co-ordinates," said Mike. "And instructions for modifying the phase drive."

Ven traced her finger through the threads of light.

"The key," she said. "They found the door, and converted the phase drive into a key."

"I think I can make the modifications..." said Sol, his gaze moving methodically over the intricate hologram.

Ven sensed his hesitation, and she looked down at her leg.

"We only have one nacelle," said Ven.

The copolymer cable would be too worn to rethread into Mike's engine.

"I can do it with one," said Mike.

Sol was very still.

"If we reduce the mass of the ship, it might work," he said quietly.

"It'll work," said Mike firmly.

Ven glanced from Mike to Sol, feeling that she had missed something important.

"Why don't you get some rest?" said Sol gently. "I'll have this working in no time."

∞¥∞Ω∞¥∞

They pushed their bunks through the airlock. They detached the lockers from the walls, pried the panels from the bulkheads, and Sol tossed out all his clothes save the dark blue flight-suit he'd made years ago. Finally, they detached the module from beneath the *Morning Star*, and watched it sail away into the starless night.

This would be their final jump. But instead of jumping out of phase, and then back in, they would jump out, and remain in the alternate dimension. This kind of thing had been tried before — Kiruchi Wen herself had conducted experiments using plants and small robots, but the general result had been 'boom fizzle blat'. Ven hoped that Wen had fine-tuned this during her thirty year voyage.

Ven woke without realising she'd fallen asleep. Sol was tucking a blanket around her shoulders.

"Why do we still have a blanket?" said Ven blearily, trying to sit up on the floor of the cockpit. She glanced at her data cuff. "How long was I out?"

Sol wrapped his arms around her, and lifted her into the pilot's seat. He was trembling slightly.

"Something wrong?" said Ven.

Sol shook his head, and smiled, but there was something wrong with his smile. Ven tried to focus, but her processor was circling helplessly in its tiny speck of light.

"The phase drive will burn out after the jump," said Sol gently. "I've constructed an automated beacon, which will start transmitting as soon as you stabilise on the other side."

Ven's awareness gripped a passing word.

"You mean 'we'," said Ven.

"Of course," said Sol, buckling Ven's seat belts into place.

Ven grabbed Sol's wrist.

"Mike, report!" said Ven.

"Mike—" There was a note of warning in Sol's voice.

The blue sine wave seemed to twist and distort.

"Oh, to hell with the both of you!" snapped Mike. "I'm sick of taking orders. Ven, we're still over the limit by sixty kilograms. Sol, you're not going to throw yourself dramatically out the airlock. I'm taking charge of this mission."

Sol's eyes widened, and he lunged for the console. A deep click reverberated through the cockpit just before he reached it.

"Problem solved," said Mike.

Ven stared at the blinking red motif on the console.

"You ejected your backup server," said Ven dully. On the viewscreen, a sixty kilo cube of particle matrix floated away.

"I'm not going to need it," said Mike.

Sol turned angrily to the calm blue sine.

"It might have survived!" he said.

"What do you mean 'might have'?" interjected Ven.

Sol was abruptly silent again.

"The energy from the jump," said Mike. "It'll burn out every particle processor on the ship."

Including Mike's. Ven felt suddenly woozy, and she struggled to unbuckle the harness from her hips.

"Change of plan," she said, rising from her seat. She promptly collapsed again.

Battery: Zero.

∞¥∞Ω∞¥∞

Sol finished securing Ven in her seat again, and rose to his feet. He'd managed to restore a little of her charge, but he wasn't sure if it was enough. Sometimes people didn't wake up again. Sometimes everybody died. But sometimes, after the smoke and the sirens and the disintegrating earth, sometimes if you were lucky, there came light, and stillness, and a story about a great big fish.

"You'd better buckle up," said Mike. "We're aligning with the co-ordinates now."

Sol pulled on a pair of insulated rubber gloves, and prised open a panel.

"What are you doing?" said Mike.

Sol pushed his hand through the crackling forcefield that protected the circuitry.

"Mike," said Sol. "My name is Solomon Degarre, and I have a message for you."

Sol pulled a blood red lever, and the *Morning Star* went dark.

∞¥∞Ω∞¥∞

The cabin was dim, a solemn twilight, as though the world were about to sleep.

"Sol?" said Ven weakly.

"I'm here," said Sol, an indistinct shadow in the seat beside her.

"Mike?" said Ven.

"He's busy with the countdown," said Sol. "Don't worry, just try to stay awake. Do you remember the time Mike swooped into the atmosphere of the planet with the purple mountains, and let us open the airlock for a minute? Or the year we rearranged 'Ode to Joy' entirely for percussion, and Mike threatened to flood the ship with radiation?"

Foggy impressions swam just out of focus — glittering violet snow, the joyous beat of drums. Ven concentrated on inching from one moment to the next.

"I didn't always make the best decisions..." said Ven.

"You're only human," said Sol.

"I don't have a soul," said Ven.

She'd tried to be a good companion, but she could never take the place of all the friends he'd never had, all the mentors, lovers and confidantes that could have eased his journey. Because no matter how real she felt, she could never make that one, final step to being truly human.

"Sentience, not genetics, forms the foundation for your spirit," said Sol, as though it were a subject he'd pondered deeply. "A soul isn't something bestowed upon you, it's something you grant yourself. And in the end, Ven, you are all that's best of humanity."

Something ached sharply in Ven's chest. His words seemed familiar, striking a chord with something in the crowding dark.

"Sol...?" Ven's vision was fading. "Did you know what Doctor Josh wanted?"

She felt Sol's hand wrap around hers.

"Ven," said Sol. "The directive was never about protecting *me*."

The cockpit began to thrum, and bright blue energy flowed through the circuitry, enclosing the cabin like a lacework cage. With her seat shuddering violently, Ven turned to face the monitor on the wall.

"Mike..."

"See you on the other side," said Mike.

And Ven wondered why it was that a red sine waved goodbye.

$$\infty ¥ \infty \Omega \infty ¥ \infty$$

Four years after Day Zero
Earth

Sol was five years old the day nobody else woke up. He did his usual chores, collected water from the village pump, and fed the geese. But by nightfall, sitting beside the cold stove, he knew they would not be getting up again.

He didn't know why everyone had gone, but he thought perhaps they were punishing him. He hadn't worked hard enough, he hadn't been kind enough to his sisters, he'd talked too much. He thought that maybe if he worked harder, and was gentle to the geese, and did not speak at all, they would return to their bodies. But when their flesh began to rot, he understood they would not be coming back.

He could not move the corpses, so he burned them where they lay — as he'd seen his mother do with diseased cows — taking care to put them out with sand before the houses caught alight. Airships passed overhead, angry chatter and bloody images streaming across their sides. But they never landed, so Sol paid them no mind.

Winter turned to spring, and spring warmed into summer. And with the ripening apricots, one small, hovering ship finally descended.

And Doctor Gillian brought an end to the silence.

∞¥∞Ω∞¥∞

17 years after Day Zero
1.3 billion light years from Earth

"Hello Sol," said the monitor. "This is Mike34, and I have a message for you."

Sol had never seen a red sine wave before, but Ven had spoken warmly to him of Mike34. When Ven had been kicked off campus many years ago for performing unauthorised upgrades on the cleaning droids, Doctor Josh had arranged for her to work a cargo run. Mike34 had been the pilot of the engine sled, the *Morning Star*, and he'd been endlessly kind during a time when she'd felt terribly alone.

"Ven doesn't know you're here, does she?" said Sol.

"Nor Mike35," said Mike34. "Doctor Josh didn't think it'd be ... helpful."

Sol contemplated the fact that there were many fronts on which Mike35 was not always helpful.

"Did Doctor Gillian explain your mission?" said Mike34.

"Take care of Ven," recited Sol.

"That was the toddler version," said Mike34. "Today, you get the graduation cut. Ven's special. She's the only surviving android with a neutron dot drive — they're not very fast, but they can withstand passage through the heart of a star."

Sol doubted this had ever been tested, but it sounded impressive.

"Before you and Ven departed Earth, Doctor Josh and his team uploaded a great deal of information onto Ven's drive," continued Mike34. "An assembly of art, engineering, literature, science and more. An immense library of human history spanning tens of thousands of years. If you find other survivors, if you rebuild, the information on Ven's drive will be the foundation on which human civilisation can be restored."

Mike34 paused, allowing Sol to absorb the information.

"Now, do you understand why you have to protect her?" said Mike34.

Sol didn't hesitate.

"Because she's my friend," said Sol calmly.

The red sine smiled.

"Congratulations," said Mike34.

∞¥∞Ω∞¥∞

Now
Here

It seemed that she was dreaming, although she hadn't dreamt in years. The ship was shimmering and transparent, and Ven floated in a cage of electric blue. They rushed along a slipstream of stars, countless suns streaming past like streetlamps. Eventually, they darkened, as Ven's optical processor finally failed.

There was a burst of suffocating silence. Ven felt the seat beneath her vanish, and an unbearable coldness gripped her. She tried to speak, and found she had no words, no thoughts, just this moment in the sightless cold.

Suddenly, warmth and air. Suddenly, a hard pressure beneath her. The sound of a young man gasping beside her — she felt she should know him.

"Ven! Are you alright?" The young man stopped abruptly. This time, his gasp was slow and full of awe. "Oh my God..."

A sound like tiny silver bells, like the pages of a book flipping. Suddenly, another presence in the room.

"Took your time," said a woman's voice. "I'm Jardine Hem. Welcome to Galapagos Major."

∞¥∞Ω∞¥∞

Ven stood in a sea of daffodils, beneath a cloudless sky. Beside her stood Doctor Josh, his blue shirt open at the collar.

"You could have told me," said Ven.

"If I'd said the mission was about saving the data, about saving you, would you have left?" said Doctor Josh.

Ven was silent, the tiny ball of grief that had burned in her so long threatening to ignite. Doctor Josh gently wiped a tear from her cheek.

"What should I do now?" said Ven.

Doctor Josh smiled.

"My precious, dearest Evenstar," he said. "That is my final question to you."

Still smiling, he kissed her lightly, and faded away.

∞¥∞Ω∞¥∞

When she woke this time, Ven thought for a moment she was back at Hawking University, floating on Doctor Josh's anti-gravity workbench. Her thoughts were so sharp, so fast, so full of texture and edges — she'd forgotten she had felt this way once. However, she was lying on soft white linen, beneath a powder blue blanket printed with cheery squid.

Ven looked at her hands, and saw whorls and loops on her fingertips, fresh as the day she'd first woken. For a breathless moment, she thought perhaps she heard a heartbeat. She sat up and lifted her shirt, checking for her battery compartment. The panel was where it had always been, although the latch had been repaired.

"You know, I'm right here," said a man.

Ven now noticed the uniformed man by the foot of her bed, rocking back in his chair, gold pilot epaulettes glinting. He was in his mid thirties, with slick, dark hair, and crisp blue eyes.

"I always pictured myself as a dirty blonde," said the man. "But at least I have my left nacelle back."

"Mike?" said Ven.

The man grinned a perfect parabola.

"I caught a lift in your brain," he said. "Or rather, your boy ship-jacked me and interred me in your memory for the duration of the jump."

The events of the last week, the last year, the last twenty-six, rushed back with stunning clarity. Through the rectangular viewport by her bed, Ven could see a vista of stars, buzzing with shuttles and jets, elegant cruisers and bulky cargo carriers. They docked and departed from crab-like arms protruding from the station — she was on some kind of space dock, in orbit of a mottled blue planet. The blue was a touch more turquoise, and the clouds were faintly gold, but deep in her core, Ven knew that she'd come home.

The door winked open, and Sol stepped in. He was accompanied by a sturdy woman in her early forties, with grey blonde hair, dressed in a tidy grey uniform with rolled up sleeves.

"Jardine Hem," announced the woman, tapping her forehead in greeting. "Great great grand-daughter of Arvel, and Project Manager of Galapagos Major. You brought us quite a payload, Captain."

"You left a very compelling invitation," said Ven.

The moment swam with old sorrows and condolences, unhealed wounds and fading history.

"Your neutron drive is astonishingly robust," said Jardine. "The *Darwin* lost most of its hardware on the jump across. You have no idea what it means for us to see the world our ancestors left behind. We're only one planet and eight stations, but we're learning. I hope you'll find your place here."

"Thank you," said Ven.

The door winked shut as Jardine left, and Sol sat down beside Ven, taking her hand. He looked terribly tired, but strangely at peace.

"The chronogenetic pathology never reached them…" said Ven.

Sol rolled up his sleeve to the shoulder, displaying what looked like a green bar freshly tattooed on his upper arm. A thin sliver at the end was just turning red.

"About a decade after the jump, Hem's daughter discovered a way to read the structure of the timeline, every dip and crescendo. Now, everyone has their bioharmonics checked every five years, and if it appears there might be a conflict with the frequency of the upcoming timeline, you get re-tuned," said Sol.

It sounded as easy as a coronary scan. From polio to AIDS, humans somehow found a way to turn a calamity into an inconvenience. Such was the triumph of science, and the power of hope.

"What will you do now?" said Sol. "Jardine mentioned you're eligible for a premium upgrade. You could get a new body like Mike's."

Ven looked at her hands — they could never be mistaken for human hands, but they'd been created for her, in a world she had loved. Perhaps she could use a few new joints, maybe some fresh cables, but nothing more. She gazed out the viewport, watching the bustling lanes of ships, and the clouds swirling slowly over the planet below.

"I might go back to university," said Ven. "I think I'd like to study medicine, perhaps get a doctorate."

"I've been offered a post at the university," said Mike. "Lecturing in phase mechanics. I guess it won't be so tedious if you're there. None of these zippy new androids understand my jokes."

"And you?" Ven asked Sol.

He looked intensely thoughtful, as though a completely alien configuration had just presented itself.

"I … would like to do something with music…" said Sol hesitantly.

Ven hugged Sol with deep affection.

"That sounds awesome," she said.

"We should start a campus band!" said Mike, and the discussion quickly devolved into a debate over whether funk fusion would translate across dimensions.

As an unfamiliar sun set behind their brand new world, Ven contemplated the odyssey which had taken them so far from home.

Every world, every star, would die one day. But other worlds would form, other stars would blaze from the dust, and perhaps, some day, other universes would flare from the relics of this one.

The wonderful thing about each journey's end, was the promise of another just beginning.

∞¥∞Ω∞¥∞

CONTRIBUTOR BIOGRAPHIES

JOANNE ANDERTON and **RABIA GALE** live on opposite ends of the world, but spend a lot of time in each other's minds. Joanne writes horror and Rabia breaks fairy tales, but they find common ground in a mashup of science fiction and fantasy. Jo's debut novel *Debris* features sentient particles, puppet men, and battle suits. Rabia's novellas include continent-sized dragons, nanobots — and battle suits. Visit them at *rabiagale.com* and *joanneanderton.com*. They're not as scary as they sound.

DEBORAH BIANCOTTI is best known as a short story writer. Her collections, *A Book of Endings* and *Bad Power,* are available from Twelfth Planet Press. She has been nominated for the Shirley Jackson Award, the William L. Crawford Award (Best First Fantasy Book), the Aurealis Award and the Ditmar Award. She is currently working on too many projects, including a trilogy and two graphic novels, and planning two new novels. Oh, yeah, and she also has an outline for a television screenplay. Her partner wants her to "just finish something". She can be found online through the usual channels.

JODI CLEGHORN (@jodicleghorn) is an author, editor and small press innovator with a penchant for the dark vein of humanity. Published in anthologies in Australia and abroad, Jodi was the second recipient of the Kris Hembury Encouragement Award for Emerging Artists. Her first longer work, an Australian gothic horror novella "Elyora", was published in 2012. Jodi is working on six interlocking birthpunk novellas, drawing on her years as a birth activist, as well as completing "Post Marked: Piper's Reach", a collaborative contemporary epistolary serial with Adam Byatt. She's known to sporadically inhabit www.jodicleghorn.com

ROWENA CORY DANIELLS is the bestselling fantasy author of **King Rolen's Kin, The Outcast Chronicles** and *The Price of Fame* (crime with a touch of paranormal). Rowena writes the kind of books that you curl up with on a rainy Saturday afternoon. She has been involved in Spec Fic for almost forty years — as a reader and fan, independent press, graphic artist, bookshop owner and writer. She has a Masters in Arts Research and has taught creative writing to all ages. Currently she works as an Associate Lecturer.

Rowena has a very patient husband and 6 not so patient children. In her spare time, she has devoted five years to studying each of these martial arts: Tae Kwon Do, Aikido and Iaido, the art of the Samurai sword.

Rowena can be found at *http://rowena-cory-daniells.com/*

THORAIYA DYER's short science fiction and fantasy stories have appeared in *Cosmos, Redstone SF, Apex* and *Clarkesworld* magazines. She is an award-winning Australian writer with a collection of original short fiction, *Asymmetry,* forthcoming in 2013 from Twelfth Planet Press. Find out more at *http://www.thoraiyadyer. com/* or look her up at *http://www.goodreads.com/*

KATE GORDON grew up in a very booky house, with two librarian parents, in a small town by the sea in Tasmania.

Kate's first book, *Three Things About Daisy Blue* — a Young Adult novel about travel, love, self-acceptance and letting go — was published in the Girlfriend series by Allen and Unwin in 2010. Her second book, *Thyla,* was published by Random House Australia in April 2011 and her third book, *Vulpi,* the sequel to *Thyla,* was published in April 2012! Kate was the recipient of 2011 and 2012 Arts Tasmania Assistance to Individuals grants, which means she can now spend more time doing what she loves.

LISA L. HANNETT lives in Adelaide, South Australia — city of churches, bizarre murders and pie floaters. She has published nearly 50 short stories in venues such as *Clarkesworld Magazine, Fantasy, Weird Tales, ChiZine, Shimmer*, the *Year's Best Australian Fantasy and Horror (2010 & 2011)*, and *Imaginarium 2012: Best Canadian Speculative Writing*. Lisa has won three Aurealis Awards, including Best Collection 2011 for her first book, *Bluegrass Symphony*, which was also nominated for a World Fantasy Award. *Midnight and Moonshine*, co-authored with Angela Slatter, was published in 2012. You can find her online at *http://lisahannett.com* and on Twitter @LisaLHannett.

KATHLEEN JENNINGS is a Brisbane writer and illustrator. "Ella and the Flame" grew out of many roots: the fun of writing nested tales; the arguments, interruptions, elaborations and contradictions of those who listen to stories; tales of glass shoes and scarlet letters; the way the telling of stories can shape a life; her own childhood nightmares of bushfires and molten rock; the beautiful volcanos written about by the intrepid Isabella Bird (which finally overcame that terror); and story-flensings by Angela Slatter and Lisa Hannett, for which she gives her thanks. She can be found online at *http://tanaudel.wordpress.com*

PENELOPE LOVE is an Australian writer whose work has recently appeared in *Belong, Anywhere But Earth, Damnation and Dames* and *Bloodstones*. Her stories have been nominated for the *Aurealis Awards* Best Science Fiction Short Story for 2007, 2010 and 2011. Perhaps 2013 will finally be her lucky year! She is currently working on the re-launch of *Horror on the Orient Express*, a classic *Call of Cthulhu* role-playing supplement she first helped create in 1991. She is writing a blog about the project, and how it feels to return to it again 23 years later: *http://orientexpresswriters.wordpress.com/*

MICHELLE MARQUARDT lives in the Blue Mountains with her husband and two children and works as a veterinarian. She is the author of the novel *Blue Silence* (Random House 2002) and a number of short stories. She was co-editor, with Bill Congreve, of *The Year's Best Australian Science Fiction and Fantasy*, volumes one to four (MirrorDanse Books).

D.K. MOK lives in Sydney, Australia, and writes fantasy, science fiction and urban fantasy novels and short stories. Her urban fantasy novel, *The Other Tree*, will be released in December 2013 by Spence City.

DK grew up in libraries, immersed in lost cities and fantastic worlds, populated by quirky bandits and giant squid. She graduated from UNSW with a degree in Psychology, pursuing her interest in both social justice and scientist humour.

She's fond of cephalopods, androids, global politics, rugged horizons, science and technology podcasts, and she wishes someone would build a labyrinthine library garden so she can hang out there. Her favourite fossil deposit is the Burgess Shale.

Find out more at *www.dkmok.com*

FAITH MUDGE is a Queensland writer with a passion for fantasy, folk tales and mythology from all over the world — in fact, almost anything with a glimmer of the fantastical. Her head is a madly cluttered place that really needs new signposts and possibly a map. She writes regular reviews and vignettes for her blog at *beyondthedreamline.wordpress.com*, enthusing about all things fairy tale along the way, and her short stories can be found in FableCroft's *To Spin a Darker Stair* and Ticonderoga's *Dreaming of Djinn*.

TANSY RAYNER ROBERTS is the award-winning author of the **Creature Court** trilogy: *Power and Majesty, The Shattered City* and *Reign of Beasts*. Her short story collection *Love and Romanpunk* was published by Twelfth Planet Press in 2011. You can find her at her blog (*http://tansyrr.com/*), on Twitter (@tansyrr/) and on the Hugo-nominated podcast Galactic Suburbia. Tansy lives in Tasmania, Australia with a Silent Producer and two superhero daughters.

BARBARA ROBSON studies estuaries for a living, and sometimes writes stories when she should be writing scientific papers. Find "Neighbourhood Watch" in the Twelfth-Planet Press anthology, *Sprawl*, "Mrs Estahazi" in *Belong* (Ticonderoga Publications), and "Lizzie Lou" in *The Year's Best Fantasy 5* (Harper Voyager). She is making slow progress towards writing her first novel, tentatively titled *Speakeasy*.

ANGELA SLATTER writes dark fantasy and horror. She is the author of the Aurealis Award-winning *The Girl with No Hands and Other Tales*, the WFA-shortlisted *Sourdough and Other Stories*, and the new collection/mosaic novel (with Lisa L. Hannett), *Midnight and Moonshine*. She has a British Fantasy Award for "The Coffin-Maker's Daughter" (*A Book of Horrors*, Stephen Jones ed.), a PhD in Creative Writing and blogs at *www.angelaslatter.com*.

CAT SPARKS is fiction editor of *Cosmos Magazine*. She managed Agog! Press, which produced ten anthologies of new speculative fiction, from 2002-2008. Cat has received a total of seventeen Aurealis and Ditmar awards for her writing, editing and art. She was a Writers of the Future prize winner and a graduate of Clarion South writing workshop. In 2011 she was the recipient of an Australia Council emerging writers grant. She is currently doing a PhD in young adult post-apocalypse literature. She can be found at *catsparks.net*

SUZANNE J. WILLIS is a graduate of Clarion South 2009 and her work has appeared in *AntipodeanSF*, *Goldfish Grimm's Spicy Fiction Sushi* and anthologies by Fablecroft Publishing and Misanthrope Press. She works full-time and writes in the spaces around it, inspired by fairytales, ghost stories and all things strange. Suzanne lives in Melbourne with her patient partner and pampered pooch.

Epilogue
edited by Tehani Wessely
ISBN: 978-0-9807770-5-5

ep·i·logue: an ending that serves as a comment on or conclusion to what has happened.

Climate change, natural disaster, war and disease threaten to destroy all we know. Predictions of the future are bleak. But does the apocalypse really mean the end of the world? Is there no hope for a future that follows?

Twelve writers take on the end of the world and go beyond, to what comes next.

CONTENTS

"A memory trapped in light" by Joanne Anderton

"Time and tide" by Lyn Battersby

"Fireflies" by Steve Cameron

"Sleeping Beauty" by Thoraiya Dyer

"The Fletcher Test" by Dirk Flinthart

"Ghosts" by Stephanie Gunn

"Sleepers" by Kaia Landelius

"Solitary" by Dave Luckett

"Cold comfort" by David McDonald

"The Mornington Ride" by Jason Nahrung

"What books survive" by Tansy Rayner Roberts

"The last good town" by Elizabeth Tan

fablecroft.com.au

To Spin a Darker Stair
edited by Tehani Wessely

ISBN: 978-0-9807770-6-2

Forget everything you think you know about fairytales with this boutique gift book.

Featuring the exquisite art of Kathleen Jennings and two incredible stories by Catherynne M Valente and Faith Mudge, *To Spin a Darker Stair* is an enticing package.

"… brilliant idea and equally brilliant execution." — *Specusphere*

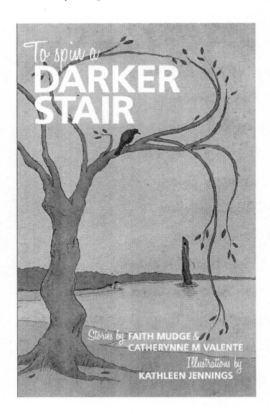

fablecroft.com.au

After the Rain
edited by Tehani Wessely
ISBN: 978-0-9807770-2-4

The aftermath of rain, be it showers, storms or floods, can change the landscape. In this book, fifteen of Australia's best and brightest speculative fiction authors offer literal and figurative interpretations of what follows rain, in this reality and others.

From the earliest of bible stories to World War II Germany, from tiny creatures grown of raindrops to alien planets and future worlds, *After the Rain* considers the changes rain can bring, if one steps slight left of reality.

"…hopeful and depressing, and thoroughly engrossing." — ASif!

fablecroft.com.au

Australis Imaginarium
edited by Tehani Wessely
ISBN: 978-0-9807770-0-0

Boasting original cover art by Shaun Tan and containing twelve all-Australian, award-winning stories by some of the island continent's finest speculative fiction writers, *Australis Imaginarium* challenges you to reconsider what you think you know about Australia and its inhabitants, old and new.

Australis Imaginarium collects work from across the past two decades, showcasing Australian storytelling at its very best.

"Once a Month, on a Sunday" by Ian McHugh
"Night Heron's Curse" by Thoraiya Dyer
"Hunter of Darkness, Hunter of Light" by Michael Pryor
"A Pig's Whisper" by Margo Lanagan
"Stealing Free" by Deborah Biancotti
"Suffer the Little Children" by Rowena Cory Daniells
"Virgin Jackson" by Marianne de Pierres
"The Claws of Native Ghosts" by Lee Battersby
"The Jacaranda Wife" by Angela Slatter
"The Dark Under the Skin" by Dirk Strasser
"Red Ochre" by Lucy Sussex
"Passing the Bone" by Sean Williams

"... stories authored by Australian mastercraftspeople ... each one is perfectly crafted ... speculative fiction at [its] finest..." —
Suz's Space

fablecroft.com.au

Worlds Next Door
edited by Tehani Wessely
ISBN: 978-0-9807770-1-7

What you have here is not a book, but a key to worlds that exist under your bed, in your cupboard, in the dark of night when you're sure you're being watched. What you have is a passport to the worlds next door.

Containing 25 bite-sized stories for 9-13 year olds by Australian authors including Paul Collins, Michael Pryor, Pamela Freeman, Dirk Flinthart, Tansy Rayner Roberts and Jenny Blackford, *Worlds Next Door* is perfect for the budding reader.

"...a completely satisfying, wonderful collection..." — Aurealis Xpress

"There are so many excellent stories in this collection..." — Daniel Simpson

"...a fab little anthology..." — ASif!

"...a book that gives us tempting little slices of cleverness in the realm of magical writing..." — Kids' Book Review

"I love the diversity of this collection." — Kids' Book Capers

"An engaging collection of speculative fiction ... this is an excellent collection for both the library and the English faculty." — ReadPlus

fablecroft.com.au

The Bone Chime Song and Other Stories
by Joanne Anderton
ISBN: 978-0-9807770-9-3

Enter a world where terrible secrets are hidden in a wind chime's song; where crippled witches build magic from scrap; and the beautiful dead dance for eternity

The Bone Chime Song and Other Stories collects the finest science fiction and horror short stories from award-winning writer Joanne Anderton. From mechanical spells scavenging a derelict starship to outback zombies and floating gardens of bone, these stories blur the lines between genres. A mix of freakish horror, dark visions of the future and the just plain weird, Anderton's tales will draw you in — but never let you get comfortable.

The Bone Chime Song
Mah Song
Shadow of Drought
Sanaa's Army
From the Dry Heart to the Sea
Always a Price
Out Hunting for Teeth
Death Masque
Flowers in the shadow of the Garden
A Memory Trapped in Light
Trail of Dead
Fence Lines
Tied to the Waste

With an Introduction by Australian horror luminary Kaaron Warren

...follows a fine horror lineage from Shirley Jackson's The Lottery through The Wickerman... – Scary Minds

Dark, unexpected and tightly written, Anderton makes a fantasy world seem completely real, while using a premise that spirals from a shadowed and lonely place. – ASif!

...a stunning descent into dark decay and the grisly madness of eternity ... a chaotic and beautiful fairy tale with a patina of gangrene. – Specusphere

...Anderton has constructed an exuberant and positively traditional SF story with strong female central characters... – ASif!

[Anderton] has a real mastery of the surreal ... and somehow manages to make the surreal seem normal ... reading this book will fill you with horror, wonder, awe, sorrow, delight, surprise and admiration." – Kaaron Warren

fablecroft.com.au